A PRICE TO PAY

Club Twist Book Two

Alice Raine

Published by Accent Press Ltd 2018
Octavo House
West Bute Street
Cardiff
CF10 5LJ

www.accentpress.co.uk

The story contained within this book is a work of fiction. Names and characters are the product of the author's imagination and any resemblance to actual persons, living or dead, is entirely coincidental.

ISBN 9781786152589
eISBN 9781786152596

Printed and bound in Great Britain by Clays Ltd, Elcograf S.p.A

For Leah Weatherall…

see? I can spell your name correctly!
Not only are you an amazing supporter of my books,
but now my friend too.
Thank you for everything you do! xx

CHAPTER ONE

Robyn

'Move in with me, Robyn.'

I was pressed against the wall in Oliver's hallway with the man himself kissing me half to death and groping me in all the right places, and *this* was the time he chose to ask me to move in with him? I could barely breathe, let alone think straight about such a monumental topic.

My man didn't half choose his moments sometimes. Mind you, this wasn't the first time he'd asked me. He'd brought the subject up multiple times since we'd been together, but being cautious, I'd decided we needed to let our relationship settle before such a big commitment.

We were eight months into the relationship now, and I'd known him at least ten, which was fairly settled, wasn't it? So really there was nothing holding me back. I'd had boyfriends before, but I'd never lived with any of them. Actually, I'd never even been on holiday with any of them, so I guess that was why this seemed like such a big step to me.

Leaning back, I gazed up at Oliver's determined expression and tried to draw in some steadying breaths and calm the dizzying lust that thrummed in my system. Jeez, when he'd pulled me into his arms five minutes ago and started kissing me I'd been expecting him to sweep me up and carry me to bed, not start a discussion about the future progress of our relationship. From my raised temperature and hammering heart my body was having just as much difficulty with the swift change in topic as my brain was.

'Umm…' I wasn't sure what to say. I loved him more than I'd ever thought possible, and of course I wanted to share my life and a house with him, but there was still one small hurdle in the way. 'You haven't even met my parents yet, Oliver.' As silly or traditional as it might sound, I wanted my parents to at least have been introduced to my boyfriend before we shacked up together.

Oliver gave a casual shrug and raised a hand to rub his thumb gently across my flushed cheeks. 'They know about me, though. And they know we've been together for eight months, too, so surely it's just a natural next step?'

Eight whole months of non-stop attention, romantic dates, and stupendous sex. I could hardly believe how quickly the time had flown by, but I was still just as much of a loved-up mess over this man as I had been at the start. 'It is, but I'd still like them to meet you.'

He smiled down at me, the corners of his eyes crinkling in that way that always made my insides melt. 'I'd like to meet them, too.' He dropped a kiss on the tip of my nose which had me leaning forwards for more with a quiet moan. 'Why don't you invite them over this weekend? I'll cook.'

I raised my eyebrows at his lovely offer, and I grinned at the idea of Oliver dashing around the kitchen in an apron as he prepared a feast for my folks. Mind you, Oliver didn't "dash". His demeanour was pure power – everything he did was done in a calm, controlled manner, even cooking. It sometimes felt like he controlled the world, and not the other way around. 'That way, if they don't like me I can try and win them over with my fantastic culinary skills.'

A gurgled laugh broke from my throat, and I looped my arms around his neck and trailed my fingers through the silky-soft hair at his nape. 'They'll love you.'

Suddenly his smile dried up and his eyes narrowed as a brief flinch of concern tweaked his eyebrows. 'Will they mind the age gap?'

Shaking my head with certainty, I lowered a hand and stroked his chest reassuringly. 'Nah, they know you're older. They don't care because they also know that I'm happy and crazily in love with you.'

'Hmm, crazily in love with me. I rather like that description.' Oliver's smile returned with a vengeance as he gipped my hips and spun us around once in a dramatic dance move that had me yelping and clutching at him to avoid tripping over my own feet.

'Saturday it is, then. Dinner and drinks with your parents at *our* house.'

'OK.' *Our house*. Blimey. That was going to take some getting used to. Snuggling into his chest, I let him get away with his assumption and instead absorbed the smell of the fresh cotton and the way it mingled with his aftershave and the delicious scent of his skin.

He smelled amazing, was handsome as sin, a genius in the kitchen, a god between the sheets, and on top of all that, treated me like I was the most important person on the entire planet. I literally loved everything about this man.

Oliver lowered his head and captured my lips in a kiss so filled with understanding and mutual adoration that I shivered in his arms and pulled him just a little closer.

'God, I love how affected by me you are.' He gave a thrust of his hips and I felt the solid heat of a building erection as he pressed it against my belly and my insides liquefied with need. 'And the feeling is completely mutual. You affect me, Robyn, on so many levels. I love you so much.' He captured my lips in a kiss which went from chaste to sinful in just a matter of seconds, our tongues meeting and tangling as we pressed ourselves as close as physically possible with clothes on.

Oliver allowed the kiss to consume us for a minute or so, and then he pulled back, smiling ruefully as we both took ragged breaths and clung to each other for support. 'And I can't wait to live with you, so if we have dinner with your parents this weekend, will you agree to move in?'

Trying not to let out a squeal of excitement, I nodded my response and gripped his biceps as my legs went wobbly from the enormity of it all. 'Yes, I'd love to, Oliver.' I was going to be living here in this gorgeous house with the man of my dreams.

I almost couldn't believe it was all real.

What *was* real, though, was the insistent pressure of Oliver's groin as it continued to throb and nudge against my stomach.

'Maybe dress down a little bit, though,' I murmured, fingering the soft silk of the waistcoat he was wearing over a pristine pale blue shirt. 'I love your three-piece suits, but you can look a little intimidating in them.' My dad was a jeans man through and through. He dressed up for weddings or funerals, but he'd definitely find Oliver and his Savile Row attire a bit over the top.

Oliver's eyes darkened wickedly, and then he lowered his lips beside my ear. 'You like me when I'm a little intimidating, though, don't you, Robyn?' His breath tickled across my ear and my eyes fluttered shut as my arousal instantly reignited and soared through my body.

'You can try to pretend otherwise, but I know that my domineering side is one of your favourites.' He spoke with complete confidence, and he was spot on, because it really was such a turn-on when he got all broody and masterful with me. A shudder ran through my entire body just thinking about it, and in response Oliver let out a wicked laugh and gathered me closer into his arms.

Glancing up, I saw that he had a wicked twinkle in his eyes, too, as if me agreeing to move in with him had calmed his concerns and set his brain off on contemplating a much naughtier prospect. A prospect that I had been hoping for all along.

'Speaking of my domineering side…' He paused and gave my hips a squeeze. 'It's been a while since we've unleashed it, hasn't it?' he murmured, his tone dropping lower and becoming more authoritative with every word.

Now that I came to think of it, it had. Oliver and I had mellowed into our relationship, and although his commanding personality meant he would never be completely separated from his need to be in control, we hadn't actually done a proper scene for quite a while.

'It has… Sir.' I added his title as my way of giving him my consent to continue and his eyes sparkled with appreciation. I watched as he stood a little taller, his eyes blazing, and I swear I could almost see his brain ticking over as he considered exactly what he wanted to do to me. As much as it might surprise some people, I found the determined focus on his face just as much of a turn-on as any physical touch.

'You look a little flushed, Robyn. Are you worked up? Hot under the collar, perhaps?' Oliver commented mildly, teasing me.

I was damp between my legs, my breath was still coming in panting gasps, and my body temperature was surely approaching that of someone with a high fever, so in short, yes, I was more than a tad worked up. As usual, he was playing it cool, so I decided that I would, too. Giving a shrug, I tried for a nonchalant expression as I replied. 'A little, Sir.'

His eyes twinkled with delight at the game we were playing, and then he stooped down and caught my right leg behind the knee. He lifted it so that when he stood up again my leg was almost wrapped around his waist. This was a far more intimate position; his throbbing shaft was now pressed against my core and my breath hitched in my throat as I looked up and caught sight of the heat in his expression.

'Let's see if we can ease that, then, shall we?' Oliver's eyes were locked with mine as he slowly ran his hand down over my boot-clad calf, and then back up my leg until he came to the exposed skin that sat between the bottom of my skirt and the top of my knee-high boot.

'Hmmm. These boots.' His fingers trailed down my leg again, and I watched as he bit down on his lower lip and let out a low groan. 'I think you know they're my weakness and wear them more nowadays just to tempt me.'

I didn't reply verbally, but my cheeks flushed with mild guilt, because his speculation was true – I *did* wear these boots more often now because I loved his reaction to them.

Up until meeting Oliver I had favoured my battered old Converse and a pair of jeans. I'd been more of a "girl next door" type as opposed to one who dressed up to the nines, and I still was most days, but Oliver's lusty response to me in knee-high boots, stockings and suspenders had made them a far more regular choice in my outfit range.

'Did you know that visions of you, these boots, and a wall will always feature at the top of my fantasy fuck list?' he asked. I did, but only because Oliver had told me rather explicitly that his favourite fantasy was fucking me against a wall hard and deep while I wore knee-high boots, stockings, and not much else. He'd also indulged in this scenario several times, and I had to say it now featured pretty damn high on my list of sexual fantasies, too.

'I also have another fantasy involving these boots that we haven't acted out yet,' he informed me.

My eyebrows rose in curiosity at his confession. 'Really? What's that?'

He gave a light swat to my thigh and lowered his brow in disapproval, which prompted me to realise that we were at the start of a scene and I hadn't used his title.

'Sir.' I added a flutter of my eyelashes to soften him and saw it instantly work as he flashed me a wink.

'My other fantasy involves leather on leather,' he replied cryptically, leaving me wondering what on earth he meant. 'I think perhaps we'll bring it to reality now. I'll need my favourite toy to assist us. Wait right here, I won't be a moment.'

Oliver strode up the stairs, leaving me panting and curious. Leather on leather? His favourite toy? He had quite a collection in his cupboard upstairs, and my mind frantically ran through the options, trying to work out which he favoured most. Paddles? Spreader bars? Nipple clamps?

Just as he was trotting back down the stairs it came to me. *Leather on leather*. His flogger. It was definitely his favoured toy, and the one he would reach for the most often in our scenes. He wanted to use the flogger on me while I was wearing the leather boots.

I dropped my eyes to his right hand, and sure enough there it was. He held the brown leather handle in a loose-knuckled grip. Falling from the stem was the swathe of leather strips that had caused me so much pleasure since we'd purchased it. They'd caused a little pain, too, on occasion, but always just the right amount to heighten my arousal and increase the intensity of my orgasm.

Out of all the sex toys available, this was his speciality, so much so that Oliver had a reputation at Club Twist for being a master with those little leather strands, and goddamn had he lived up to it on the occasions we'd used it together.

A shudder of excitement ran through me, but it was accompanied with a tug of frustration, because as amazing as he was at using the flogger to make me come, Oliver had also proven that he could play a wicked game with it and keep me hanging on the edge until I was desperate and begging for him to let me climax.

Which would it be tonight?

He paused in front of me, slid a hand around my waist, and then silently led me into the dining room where he turned the lights on and dimmed them so the room was swathed in the sensation of candlelight. We stopped inside the doorway, both glancing around the large room and taking in the walnut table, soft chaise longue in the corner, and huge windows looking out onto the garden.

'I'm not sure we've christened this room in our house yet,' Oliver murmured hotly.

Our house. Once again, the words made my heart give a thrilled leap. We had christened this room, multiple times, and from the grin on his face he damn well knew it, too; we'd had sex on the small sofa in the corner, a quickie on the rug by the fireplace, and sex against the wall just inside the door, but I certainly wasn't going to stop him if he had his mind set on it.

'Well, not the dining table, anyway,' he clarified with a wink. The table? Well, that certainly was a new location.

'Perhaps we should rectify that, hmm?' He lowered his mouth to trail kisses along my jawline as he moved his free hand to my other leg and began to lift my skirt up inch by inch.

'I think we definitely should, Sir,' I agreed breathily.

One of his hands caught in my hair, giving a tug that was just hard enough to send a thrill of pleasure-laced pain across my scalp and skittering down my body, and then Oliver used his grip to angle my head as he kissed and licked at my neck and pulse point until I was heavy with desire and almost sagging in his arms.

He let go of my hair, slid his hand back down to my waist, and dropped to his knees before me. He made quick work of the zip of my skirt and groaned as he discovered the suspender belt below, and the fact that I wasn't wearing any knickers.

'You're knicker-less? *Dios*, Robyn.' His words were muffled, because he'd buried his face in the soft skin at the top of my legs and was now alternating between kissing me and tugging at the suspender belt with his teeth like a man well and truly on a mission.

Oliver sucked hard on the tender skin at the top of my thigh and paused briefly to look up at me. 'Undress. Top half only,' he added with a smirk. 'The boots and suspenders can stay.'

My fingers were shaking, but I complied immediately,

pulling my blouse over my head and then dispensing with my bra in record speed. I chucked it aside where it flew through the air and hooked over the brass fire pokers.

Leaning back, Oliver glanced up at me. 'Present yourself for me. On the table,' he instructed quietly, jerking his chin towards the huge dining table.

On the table? That might be a bit of a challenge, seeing as I was basically naked apart from my heeled boots and the stockings. As if reading my thoughts, he smiled.

'Don't worry, it's solid. You won't fall.' He stood up and held out a hand to me and helped me step onto a chair and up onto the table top. He was right, it didn't wobble or move at all under me, and I quickly set about presenting myself to him. I dropped to my knees at the edge closest to him, carefully folding my boot-clad legs below me. I kept my back straight but eyes averted as I placed my hands on my thighs before parting my knees wider, just as he liked.

A heavy moment of silence passed between us where I was desperate to raise my eyes and see if he looked pleased or not with my display, but then I got my answer in the form of a lusty growl. 'You really are the ultimate temptation, Robyn.'

Oliver placed his hands on my thighs and ran them down to my knees before hooking his fingers into the tops of my boots and using his grip to drag me forwards to the very edge of the table. His hands then took the trip up and down my legs again before he dropped to a crouch before me. As he lowered himself, my averted eyes met his and I watched in delight as he grinned up at me.

Remaining crouched there, he kept his gaze locked with mine and then slowly slid his hands up my thighs, over my stomach, and across my ribs until he reached my breasts. His arms were almost at full stretch now, but he still managed to expertly tease my nipples into solid peaks and cause me to moan loudly.

Continuing with rolling and tweaking my nipples, he

blinked and lowered his eyes to my knicker-less pussy, and with a growl leaned close to press his lips against my clit in a hot, open-mouthed kiss. He used his chin to nudge at my thighs in a silent command to widen my legs, and so, on a pleasured whimper, I complied, leaning back onto my palms to aid my balance and make sure I didn't topple off the table from the pleasure of it all.

My head fell backwards, my eyes rolling closed as Oliver's skilled tongue lashed at my skin and whipped me into a frenzy so quickly that I felt instantly dizzy. He was alternating between sucking on my clit and hard, long licks through my sensitive flesh, knowing just what my body needed to send me spinning towards a speedy orgasm.

'Oliver, Sir… I'm so close.'

Oliver gave one more suck to my clit, then began to rise. I let out a moan of desperation as my orgasm swirled on the cusp but hovered just out of reach. He silenced my plea by trailing kisses across my body as he rose, before finally standing before me and staring me straight in the eye as he picked up the flogger from the table beside me.

'I know you are, but I wish for you to indulge me for a few more minutes.'

I could argue, desperately try to plead my case, or perhaps just lower my hands and finish myself off, but I wouldn't. I would never go against Oliver when he was as in the zone as he currently was, and so, with a breath for composure, I nodded slightly.

'Whatever you wish, Sir.'

Oliver smiled at my reply and trailed the strands of the flogger across my thighs. 'So fucking perfect in your submission.' He raised the flogger and lazily draped it over one of my shoulders, then slowly across the other, the cool tickle of the strands sending goose pimples rushing across my skin.

Standing back from me, he tucked the flogger into the belt

of his trousers and took his time unbuttoning his shirt sleeves. I knew what was coming next – it was one of his custom moves and I bloody loved it; before a scene he would always undo the sleeves of his shirt and roll them up to expose his lovely muscled forearms. It was his way of adding to the anticipation and drawing things out a little, and as I watched him form each perfect chunk in the cotton, my clit pulsed as my arousal mounted.

Oliver's eyes remained glued with mine. Once he was satisfied that his shirt looked perfect he gave a single nod and walked over to the couch in the corner to retrieve the blanket that hung over it.

He spread the blanket on the table behind me then moved in close to place a kiss on my temple. His lips hovered by my skin, and I couldn't resist leaning in for more, a move that was rewarded by Oliver tipping my head back and placing a lingering kiss on my lips. 'Lay back, *cariño.* Show me that beautiful body.'

I lowered myself back onto the soft blanket and tried to imagine how Oliver might like me to position myself. Laying my arms loosely by my sides, I parted my legs slightly and then let my head tilt to the side to look at him. I was sprawled across the fancy dining table like a hooker in my leather boots and suspender belt, so I felt a little self-conscious, but the low lighting helped relax me, as did the appreciative heat in Oliver's eyes as he ran his gaze up my body.

'Now just lie still and enjoy,' he murmured, moving towards the end of the table where my feet were, trailing the strands of the flogger across my body as he did so. Every inch of my skin was caressed with the leather as he dragged it over me, and the soft movements were lulling, making my limbs and eyes feel heavy.

'Leather on leather,' Oliver murmured with appreciation as he gave several swats to my boot-clad calves. I'd thought that my boots might dull the sensation of the flogger, and they did to some extent, but I could still feel each stroke, and the cracking noise created as the two leather surfaces met was quite a turn-on in itself – I could see why he'd wanted to try it.

The first slightly harder swat came to the inside of my thigh. After the previously gentle touches, it was shocking enough that I let out a yelp and jerked my leg. The warmth of Oliver's palm encircled my knee and pressed it back to the table, and when I raised my head and looked down at him I saw a warning expression on his face.

'Lay still, remember?' he reminded me softly, but the lowering of his tone was commanding enough that I knew it wasn't a request – he had asked me not to move, and he expected me to comply, otherwise there would be consequences.

'Sorry, Sir,' I apologised croakily, my throat dry from the intensity of the scene.

Oliver remained silent but nodded in acceptance and then gave my thigh a harder swat again. This time I was prepared for the slight sting from the leather and managed to stay still. He began moving around my body, swatting at me with deft flicks of his wrist until my skin felt heated and over-sensitised.

Every touch sent a flicker of pain through me but also sent my arousal soaring, and as the minutes passed my body started to feel like it was deliciously alight with awareness. It was an addictive high, and something that I'd never experienced before Oliver. I'd never imagined that a lick of pain could be so thrilling, and yet with him, it was.

His movement with the flogger was graceful, almost hypnotising as he continued to work my body until I was desperate to writhe around and moan my desperation to come. Oliver must have read the signs in me, just as he often did, because his lips twitched with a smile. 'You may move, if you need to.'

My entire body jerked as I released the tension in my muscles and a moan rose from my chest that was so throaty and low I almost felt embarrassed. Oliver let out a small chuckle and watched in anticipation as he moved towards my feet again.

He laid the flogger across my belly, took hold of my ankles, and ran his hands up and down my leather boots again. He pulled me closer towards him until my knees were bent and hanging over the table edge, and my pulsing core was within touching distance for him.

Oliver placed his palms on my thighs and took a moment to just look at me. His eyes moved from mine to trail down my body and focus on my pussy before moving back to my face. He had a gigantic hard-on tenting his trousers, and his expression was one of barely controlled lust, and a thrill of excitement ran through me, knowing that I could affect him to this degree.

He looked like he was desperate to bury himself inside me, but I knew Oliver and his supreme self-control, and he wouldn't be doing that until he was content that he'd finished the scene he'd had planned.

He reached for the flogger again and tightened his grip on the handle. I instinctively grabbed a handful of blanket in each hand to help ground me for what was to come. The first sharp flick landed on my right breast, hardening the nipple to an impossibly tight peak before sending a jab of desire shooting to my core. My left breast was next, his touch with the flogger having similarly incredible effects and making me cry out from the pleasure now pulsing around my body.

He continued to tease my breasts like this for what felt like hours, and then, just when I thought I couldn't take any more, his palms pressed my thighs wider. 'Beautiful. So ready for me.' He hummed in appreciation and started to work my pussy over with the flogger, gently at first, but his swats quickly built in their intensity. As he homed in on my clit and gave several shorter, sharper swats, I knew I was a goner.

The third hit to my clit sent me rushing over into the climax that I had been longing for all along, and my muscles contracted as my entire back arched away from the table from the intensity of my release. The pulsing bursts of pleasure seemed to go on and on, and it was only when Oliver swapped from the flogger to his thumb and began to gently work me down that my spasms started to slowly fade.

Ho-ly fuck. So he'd chosen the long drawn-out use of the flogger, then. Not that I could say I minded, because that climax had been so powerful my whole body felt jellified from it.

Oliver was still standing between my legs, and as I gazed down at him with a contented smile, he lowered his hands and released himself from his trousers. I couldn't help but stare at his cock, and I bit down on my lower lip to stifle a lusty groan as I watched him palm his solid erection and run a slow drag up his shaft and back down again.

I might just have climaxed, but God, that was a seriously hot sight, and immediately put me in the mood for round two.

Oliver didn't bother to remove any clothing, but as soon as his cock was free and bobbing urgently towards me he gripped my hips and slid me the last few inches down the table where the broad head of his erection nudged at my entrance, causing us both to groan.

He ran his hands over my boot-clad calves again with a moan, and then traced the suspender belt with his fingertips. I could see from the twitching muscle in his jaw that his self-control was spent, and as soon as his cock made contact with me he groaned and began pushing inside.

'Wrap your legs around my waist, *cariño*,' he urged, but he needn't have worried, because I was already moving my legs into position as he spoke and locking the heels of the boots behind him.

Oliver buried his cock inside me inch by glorious inch, in one deep, slow thrust and held us pressed together. He threw his head back, and I could see the tension in his neck as he tried desperately to keep the movement slow for my benefit and not give in to the urge to just smash forwards into me.

Staring into my eyes, Oliver leaned over me, placed one short, hard kiss on my lips, and began to move. He started off gently, just rolling his hips so that all the right places were rubbing and creating a delicious friction between us. It was so good that if he'd just carried on like that it would have been enough to make me come again, but I could tell from the bristling tension in his shoulders and the intent look in his eyes that Oliver had something a little harder in mind tonight.

Barely a few seconds after the thought had crossed my mind, he began to move with more purpose, his hips jolting back and forth with harder thrusts that slid me up and down the table with each movement. Luckily, with my legs circled around his waist and his grip on my hips, the towel slipping across the shiny wood didn't affect our rhythm.

Oliver upped it another gear, his hips now moving with sharper, harder thrusts that forced his entire length deep inside me on each move. He was so deep it was almost painful, but as always, Oliver seemed to know how much I could take and managed to keep it all just balanced on the pleasurable side of pain. My hands were clawing at his forearms as I tried to move with him and increase the friction, but in this position, it was Oliver who was in control and he didn't disappoint.

The sounds of us groaning and panting were joined by the dull creaking of wood as we banged into the table with each of his hard, jabbing thrusts, and the very eroticism of the whole scene sent a fresh wave of lust pouring through my body. I was still so sensitised from my last orgasm that a second one was already rolling up on me.

'You're close… so am I… Wait for me, Robyn.' Oliver ground out, his hips losing some of their coordination as he neared his climax.

I tensed my inner muscles in a desperate attempt to hold back the orgasm that was swelling low in my belly, but just when I thought I wouldn't be able to comply, Oliver jerked his hips into mine with a deep groan.

'Now… Robyn, come with me.' He buried himself deep, over and over again, as I started to fall apart around him, my climax shattering me physically and emotionally as I clung to him and tried to cope with the waves of pleasure clenching my muscles.

Only when I was in the height of my orgasm did Oliver allow himself to let go, too, and he slowed his thrusts as he began flooding my insides with pulse after pulse of his hot release.

Oliver collapsed forwards onto me, his face buried in the crook of my neck and his warm breaths panting rapidly against me. After taking a moment to compose himself, he stood up and slid me towards him so he could lift me into his arms. He staggered over to the sofa where he collapsed down with me wrapped around him and his softening erection still nestling inside me.

He got us settled so we were both comfy, and then stroked one of my boots while giving me a rueful smile. 'Once you move in we're going to have to limit the days that you're allowed to wear these or else I'm going to be buried inside you twenty-four seven.'

I giggled at his joke, but having Oliver inside me non-stop sounded pretty bloody fantastic to me.

CHAPTER TWO

Robyn

'I can't believe you're leaving me,' Sasha complained with an exaggerated groan. She was supposed to be helping me pack up my stuff, but instead plopped down onto the bed and carelessly chucked one of my jumpers into an open packing box beside her. 'Although, actually, with the way you and Oliver are always all over each other I suppose I should be glad you lasted this long living here.' She gave a knowing wiggle of her finely shaped eyebrows and pouted at me. 'Knowing his penchant for dominance, I thought he'd have dragged you off to live with him months ago so he could get your undivided attention twenty-four seven.'

Her mention of Oliver's dominance made me recall his comment last week about how he'd like to be inside me twenty-four seven, and I giggled, before hiding my blushes by standing up, retrieving the jumper she had carelessly chucked, folding it, and laying it in an open suitcase.

'It didn't feel like something we should rush. Besides, I wanted him to meet my parents before we moved in together.'

'Yeah, I get that. Bet he charmed the pants off them, huh?'

Amusing visions of my parents ripping off their pants and throwing them at Oliver filled my mind and I chuckled. 'Not literally, thank goodness, but yes, he was in full suave and sophisticated mode, and they loved him.' I smiled, remembering the expression on my mum's face when I'd first introduced her to Oliver. Her mouth had dropped open and she'd looked almost starstruck, like he was some Hollywood actor or something. I suppose with his chiselled looks, sparkling eyes, and calm confidence he did have that kind of vibe about him.

The evening had been lovely, much more relaxed than I'd expected, and had thankfully finished with both my parents giving their wholehearted support to our relationship.

Sasha threw another jumper into the box and scrunched her face up like a petulant child. Some help she was being, I was having to repack every item she touched! 'What am I going to do without you? Who am I going to drink endless bottles of wine with?'

Retrieving the screwed-up jumper with a smile, I rolled my eyes. 'I'm sure you'll survive. Besides, you still have Chloe.'

Sasha let out a dramatic sigh and lay back on the bed, flopping an arm over her face. She'd obviously decided that she'd had enough of helping me pack. 'I know, but all she drinks is Chardonnay, for God's sakes. *Char-don-aaay.*' She drew out the word to highlight her absolute disgust of the beverage. 'It's like the devil's piss. I'm going to have to do some serious training with her to get her to your level of drinking buddy compatibility.'

Letting out another laugh, I also gave up on my packing and joined Sasha on the bed. 'It's not like I'm moving to Iceland, Sash. I'll just be a few Tube stops away. We'll still see each other plenty.' Even as I said the words, I knew I was going to miss having Sasha around every day. I was so excited about moving in with Oliver, but these few years of living in a girly flat had been lovely, and I would definitely miss Sasha's wicked sense of humour and filthy jokes, not forgetting her amazing skills with Thai food.

'Yeah, yeah, you'll be too busy being humped senseless by the big bad Wolfe to spare time for lil' old me.' She gave me a cheeky wink and grinned like a Cheshire Cat as she used her favourite nickname for Oliver. 'I mean, sharing a glass of *vino* with me can hardly compete with being sexed silly until you can't walk straight, can it?'

My cheeks filled with heat and I grinned at her blatancy before deciding to join in with her teasing. 'True, but I am occasionally going to need to rehydrate and come out for air, probably once every few months… so that's when I'll squeeze you in.'

Sasha spluttered out a giggle and lobbed a pillow at me. 'Ha! You better see me more frequently than that!'

Playfully grabbing the pillow off her and returning the favour by flinging it back at her head, I grinned. 'Of course I will! We'll see each other each week, I promise.'

She caught the pillow with a laugh. 'I should bloody well hope so!'

'Maybe we could make Thursday our new night to meet up,' I suggested as I stood up and carried on packing clothes into the cases.

'Sounds good to me. Why Thursdays in particular?'

'Oliver plays squash with Marcus on a Thursday and then goes for a beer with him at Club Twist. Me and you could do a girls' night somewhere while they're out.'

Sasha thoughtfully absorbed my suggestion and then nodded slowly. 'Sounds like a plan.'

She put the pillow aside, stood up, and opened my jewellery box before starting to collect the earrings and bracelets that were scattered on my dressing table and carefully stowing them in the box. 'I'm thinking that now you're moving out it might be time for me to look at buying a place of my own. What do you think?'

I perked up at her news and nodded. 'I think it's a great idea, Sash.' Sasha's inheritance from her parents meant she had plenty of money in her bank account, but even with her sizeable savings she hadn't had enough to buy a three-bedroom place in the extortionate London property market. She hadn't had the heart to chuck me or Chloe out, so she'd just carried on renting so we could all stay together. 'What areas are you going to look at?'

Before she could answer we were interrupted by the doorbell, so I gave her a "hold that thought" look and jumped up. Once I'd navigated the stacked boxes in my room, I jogged out through the flat and peered through the spy hole to see Oliver outside holding a large cardboard box in his hands.

I pulled the door open with a broad smile, ushered him in, and was immediately swamped with the delicious smell of Chinese food. 'Hello, gorgeous,' he murmured, dropping a kiss in the top of my hair as he passed. He slid the box onto the sideboard. 'I thought you might be busy packing, so I brought lunch. Chinese, I hope that's OK?'

'It's bloody brilliant!' Sasha declared, joining us in the lounge area and eyeing the box hopefully before wincing in embarrassment. 'If there's enough for me, I mean. Sorry, didn't mean to invite myself to eat your food.'

Oliver smiled at Sasha and prodded the large box which didn't budge an inch. 'I wasn't sure who was helping Robyn with her packing, so I brought enough food for a small army.'

'God, you really are the perfect man. Don't you have any flaws?' Sasha asked, plucking a prawn cracker from a bag and popping it into her mouth.

Oliver narrowed his eyes and smiled. 'Oh, I have plenty, but none I'm going to share with you until I have Robyn living with me. Once she's safely ensconced under our roof I can let her see all my bad habits.' He flashed me a wink, and from the intensity of the look he followed it up with I had a feeling that he wasn't talking about his flaws any more. Instead, he was hinting at all the naughty sexy habits he was going to share with me. My stomach gave a little flutter of excitement and my cheeks burned as I returned his gaze.

As Sasha began digging in the box of food, Oliver watched my reaction and laughed softly, before moving closer to me and pulling me into his side. 'That expression on your face looks decidedly promising but save that thought for later. You need to eat.' His words were murmured in a low, heated tone that only I could hear, but judging from the smirk on Sasha's face she'd picked up the gist of our private conversation just fine.

Oliver gave my arse a squeeze that was hard enough to make me yelp, and then released me from his grip to start unpacking the food. He laid out trays of chicken wings, beef in black bean sauce, chicken and cashew nuts, spare ribs… On and on he went, and to my disbelief the food pile just kept growing. He hadn't been kidding when he'd said he'd bought extra. This would keep us going all week in leftovers.

Once we all had plates piled with food, I decided to return to my earlier conversation with Sasha as a means of distracting myself from the thick sexual tension that was now hanging in the air between Oliver and me.

'Sasha's thinking of buying a place in London. We were just talking about it when you arrived,' I told him, before turning to Sasha. 'So which areas are you considering?'

After finishing off the spare rib she was munching on, Sasha shrugged and licked her fingers clean. 'I don't really know. I don't want to be too far from work, and it would be nice to have a bit of an easier journey to see you, but I think it'll probably come down to what I can afford.'

'How many bedrooms are you after?' Oliver asked, helping himself to a duck pancake and starting to roll it. Something about the way his fingers smoothed the delicate pastry and lifted it to his mouth grabbed my attention, and as he licked some plum sauce from his thumb I felt a sudden tingling between my legs and had to shift on my chair. God, I was getting turned on just watching him eat! I really did have it so bad for him.

'Ideally two, as I don't want Chloe to feel like she needs to find a new place to live. A tiny bit of outside space would be amazing, too, but I know how hard that is to get in London, so

I won't hold my breath,' Sasha said sagely. Outwardly she might appear loud and a bit of a party girl, but she was extremely intelligent and very shrewd when it came to her savings and investments.

Oliver nodded thoughtfully and wiped a napkin across his lips. 'My friend lives across from me and he's just getting ready to put his apartment on the market. Two-bed flat with a small balcony. Do you want me to find out how much he's going to be asking?'

The same street as Oliver? So Sasha could be my neighbour? We shared an excited glance, and she almost spat out her mouthful of food in her hurry to speak. Swigging down half a glass of water to clear her throat, she nodded frantically.

'I'd bloody love to live on your street, but fuck, Oliver, a flat in that area will be way out of my budget.'

Oliver smiled, no doubt amused by her colourful language, and shook his head. 'Not necessarily. It's in a more modern building, so it won't be as pricy as the Victorian ones on the street, and it's not a huge flat, but it is nicely done out. He's just found out that he's being moved to America with work, so he needs a quick sale. I'll message him now and ask; there's no harm in finding out.'

After we had all stuffed ourselves with delicious egg fried rice and chicken chow mein, Oliver left to go back to work and Sasha and I continued with my packing, being much more productive now that our stomachs were content.

Once we had a sizeable stack of boxes and suitcases by the apartment door we decided to load her car up and take the first trip across to Oliver's house. Or maybe I needed to start calling it "our house" – that was how Oliver kept referring to it.

Our house. Together. It would take some getting used to, but I definitely liked the sound of it. Grinning, I shook my head as I tried to absorb the idea and help Sasha lug the boxes down the stairs and into the car.

Just as we were pulling up to the kerb outside Oliver's house – *our house,* I corrected with a grin – I felt my phone buzz in my pocket and pulled it out to see a text from the man himself. Quickly scanning the words, I winced at the huge figures included and then read it out to Sasha.

'Oliver heard back from his friend. Apparently if he sells through an agent it's going on the market at four hundred and fifty thousand, but if you're willing to do a private sale he'll drop fifty grand off the price.' Those amounts of money were hard for me to even comprehend, so I expected Sasha to let out a shocked choke when I said them, but to my surprise she raised her eyebrows and nodded.

'Sounds pretty cheap for a two-bed in this part of town.'

In the end it was me who let out the choking noise as I turned to gawk at her. Was she nuts? '*Cheap*?' I squawked. 'Did you hear me correctly, I said *four hundred and fifty grand*!'

Sasha smiled at my outburst and shrugged. 'I heard you perfectly. I know it's a lot of money, but this is central London and the flat's on a really nice street close to a Tube station. To be honest, I'm surprised it isn't double that price.'

'And… you… you can afford that?' I spluttered. I'd known for ages that Sasha had a large inheritance from her parents, but I'd never realised the sums of money involved were quite in this league.

'I can,' she replied a little sadly, perhaps thinking about her mum and dad. As much as her money made life easier for her, I knew for a fact that Sasha would give up every last penny if it meant she could have her parents back.

Glancing out of the car, she looked over her shoulder at the houses on the opposite side of the street. 'Which one do you think it is? For that price it must be tiny.'

'I'm not sure…' Looking at my phone again, I saw that I had now received a second message. 'Oliver's sent the address now… House number 220, the flat is 220a. He said his friend won't be home, but apparently he's left a key with the neighbour downstairs and if we tell her Mr Stokes sent us she'll let us in to have a look around.' I peered across the street but couldn't make out any building numbers from here.

'Well, what are we waiting for, then? Let's get your stuff inside and then go and have a nosy around my potential new pad!' Sasha pulled the keys from the ignition and grinned. 'I'm not going to get too excited, though. I don't want to live in somewhere the size of a matchbox, even if it would mean I'd get to be your neighbour,' she announced, before jumping from the car and practically ripping the boot open in her excitement.

So perhaps she was going to let herself get a little bit excited, I thought with an amused chuckle as I followed her and started pulling boxes from the car.

Opening the door to Oliver's house, I smiled fondly as I saw the moss-coloured paint that now adorned the hallway. Months ago, Oliver had casually asked me what my favourite colours were, and I'd mentioned a fondness for moss green, silver grey, and teal, not realising that he was going to use my choices to steer the direction of the decorators who had been working on his home.

Moss green now lined the hallway, silver grey flanked the walls in the kitchen, and there was a teal feature wall in the master bedroom. It had been quite a surprise, but I secretly loved the fact that even so early in our relationship he had been trying to make me feel at home in his house.

I wanted to give Sasha a full tour, but it was obvious that she was excited about looking at the flat across the road, so we piled my stuff just inside the front door and set off in search of her potential new abode.

CHAPTER THREE

Sasha

The numbering wasn't very clear on this side of the road, so it took us a few minutes to locate the building, and when we did I paused and gave the exterior a critical examination. It was modern, but had bay windows on the lower floors, a central front door, and a high peaked roof. I liked it. Turning to Robyn, I saw that she looked as pleasantly surprised as I felt.

'When Oliver said it was a modern building I thought it might be a seventies monstrosity, but it's pretty nice.' And it really was. Even though it was clearly a more recent build than some of its Victorian neighbours, it had been well designed and fitted snugly with the architecture of the street. I could only hope that I liked the inside as much as the outside. I was sceptical, though, because four hundred and fifty thousand for a two-bed flat in this postcode was an absolute steal.

After ringing the doorbell for several minutes, we discovered that the occupier of 220c – Mrs Linden – was eighty if she was a day, with thick-rimmed glasses and a pronounced stoop in her shoulders that looked like it might be quite painful.

Pasting a bright smile on my face, I gave a quick wave. 'Hi, we're here to look at the top floor flat. Mr Stokes said you had a key we could use.'

Mrs Linden might have looked old, but she was obviously still very with it, because she gave the two of us a long once-over before narrowing her eyes. 'Are you two a couple?'

Realising that my statement of "*we're* here to look at the top floor flat" might have implied that Robyn and I were together, I snorted out a laugh and shook my head. 'Fuck no!'

Mrs Linden's eyes widened and her mouth dropped open. 'I beg your pardon?' As she wheezed her words I winced, realising that I'd just done my usual and sworn like a trooper.

Beside me, Robyn tried – and failed – to disguise a laugh as a cough, and an uncharacteristic blush rose to my cheeks. I didn't blush that often, but for some reason Mrs Linden's surprised look was making me feel guilty, as if I needed to cover up my mistake pronto.

'I said, "*what?* No!"' I clarified quickly, ignoring Robyn's continued chuckles and hoping that Mrs Linden might be hard of hearing and accept my botched attempt at a cover-up.

The old lady narrowed her eyes for a second. Just when I thought she was going to call me out on my language she shrugged. 'Oh. I wouldn't have minded, I was just curious. Big people-watcher me, you see. I'm afraid I'm a bit of a nosey neighbour,' she confided with a grin that was growing friendlier by the second.

Relaxing, and deciding that I could grow quite fond of Mrs Linden and the curious twinkle in her pale blue eyes, I smiled again. 'It's just me who's interested in the flat. I'm Sasha, by the way.' Waving a hand at Robyn, I did a quick introduction. 'This is my best friend. She's just here to give me a second opinion.'

'Nice to meet you both. Would either of you like a cuppa? Or a biscuit? I baked some gingerbread fresh this morning.'

She looked like she wanted company, and as bad as I felt rejecting her now, I made a mental note to stop in on her if I did end up buying the flat. Although at this point, having not even seen the place, it was still a pretty big "if".

'If you do end up living here, you should know that the back garden technically belongs to my flat, but I can't tend it properly any more with my bad back, so I've told everyone they can use it as communal space as long as they tidy up after themselves.'

Nice kerb appeal, excellent postcode, *and* use of the garden? This place was getting better and better… It would be just my luck if the flat turned out to be an absolute dump.

'Wow. That's brilliant. Would I be able to grow some herbs to use in my cooking?' I could save a fortune if I could grow some of the ingredients I used on a weekly basis.

Mrs Linden looked thrilled by my enthusiasm and nodded. 'Oh yes! I have some raised beds for my vegetables, but there's plenty of space for some herbs, too.'

With some difficulty, Mrs Linden reached up to a hook beside her and pulled off a key ring. 'Here's the key. I hope you don't mind showing yourself up. The stairs are a bit much for me these days.'

'Not at all. I'll bring it back when we leave.'

The three flights of stairs didn't bother me at all, and to my utter amazement I loved the flat as soon as I walked in. It wasn't big, or flashy, but it was so cosy and homely that I instantly felt comfortable in the space.

Oliver had sort of been right when he'd said the place was small, but that was just because it was in the eaves of the building, so the ceilings were all sloped. But the floor space was big, and the sloped ceilings gave a lovely quirky feel to the place.

Whoever designed this flat had certainly made the most of the limited space, because instead of making it boxy and putting up lots of dividing walls, they'd kept it open plan. They'd also installed skylights all over, so it was bright and airy.

Most of the main room was devoted to a lounge diner, and bi-folding doors separated off a kitchen to the rear. The doors were currently open and pushed back, making the space feel even larger, but I supposed they would come in handy if you were cooking something smelly like fish, or one of my many

Thai creations. There was one decent-sized double bedroom, a slightly smaller second bedroom, a nicely fitted bathroom, and tons of storage space in some of the roof cavities.

All in all, it was pretty perfect.

'My God, have you seen this balcony?' Robyn's shocked voice travelled in from outside and I realised that in my excitement I hadn't actually looked out of the double doors in the lounge. I jogged to the doors and gasped excitedly and stepped out to join her.

'It's more like a roof terrace!' Which was perhaps a bit of an exaggeration, but it would certainly be big enough for a small table and chairs, and would look great once I'd decked it out with some fairy lights and a few plant pots.

Robyn gave me an excited look and nodded. 'The whole place is gorgeous. Are you interested in buying it?'

I could barely contain my excitement. 'Fuck yes! It's bloody lovely! It's near the Tube for work, on a gorgeous street, *and* I'll be your neighbour!'

I dragged her back indoors, grabbed her bag, and dug out her mobile phone before shoving it into her hands. 'Call Oliver and ask him to see if he can set up a meeting with his friend for me!'

Robyn

I loitered outside on the balcony enjoying the sunshine while Sasha had a conversation with Oliver's friend to set up a meeting. Minutes later, she bounced out looking excited. 'I'm meeting him next week when he gets back from a business trip, but he's promised not to show it to anyone else until then.'

We locked the flat up, and after saying goodbye to Mrs Linden and handing the key back, we jogged down the steps to the street feeling positively buoyant. I was going to be living with Oliver, and Sasha could be just across the street!

'So, now we've hopefully set my new move in motion, let me get a look at Mr Wolfe's swanky lair.' Sasha linked her arm with mine and practically skipped across the street.

Giggling at how she continuously referred to Oliver as a wolf, I slid the key in the front door and ushered her in before me, just knowing that Sash was going to love Oliver's house. My man had better taste than most top interior designers, so to be fair she'd be hard-pressed not to love it.

Sasha was barely past the mountain of my boxes when she stopped abruptly and dumped her handbag so she could flail her arms wildly in the air.

'Shit a brick! This place is amazing!' She spun on the spot, her eyes darting around Oliver's lovely light hallway, no doubt taking in the stained-glass windows above the door, the antique coat stand, and the wide staircase complete with beautifully turned wooden detailing. To use Sasha's own words, it was pretty swanky.

With gushed words of praise, she dragged me around his house, getting more and more excited as she went; stroking cushions, gasping at his lovely furniture choices, and "ahhh-ing" over the gigantic walk-in shower and twin sinks in the main bathroom.

Finally we reached the kitchen, and Sasha released my arm and came to a standstill in the centre of the space. 'My God, this is like my dream room… The marble surfaces are gorgeous, and wow, he has so many cool gadgets! Have you seen this coffee maker?'

Laughing at her boundless excitement, I leaned back on the counter and smiled. 'Yes. You know me and my intimate relationship with coffee. It was practically the first thing I discovered when I stayed over.'

Sasha grinned and narrowed her eyes. 'I bet it wasn't the very first intimate thing you discovered…' she said with a teasingly suggestive lilt to her voice, and a wicked twinkle in her eye. 'I'm sure your first visit involved popping into that incredible master bedroom, not the kitchen, and I'm sure the gadgets he has in his bedroom weren't food-related either… Not that you would let me poke around in the cupboards up there, you spoilsport.'

While we were in the bedroom Sasha had tried to have a nosey around Oliver's wardrobes and drawers, no doubt hoping to uncover something to tease me about, but I'd stopped her. It was an invasion of his privacy, and while we might be best mates there were some things that I liked to keep private. Besides, even I hadn't delved into all the drawers in Oliver's bedroom yet… He might have a stash of kinky stuff I didn't know about, and I didn't want to discover it for the first time with Sasha by my side.

Glancing around us, Sasha suddenly frowned. 'Actually, thinking of Mr Wolfe and his penchant for all things kink, I'm quite disappointed there isn't a sex room in this mansion of his.'

'A sex room?' I squeaked, my cheeks heating at the images her statement brought rushing to my mind.

Just at that exact moment, Oliver shocked the heck out of me by sauntering into the kitchen, and the flush on my cheeks erupted down my neck and heated my chest as we were caught talking about his bedroom tastes.

'Ah, but Sasha, you haven't seen the sex cellar yet...' he commented mildly, prompting Sasha to choke out a stunned cough. He placed his car keys down on the table, then turned his eyes onto me and stalked towards me with a dark smile on his lips that instantly turned my legs to jelly.

He didn't seem bothered in the slightest that we'd been talking about him and his preference for a bit of dominance, but his words seemed to stop Sasha and me in our tracks as we both turned and gawked at him. 'There's a sex cellar?' I squawked, my eyes opening so wide it felt like they might explode.

Oliver reached my side and paused, dropping a kiss on my lips and then standing back and slipping his hands in his pockets as he continued to observe the two of us with an amused smirk.

'No... Unfortunately not. But that look on your face is priceless. I really wish there was a door somewhere so I could at least pretend for a little longer.'

Normality was returned. There *wasn't* a sex room in the house. My God. My legs felt rubbery and my heart was pounding, but I couldn't quite decide if it was from relief or disappointment.

CHAPTER FOUR

Robyn

I glanced around Club Twist and could only count about twenty people in total, and that included David and Natalia behind the bar. Taking a sip of my chilled white wine, I checked my watch, shook my head, and looked at Sasha.

'I don't know why you dragged us down here so early, Sash. I told you it would be dead at this time.' I had my suspicions of why we were here so early on a Thursday night, and they involved Sasha's long-standing crush on a certain blond-haired friend of Oliver's. But, seeing as she wouldn't openly admit it to me, I decided to do what any good mate would do and rib her about it instead.

'You should just be upfront with Marcus, tell him you fancy him. You never know, he might like it if you took the lead.'

'I don't fancy him!' she replied immediately. Denial had become her automatic response to any questions relating to Marcus, and it was starting to grow decidedly old with me. Raising my eyebrows, I gave her a stern "that won't wash with me" look, and to my surprise Sasha's shoulders sagged and she let out a sigh as if finally relenting.

'There's no point. He'd have to be blind not to see how I feel. I've approached him enough times.' Sasha shrugged and chewed on her lip.

'And he definitely knocks you back every time? You're not just reading his signals wrong?' Sasha was gorgeous, and

Marcus would have to be nuts not to be interested in her.

'Nooo. He is more than clear in his rejection. From what Oliver said, Marcus and I just aren't going to be compatible. Marcus doesn't do one-night stands, and that's all that I do,' she stated simply.

'Hmmm.' I was in mid ponder when Sasha gave me a slap on the arm that broke my concentration and caused my eyes to shoot to hers. 'Besides, coming here tonight has nothing to do with Marcus bloody Price!' She flashed me an outraged look as her custom denial surrounded her again and then averted her eyes in a tell-tale sign that she was indeed telling me a fib. I loved her so much, but her pride was going to drive me insane one day.

'So, the fact that we're here this early on a Thursday night has nothing at all to do with me telling you just days ago that he and Oliver play squash on a Thursday afternoon and head here for a quick beer afterwards?'

'Nope.' Her denial was adamant. 'Although being my best mate you should have told me that *months* ago,' she added, flashing me a mildly disapproving look.

Giggling, I took a sip of my wine and shrugged. 'Sorry. You'd been quiet on the Marcus subject recently, so I didn't think it would be of interest to you.'

'It isn't.' She flicked her hair from her shoulders and pretended to examine her nails while actually glancing at the entrance doors for what must have been the hundredth time since our arrival, presumably on the lookout for Marcus.

I grinned and rolled my eyes. 'Hmm. Sure it isn't.'

Letting out a heavy sigh, Sasha looked up and threw her arms into the air. 'OK! OK! Fine. I admit it. I do still have a crush on him, but it seems that neither of us will give in and change our outlook, so it's never going to go anywhere. It's driving me bloody nuts!'

Both Oliver and I had noticed the way our two mates always gazed at each other, but to our continued surprise, nothing had ever happened between them. 'It's such a shame. It seems pretty obvious to me that he likes you. He certainly looks at you a lot.'

'I know, right? We have some seriously hot chemistry going on, but every time I try and initiate anything he finds a reason to leave or move away. I've never met a man who'd turn down sex,' she mused, as if this made him an alien species of some kind. 'I have no idea why he's a member of a sex club if he doesn't actually want to have sex!' Sasha held her hands up in an "I give up" gesture.

It was quite an amusing observation, but from what Oliver had told me, Marcus *did* want to have sex, just not *casual* sex. It did seem that perhaps Sasha was right, though; if he wanted a relationship then maybe Club Twist wasn't the best place to be pursuing it. He'd probably have more luck on an online dating site.

'He's definitely single. I asked Oliver.'

Sasha nodded. 'You know me, Rob, I don't date, but the fact that Marcus won't give it up for a night of passion with me is driving me crazy. I'm not used to being rejected!' Her statement wasn't said in a big-headed way, it was just the truth. Sasha had never had an issue picking up a guy; they seemed to practically fall at her feet on a weekly basis. Laughing at her own statement, she shrugged. 'I think that's why I'm still lusting after him. He's turned himself into the fucking forbidden fruit. I can't have it, so I want it even more!'

Nodding sagely, I wondered how I could help my friend, but drew a blank. If Sasha and her supreme seduction skills hadn't worked on Marcus so far, then I had no idea how she could make a breakthrough.

'Are you sure you couldn't consider trying more with him? I think you'd make a great couple,' I ventured carefully, well aware of why Sasha didn't date, but wondering if Marcus could possibly be the man to persuade her otherwise. Unfortunately, Sasha was already shaking her head before I'd even finished my sentence.

'You know my rules, Robyn. No relationship means no emotion which means no pain.'

I'd known Sasha since school, and I was well aware she had some pretty major emotional issues left over from the early deaths of both her parents. Being a young teenaged orphan had broken her for a while, and unfortunately, she'd somehow concluded that if she never got attached to anyone emotionally she'd never have to go through the heartbreak of losing someone again. Hence her "no relationship, no emotion, no pain" rules.

Sasha downed the last dregs of her drink and then slammed the tumbler down on the bar with such force that I was surprised it didn't break. 'Bloody man. He's thrown my mojo right off. I've been off my game for months now. Did you know I've only slept with two guys in the last twelve weeks? Two! And they were both lousy,' she added, her lip curling in irritation.

Jeez. Two men in twelve weeks might not sound a particularly low figure to someone like me, who had only had six lovers in my entire life, but for Sasha, who usually warmed her bed with a different guy every weekend, it counted as a significantly dry spell.

'Anyway, that's enough about me. What's it been like living your first two weeks in the Wolfe's Lair?'

I chuckled at her joke and grinned broadly. I was so happy at the moment that it was difficult not to look really smug about it. It might only have been a fortnight so far, but I was loving every second of being with Oliver.

'It's been amazing.' I hadn't thought I could love Oliver any more than I already did, but sharing his private space had allowed me to get to know him on a whole other level. I'd known he was a romantic deep down, but I'd now discovered his sweet, thoughtful side, too. He did little things on a daily basis to make me smile; things like bringing me a coffee to the bedroom if he was up before me, sticking little notes around the house in places he knew I'd see them, or leaving single flowers in vases for me to find.

'I bet he still looks hot in the morning though, huh? He seems like one of those guys who never has a hair out of place, regardless of what time of day it is.'

When I'd first glimpsed Oliver in Club Twist his seemingly flawless appearance had made him look dauntingly unapproachable. Not that I had approached him, I thought with a smirk – in the end, Oliver had done all the chasing – but I still laughed at her description of his hair, and I could see why she'd think it; he did look immaculate *most* of the time. More than immaculate. His hair was always wild, but in an "I styled it to look like this" kind of way. However, in the last two weeks I'd discovered that his hair took on a complete life of its own after a night's sleep – it literally stuck out everywhere with none of its usual sleekness or intentional tousle.

'Oh no, he gets bed head just like the rest of us,' I confided with a smile. Oliver had been surprisingly self-conscious about his morning hair until I had declared how cute I thought it was, and now he knew I liked it he seemed to keep it deliberately ruffled until he had to leave the house.

'And he's still kissing you breathless and shagging you senseless on every available occasion and surface?'

Her words made me laugh so hard that my recent sip of wine stung at the back of my nose and threatened to spray out of my nostrils. Swallowing with difficulty, I chuckled again and nodded. 'He is. But you already know that, Sasha, because you demand inappropriately explicit details of my love life practically every time I see you.'

'I do, but I haven't seen you all week and so I have yet to hear if you've christened all the rooms in his house. I bet you have, haven't you?' she declared with a wicked leer and an expectant wiggle of her eyebrows.

We had, on multiple occasions, and some more than

others – Oliver's favourite locations seemed to be the kitchen and the hallway – but instead of answering I just rolled my eyes and grinned at Sasha's keen expression.

'Seeing as my own sex life is in the shitter at the moment, I'm living vicariously through you, Robyn. Hearing details of all the kinky things you do with Oliver is better than watching porn.'

I recoiled in my seat with a grimace and waved a hand at her to stop. 'Ugh, God, Sasha!' Before I could moan at her any further, the music in the club changed and I heard the familiar strains of *Better Together* starting up. It was one of my favourite songs, and I grinned. 'Ah! Jack Johnson! I love this song!'

'It's a bit unusual for the club, though, isn't it?' Sasha commented with a peculiar smile, and I realised she'd made a good point – Club Twist constantly played upbeat dance music, never acoustic tracks like this one. I had no idea what her grin was about, but I ignored it for now and focused on listening to the music.

This particular tune had leaped to the top of my all-time favourites when Oliver had included it on the playlist that he'd made for me a while back, and I still loved it. The lyrics were just so perfect.

As if Oliver knew I was thinking about him, he chose that very moment to sweep through the entrance doors of the club with Marcus by his side. Instead of looking flushed from their recent squash game, they were both impeccably suited and booted. Oliver's wild hair looked a little more tamed than usual as if he'd put even more effort into neatening it up. Ignoring everyone else, he strode straight up to me, and then, without saying a word, took my hand and pulled me in the direction of the dance floor so swiftly that I only just managed to hand my sloshing glass of wine to Sasha as he dragged me away.

'Oliver! The dance floor's empty!' I protested desperately,

wondering what on earth had got into him. I wasn't exactly a huge fan of dancing at the best of times, and seeing that not a soul was so much as tapping a foot, every single person here was probably now watching us, which just made me feel even more uncomfortable.

He lowered his lips to my mouth and placed a brief kiss there before speaking. 'But it's our song, *cariño*. Humour me.'

It was kind of our song, I suppose, and his kiss had softened my nerves, so with a nod I relented and let Oliver wrap me in his arms and sway us to the music.

Halfway through the track he kissed me again, but this time it was soft and lingering and had me just starting to pant when he broke our lips and took a small step back.

'It's not often you'll see me on my knees, so make the most of this.' After this cryptic comment, he reached into his jacket pocket and then dropped to one knee before me.

My eyes widened and my mouth went instantly dry as I looked down at him. He opened a small velvet box and gazed up at me with hopeful eyes.

Oh my God.

I might be slightly naïve when it came to relationships, but even I couldn't misunderstand what was going on right before my eyes. My heart was pounding in my chest and my legs were distinctly rubbery below me as I continued to stare down at him with bated breath as I waited for him to speak.

'Robyn, you are my lover, my submissive, and my best friend. You have made my life complete. Would you make me the proudest man alive by agreeing to marry me?'

Oh! My! God!

I'd known the words were coming, but they still shocked the hell out of me. I also understood the enormity of this moment, but I was so overwhelmed that for several seconds I stared at him as if he'd just sprouted a second head.

When I did try to answer, I found my throat was so swelled from emotion that I couldn't actually speak, and my reply of “yes” came out as a high-pitched squeak. Oliver’s eyebrows quirked in amusement, so I nodded my head frantically and watched in fascinated shock as he pulled a beautiful diamond ring from the box and carefully slid it on my ring finger before placing a lingering kiss on top of it.

I was vaguely aware of the sound of Sasha screaming excitedly somewhere behind me, but right at this moment all my focus was on the beautiful man kneeling before me.

Swallowing hard, I finally managed to find my voice. ‘I love you so much, Oliver.’ He gazed up at me with a broad grin and eyes twinkling with delight, but when he made no attempt to move I gave a tug on his hand. ‘Stand up, it’s weird seeing you on your knees. That’s supposed to be my spot.’

Flashing me a wink, he obeyed and stood up. He encircled me in his arms and laid a kiss on me that was at once both so tender and deep that happy tears leaked from my eyes as I clung to him.

‘I’ll warn you now, Robyn, that I don’t want to wait long…’

I didn’t either. Now that he’d proposed I realised just how much I wanted to marry him. I could barely believe this was all happening, but before I could say anything else, we were hit from the side by Sasha as she came charging over to us and smacked straight into us with a congratulatory hug.

This was followed by firm slaps on the back from Marcus, David, and Nathan and a tray of champagne which appeared from nowhere shortly before a glass found its way into my hand.

‘That was just as perfect as I’d hoped,’ Sasha gushed, giving Oliver a playful punch on the arm. ‘Well done!’

Ah, so that was why Sasha had been grinning at me earlier – she’d been in on it all along. It must also be why she’d dragged me here so early, and nothing to do with Marcus as I had assumed.

Looking down at my ring finger again, I shook my head in

amazement as the diamonds sparkled up at me. My God, I was engaged! Talk about a whirlwind. Oliver Wolfe, the enigmatic man who had captured my attention all those months ago in this very bar, was now my fiancé.

CHAPTER FIVE

Sasha

Robyn was busy with Oliver tonight – no doubt doing sickeningly-romantic-recently-engaged-couple shit – but I'd thought that I'd be fine coming down to Club Twist without her as my sidekick. I was confident being here on my own, and I now knew quite a few of the regulars to chat to, but it wasn't turning out to be as much fun as I'd thought.

All I'd wanted to do was have a few drinks and dance my arse off, but none of the girls I was friends with were here tonight, not even Natalia, and I wasn't in the mood for chatting up a random guy, even though I'd already had to knock back three who had tried.

Dancing on my own like a loser was a step too far even for me, so I'd found myself sitting in a booth fiddling with my phone and messaging Chloe to see if I could persuade her to join me.

'Hey. You want some company?'

A deep voice mingled with the bass of the music and interrupted me, and I sighed heavily, irritated that yet another bloke was clearly set on trying his luck. I might be a single girl spending the evening in a sex club, but that didn't necessarily mean I wanted to be hassled. Pasting a defensive scowl on my face, I prepared to give the guy the same dismissive brush-off as I had his predecessors, but when I looked up my eyes nearly boggled out of my head.

It wasn't just a random guy, it was Marcus.

Marcus Price, my long-running crush, the man I'd been aiming flirtatious glances at for weeks with no luck whatsoever, and suddenly *wham*, here he was, standing right beside me, looking gorgeous in a black polo shirt and grey jeans and asking if I wanted company.

I definitely wanted *his* company.

Marcus gave me a wary look and took a step back. 'Actually, that scowl says you want to be left alone… I'll go.'

Quickly wiping the bitchy expression from my brow, I held up a hand. 'No! Wait! That was just because I thought you were another random bloke trying his luck. I've had to knock a few back tonight, and my scowl usually works a treat.'

One of Marcus's eyebrows rose in amusement. 'I can see why, it's quite formidable,' he commented dryly. 'So, can I join you?'

This was certainly a turn-up for the bloody books. I'd tried and failed to get closer to him over the past few weeks, and even though I'd seen heat in his eyes as he looked at me and returned my smiles, he'd always found an excuse to leave or move away if I'd tried to initiate anything more.

In the end, I'd had to reluctantly draw the conclusion that he just wasn't interested in me, and yet here he was in all his glory asking if he could sit with me.

Reeling in my shock, I smiled and nodded as I slid across the booth and patted the space beside me. 'I'd like that, Marcus, thanks.' Stupidly, my heart rate had accelerated to near lethal levels in my chest and I had to draw in several shaky breaths to try to calm myself.

As soon as he was settled he took a deep breath as if also steadying himself, and I felt reassured that he was apparently finding this just as nerve-wracking as I was. There was a slightly awkward silence between us and then he offered me a small, sweet smile and broke the quiet. 'So, how's things?'

"*Things*" were seriously weird – my pulse was still going wild and I could feel a nervous flutter in my stomach at his proximity. Not that I would admit that, but with the way my body was going crazy for him, small talk was probably sensible to give me time to calm down.

'Really good, thanks. I'm in the process of buying a flat, actually.'

'Wow, that's exciting.' Marcus looked surprised, so Oliver obviously hadn't told him about my meeting with his neighbour.

Sipping my drink, I lifted my free hand and crossed my fingers. 'As long as the survey goes through it should be full steam ahead in the next few months.'

'Good luck.' Marcus chinked his glass against mine in a toast, and after we had both taken a drink and placed our glasses down he looked up at me intently. 'I've been holding myself back from doing this for months.'

He'd been holding himself back from talking to me? I'd made enough attempts to start up conversations with him, so his words made absolutely no sense. 'Doing what?'

Marcus didn't answer me audibly. Instead, he slid closer in the booth, looped a hand behind my head, and then, with no further pause, crashed his mouth down onto mine.

Desire exploded in my system at his desperate touch, my skin going wild at his closeness, and a flare of heat rushed up my neck as his lips started to move insistently over mine.

Holy fuck! Not that I was complaining, but where the hell had this come from?

All the months of pent-up frustration suddenly seemed to ignite between us like a petrol-soaked rag to an open fire, and I groaned in pleasure and shifted in my seat so our bodies were at the perfect angle to deepen the kiss. Marcus took my cue and used my groan to press his tongue inside my mouth, extending the kiss into something far more erotic as his tongue began twining with mine in a lusty duel that had us both panting within seconds.

My God, he was a seriously fucking good kisser, and this

was seriously fucking hot.

He was kissing me like I was the very thing he needed to survive, like I was some rare and beautiful creature he wanted to capture and keep, and the feeling was so potent that my head started to spin and I had to reach up to steady myself on his forearms.

I dragged him closer, needing the feel of him under my fingertips. I felt as if I couldn't get him near enough, like *he* was the very thing *I* needed for survival, too. I wanted him touching me all over, pressed against me, inside and out.

As soon as I touched him, though, Marcus tensed below my fingers, but without breaking the contact between our lips he managed to take both of my hands in his and link them behind my back, where he gripped them in one of his large palms. Holding my wrists with one hand, he moved his other hand up to cradle the back of my head as his lips continued to devour me.

Hmm, into a bit of restraint, was he? The hold on my wrists and tension in my arms was a new sensation for me – though I'd had a lot of sex in my adult life, bondage wasn't something I'd experimented with – but now I was experiencing it at the hands of Marcus I had to say it was pretty damn hot. The new position made me feel deliciously wanted by him, and the pull on my arms arched my back slightly pressing my breasts into his chest, which was just fine by me.

We kissed like this for an age, both of us breathing heavier and getting more and more aroused with each passing second. His lips left mine and began to explore along my jawline and I took the opportunity to pull in a ragged breath. As much as I was enjoying the sensation of being controlled by him, I started to get fidgety in my capture. I wanted to touch him; explore the firm chest I could feel against my breasts, run my hands through his wild blond hair, and feel the roughness of his stubble under my fingertips.

While my lips were free I vocalised my desires, giving a

tug of my wrists at the same time. 'I want to touch you.'

Marcus paused, his lips hovering just beside my ear and hot breath tickling the sensitive lobe. 'No. No touching.' His lips landed on my skin again, peppering kisses across my cheek as if that might make me forget my request, but as he reached my lips I twisted my head away so I could look into his eyes.

'I can't touch you?' I asked, confused by his odd statement. Did he mean no touching now, or never? Perhaps this was a scene he wanted to play out tonight. We were both members of a sex club, after all, and I had no idea what his bedroom tastes were. He might be like Oliver and enjoy domination and restraint.

A troubled look flickered in his eyes and reflected in a frown lowering his brow. 'No.'

In one fluid movement he stood and shifted us to the side of the booth so we stood in a darkened nook hidden away from the rest of the club. He backed me into the wall and adjusted my wrists, interlinking our fingers and pressing our joined hands against the wall on either side of my head.

Our faces were now level, and he gave a squeeze on my hands. 'Apart from hand-holding.'

So I could hold his hand but nothing else? How the hell would that ever work if we had sex? He shifted his stance so that his body pressed against mine, and now we were standing the jut of his arousal pressed insistently against my stomach, notching up my own desires.

He was so close like this that I very nearly lost myself to the feel of his body, the scent of his skin, and the gorgeous green of his eyes, but there seemed to be a trace of something in his gaze, some sort of sadness or regret, and it made me question him further.

'No touching at all? Like ever?'

The sorrow in his gaze seemed to increase at my words, and then he slowly shook his head. 'No, only me touching you.'

I blinked in confusion, struggling to understand his bizarre rules. 'Why?'

His nostrils flared, and he gave a marginal shrug, clearing his expression as if he hadn't just requested something so peculiar. 'Because that's the way it has to be.' Marcus's tone made it clear he'd decided that was the end of our discussion, but even though I didn't ask any more questions my mind was still racing, and I wondered if he'd always been like this.

His kiss and confidence screamed of experience, so I could only assume that he'd had many sexual partners in the past. Had his previous lovers not been allowed to touch him either?

As these questions floated in my mind his mouth found mine once more, and his lips were so warm and persuasive that I started to forget about my queries and my earlier urge to touch him. My body was instantly alight for him again and I moaned as he rolled his hips against mine and tilted his head to deepen the kiss. He was clearly more than capable of turning me on without the need for my touch, because my body was on fire for him, so I gave up my questions and just allowed myself to sink deeper under his spell.

Electricity felt as if it was sparking in the air around us and crackling across my skin, and our breathing was so frantic that I could hear it echoing around us above the beat of the music. Marcus was kissing me like a man possessed, and after so long craving him I was giving back just as much.

Pulling back for a breath, Marcus grinned down at me, looking relaxed again now that I had stopped my questions. I took a moment to absorb just how bloody handsome he was; his green eyes were clear and possessive, and his blond hair was wild, reminiscent of Gordon Ramsay's, only thicker and even less tamed.

Licking my lips, I tried to calm my breathing as I returned his smile. 'I'm not complaining at all, but what's caused your sudden change of heart?' I asked, wondering why he had chosen now to kiss me, when I'd tried it on with him so many times over the past few months and been rejected every single time.

Marcus gave a shy smile and lowered his head so the tip of his nose briefly brushed against mine. It was an oddly romantic gesture, and for a girl who only ever did connections that involved no feelings or emotions I was surprised at how much I liked it.

'Unlike many other men here, I don't do one-night stands,' he admitted quietly. 'From what I saw of you when you first joined Club Twist that was all you did.' Marcus brought himself up short, and a blush reddened his cheeks as he gave me a rueful smile. 'No offence.'

'None taken.' I shrugged, a little embarrassed by the accuracy of his observations, but honest enough to admit that yes, that was exactly how I chose to conduct my sex life. I liked sex, but I didn't like relationships, and there was no point being prim about it.

He nodded once, and his hands gripped mine a little tighter as he lowered his face closer again. Our breaths mingled, and as I smelled a faint trace of rum all I could think about was him kissing me again.

'I've noticed a change in you over the last few months, Sasha. You're not with a different guy every time I come in here any more, I even watched as you knocked back three separate guys tonight, one after the other.' He smiled, and it was almost shy, then he gave a small shrug. 'You and I have been exchanging some pretty heated glances over the past few weeks, so I figured maybe you felt the thing between us, too, and that I could finally tempt you into forgetting your one-night rule and give me a chance.'

Visions of him kissing me again evaporated as his words sunk in.

Give him a chance?

What. The. Fuck?

So, within the space of five minutes we'd gone from barely

ever speaking, to kissing like maniacs, to him asking me to give him a chance? A chance at what, exactly? Did he mean a relationship?

My hands were still trapped, and my body was pressed against the wall by the firm heat of his, but I used my limited wiggle room to shake my head.

'Marcus… I don't date. I don't do relationships.' I knew Robyn had told Oliver this much; had he not in turn told Marcus? 'Oliver must surely have mentioned that?'

Rolling his eyes as if my statement was ridiculous, Marcus blew out a long breath. He let out a groan and lowered his mouth to mine again as if there was no possible way he could resist me for another second.

I rather liked the idea that he seemed to find me irresistible, and no matter how much I knew we needed to continue our conversation and not snog each other's faces off, I couldn't seem to ignore the sizzling bond between us. This was chemistry like I'd never experienced before; addictive, hot, and passionate, hinting that we'd be seriously explosive in the sack together. As he continued to kiss me with hot, open-mouth kisses that skimmed across my lips I gave up on conversation and enjoyed the sensation of our tongues duelling and our heated breaths mixing in the sex-drenched atmosphere around us.

Marcus trailed his lips up my neck and then pulled back just slightly, his cheeks flushed and his eyes so dilated that they looked almost completely black.

'There's something between us, Sasha, you feel it, too. I know you do.' His kiss began all over again as if trying to persuade me to his way of thinking, and I was so foggy-headed from the desire coursing around my system that I once again allowed it to blind me and continued kissing him back.

I'd wanted Marcus for months, but his kiss was all-consuming, sucking me in and shocking me with the intensity of what I felt for him. The longer our mouths were joined, the clearer it became to me that this was more than just a kiss. He was right, there was something between us, a deeper connection of some sort, and from the way he was clinging to me and kissing me so desperately it seemed like he was just as affected by the emotions as I was.

Emotions. The word echoed around inside my lust-fuddled mind, and if I hadn't been so hazy from desire it would probably have caused alarm bells to sound.

'We could be so good together. The connection between us is incredible,' he murmured against my lips. He ground his hips against mine to make me completely aware of just how large he was in the trouser department, and how good it would no doubt feel to be joined with him intimately.

One word stuck in my mind and finally broke through the cloud of yearning engulfing my body. *Together*. I didn't do "togetherness". The only version I did was two bodies banging together in the heat of passion for a short period of time and then going their separate ways.

'Just admit that you feel it, Sasha. The connection between us is too good to ignore.'

Suddenly everything started to feel as if it was spiralling out of control. Once again, he was speaking against my open mouth and I tasted something sweet like rum and Coke on his breath. The move would have been so erotic if he'd been murmuring sweet nothings or talking dirty to me, but he wasn't; he was digging into my insecurities, talking about feelings and trying to get me to open up.

I didn't do deep feelings or connections, and I didn't let anyone see my vulnerabilities, especially not a man.

Nothing with emotions could ever last forever. It would always end in pain; I knew that from bitter experience.

All this talk of emotions, togetherness, and connections had doused my arousal more effectively than if a bucket of iced water had just been thrown over me and I tilted my head back to look up at him.

Marcus was gazing at me with such intensity that it was as if I could be the answer to all his problems, the girl to take away the pain in his eyes.

He was looking at me as if I could be his everything, and it fucking terrified me.

'This could be amazing if you'd just let it.'

This would be amazing if *I* would let it? He was blaming *me* for holding things up? His words made me pause, and finally I came to my senses a little and twisted further away from him. How dare he turn this around onto me?

'If *I'd* let it?' I knew I was avoiding the real issues here – my fear of getting closer to someone and getting hurt – but turning the blame onto him seemed an easier option, so I allowed my brain to run with it and fire out an accusation of my own. 'What about you, Marcus? You've made a run for it every single time I've tried to come close to you!'

'Because I knew you only wanted a one-night stand and I'd place money on the fact that this thing between us is worth more than just a quick fuck.'

'Quick fucks are what I do,' I stated bluntly, ignoring the wince that my tone caused on his face.

'Why can't you even consider the possibility of something longer than one night?' He sighed, his body still pressing heavily against mine, and his groin just as hard as it jerked and pulsed against my body. Clearly his dick hadn't quite got the message that we were now arguing and not making out.

'Because that's what I do,' I repeated sharply, not willing to explain my reasons to him. Two could play at that game – he hadn't explained why he wouldn't let me touch him earlier, so I wouldn't explain my intimacy issues, either. 'Can't you just change your rules for one night?'

His head shake was immediate and resolute. 'No. I don't do one-night stands, I already told you that.'

'Why?'

'Because I see you as more than just someone to fuck for

an hour or two. Is that so bad? It should be a fucking compliment.' To be fair to him, it probably was complimentary, but I just couldn't do it… I'd never done more than one night with a guy. *Never*.

Finally seeing the frown still on my face, he sighed and let go of my hands as he moved back towards the booth, his entire demeanour changing and shuttering off in a split second, even if I could still see the large bulge in the front of his trousers.

'I have issues, Sasha, and I'd need to explain them to you before anything could happen between us. I'm not going to put myself through the stress of that conversation just for a few hours of sex.'

His words made me pause, but then the champagne bubbles from earlier boosted my confidence and now that my hands were free I reached down and lightly gripped his rock-solid groin. 'It doesn't feel like you have any issues to me.'

Marcus tensed, let out a low growl, and knocked my hand away before shaking his head. 'I'm not talking about performance issues,' he grated. 'My tackle works just fine.'

I lowered my gaze and smiled. Even through his jeans it was obvious to see that Marcus was gifted in that department. *Very* gifted. 'So I can see, big boy.'

'Sasha, stop it.' His tone was resigned now and full of frustration. 'I guess this thing between us has to stop here, then.' His words held a note of finality, and as I realised that he wasn't going to change his mind about it I tried to protect myself and reply with a flippantly dismissive comment like I always did.

'It doesn't. Not if you weren't so stuck up.' Flicking my hair over my shoulder, I levelled my gaze on him and slowly licked my lips. 'It could stop tomorrow morning, after we've spent the night together fucking each other's brains out.'

Marcus shoved his hands into his jeans pockets and scowled at me. 'No, no, and three times no, Sasha.'

Gah! This guy was so frustrating! Why did he have to be so

bloody attractive?

He let out another heavy sigh and stepped back from the booth with obvious reluctance. 'I wish we could work this out, because the chemistry I feel with you is incredible,' he murmured softly, his eyes dejected. 'I just wish you would admit to feeling it, too.'

It *was* incredible, and I *did* feel it, ridiculously so, almost to the point where I was tempted to say it out loud and ask him not to go. But what then? He clearly wasn't going to change his mind about coming home with me for the night, and so I'd have to consider his option – more. I didn't do more, literally never had in my entire life, so instead of saying anything I stayed silent and clenched my hands at my sides to stop myself reaching for him.

Marcus smiled sadly and nodded once. 'Fine. This just isn't going to work, Sasha. I'm sorry I interrupted your night.' With that, he turned and walked away, his shoulders hunched and the usual spring noticeably missing from his step.

Fuck, fuck, fuck! Why was he so bloody stubborn? A dry laugh left my throat when I realised that he was quite probably thinking the exact same thing about me at this very moment.

As I watched him cutting through the crowd in the bar a nagging voice at the back of my head told me to call to him, stop him, and explore these strange feelings inside me, because as much as I might not like to admit it, he'd been right – I *had* changed over the last few months. My mind frequently wandered to him these days, and my attention was definitely focused more on him during my trips to Twist, and as a result I hadn't pulled nearly as much as I had in the past. I just hadn't had the inclination to spend time with another man when Marcus had been in the same room. Watching him and wondering if I could get closer had become like a challenge to me.

Now I'd had a taste of the challenge, only to be firmly thrown to the side, and it wasn't a sensation I liked in the slightest.

Finally, he disappeared from sight, and I plopped back down into the booth and started anxiously twirling a strand of hair as I fell deeper into thought.

After sitting there for five minutes playing back how incredible his kiss had felt I found myself just as confused as I had been to start with. I'd always been so resolute in my belief that relationships could only ever lead to one thing – pain and broken hearts – but now I'd had a taste of how good it could be with Marcus, I was left feeling distinctly confused about my long-held outlooks.

CHAPTER SIX

Marcus

The weights bar landed back into the cradle with a resounding crash, and as I tried to regain my breath I stood back and ruefully looked at the load I had been lifting. One hundred and sixty kilograms. I was a regular here at the gym, and a pretty skilled weight lifter, but pressing one-sixty was pushing it, even for me. I'd needed a challenge today, though, something physically tough to consume my mind and help take my thoughts off Sasha and the kiss we'd shared last night.

It had worked, but only for the five minutes I'd been struggling with my lifting reps, and now the weights were down again I was left with aching muscles and a head full of *her*.

Cursing under my breath, I grabbed my water bottle for a drink and then threw it back down onto my gym bag with an irritated grunt. I'd literally never been so fixated on a woman in my entire life, but Sasha, the one woman who I couldn't have, had taken over my mind and now seemed to reside in my head twenty-four seven.

Huffing out a breath, I stepped back to the weights rack and took hold of the bar, again twisting my grip around the roughened metal until I felt the burn of it tearing at my skin. The rack was set so that the bar was at my shoulder height, so I settled myself under it and prepared my grip on the bar, making sure my elbows were at a safe ninety-degree angle.

Thinking through each step of the process was good. It was

focusing my mind into the here and now, so I continued with it.

I widened my stance a little so it was just over shoulder width, bent my knees slightly, and braced my core for the weight I was about to lift onto my shoulders. Tensing my mid-section, I breathed out and pressed the bar up above my head. I kept raising the weights until my arms were straight and my muscles were screaming at me to stop, and then I lowered the bar back down to collarbone height and set myself to repeat the action again.

Breathe. Lift. Forget about Sasha Mortimer.

And repeat.

Once I'd lifted it ten times I set the bar back in the cradle and stepped away with a tired groan. I was pushing myself too far, I knew that, but I needed the muscle stress and pain as a distraction.

God, her kiss had been *in-fucking-credible*. Her mouth was so soft, and the little moans of pleasure she'd made had been…

'Fuck!' I spun away from the weights with a loud curse and only just resisted the temptation to hit out at something, *anything*, in my frustration. Seeing as I was surrounded by very heavy metal things, it was just as well that I did resist, because I would no doubt have come off worse from any outbursts.

Why the hell couldn't I get Sasha out of my mind? Closing my eyes, I finally gave in and let my evil brain go to where it wanted to. My vision was immediately flooded with images of Sasha and her blonde hair, teasing smiles, and gorgeous blue eyes.

She was beautiful, and no doubt most men's idea of a perfect woman. A defeated sigh slipped from my lips as I allowed memories of our kiss to flood back to my mind. Her lips had accepted mine as if they were made to be together, and the groan of pleasure she'd made as I'd pressed my tongue inside her mouth had been such a fucking turn-on that my cock had felt like an aching slab of granite behind my zipper.

She hadn't even minded when I'd held her hands behind her back. In fact, she'd arched into me enthusiastically and practically purred her agreement against my neck.

Glancing down, I growled in irritation when I realised I was standing in the middle of the gym sporting a raging hard-on. My flimsy shorts really did nothing to hide it at all, so it was just as well it was early, and the gym was deserted.

I dropped down onto the floor, took up a press-up position, and tried to divert the blood away from my cock by racking out as many reps as I could manage, grunting with each move and forcing my brain to think about something else apart from Sasha bloody Mortimer.

By the time I had reached fifty repetitions I was dripping with sweat and my shoulders were in agony but at least my cock had finally calmed again. I stood up and rolled off my stiff shoulders, then grabbed the hem of my workout vest to pull it up and wipe at the sweat on my forehead.

As I did, I caught a glimpse of my scarred torso in the mirror. Scowling, I glanced around to check I was still on my own and then lifted the vest higher and examined my reflection in the mirror. Thanks to my weekly gym sessions, I had a six pack that a lot of men would kill for, but I was fairly sure that my gym buddies wouldn't be so keen to crave the other things that adorned my torso – my scars, and there were a lot of them.

My eyes traced the criss-cross of furrowed lines that were scattered across my stomach and then moved around to the side of my body where the deeper, more pronounced scarring was. The bright lights of the gym were particularly unforgiving, and I winced as I took in the dark purple puckered lines above my hip bone. I'd gotten so used to seeing them in the mirrors of my bathroom on a daily basis that I'd almost forgotten how horrible they were when viewed in proper lighting.

It might be just as well that things with Sasha hadn't gone

any further last night. She'd probably have taken one look at my ruined body and run for the hills. I dropped my vest down again with a grimace and moved back to the weights bar ready to punish myself again and try to force thoughts of my kiss with her from my mind once and for all.

CHAPTER SEVEN

Robyn

I always found it weird when I came to the club before opening time. Bright lights illuminated the spaces that were usually filled with darkness and illicit behaviour, the dance floor was empty, and the entire premises just felt bigger, airier, and more… normal, I suppose.

The most amusing thing was always the swarm of cleaners that I found here when the doors were locked to the public. The place was literally gleaming. David Halton, the owner of Club Twist, might be a muscly tattooed guy with the rough and ready air of a biker, but the level of hygiene he demanded was top notch.

I supposed it needed to be, seeing what went on in the private rooms and dark corners.

A quick glance around the empty space seemed to indicate that Oliver wasn't finished in his meeting with David yet, so I pulled my iPad out to do a bit of writing while I waited. I'd only just got myself settled at the bar when Alex pushed her way through the door that led to the storeroom behind the bar and came to an abrupt stop.

Our eyes met, and her features momentarily tensed as she joined me, as they frequently did. It would be fair to say that Alex and I still didn't exactly get along; I didn't really like her because of the fact she'd once slept with Oliver, and I suspected that she disliked me because I now slept with Oliver.

What it came down to between the two of us was jealousy,

plain and simple. Although seeing as I was the one sharing my life with Oliver I always tried to be an adult about it and play nice. 'Hey, Alex.'

She placed down the box she was carrying and greeted me with a nod. 'Robyn.' Her lips briefly puckered into a pout and then her eyes flickered to my engagement ring. 'I hear congratulations are in order.'

It wasn't exactly a glowing exclamation of good wishes, but I guess coming from Alex it was probably the best I could hope for.

I wasn't enough of a bitch to rub it in her face, though, so I gave a small smile and nodded before tucking my hands into my lap and hiding my ring from her stare. 'Thanks.'

Her mouth opened as if she wanted to say something else, but at that moment we were joined by Oliver and David as they trotted down the stairs from the offices.

'Evening, ladies,' David greeted us, flashing us both a charming wink that would make a lot of women weak at the knees, but seconds later I was engulfed in the delicious scent and feel of Oliver as he swept me up into his arms and landed a kiss on my lips.

Hmm, now this was the man who made *me* weak at the knees.

'Good evening, *cariño*.' His words were peppered across my cheek as he kissed a trail to my lips. Alex frowned at his affection, and then dismissed us with a roll of her eyes as she walked away.

'I'll open up,' she muttered, leaving us to our embrace. Maybe now we were engaged she'd finally move her attention away from him and things between the two of us would become a little less prickly.

The lights flicked off, deep booming music began to play, and then, as was always the case on a Friday night, the club was swamped with people flooding in the second the doors opened.

What had been a light, bright, clinically clean interior just seconds ago was now dark, throbbing with atmosphere and filled with that unmistakable feeling of expectation.

Frowning, I asked a question I'd been pondering this week. 'Are we inviting Alex to the wedding?'

Oliver scoffed and shook his head. 'No.'

'But you want to invite everyone else who works here, right?'

'Yes, but I haven't forgotten how she treated you when we thought you were pregnant, Robyn. We don't have to invite her.'

Seeing as Oliver was a part-owner of this place the club was always likely to be a feature in our lives, so having a better relationship with Alex would make things easier for everyone involved.

'I think we should invite her. Let bygones be bygones and all that.'

Oliver looked down into my eyes. He smiled fondly and shook his head. 'You are one of the sweetest people I have ever met.' He dropped a kiss on my temple and gave a shrug. 'We don't have to decide now, do we? We can discuss the guest list at a later date,' he said, neither agreeing nor disagreeing with my idea. 'So what time is Sasha getting here?' He released me from his grip only to sit down on a stool and then reinstate me on his lap.

Glancing at my watch, I shrugged and snuggled closer. 'Not sure. Any time now, I guess. I'm looking forward to seeing her.'

It had been such a busy few weeks that I hadn't managed to see Sasha since the night Oliver had proposed to me. So much for our plan of a Thursday girls' nights out – Sasha had cancelled last week due to a work deadline, and the week before that it had been me calling it off because Oliver and I had been attending a wedding fair.

I was so excited to see her tonight. We had so much to talk

about; I needed her advice on dress shopping, flower choices, cake types… basically everything. There were so many on my favourites list that I was having a really tough time scaling down my options.

Plus, I needed to ask her an important question – I wanted her to be my bridesmaid. It wasn't the type of thing I had wanted to ask over the phone, so I had saved my question for tonight.

Oliver also wanted Marcus to be his best man but hadn't asked him yet, either. We were planning on asking them both tonight in a joint announcement, so having the four of us together privately would be perfect.

Marcus arrived first, grabbed a beer, and joined us with a smirk as he took in my position on Oliver's lap. Feeling a little embarrassed, I pushed myself to standing, much to Oliver's displeasure, but I soothed him by immediately sliding a hand around his waist.

Sasha arrived just a few minutes later. As always, she looked gorgeous; her wavy hair had been tamed into long, sleek submission with some skilful use of her straighteners, and she was wearing a short, fire engine red dress and matching lipstick.

I could never carry off a dress like that, but with Oliver's firm grip wrapped around my hand I didn't feel any envy at the appreciative looks she drew as she walked across the bar towards us. Marcus's gaze was one of many that latched on to her, and I noticed he didn't seem too keen on the stares she was attracting.

Something flickered across Sasha's face as she broke through the crowd and saw that Marcus was with us, but then she cleared her expression and headed towards me.

I watched in horror as she slipped when her high heel hit something wet on the floor about a metre away from us. I gasped, and as Sasha's arms briefly flailed both Marcus and I made a grab for her to stop her falling. I was too far away, but luckily, Marcus managed to place a hand on her waist and grab one of her hands to give her just enough stability to right herself.

Sasha steadied her balance and I watched with interest as she and Marcus exchanged a heated glance. Things seemed to slow down as Sasha pulled in a ragged breath, and then Marcus slid his hand from her waist but seemed to cling to her hand as if he didn't want to let go.

Oliver nudged me in the shoulder and gave me a curious look to show that he'd also noticed the weird moment between our friends, and so I nodded and tried to work out what was going on between them.

Even as a bystander the chemistry that had sparked had been obvious to see, but as far as I was aware things between Sasha and Marcus were still just that of an awkward friendship because they were attracted to each other but wouldn't act on it.

Sasha stared at their joined hands, and because I was watching them carefully, I saw the exact moment that my best friend shut herself off again; she lowered her eyebrows, straightened her shoulders, and started to shake her arm, trying to free her hand from Marcus's grip.

'I don't need your help, Marcus.' Her tone was acidic enough that even I winced, and poor Marcus drew in a shocked breath before his expression morphed from one of concern to a look of sour irritation quicker than I could even blink.

'Well, excuse me for trying to be a gentleman.'

My jaw dropped open at the frostiness in both of their voices and I stared in surprise at the unexpected confrontation unravelling before my eyes. Sasha gave her arm another tug, and finally succeeded in getting her hand back. She glowered at him. 'If I can't touch you, then you can't touch me, either. It goes both ways.'

Marcus's shoulders rose, and he crossed his arms over his chest as he returned her stare just as fiercely. 'You walked away from something good, not me, Sasha. Don't take it out on me if I was just trying to help you.'

Before Oliver or I had even had a chance to intervene, Sasha pivoted on her toes and stormed off in one direction, followed by Marcus a second later going the opposite way.

I felt like I'd just witnessed a hormone-induced strop from a teenage film and both Oliver and I stood frozen to the spot, gawking at the retreating backs of our friends. Oliver turned to me with a stunned expression on his face that matched my own astonishment. 'Do you have any idea what that little yelling match was about?'

Shaking my head, I watched as Sasha disappeared into the ladies' loos, and then looked up at him. 'Nope. No idea at all. Kinda ruined our idea of a joint announcement, though, huh?'

Oliver gave a tight smile and nodded. 'It did rather. It would seem our potential best man and bridesmaid hate each other's guts.'

After that angst-filled performance, I had to say that yes, it really did. They'd gone from sharing a heated glance to shooting daggers at each other within the blink of an eye.

'I have no idea why. I didn't think they even spoke to each other that much. Sasha seemed pretty upset, though. I'm going to go and find her.'

Nodding, Oliver buttoned his suit jacket and scanned the crowd in the bar. 'Good idea, I'll hunt down Marcus.'

Sasha was in front of the mirror reapplying her lipstick when I entered the toilets. Her eyes flicked towards me and then dropped away again self-consciously, and I immediately knew she was in high defence mode. I also knew her well enough to be aware that I probably wouldn't get any honest answers from her when she was in this type of mood, but I had to at least make sure she was all right. 'Hey. You OK?'

'Yup. Why wouldn't I be?' She puckered her mouth and ran a slick of red across her lips before smacking them together a few times to make sure the lipstick was evenly spread.

Sighing in resignation at my friend's stubborn ways, I leaned on the sink beside her, determined to persevere. 'I dunno. Maybe because you practically gouged out Marcus's eyes back there for no apparent reason.'

'Gouging would require touching, which isn't allowed, apparently,' Sasha murmured darkly as she continued to perfect her already flawless makeup.

I frowned and slid a little closer. 'That's the second time you've mentioned no touching. What do you mean?'

Shoving her lipstick back into her bag, Sasha stood tall and looked me in the eye. Her expression was still closed off, but I could see a trace of what looked like frustration in her features. 'Nothing, Rob. Just leave it, OK?'

I shook my head and stepped sideways to block her exit from the bathroom, holding up a hand to stop her. 'No, it's not OK. You're obviously upset, and so was Marcus. Something must have happened between the two of you, and judging from that little show just now, it wasn't something good.'

Sasha tipped her head back and gazed at the ceiling for a second, and then levelled her gaze on me again. 'You're wrong there, it *was* good. For about five minutes,' she replied cryptically. Seeing my confused look, she let out a breath and closed her eyes. 'We kissed last week, all right? It was great, but then we decided to go our separate ways.'

Wow. OK, I hadn't been expecting that.

'If it was good, why didn't things carry on?'

Sasha rolled her eyes and shook her head. 'He doesn't do one-night stands, and I don't do relationships, so we're totally incompatible.'

Placing a conciliatory hand on her shoulder, I tried to soothe her obvious tension. 'And the no touching thing?'

Sasha made a disgruntled face. 'I have no bloody idea.' Blowing out a breath, she shrugged. 'I tried to grab hold of him in the heat of the moment, but he held my hands behind my back.'

I let out a low hum and nodded. 'Oliver does things like that sometimes,' I admitted, feeling a blush colour my cheeks. 'I like it… did you?'

Sasha bit down on her lower lip, and I could immediately tell from the look in her eyes that yes, she had enjoyed it just as much as I did.

'Yeah. It was hot.' She shrugged. 'When I asked him about it he said he had some weird rule where I couldn't touch him, apart from holding hands, but he wouldn't tell me why.'

'What, never?' I asked in surprise.

She shook her head. 'Nope. He said there could be no touching at all apart from hand-holding.'

'Huh. That is strange.' There surely must be more behind it, and I wondered if Oliver might be able to enlighten me.

'So anyway, now you know that my love life is a fucking disaster do you want to tell me about the "important chat" you wanted to have with me tonight?'

I'd texted Sasha earlier, telling her I needed to speak to her, but I wasn't sure that now was the right time to tell her I wanted her to be my bridesmaid. I debated it for a few seconds and decided that something exciting might brighten her mood, so I took her hand and led her from the bathrooms – it was hardly a nice setting for my announcement – and dragged her towards the bar.

I ordered two glasses of fizz from Natalia, handed one to Sasha, and chinked the rim of my glass against hers. 'My important chat is this…' I paused just long enough to make it a bit dramatic, but Sasha interrupted me with a loud gasp.

'Oh my God, you've not got a bun in the oven, have you?' Her eyes widened and she lowered her gaze to my stomach and she yelped again. 'Are you preggers? Fuck me! Has Oliver got you up the duff before you're even married?' We were in a crowded bar surrounded by people, but of course that didn't stop Sasha yelling her assumption for all and sundry to hear.

'No! Bloody hell, Sasha! Sshhhh! Keep your voice down!' Her incorrect guess and matching expression of gawking shock were so amusing that I couldn't help but throw my head back and laugh long and hard, which no doubt confused anyone around us who was trying to listen in and get some juicy gossip.

'I'm not pregnant. My important chat was that I wanted to ask you to be my bridesmaid, you silly cow!'

Sasha raised her eyes from my stomach and her shocked look was quickly replaced by a grin as broad as the River Thames. 'Really?'

Nodding, I returned her broad smile. 'Really!'

After a characteristically over the top shriek, Sasha did a little jig on the spot and nodded frantically. 'Of course! I'd love to!'

The next minute passed in a blur of hugging, where we spilled bits of our drinks all over each other and giggled like kids until Sasha finally disengaged herself. She flicked her long hair back over her shoulder, smoothed down her dress again, and flashed me a wink. 'To be honest, I'd have been bloody offended if you hadn't asked me.'

Laughing at her typically blunt comment, I chinked my glass with hers a second time and took a sip, enjoying the fact that she was looking relaxed and happy again.

The weird situation with Marcus might still be hanging over her, but at least I'd managed to put a smile back on my best mate's face for the time being.

Oliver

I'd been looking for Marcus for so long that I was just starting to think he'd gone home when I finally spotted his unmistakable mop of blond hair disappearing into a far corner.

I made my way through the packed dance floor and found that he'd chosen to hide away in probably the darkest, most secluded area of the club. The amount of people who'd had sex in this corner over the years was probably uncountable, but I ignored that unsavoury thought and strode towards him.

Marcus was leaning on a wall with his head tipped back and eyes closed. At first you might be mistaken for thinking he looked quite serene, lost in the music, perhaps, but knowing this man as well as I did, I immediately saw signs of his stress. His hands were clenched at his sides, he was grinding his jaw, and his entire body bristled with tension.

In short, he looked like he wanted to hit something really fucking hard, and I just hoped that it didn't end up being me on the receiving end.

Tucking my hands into my trouser pockets, I coughed loudly to announce my presence. I propped myself against a tall stool and waited patiently until his eyes opened and he acknowledged me by briefly flicking his gaze towards me.

'Want to tell me what that was about?' I asked.

Marcus let out a sigh and clenched his teeth again. 'Nothing.'

'Nothing?' I gave a disbelieving roll of my eyes. 'Really?

Because from the sparks flying it looked a lot like the two of you were seconds away from ripping each other's clothes off and getting down to some hot angry sex right there in the middle of the club.'

Marcus let out a dry laugh and dropped his head forwards to look at me. 'We probably were.'

I had made the comment as a joke, so his quiet admission shocked me. 'Has something happened between you two?'

Marcus pushed off the wall and took the stool opposite mine. He lifted his big body up slowly as if exhausted from the stress of the evening. 'Yeah.' Running a hand through his hair, he rolled his eyes. 'We kissed last weekend.'

I could sense there was more to this story, but instead of prying I sat silently and let Marcus decide how much he wanted to share.

'Just kissed. It was fucking hot, but after making out for a while I chose to walk away because she only wants a night of sex and I want more.'

He wanted more? That was quite a confession, especially seeing as he and Sasha hadn't even been out on a date as far as I was aware.

Marcus must have seen the surprise on my face, because he gave a wry smile and nodded. 'Yeah, yeah, I know I used to sleep around, but I've changed. I'm not like that any more.' He rested his elbow on the table and propped his chin into his palm dejectedly. 'There's a real connection between me and Sasha. I don't just want a casual night with her. It feels like we could have something really good together.' Dropping his eyes away, he sighed. 'I like her, Oliver.' After another pause he looked up and his expression was grim. 'A lot. But she refuses to consider anything other than a one-night thing.'

Marcus and I used to be quite the players when we were younger, wooing a different girl most weekends, but now I'd met Robyn I could completely understand where he was coming from. 'From the little Robyn has said I think Sasha has some emotional issues when it comes to relationships.'

'Yeah, I assumed it was something like that. She won't tell me for sure, though.' He nodded and took a swig on his beer which turned into him downing half of it in one go. 'The stupid thing is, since things with Celia ended I have trust issues, too, so Sasha and I would probably be a perfect pair. We could sort our hang-ups out together.'

Once again, I wanted to push for more details on what had really happened between him and his ex, but I respected his privacy and didn't force him. I knew he'd tell me when he was ready. We contemplated it all in silence for a moment or two, but as much as I wanted to offer him some helpful advice, I couldn't really see a way around the impasse that he and Sasha had reached.

'Can I ask what she meant when she said if she couldn't touch you, you couldn't touch her either?'

Marcus gave a thin smile and shrugged. 'I like restraint these days. I held her hands behind her back when we kissed.' He hesitated, picking briefly at the label on his beer, and it seemed to me to be a way of avoiding eye contact for a minute or two. 'There's a little more to it than that, but it's not something I really want to discuss, if that's OK.'

'Of course.' Marcus and I might be best mates, but that didn't mean we had to share all our deep dark secrets. 'So, you're sure there's no future for the two of you? The looks you exchange are pretty potent.'

'Nope. Not unless she changes her mind, because I sure as hell won't be changing mine.' Sitting up straighter, he offered me a tired smile. 'It'll be fine. Sasha and I just need to avoid each other for a while.'

Nodding, I smiled apologetically. 'That might be a little tricky.'

He shook his head. 'Nah, I know we both come to the club, but I can stay away from her. It's fine.'

'That's not quite what I meant.' Shifting on my stool, I

looked him straight in the eye and decided to ask my question. 'This isn't exactly the situation I wanted to be in when I asked you this, Marcus, but I was hoping you'd agree to be my best man?'

Marcus's eyes widened in surprise, and then he grinned and reached across to slap me affectionately on the shoulder before grabbing my hand in a firm shake. 'Mate! I'd be honoured!'

'Thank you. I'm asking Nathan, David, and my good friend from Spain, Matías, to be part of the wedding party as groomsmen.' Nathan and Marcus were my closest friends these days, but as Nathan and I had met via a slightly different route than the norm – I'd trained him to be a dominant – he still retained a slight professional distance from me, so Marcus had seemed like the perfect choice for my best man.

'Awesome, thank you so much for asking me, Oliver.'

'I wouldn't want it any other way.' I paused, wondering how to break my bad news to him, and deciding that the only way was to come right out with it. 'The only slight issue is that we're planning on having the wedding quite soon and Sasha's going to be a bridesmaid, too.' Robyn didn't know quite how quickly I wanted to have her as my wife, but if I got my way we'd be married before the end of summer. 'We'll have planning to do, so avoiding Sasha might not be quite as easy as you'd hoped.'

Marcus drew in a long breath through his nose and then gave a dismissive shake of his head. 'We'll make it work somehow, don't worry.'

After their fiery outburst earlier I had my doubts, but only time would tell.

CHAPTER EIGHT

Robyn

Oliver filled both of our wine glasses and then joined me on the sofa. He chinked his glass against mine in a silent toast. I took a sip, enjoying the cool crisp wine he had picked. I was no connoisseur, but since meeting Oliver I'd discovered that I was particularly partial to a Sauvignon Blanc from Marlborough in New Zealand. Luckily it was also one of his favourites, too.

After taking a sip he placed his glass down, and then gave me one of his characteristically intense looks that always made me shiver with desire and wonder if he were going to initiate something sexual. 'So, I've been thinking about wedding venues.'

Not a sexual interlude, then, but an interesting topic nonetheless. I'd been pondering venues, too, scanning websites and nosing around in the stack of wedding magazines that I'd purchased, but I still had no idea where we should choose. 'Oh yeah? Any good ideas?'

Oliver nodded slowly, and I found myself staring at him, almost hypnotised by his handsome features. 'I have, but I want you to be totally honest and tell me if you don't like it.'

He suddenly looked really thoughtful, verging on concerned, but I couldn't for the life of me imagine what he could possibly suggest that could provoke such a serious expression. 'Um, OK.'

'I was wondering how you'd feel about getting married in

Spain.'

My eyebrows rose in surprise, but then I smiled with excitement. I'd loved our visit there. It was a beautiful country, warm and characterful, and his home; it could be a perfect location for a wedding.

I was so deep in thought I didn't reply immediately, which Oliver obviously took as hesitation because he frowned and leaned in to take my hand. 'I completely understand if you'd rather marry here in England. I know all your family are here.'

Shaking my head, I grinned. 'No, no, that wasn't why I didn't reply. I was just thinking it through. I like the idea, a lot.'

'Really?' He looked so expectant it was as if he was hanging on my every word. Bless him, my usually confident man actually sounded unsure for a change, so I immediately set about reassuring him.

'Really. It was so beautiful over there and the weather was amazing.' I gave his hand a squeeze and my heart clenched as a look of boyish happiness burst across his face. Sometimes I still couldn't believe that this was real – that I was really going to be marrying Oliver – but talking about it was setting off an excited fizzle in my belly and I matched his grin with one of my own. I loved him so much, and it was all starting to become real.

Oliver's face was completely relaxed now, a lazy smile putting crinkles at the corners of his eyes and a dimple in his cheek which I adored.

'It is. I was thinking… well… I was wondering how you'd feel about marrying in the citrus grove at my parents' house?'

A small, excited gasp left my lips as I took in his words. The citrus grove. As soon as he said the words I was instantly transported back to the day when he had first introduced me to his family. Oliver had given me a tour of their beautiful stone farmhouse and the well-tended back garden before taking me out to see the larger estate beyond the garden walls. There had been neat vegetable gardens and some chickens and goats in a grassed area, and then, after walking through another gate, we'd come to the citrus grove.

Orange and lemon trees had lined a narrow path through the grove, and beyond them was an open terrace that had taken my breath away with its views. The terrace showed just how high up we'd been in the village and overlooked lush hillsides with no other houses even visible. Oliver had told me that you could see the lights of Barcelona from up there at night, but even squinting and shielding my eyes I hadn't been able to see the city in the bright sunlight.

From memory there was a stone bench and table under a larger tree to the side of the terrace. Oliver had told me that was where he'd sat with his grandfather to have lunch when he was a child and helping harvest the fruit.

It had been my favourite spot on his parents' estate, and I couldn't really think of anywhere more perfect to exchange vows with him.

'Oh my God, Oliver, that would be amazing!'

He grinned at my response, and leaned forwards to place a lingering kiss on my lips. My mouth parted, and I indulged in a few moments of lazy kissing as his tongue explored and threatened to completely distract us from our conversation. Oliver pulled back with a rueful chuckle, rubbed the tip of his nose over mine, and smiled.

'I saw how much you loved it there, and I have very fond memories of that spot, too, so it immediately sprang to my mind when I was considering places significant to us that we could marry in.'

It was such a small thing, but I loved the fact that he'd been spending time trying to plan the perfect spot for us to marry. He really was such a soft romantic under the dominant façade he wore.

'It would be perfect. But can we do it there? Doesn't the land have to be consecrated or something?'

Oliver picked up his wine again and took a long sip before nodding. 'There are certain papers we'd need, yes, but for a fee that can be arranged.' I wasn't used to having access to money, but I supposed pretty much anything could be bought for the right price.

He extended his free hand along the back of the sofa and trailed his fingers through my hair, sparking tingles across my scalp and causing a lusty moan to creep up my throat as the heat from his earlier kiss reignited in my veins.

'And don't worry about flight costs. I'm more than happy to cover them for your family seeing as it was my idea to marry abroad.'

We might not be as rich as Oliver's family, but I knew that with the new low-cost airline flights to Spain it wouldn't be a problem for my clan to make their way out there. 'Don't be silly, they won't mind at all.' Leaning my head into his touch, I closed my eyes with contentment as he continued to massage my scalp. 'We need to think about guest lists, too,' I murmured, his caresses making me feel sleepy. 'I don't have a very big family, but I know you do.'

'Hmm, yes, us Spanish are known for our huge extended families,' Oliver agreed with a wry smile.

'I don't mind if you invite them all. I'd like to meet them,' I offered groggily.

A loud laugh from Oliver made me open my eyes again and I saw him shaking his head in amusement. 'If I invited every uncle, aunt, and cousin we'd have to find space for about three hundred people, so I was thinking perhaps we could keep it quite small. Perhaps just parents, siblings, and close friends?'

Three hundred? Wow. That certainly woke me up again. I think if I counted up all my extended family it wouldn't even exceed thirty, let alone enter triple figures.

'Sounds good to me, if you're sure you won't offend anyone?'

'No, we can have a party at a different time and invite them all to that.' Oliver's fingers sunk deeper into my hair, and then he suddenly took a firmer hold, tilting my head back further so he could lean over and look deeply into my eyes. He hovered there, his eyes darting across my features as if absorbing every tiny detail to memory.

'I love you so much, Robyn.' Discussing our wedding was obviously having a similar effect on Oliver as it was on me, because he'd almost blurted the words out as if he physically couldn't hold them back for another second. I didn't care when or how he said them, though – I would never tire of hearing him say he loved me.

My cheeks heated as they often did when in his company and I gave a shy smile. 'Me, too, Oliver. I can't wait to marry you.'

Oliver moved in even closer, his eyes burning with desire and clearly showing every single ounce of what he felt for me. 'I was hoping you would say that… you know I can be an impatient man, and I don't want to wait long to have you as my wife. How does July sound?'

July? That was less than two months away! Mind you, now that Oliver and I had decided to take this next step I wanted to get started on our new life together as soon as possible.

Would we be able to get it all arranged at such short notice, though? The venue was the big thing, but if we were marrying at his parents' house we wouldn't need to worry about finding somewhere that was available, and everything else would be relatively simple.

'Sounds good…'

He narrowed his eyes and maintained his proximity to me. 'But? I can hear the hesitancy in your tone. What is it, *cariño*? Is it too soon?'

I immediately shook my head. 'No, there's no but. All I was going to say was that I'd have to check my parents and brother can all make it, because I couldn't get married without them there, that was all. As long as they can, then I say we go for it.'

Oliver growled his appreciation of my answer, and then his expression darkened. He ran his tongue along his lower lip slowly as if deliberately trying to draw my attention. It worked a treat, and suddenly all I could think about were Oliver's lips and all the wicked things he was capable of doing with them.

'Talking about you becoming my wife is making me really hard,' he muttered, shifting on the sofa and adjusting his trousers. He extended his hand in a silent demand for my wine and when I passed it to him he placed it on the table and shifted so he had one hand on each side of my head and I was caged in against the sofa.

'Enough talking for now. Let's work on how we're going to consummate the marriage. After all, practice makes perfect, doesn't it?'

I was now hot and lusty and wanted to do exactly as he suggested, but I flashed a nervous glance at the door. 'But what about your aunt? Isn't she home?'

Oliver also flicked a look at the door and shrugged. 'She is, but she's tucked away in the spare room painting. She'll be up there for hours.'

I was about to continue my protest, or maybe suggest that we at least moved to his bedroom, but his mouth was on mine before I could let out a single word, capturing my breath and sending me to heaven with his skilful tongue.

When he was kissing me with this much passion my concern about his aunt being in the house somehow faded away into nothingness.

Oliver kissed me until I was panting and ready to just submit to whatever he had planned for me, but to my surprise, he suddenly pushed himself away and sat on the opposite end of the sofa. Looking at me from under a hooded gaze, he curled his mouth into an utterly devilish smile and gave his lap a rapid tap.

'Come here, *cariño*, I want you riding me.'

Oliver was frequently in charge in the bedroom, meaning I didn't often get the chance to be on top, so I didn't pause for long when he gave me the opportunity. I leaped across so exuberantly that he let out a small shocked grunt as my body collided with his, and then chuckled darkly before sliding a hand to the nape of my neck and dragging me down for a kiss.

Over the course of the next few seconds we kissed like the world was about to end; our hands clutched desperately at clothing, lips explored, tongues twined, and heavy moans filled the air until I was like a boneless mass of desire poured across his lap.

This was lust at its most potent, and even though we'd only just been talking about the romantic topic of our wedding, I knew that what was about to follow wasn't going to be slow and romantic at all. It was going to be hard and frantic and about one thing: sex, sex, sex.

I was straddling Oliver's lap with my skirt shucked up around my hips so that I was in the perfect position to grind myself down onto the raging erection trapped within his trousers. I greedily slid my fingers through the silky strands at the back of his head and tugged, eliciting a rough groan of pleasure from him as I cupped his face with both of my palms to pull him even nearer, not satisfied with the fact that we were already practically plastered together.

Oliver took hold of my hips and jerked me down upon him. He gave a sharp, upward thrust of his hips. We were joined at the crotch area so firmly now that I could feel every inch of his cock pulsing through his trousers. He gave another hard thrust that hit my clit with perfection and I moaned and clutched at his shoulders, causing him to hum his appreciation into my mouth.

Oliver trailed his kisses from my mouth across my jaw and then down onto my neck, each and every one sending a flurry of goose pimples in its wake and leaving me shuddering with need on his lap. One of his hands left my hips and pressed down between us, digging underneath my skirt until his fingers found the damp panties at my groin. 'Hmmm. Lace,' he muttered appreciatively, as he pulled the fabric aside and slid a finger along my quivering flesh to my clit.

My eyes rolled back in my skull at the unbelievable pleasure as a gargled groan left my throat. It felt so incredible that I lifted myself onto my knees to give him even better access. Oliver flicked my skirt up and cast a quick glance down between my legs, giving my nether regions an inquisitive look.

'What are you doing?' I panted, suddenly feeling slightly self-conscious.

'Checking the colour so I know what to replace them with.'

'Why would you need to...?' But before I'd even finished asking why they would need replacing, Oliver had dug his fingers through the lace and ripped the knickers from my body with one hard tug that had me falling forwards onto him with a shocked gasp.

His hand was trapped between us, but his fingers immediately sought out my opening and circled it before plunging in with one finger. 'Oh fuck... so wet... you're so ready for me, Robyn.'

I was. I was wet, horny, and more than ready. I simply didn't care if his aunt was home, I wanted him. *Right now.*

Oliver shifted me slightly, so I was back on my knees, and then added a second finger to my channel. He pumped them rhythmically in and out and circled my clit with his thumb until I was well on my way to heaven.

Not wanting to just sit there limply, I reached down and took advantage of the gap between our bodies to quickly undo his zipper and dip my hand inside. From the moment his hot, hard cock surged free into my palm and Oliver swore in Spanish under his breath I just knew that it was going to be inside me within a matter of seconds.

And it was. One moment I was palming his cock and

running my fist up and down the steely length while he buried his fingers inside me, and the next second, he'd ripped his hand from within me, lifted me, and lined up my entrance with his waiting cock.

'I can't wait a moment longer,' he muttered hotly before staring deep into my eyes and lowering me down the first few inches of his shaft.

The sounds of my moans and Oliver's deep groan reverberated through the room. I practically gurgled with desire as he let me slip down the rest until we were almost fully joined. The root of his cock was far thicker than the rest, so I impatiently wiggled on his lap, trying to push myself down and causing Oliver to growl against my mouth as he gripped my hips to slow me.

'Take it easy, Robyn. Just relax, let me do the work,' he murmured, licking a path across my lips as he gently circled his hips, stretching me for him.

Oliver kissed me again, his tongue sweeping through my mouth lazily as he held me half impaled on him. His lazy, languorous kisses worked their magic and I began to slip down him, accepting more and more of him until finally I was seated on his lap and he was fully inside me.

Our eyes met, and his were burning with desire and so dilated they almost looked black. Grinning at me, he placed a peck on my lips as we both took a second to appreciate how good we felt when we were joined like this.

I could feel him so deeply in this position it was almost too much. Almost, but not quite. Oliver would make sure of that; he always did, manging to push me right to the edge of comfort with his deep penetration, but never over into pain.

The noise of a floorboard squeaking above us was like a bucket of cold water being thrown over me and I tensed, my eyes widening as I let out a panicked yelp and looked at Oliver to see him glancing towards the door. He didn't look nearly as worried as I did, but there was no way I could let his aunt catch us in this position; I'd be mortified. It was bad enough she'd seen me wrapped in a bed sheet, the last thing I wanted was for her to find me on the sofa with her nephew balls deep inside me!

I tried to push off his lap, but Oliver gripped my hips and gave a small, decisive shake of his head.

No? Seriously? He was saying no?

'Oliver! Your aunt could be coming down here any second now!'

His gaze flicked back from the door and as it landed on me I almost gasped from the determination in his gaze. 'You'll stay exactly where you are, *cariño*. Understand?'

His tone, expression, and the slight tilt of his head all carried such dominance that I immediately stopped my struggling and gave a meek nod of my head. God, he was hot when he flicked into this persona.

We sat there silently, both straining our ears to listen and discover if we could hear Oliver's aunt coming down the stairs, but while I was still panicking about being caught in a compromising situation, Oliver's dick was twitching away happily inside me. I was still panting, and my expression must have been very much "deer caught in headlights", but when I glanced at Oliver I found him looking relaxed and almost carefree. Was he not worried about his aunt walking in any second now?

His solid cock gave a huge lurch, sending waves of pleasure through me, and I lowered my head and groaned quietly, wondering how the hell we could get out of this when Oliver was being so bloody stubborn. Just then there was the noise of a toilet flushing upstairs followed by some creaking floorboards and a door closing.

'See? Nothing to worry about. Val has gone back to her painting,' Oliver replied, sounding cool, calm, and in complete control.

I gave him an astounded look, still unsure how he hadn't

freaked out like me, *and* how he'd managed to maintain a solid erection throughout the entire thing. He smirked at me and moved his hips in a slow circle which had me whimpering and taking a fistful of his shirt.

'I'm always hard when you're near. Nothing can stop that, not even the risk of being interrupted,' he informed me, having once again accurately read my mind. 'Now. Where were we?'

A huge breath left my lungs as Oliver gave a sharp upwards jerk of his hips and my heart clattered in my chest. My raised pulse was half from desire and half from my leftover panic.

'She's at the back of the house, she can't hear us from there. Can you relax again, *cariño,* or do you want to stop?'

Stop? I might have been recovering from shock, but I definitely didn't want to stop, so instead of answering his question audibly I simply raised myself onto my knees and circled my hips until he was groaning and staring up at me with wide eyes.

Lifting myself higher, I paused with the final inch of him just inside me and then let my body drop back down. Our hips clashed as I seated myself fully on his lap and once again had him imbedded inside my clenching body.

'*Dios*! Robyn!' His head fell back against the sofa and Oliver's hands flew out and gripped my hips with bruising strength. 'Some warning would have been nice, but if that's how you want to play it...' he muttered hotly. Using the grip on my hips he began to move us at a far harder pace, our bodies banging together until the air around us was filled with slapping sounds and moans.

He dug one of his hands into my hair and wrapped a portion around his wrist before pulling my head backwards to expose my neck. Somehow, he managed to continue to grind inside me while also licking and kissing along the sensitive column of my neck.

Loosening his grip, he dragged me forward to meet his lips and our mouths collided so feverishly that our teeth briefly clashed before we settled into our familiar practised kisses.

He hit me with another of his punishingly hard upward thrusts and I cried out, my orgasm starting to build deep in my belly.

'You feel so good… I'm going to fuck you until you scream the house down,' he added with a devilish grin.

I might have been the one on top, but there was no doubt who was leading this encounter. Oliver's dominance was never far from the surface, but with his hands gripping both my hips and my hair and him leading the movements of our thrusts it really was just a case of me clinging on for the ride.

And what a ride it was.

Oliver slowed the movements and removed the hand from my hair before lifting it to his lips and sucking on one finger. He stared into my eyes as he took it around my back and began digging under my skirt. His hand trailed down the crack of my arse and then the wet digit began to gently circle and tease at my rear opening, prompting me to gasp.

This was new. We hadn't explored this area yet, but I'd always had the feeling that a man of Oliver's experience would perhaps take us there one day.

It would seem today was that day.

His finger circled again, this time with a little more pressure, and I couldn't help but tense at the feeling of resistance, not sure how to cope with it.

'Just relax, *cariño*. Touch yourself for me. Rub your clit,' he urged, and his voice was so assured and confident that I immediately did.

I licked two fingers on my right hand and lowered it between my legs to find my clitoris swollen and sensitive. I ran a slick circle across the tight bundle of nerves that immediately made me feel like exploding as pleasure flooded my system and slackened my tension.

Oliver took advantage of my body relaxing and pressed the tip of his finger inside me, once again circling the tight hole and sending a rush of new sensations through my body.

It felt alien and new, but… good. It felt really good. Oliver's eyes were glowing with intensity, but his enjoyment was obvious as he bit on his lower lip and began to gently thrust his finger inside me to the knuckle and back.

'Keep your fingers moving,' he reminded me, and as I once again began to play with my clit he started a slow circle of his hips that was in time with the movement of the finger in my back passage. His cock seemed to have swollen even larger than usual, and with his finger in my arse as well I felt really full and, to my surprise, really close to climaxing.

'Feel good?' he asked on a raspy breath, and I brought my eyes up to his and nodded shyly.

'Yeah. Really good.' We'd done a lot of stuff together now, and a lot of it was kinky, so it was stupid to feel embarrassed to admit it to him, but I did, nonetheless.

Oliver grinned at my admission and began to up the pace. The finger in my rear always kept up with the movement of his cock, one going in as the other pulled out, and I quickly started to feel dizzy from the overwhelming sensations flooding through my body.

My channel gave a sudden spasm and Oliver moaned in response, a smirk curling his mouth. Sensing our impending climaxes, he upped the effort, moving faster, thrusting harder, and burying his finger deeper still until I was panting and clinging on to him for dear life.

Just as I was about to fall into my climax he pressed his mouth against mine in a heated kiss, catching my moans and swallowing the noise of my pleasure as I tipped over the edge and started to come undone around him. My channel gripped him like a fist, and my rear clenched around his finger as if I never wanted to let it leave my body.

Oliver growled and continued to twine his tongue with mine as he ground his cock deep and hard inside me and began to come with such force that I could feel the heat of his release flooding my insides in a series of jerks and twitches.

He worked us both down from the high, and then we sat in contented, exhausted silence for several minutes, happy to just hold each other and absorb the power of what we had shared. I flopped forwards, my body liquefied, and rested my sweaty brow onto his with a small chuckle.

Anywhere, anyhow, Oliver always managed to surprise me with the undying intensity of our connection. Sex between us had always been potent, and even after all our time together it was still just as intoxicating.

When I finally mustered the strength to lift my head from his, Oliver lifted a hand and cupped my cheek. 'OK, *cariño*?'

'Hmm,' I murmured and blinked, trying to wake myself from my post-coital bliss, but Oliver gave me a wry smile and continued talking. 'I may have gotten a little carried away…' He raised his other hand and wiggled a finger, *the finger,* the one that had been… well… buried where the sun doesn't shine just a few minutes ago. 'Was it OK, or too much?'

My cheeks heated with embarrassment; we'd just fucked while his aunt was God knows where in the house, he'd had his finger shoved up my arse, *and* he was still buried inside me, but then I brought myself up short – this was Oliver, the king of kink, and a man who had chosen to share his bedroom skills with me and no one else for the rest of our lives, so really I had nothing to be self-conscious about.

'I liked it.' Pausing, I placed my hands on his chest and ran my fingers over the material, loving the firmness of his pecs below.

Leaning forwards, he offered his mouth for a kiss which I immediately took, placing my lips upon his and humming with pleasure when he lazily ran his tongue across mine. 'I'm glad.' He flashed me a cheeky wink. 'I enjoyed it, too. Very much,' he mused, a smile pulling his lips up as he raised a hand and ran it gently through my tangled hair, attempting to smooth it after his earlier grabbing.

There was another creak of floorboards above us and we both looked up at the ceiling before sharing a joint chuckle. 'Perhaps we better not push our luck, hmm?' With another wink, Oliver reached across the sofa and grabbed a box of tissues for our clean-up. Helping me lift myself up, he let out a moan of pleasure as his softening length slipped from my body, and then we wiped ourselves clean and sorted out our clothes.

I shifted from his lap and he snuggled me into his side and lifted my destroyed knickers in his hand, giving a satisfied chuckle as he did so. 'I owe you an underwear shopping trip.'

I laughed and grabbed the scrap of lace from him, looking up at him with mock disapproval. His hair was a mess from where my fingers had explored it earlier, but with the relaxed expression and grin on his face he looked devastatingly handsome and impossible to stay mad at.

'So that was a practice of how we might consummate our marriage, was it?' I asked lightly as I curled deeper into his embrace.

'Hmm. Yes, it was rather good, I thought.'

I nodded in agreement, a laugh bubbling up my throat.

'What's so funny?' Oliver shifted slightly so he could look down at me in confusion, but his perplexed expression only made me laugh harder.

'So you're planning to celebrate our marriage union by sticking your finger up my bum, are you?' I asked, attempting to keep my face serious, but not managing it in the slightest.

As soon as he realised what I'd been laughing about Oliver's face relaxed and he chuckled along with me. 'It hadn't been my intention, no, but I got caught up in the moment,' he admitted, looking uncharacteristically sheepish.

'And they say romance is dead.'

Oliver turned in his seat and began to tickle me on the underside of my ribs. 'I'll stick more than just a finger up your arse if you don't stop teasing…' he promised darkly, thrusting his groin against my thigh as he did so.

Oh. That idea stopped me in my tracks. Oliver was very fortunate in the manhood department and I'd felt full to the brim with just his finger inside me. Would he even fit back there? I'll be honest, after enjoying what we'd just done together I wasn't averse to giving it a go one day.

Oliver tilted his head and narrowed his eyes, assessing my expression and no doubt reading every single filthy thought that was going through my mind.

'Although judging by the look on your face you're not opposed to the idea, so maybe I'll do it anyway…'

A huge breath filled my lungs as I sought out his hand and linked our fingers. 'We could certainly experiment…' I offered softly, enjoying the way his eyes lit up as I did so. 'But perhaps not on our wedding day.'

This time Oliver didn't just chuckle; he let out a full-blown belly laugh and nodded in agreement. 'No, I agree. Romance only on our wedding day. I plan on worshipping you from head to toe.'

Romance and full body worshipping. Now that really did sound like a perfect way to consummate our marriage.

CHAPTER NINE

Robyn

'Engaged! I can't believe it!' My mum took hold of my hand and examined my ring again with a fond smile on her lips. Oliver and I had just met up with Mum and Dad to break the news of our engagement, and as I'd hoped, my parents were thrilled with the development.

Dad and Oliver were at the counter in the restaurant ordering our lunches, leaving Mum and me to a few minutes of girl time.

'I'm going to need to get on a wedding diet, pronto,' Mum declared, giving her stomach a small pat. 'This man of yours certainly doesn't hang around, does he?'

I smiled, but couldn't pass any comment, because she was spot on. When Oliver set his mind to something it would take a bulldozer in his way to stop him, as I had found out many times since we'd been together.

'You've only been living with him a few weeks and now you're getting married in just over two months!' Mum gushed, shaking her head in amusement, but then her eyes widened and her cheeks took on some extra colour.

'Goodness… you're not… you're not pregnant, are you, love?' she whispered urgently as her eyes flicked to my stomach and back to my face. 'Do I need to prepare myself for becoming a grandma as well as a mother-in-law?'

Really? I'd thought it was amusing when Sasha jumped to the pregnancy conclusion, but now my mum was thinking the same thing, too? Was everyone going to make this link and think I was up the duff just because we wanted to get married quickly?

'No, Mum!' I shook my head and rolled my eyes. 'I'm not pregnant. We just really want to get married and don't see any reason to delay it.'

'Are you sure?' She gave my hand a squeeze. 'You know that your father and I wouldn't mind if you were pregnant before marriage. It's not like we're traditional like that, I mean, you live with him, so you and Oliver obviously sleep together already…'

God, were we really having this conversation? 'Mum!' Holding up a hand, I scrunched my face up in embarrassment. Mum and I were close, but we weren't "let's talk about sex" kind of close. The last time I'd discussed anything vaguely sexual with her was when I was sixteen and she'd given me the birds and the bees talk and that had been mortifying enough.

'Please, let's not discuss that, OK? I promise you, I'm not pregnant.'

Mum finally seemed satisfied, and amusingly didn't look anywhere near as mortified by this whole conversation as I felt. *If Mum knew exactly what Oliver and I get up to together behind closed doors she might not look quite so relaxed*, I thought with a smirk.

'Your father and I had a very short engagement, too, did I ever tell you that?'

Relaxing slightly now that she wasn't attempting to delve further into my sex life with Oliver, I shook my head. 'No. You guys met at a dance class when you were eighteen, I think? But that's all I can remember.'

Mum smiled and glanced towards where Dad stood in the queue with Oliver. They were both currently engrossed in assessing the wine list, but I suspected that Oliver would make the final decision.

'We did. Your father was quite the dancer back in those

days. He had a right set of twinkle toes on him and he literally swept me off my feet.'

'And you guys fell head over heels in love and so got married quickly?' I guessed.

'Not quite.' Mum licked her lips and shrugged. 'We fell madly in lust first, but my mum, your gran, God bless her soul, could be so strict and she'd barely even let me hold his hand when we first started dating.' Faffing with her napkin, Mum flashed me a wicked, almost dirty smile, an expression I'm not sure I'd even seen on my mother before. 'It was very frustrating.'

Reading between the lines I let out a gasp. 'So… so you married Dad so you guys could have sex?' I blurted, my eyebrows jumping up towards my hairline.

'No!' Mum laughed and flushed an even deeper shade of red. 'Well… sort of, yes,' she confessed, almost looking like a teenager again as she giggled and flashed another look across at my dad. Wow, this was all quite enlightening. It was also a bit yuck – I mean, no child wants to think about their parents having sex, do they?

'Luckily for us, lust and love came hand in hand and here we are, years later and still happily married.' Giving my hand a squeeze, she brought my attention back to her gaze. 'I predict the same outcome for you and Oliver. I can see the way he looks at you and it reminds me of how your father used to look at me.'

We both turned our gazes towards the queue, and this time I found Oliver staring straight at me with an expression on his face that was hot enough to melt my panties.

'That, Robyn, is the look of a smitten man,' I heard my mum murmur to me, but I was so caught up in his magnetic stare that I couldn't find any words to reply, because quite simply, I was a woman smitten, too.

CHAPTER TEN

Marcus

Flicking through the pages on my phone, I tried to decide which location would be best for Oliver's stag do. Amsterdam certainly had some appeal; it was close, cheap, and the local beers were great. Barcelona was another option, but Oliver knew the city inside out and I'd decided it might be nice to go somewhere a little different. I also had Luxembourg, Prague, and Budapest on my list, but ideally I needed Oliver's input in choosing the perfect place.

We had been set to meet tonight to discuss it, but he'd just text me to rearrange, so I was now sitting in Club Twist with a nearly full pint and no one to talk to.

It was as if fate had decided I needed company tonight, because I'd barely put my phone down after receiving Oliver's text when I saw Sasha coming over to me. She had a nervous smile on her face, and to be fair she was right to look anxious. We'd basically avoided each other for the last few weeks since our very public argument, and things between us were now awkward as fuck.

I took in her long hair, wide eyes, and slightly parted lips and then sharply turned my gaze away. She was so beautiful it was almost painful being close to her, and such a bloody shame that we were so incompatible in our views on sex and relationships.

'Hey, big boy,' she said cautiously as she joined me at the bar and slid up onto the stool beside me. Her words had been jokey, but I could hear a nervous hesitancy in her voice which was a million miles away from her usual bravado.

David behind the bar heard her nickname for me, and grinned at me while jokingly grabbing his crotch before seeing my scowl and wandering off to the other end of the bar. Grimacing, I shook my head – it might be a complimentary nickname, but I really hoped it didn't stick for too long.

Once she was settled, she angled her head and gave me a small smile that made something inside me clench. This girl really did affect me like no other, and I had to draw in a deep breath to compose myself.

'So, look, I wanted to apologise for being a bitch the other week. I… I was feeling a little oversensitive and I took it out on you. I shouldn't have done that.'

I knew how stubborn Sasha was, so I genuinely hadn't been expecting her words and suspected that they must have been quite hard for her to say. 'Apology accepted. I reacted badly, too, so I also apologise.' I took a sip of my beer, hoping we could keep this conversation short and sweet – being this close to her was driving me insane with the need to touch her. The tips of my fingers literally tingled with the urge to reach out.

Unfortunately, she settled herself more comfortably on the stool, not looking as if she was planning on leaving anytime soon, and I had to focus on my beer to avoid staring at her. 'We need to try and play nice, for the sake of Robyn and Oliver's wedding.'

Nodding, I drew in a deep breath. 'I know. I *am* being nice.' We shared a long glance that made my groin give a kick of lust, and I sighed heavily. 'Sorry if it sounds harsh, but it's just easier for me if I avoid you.'

A long silence fell between us. After several moments where we both looked away, our eyes joined, and some seriously intense shit passed between us, but this time it was Sasha who broke the bond and looked away. 'You sure I can't change your mind about having a little fun with me? I'm sure it would magically make all this awkwardness go away.'

This topic, *again.* But tonight, her words sounded more jokey than serious, as if she was finally getting the message that I wasn't interested in casual sex with her. I smiled wistfully, wishing things could be different between us, but knowing that with my issues, this was how it had to be. Just friends. Albeit friends who seemed to share an insanely hot chemistry.

'Nope,' I fired back, before taking a slow sip of my beer. 'Have you changed your mind about only doing one-nighters?'

I was surprised to see Sasha's bravado drop away slightly. Her expression became more open than I'd ever seen it and she chewed briefly on her lower lip, exposing a minute show of vulnerability. A brief glimmer of sadness crossed through her eyes, hinting at what I'd long suspected – that Sasha might well have a few demons of her own buried beneath the polished front that she seemed to put on for everyone around her.

It would seem we were both a little broken inside. In another time and place we could well have been a perfect match for each other; two broken pieces coming together to form one whole.

'No.' Just like that her moment of weakness had passed and her armour slid back into place seamlessly, and she scrunched up her nose and twirled her wine glass between a finger and thumb. 'Why would I want a relationship and all the painful shit that comes with it?' Pulling in a low breath, she shook her head, seemingly lost in a world of her own for a few seconds. 'Emotions just lead to you getting hurt.'

Her last words were almost a whisper, as if she hadn't meant to say them aloud, but they seemed to be the most honest statement she'd ever made to me. I frowned and examined her expression more closely. She was staring ahead resolutely now, seeming determined not to make eye contact with me, but I swore I could see that trace of pain flickering in her eyes again. Had someone hurt her in the past? Was that why she fucked around and wouldn't date? Maybe she'd been in love and had her heart broken, leaving her to think that it was easier to just not let anyone close again.

If either of us had a right to be scared senseless of entering another relationship, it was me. Not that Sasha knew about my past, but with my history it was a bloody miracle I hadn't decided to be completely celibate for the rest of my life.

'You can't think that relationships are all bad. Look at Robyn and Oliver, they're a great match. They're so loved up it's almost sickening, but there's no pain or hurt there, just support, love, and comfort.'

Sasha frowned and finally looked across at me and met my gaze. She seemed to be weighing up my words, and agreeing with them, even though it went against her own long-held beliefs. 'That's true, I guess.'

'True, but not enough to make you change your ways, huh?' I murmured quietly, wondering if we might be on the verge of making a breakthrough in the honesty between us.

Sasha fiddled with her wine glass again, her face tense with thought. 'No… I… I won't do that. I just can't.' Her voice was pained, as if saying she couldn't be with me hurt her physically, and I once again wondered what on earth could have happened to her to make her so tough in her beliefs.

'In which case we're both just going to make the best of this situation for the sake of our friends. I'm not having this rift between you and me ruining Oliver's big day.'

Sasha nodded immediately. 'Ditto.' Sighing, she stood up and downed the last dregs of her wine. 'Polite and friendly it is, then. See you around,' she muttered as she dumped her empty glass and left my side.

I raised my glass in a mock toast to our agreement, but as I watched her walk away from me, my heart aching at the loss, I knew it was going to be way harder to stick to than it sounded.

CHAPTER ELEVEN

Robyn

I opened the door to find Sasha on my doorstep with her arms folded and a determined expression on her face.

'I need a drinking buddy tonight, and don't give me any excuses that you're doing something for the wedding with Oliver. It's girls' night.'

The fact that she hadn't even bothered to say hello before launching into her demand made it fairly clear there was no way she was going to be diverted on her plans, so even though it was Tuesday and most definitely not a designated "girls' night" as she had proclaimed, I shrugged, grabbed my jacket from the rack, and stepped outside to join her.

'Lead the way.'

'Oh.' Sasha paused and glanced over my shoulder into the house. 'That was easier than I'd thought. I expected you to say you couldn't come out.'

'I'm not a kid who needs permission for a play date, Sash. Besides, Oliver hasn't arrived home from work yet, so a drink sounds great. Where are we going?'

Sasha smiled and linked her arm with mine before guiding us down the pavement. 'How about that wine bar on the corner? It'll be my local once I'm moved in; I may as well give it a trial run.'

'Cool. It's nice in there. I've been with Oliver a few times.' With our destination planned, we set off. 'How's the flat sale coming along?'

Sasha smiled and glanced back over her shoulder in the direction of what would hopefully soon be her new home. 'Good. The survey came back today clean as a whistle, so now it's just a case of getting our solicitors to finalise the exchange of contracts. Completion should be within two weeks.'

'Oh my gosh, Sasha! That's brilliant!' Giving her arm a squeeze, I grinned. 'Just think, soon this little walk to the local wine bar could become a regular occurrence.'

'Could?' Sasha spat in mock disgust. 'There's no could about it; it bloody well will!'

The first few minutes of our walk passed with small talk as we caught up on how each other's week had been so far, but the whole time we were chatting I could sense an underlying tension in Sasha.

Once we were settled at a table in the wine bar and both had a chilled glass of Sauvignon Blanc in our hands, I turned to Sasha and gave her a look. 'So, it's lovely to catch up and everything, but I'm suspecting there is an underlying reason that we're here on a Tuesday night. What's up?'

Sasha frowned and straightened her shoulders defensively. 'Can't I just want a drink with my best mate?' I'd known Sasha long enough to know how stubborn she could be, but I also knew that all her bravado and bluntness were hiding her vulnerability, and so I smiled supportively and nodded.

'Of course, you can, and this is lovely, but if you want to talk about anything you know I'll always listen.'

Sasha hid her initial response by taking a gulp of her wine, but then she put the glass down and her shoulders slumped a little as she relaxed her guard. I was one of the few people who she would do this around, and as frustrating as she could be with her aggressive defensiveness, I was always grateful that she would let me in. Even if she often made me work for it.

'You always manage to read me so well,' she murmured quietly before placing her glass down and looking up at me with a sad expression.

'Yeah, well, we're buds, that's what I'm supposed to do.' Shifting my seat closer, I gave her a playful nudge with my shoulder. 'So, what's with the face? I'm going to take a shot in the dark and guess that it's Marcus related.'

She snorted out a dry chuckle and nodded. 'He definitely wants more than just one night!' she blurted with no other preamble.

'So, you've finally sat down and spoken to him?'

She nodded and curled her lip in irritation. 'Yeah, just now at the club, but it was pointless. I've never met a man like him before. Most of them jump at the idea of casual sex!'

I chuckled, because surely having a man as handsome as Marcus Price wanting more with you than a quick, easy lay would be a good thing to most girls, just not my stubborn bestie. 'I think it's actually really sweet. It shows how much he respects you.'

'Pfft.' Sasha made a dismissive noise in the back of her throat. 'I don't want his respect, I want a fuck!' she exclaimed, but almost as soon as the brash words were out of her mouth her shoulders slumped again. I could see how torn she was. She was fighting with her own long-held beliefs and considering going against them, and for someone as dogged as Sasha that was probably scaring the shit out of her.

'Hey, this is me, Sasha, you don't need to put on a front with me.'

Pulling in a long breath, she nodded, and started to chew on a fingernail. 'Sorry. You're right…' She took a deep breath and finally the real Sasha emerged from behind the defensive walls that she kept built so high. 'It is sweet that he wants more and won't just sleep with me. It's kinda traditional, I guess.'

Nodding, I smiled, glad that my original views of Marcus as a good guy hadn't turned out to be incorrect. 'He's a really nice guy, Sasha.'

Her eyes closed briefly, and she gave a small nod. 'I know.

He's nice, and decent, and I'm so bloody attracted to him… but I'm just… I don't want to get hurt, Rob.'

The strain in her voice was almost too much to take, and I slid a supportive arm around her shoulder, shocked when she suddenly turned and buried herself in my arms for a full-on hug. Locking her in a cuddle, I gave her back a reassuring stroke and tried to think what the heck I could say to make her feel better.

'The pain when I lost my parents…' She spoke into my shoulder, and even though her words were soft I heard the agony in each and every one of them. 'I can't go through heartbreak like that again. It terrifies me.'

My heart clenched for her and I squeezed her even tighter until she let out a teary giggle in my arms and pushed back. 'You're a good hugger, but enough with the sympathy squeeze, I can hardly breathe.'

Sasha on the verge of tears was not a familiar sight. She hardly ever allowed herself to cry, and seeing the glassiness in her eyes now made it clear to me just how much of a big deal her feelings for Marcus were. This was more than a crush or a craving for a one-night stand. She liked him, *a lot.*

Reaching up, I used my thumb to wipe away a lone tear that was making its way down her cheek. 'I totally understand, and I can't give you any guarantees that something between you and Marcus would last forever, but surely if you're getting yourself this worked up about it, it might be worth taking a risk?'

Sasha immediately shook her head, but the action wasn't strong or determined and I took it as a show of her indecision. Pressing on with my argument, I took her hand and squeezed. 'You say you won't risk anything in case you get hurt, but from the pained look on your face you're already hurting as it is.'

Sasha swallowed, and it sounded as if she had been trying to choke down a tennis ball. 'I know you're right, Robyn.'

From her expression, she clearly knew that she could potentially be missing out on something good with Marcus, but I could still hear the "but" hanging in the tone of her voice, before she even said it. 'But that doesn't make it any easier for me to accept these feelings, or act upon them.'

I didn't have a clue what to say to help her out, so I topped up our glasses and gave her another supportive hug. I guessed for someone like Sasha with her strongly built defences it would be difficult for her to change her ways, if not impossible.

CHAPTER TWELVE

Sasha

Taking a deep breath, I sidled up to Marcus, but even though he must have sensed me right beside him he continued to stare rigidly forwards. It was a week on from our last chat, and I didn't know what to say to him yet, so I casually bumped my shoulder into his in way of greeting which made him glance towards me, and then I flashed him a nervous, almost shy smile.

"Shy" wasn't a word that could usually be associated with me – brash, loud, rude, or confident would be more fitting, but shy? No. Which showed how monumentally this guy was affecting me.

He nodded in greeting but seemed to be intent on remaining silent, so I pulled in a deep breath and then just came out with it. 'Hey. Can we maybe go somewhere quieter for a drink, or something?'

Marcus finally gave me his full attention and swivelled on his stool to look at me with a confused frown. 'Is everything OK?'

'Yeah. I'd… I'd just like to talk to you about… well…' A lump of nerves the size of a watermelon suddenly clogged my throat, but I forced myself to carry on. 'About us.'

Us. That final word seemed to drop like a bomb into the otherwise calm air and settled heavily on my chest as Marcus simply contemplated me for several seconds and then let out a deep sigh.

‘I’m not sure we have much else to say, Sasha. It’s clear that our outlooks just don’t match.’ He took a swig of his beer and gave a shrug which seemed to be forced and not as casual as the gesture usually was. ‘Maybe we’re better leaving things as they are? We’ve coped so far.’

His eyes flickered with a myriad of emotions that matched how I felt – lust, pain, hurt, hope – so even though his words were basically a great big knock-back I wasn’t going to let them stop me.

Sucking up my courage, I decided to whisper my confession and get it out in the open. ‘But I’m not coping, Marcus. That’s the whole problem.’ I ran a hand through my hair, feeling horribly exposed but knowing that I had to open myself up if I stood any chance of persuading him to give things a try. ‘I… I can’t stop thinking about you,’ I admitted, my voice dry with the stress of the conversation.

A moment of silence fell between us and then Marcus closed his eyes and briefly lowered his head.

‘Same,’ he agreed, his voice hoarse. Opening his eyes again, he picked his head up and stared at me with such intensity that I almost lost my breath.

‘You’re on my mind constantly.’ He raised a hand toward me as if he were going to cup my cheek, but then withdrew as if having second thoughts and instead gripped his beer bottle with both hands. ‘I still wouldn’t want just one night, though.’

He was holding himself back because he thought I was still just after sex. I could totally understand that. I had been adamant about only doing one-night stands up until now, and I was going to have to say some very unfamiliar words in just a few seconds.

I drew in a deep breath, still shocked that I was about to utter the sentence on the tip of my tongue and then I opened my mouth and let it spill out. ‘I know. I want to try for more.’

For a few seconds Marcus stared at me with wide eyes as if I’d just sprouted ears all over my scalp, but then, recovering his composure, he tilted his head and frowned. 'You're sure?'

'I am,' I replied, before I could let my inner fears overwhelm me.

'And this isn't just a ruse to get me into bed so you can have your one night of fun?' he asked, one eyebrow raised high. The look he gave me was laced with amusement but full of curiosity and hope.

I let out a coughed laugh, slightly offended by his question but amused by his bluntness. 'Christ, Marcus, no. I know I put on a brash front but I'm not that much of a bitch.'

Marcus relaxed his shoulders slightly and offered me a small apologetic smile. 'I know you aren't. I'm sorry, I shouldn't have said that.' A heavy silence fell between us, broken when he huffed out a breath. 'I'm not an easy guy to be with, Sasha. Like I said when we kissed, I have rules that we would have to stick to.'

Moving carefully so as not to freak him out, I reached down and placed my hand on top of his, prompting his eyes to widen and then lock with mine.

My heart was thundering, and I was overly hot, but as soon as we touched, sparks tingled and danced across my skin and from his small inhale I could only assume that he felt the connection between us ignite, too. 'You mean no touching except for holding hands, those rules?' I whispered.

Marcus looked down at where my hand was resting on his and nodded slowly. 'Yeah.'

He made no move to join our hands properly, so neither did I; I just left my hand resting on his and enjoyed the sensation of heat flowing between our skin. Being in contact with him had relaxed me somehow, and now I felt completely content. The connection between us really was insane; it was like our bodies were already linked, drawn to the other as if they were matching pairs.

'Why are they so important to you?' I asked softly, knowing that I was probably pushing my luck, but wanting to find out nonetheless.

Marcus swallowed hard and then carefully turned his hand. Our skin slid together, tingles rushing up my arm as it did so, and he settled our hands so we were connected palm to palm. After flashing me another heavy, lust-laden look, he slid his fingers between mine so they were intertwined. It was a small move, but it suddenly felt so much more intimate and a sigh feathered across my lips as my skin continued to heat and sizzle from the contact. From the way Marcus gave my hand a squeeze I'd place money on the fact that he was feeling it, too.

'It's a long story. I will tell you… eventually.' He sighed, his smile forced. 'But not now. It's not a fun story and I don't want to spoil the evening with it.'

We seemed to be making progress, and even though his hand had tensed from this subject I decided to push just a fraction more. 'Did someone hurt you in the past?'

Marcus's expression darkened and turned grim at my guess, his eyes becoming half lidded as he turned his face away from me. From his reaction I could only assume I'd hit the nail on the head.

The grasp on my hand that had been gentle a second ago tightened as he drew in several shallow breaths in an attempt to control himself. Guilt rushed over me at his panicked reaction, and I started to wonder if he had been hit in the past? Abused, perhaps? People always thought of domestic violence as the woman getting hurt, but it could easily go both ways.

'This is just how I need it to be with a woman, OK? No touching, no staying over, no romantic lie-ins.' He let out a sigh and opened his fingers before tugging his hand away from mine. 'You deserve better than that.'

I took his words to mean "you deserve better than *me*". My entire body felt chilled from the loss of his touch, and so, with a determined frown, I reached over and grabbed his hand again, linking our fingers and increasing my grip so he couldn't push me away.

'What if I don't care about all of that?' I pulled his hand into my lap and placed my other hand on top, capturing him. 'What if I want to try anyway?'

Marcus's jaw was tense as he stared at our hands, his frown deepening until he had two perfectly parallel lines of worry creasing his forehead in between his eyebrows. I desperately wanted to reach up and soothe them with my fingertip, but I didn't dare move. He looked completely torn, but he had begun to run his thumb gently back and forth across the side of my knuckles, and this tiny gesture of affection pushed me on. 'I have my own issues with relationships, Marcus. I'm not exactly going to be the easiest person to be with either.'

He took a long, slow sip of his beer as he considered my words. Finally, he placed the bottle down and stared at me. 'So just to clarify again, even with whatever issues it is you have, you still want to try something proper between us?'

This whole conversation was just as hard for me as it seemed for Marcus, and I had to draw in a deep breath before I could speak. 'Yes.'

'And my rules… you're OK with those?'

If things between us in bed were anywhere near as hot as the kiss we'd shared in the club, then I was more than OK with it. Who cared if he liked a little restraint? I'd certainly enjoyed the way he'd captured my hands and kissed me, so there really wasn't an issue. Perhaps once we learned to trust each other more he might relax his no touching rule anyway.

I nodded slowly and clearly and increased my grip on his hand. I wanted to lean in to his body and kiss him or reach up and slide a hand around his neck to feel how soft the hair at his nape was, but I knew that would immediately go against his ground rules, so I held back, hoping that he would make the first move for us.

'There's more you should know…' Marcus started to speak again, but with the sexual tension growing between us with every passing second, I couldn't hold myself back.

'It won't matter, Marcus. I want to be with you.'

Once I'd made my declaration, I simply sat back and waited for my words to sink in.

Marcus

'It won't matter, Marcus. I want to be with you.'

She wanted to be with me. My eyes fluttered shut for a second as I absorbed her words – the ones I'd wanted to hear Sasha say for months now – and then, on instinct, I shifted closer to seize her other hand and move them both behind her so I was holding them firmly against the base of her spine. Our faces were just centimetres apart now and her breath hitched at our sudden closeness. The sexy little gasp that escaped her lips was such a turn-on that sparks ignited across my body, heating my skin and raising my pulse until it was thundering in my ears.

She was so fucking beautiful that I couldn't stop staring at her. I was instantly hard, my dick pushing uncomfortably against my jeans, so I gave in to the pressure and leaned forwards, grinding my hips against hers. Sasha groaned, pressing her stomach forwards keenly and making it obvious that she was just as affected as me. Her eyes were wide and desire-filled, and her lips damp and still parted in shock, and I couldn't help but imagine she might make that exact same expression later when I was thrusting up between her legs for the first time.

My brain conjured up erotic images in my mind; ones of Sasha naked and laid out on my bed, her arms and legs fastened to the bedposts so that she was open and ready for me, her gorgeous hair cascading across the pillows, and her eyes begging me to come closer.

A hoarse groan rose in my throat and my cock lurched desperately, throbbing with need. I wanted to savour the moment and take my time, but I was so turned on that I couldn't resist leaning in and capturing her mouth with mine. Her parted lips meant I could slide my tongue straight inside and deepen the kiss, something which Sasha seemed to appreciate, because she kissed me back fiercely and arched her back so that her breasts were now pressed against my chest.

'Marcus… please. I want you.'

Christ, the sound of her begging nearly undid me. I was so desperate for her that I nearly gave in to her soft demands and dragged her to a darkened corner where it would have been easy to rip her dress off and fuck her right here in the club, but at the last second, I pulled myself up short.

This was about more than just sex. At least it could be, if I could just get my raging hard-on under control.

Pulling back, I gazed down at her as she tried to suck in some steadying breaths. Her cheeks were flushed, eyes wide and wild, and mouth reddened from our kisses. She looked sexy as fuck, but as much as I wanted to fuck her right here, right now, I knew that we shouldn't rush into a hasty shag.

This was Sasha; I had lusted after her for months, but as well as the physical attraction I felt, I wanted to get to know her properly, too. The girl behind the mask that she put on in public for everyone else.

I wanted her in my life, not just my bed. Besides, I wanted our first time to be special. Private. Not some quick cheap fuck in a kink club.

I dragged my lips from hers and grinned as I took in her needy expression, and then placed another kiss on her lips before leaning back. 'Hold that thought for just a little longer.'

As much as I wanted to trust Sasha when she said she was now willing to try more, I was going to need a little proof of her changed mind-set, so I released her hands and took a deep breath. 'Let's do this properly… You wanna go somewhere quieter to talk? Maybe I could cook you some dinner? We can get to know each other a little more.'

Sasha gave me a rueful smile and peeled her body back away from mine. 'Sorry. I guess old habits die hard.' Running her hands through her hair to flatten it after our passionate encounter, she took a second to steady herself and then nodded, smiling up at me with a look that was almost shy. 'Dinner would be lovely, thank you.'

Shyness wasn't an expression I'd ever seen on her before, but she looked so sweet and hopeful that it was almost like Sasha had been replaced by a different version of herself, one who was willing to try something with me, even though we'd both admitted to having issues. I was so excited by this turn of events that I couldn't help but grin down at her.

'So, food. Eating together. That's like a real date, huh?' she asked, a touch of nerves lacing her tone.

From her expression I could only assume that perhaps she'd never been on a real date, and I felt a small tug of sympathy for her, even though I didn't know her history yet. It didn't feel like the time or place to show pity, though, so I simply nodded. 'It is.'

She didn't freak out at my confirmation, which I took as a good sign. Instead, she patted her tummy. 'Your restaurant has a Michelin star, right?' She gave me a cheeky flutter of her eyebrows that sent another lurch of lust to my cock and I couldn't help but grin at her playfulness.

'Yup.' I might be successful, but I'd never been one to brag and my cheeks heated with pride as she mentioned my restaurant. It was stupid, but I was glad she knew a little bit about me; it showed that even though she'd been feigning disinterest up until tonight, she'd been keen enough to do a little background digging on me.

'But if it's OK with you, I'd like to cook for you at home?' As I suggested it, I realised it might sound like I was changing my mind and trying to get her back to my place for a shag, which would be so easy to give in to, but knowing Sasha's potential for being flighty I wanted to make her see there was way more between us than just one night. 'That way we can talk with a little more privacy,' I added, to clarify my good intentions.

This time it was Sasha's turn to blush, and with that sweet shy smile again, she nodded. 'OK, that sounds great.'

My chest swelled with hope as I grabbed her hand again and slid from my seat. 'That's settled, then. Let's get out of here.'

I wanted her so badly that taking her back to my apartment was seriously risky, but I'd have to try my best to behave. I would cook, and we would talk over dinner. Then maybe if things were going well we could see where the night took us.

Just because I wasn't going to take her straight to my bed didn't mean I couldn't allow myself to fantasise about everything I would do to her once we did move things to that level. Keeping her hand locked with mine, I led Sasha from the club and towards my car with the biggest shit-eating grin stretching my face.

CHAPTER THIRTEEN

Marcus

'Notting Hill, eh? Fancy,' Sasha murmured as we arrived at my house and I parked the car. I didn't reply, because I knew the house was pretty impressive, and any comment I made would either make me sound big-headed or blasé. I lived on Lansdowne Road, one of the original streets built in this area when development first started, in a three-storey Victorian property with bay windows on the ground floor and small terrace balconies on the upper floor. The house was divided into three flats; basement, ground floor, and first floor, which was my apartment. Being on the top floor I had a balcony but didn't have use of the small back garden, not that it mattered, because as residents we had keys to the large private gardens that took up the square in front of the house.

Once we had climbed the stairs, I opened the front door and stowed my keys in a bowl by the door before standing back to watch Sasha as she looked around my apartment with keen curiosity. I gave it a quick glance myself to check it was tidy enough for guests and thankfully found everything pretty much in order. My space was neat and simple, with warm wooden floors. White and pale greys were painted on pretty much every wall, and my only real décor were the metal signs and neon adverts that I'd collected on my travels in America and shipped home.

Having Sasha here in my private space was giving me a strange feeling in my chest, and I couldn't help but stand there and stare at her like an idiot. She was smiling at my artwork and nodding her approval of my furniture and the minimalist décor I'd chosen, and as hard as I tried to pull my gaze away, I just couldn't. It seemed she'd completely dropped her guard and was allowing me to see a whole new side to her now. Her posture was still tall and confident, but her expressions were much more open than usual, letting me see beyond the public mask she always wore in the club.

Once I'd given her a quick tour I decided to steer us away from the temptation of the bedroom, or a quick fondle on the sofa, and led her towards the large, bright kitchen. There were still plenty of surfaces in here that I could ravish her on but, distracting myself from my lusty thoughts, I dug through the fridge and assessed what I could make before turning to her.

'Do you like fish?'

Sasha was standing at the window, gazing out at the view over the small park, but turned to me when I spoke. 'I love it. I eat more fish than meat these days.'

I absorbed every nugget of information she gave me, keen to learn as much about this intriguing woman as I could. 'Is that a dietary choice, or because of the treatment of the animals?'

Leaning back on the window sill, she shrugged. 'Purely a dietary thing. I love duck, and I eat chicken, too, and pork every now and then. I just started to find beef too heavy, so I cut it out, and once I'd done that fish seemed to start filling its place in my menu choices.'

'So how does a fillet of brill with lobster sauce, fresh asparagus, and a polenta cake sound?'

Her eyes widened comically and her mouth dropped open in surprise. 'Bloody hell, it sounds amazing!'

I chuckled at her swearing, glad that in this new version of herself she hadn't lost any of her sass.

Sasha grinned. 'Lobster sauce and polenta cakes? Are you trying to impress me, Mr Price?' She giggled, coming closer and looking inside my packed fridge.

'Not at all. I have the sauce and polenta left over from yesterday, so it's a quick, easy meal to prepare.'

Sasha leaned closer, inspecting my food choices, and in doing so she inadvertently brushed her shoulder against mine. Heat ignited between us and I could have sworn that I felt her tense and then rub a little closer. We shared a quiet moment like that, before she shifted slightly and shook her head in apparent amusement. 'Wow. I can tell you're a chef. Everything's packed in neat little boxes and labelled. Control freak much?'

'You have no idea.' I laughed and pulled the ingredients from the fridge, but couldn't resist a little teasing, so I leaned in closer as I passed her. 'You've not seen how much of a control freak I am in the bedroom yet, either.'

Sasha let out a small excited gasp, and I chuckled to myself as I placed everything on the counter and pulled out some chopping boards. My smile faltered slightly as I recalled how Sasha hadn't let me finish telling her about my rules earlier when I'd tried. I really *was* a control freak in the bedroom, so I just had to hope she'd been true to her word when she'd said nothing would change her mind about me.

I guessed only time would tell.

Sasha joined me at the counter and picked up the bunch of asparagus. 'I'll help. Shall I cut the ends off these? Where do you keep your cutlery?'

For a second, it felt like a thin string of ice had passed through my veins, chilling me from the inside out and causing goose pimples to pop up on the skin of my arms. With an effort, I pushed away the unpleasant sensation and shook my head as I tried to give her a relaxed smile.

'It's fine… I can do it.' I desperately didn't want her to see that I was on the verge of freaking out, so I offered up a distraction. 'How about you pour us some wine? There's a nice bottle of white in the fridge, and glasses are in that tall cupboard to your left.'

Nodding, Sasha pulled down two glasses and smiled. 'Wine – now you're talking my language.'

As Sasha started to busy herself with our drinks, I went to the cutlery drawer and placed my thumb on the small scanner to release the lock.

'Woah. You lock your cutlery away?' Sasha asked in surprise from behind me, and I glanced over my shoulder to see her gawking at me with a frown on her face. Shit. I'd hoped she'd be busy with the wine and wouldn't have noticed.

Thinking on my feet, I nodded. 'Yup. It's a security thing.' Which it was, just not for the reason I was about to give her. 'I have a set of chef's knives here and they're worth over ten thousand pounds.' I pulled a chopping knife and fish knife from the sheath of blades and quickly shut the drawer, relaxing when I heard the lock click back in place.

'Ten grand? Jesus. No wonder you lock them up.'

Luckily Sasha didn't question me any further, so I set about preparing the fish and asparagus and then washed the knives by hand before stowing them back in the drawer. While I gently oven-cooked the fish and polenta cakes, I heated the sauce through and stacked everything else into the dishwasher, before turning and finding Sasha watching me with a fond smile on her face. 'What?'

'Nothing, I was just enjoying watching you. You're very exact, Mr Price.'

'Exact?'

'Yeah. Precise. You're midway through cooking dinner and yet the kitchen is as spotless as when you started. Remind me never to invite you into my kitchen when I'm cooking; it always looks like a bomb site.'

I chuckled, but decided to take her words as a compliment, and moved towards her to express my thanks with a kiss that I'd been dying to take from her ever since we'd got home. As I moved closer her eyes went wide and her tongue dashed out to wet her lips and I deduced from her changing expression that Sasha had correctly read my intentions.

Reaching her side, I leaned down and pressed my lips to hers. As soon as our mouths touched Sasha's body shifted as if she were about to reach out and touch me, so I did the same as I had before and captured her hands. I held them between us as I explored her mouth with mine. She genuinely didn't seem to mind about me holding her captive like this, so perhaps she really would be fine with the way I ran things in the bedroom, too.

Our bodies seemed to meld into one. The kiss felt so good, so right, that I would have liked it to go on forever. But just as I was contemplating abandoning dinner along with my plans for being good and whisking Sasha off to my bedroom, a timer sounded behind me, making me jump and informing me that the fish was cooked.

Leaning back with a rueful smile, I tried to catch my breath, and saw that Sasha was just as affected as me; her eyes were dilated, cheeks flushed, and her lips slightly swollen from our kiss.

These blushes of hers seemed part of the "new Sasha", too; at the club she was always completely in control of herself. Yes, I'd seen her throwing some pretty spectacular dance moves, and yes, as much as I'd hated it, I'd also seen her kissing other guys, but I had never, ever seen her blush or lose her cool. She was always inside that defensive box of hers, always completely in control.

And yet here she was, flushed and expectant and standing in my kitchen looking utterly fuckable. It literally took every remaining shred of my self-control to force my feet to step back from her.

'You are fucking gorgeous,' I growled, lifting a thumb and rubbing it across her swollen mouth before watching with pleasure as she blushed even redder at my compliment.

I stepped back to briefly check the fish. Upon finding it

perfectly cooked I left it to rest and plated up everything else before finally unlocking the cutlery drawer again and laying the table. As I did this, Sasha topped up our wine, and then quickly lit the candle on the centre of the table as we sat down to eat.

We shared a brief, heated glance as if we both knew full well how close we'd come to screwing on the kitchen floor seconds ago, and then, after exchanging an embarrassed smile, we turned to our food.

Silence fell as I watched Sasha tuck in. Then she let out a low moan that was so innately sexual it instantly had me hard under the table. 'My God, this is so delicious, Marcus,' she commented with appreciation.

She continued to eat, and it was clear that she was oblivious to how badly her little moan had affected me.

Having Sasha here with me, a beautiful woman who might well end up in my bed later, I hadn't thought I'd have much of an appetite, but when the rich fragrance of the lobster sauce hit my nose, my stomach rumbled and I picked up my fork. As soon as the first forkful hit my tongue I realised just how hungry I was and tucked in with gusto.

Once I had managed to get my hard-on under control we passed the meal with general chat, learning little snippets about each other and discussing our favourite foods and films. As she placed her knife and fork down, Sasha gave me a more flirtatious look that stopped me in my tracks and instantly restarted the restricted space issues in my jeans.

'So, do you follow the three-date rule, then?' she mused with another of her shy smiles. This softer, quieter side to her was still quite a shock for me, but it hadn't faded, and I had to say her being open and sweet with me was much more preferable to being sniped at. It was as if she'd been desperate to relax her guard around me, but just hadn't dared do it within the walls of Club Twist, or perhaps in front of other people.

The confidence and brashness she always portrayed in the

club had attracted me from day one – we wouldn't be sitting here sharing an intimate meal if it hadn't –but seeing glimpses of the real Sasha that she kept so carefully hidden was a real fucking turn-on, too.

Thinking back to her question, I frowned. 'Three-date rule?'

Letting out a giggle, Sasha nodded. 'Yeah. I mean, I don't really have much experience of proper dating, but there's an unstated rule among girls that if you don't want to look like a slut, you don't have sex with someone new until the third date.' Her cheeks heated, and a flash of wariness crossed her features as she looked away from me awkwardly. 'I obviously didn't follow the girl code,' she mumbled, sounding embarrassed. She'd never seemed bothered by her casual attitude to sex before, but right now it looked like she was uncomfortable with it. She might possibly even be thinking that I considered her to be a slut, which was far from accurate.

'I have no issues with how you choose to lead your sex life, Sasha. I was very similar up until I left to go to America.' I reached across the table and took her hand, giving a squeeze of reassurance. As her eyes tentatively rose to meet mine again I smiled. 'But if we're going to do this thing between us, if we're going to try for more, then I'd want to be your only partner. Could you do that?'

Her face relaxed, and then she gave a slow, sure nod. 'I could… it's a deal.' Licking her lips, she smiled again and wiggled her eyebrows. 'So, three-date rule, yea or nay?'

Blowing out a breath, I raised my hands. 'Who knows? I've never had set rules regarding that side of things before.' I ran my free hand through my hair and shrugged. 'To be honest, after Celia I didn't really think I'd ever bother dating again so this is all new territory for me.'

As soon as I saw Sasha's posture straighten with interest I realised I'd just given away a little more than I had intended to at this early stage, and I dropped my eyes away towards my glass.

'Celia? Is that your ex? The one from America?' I couldn't remember if I'd mentioned having a girlfriend in America, or if she'd found that out from Oliver, but either way I supposed it didn't matter – if we really were going to try something proper between us then Sasha would find out about Celia eventually.

'Yes.' Pulling in a deep breath, I tried to calm my heartbeat, which was now drumming in my veins and threatening to make me dizzy. 'She was from the UK, but she's still in the States now.'

'Can I ask why you guys split up?' To be fair to her, Sasha was being a lot more delicate than usual, but I still wasn't ready to discuss this particular topic.

'I hope you don't think I'm being rude, but I don't want to talk about it, Sasha. Not yet, anyway.'

She gave an understanding nod and pushed the topic away by smiling brightly and glancing down at her empty plate. 'That was the best meal I've had in a long time, Marcus, thank you.'

I was immensely glad of Sasha's smooth change of topic, and nodded with a smile, feeling myself relax again. 'I'm glad you enjoyed it.'

As Sasha began chatting away about her love of cooking and favourite restaurants in London, I thought back to her earlier question about the three-date rule. I was so attracted to her, had been from the day I'd set eyes on her, and with desire pulsing in my system one thing was becoming very clear – I wanted to finish the evening in my bed with Sasha beside me. Or beneath me. Or on top of me. I was so aroused that any damn position would do, as long as her hands were tied up, of course.

With a smirk, I sipped my wine. It looked like Sasha would be getting the answer to her own question very soon.

CHAPTER FOURTEEN

Sasha

The sexual tension between Marcus and me had been ramped up high all night, but I honestly hadn't expected him to initiate sex. He'd been so insistent that he wanted to "do this properly" that I'd half expected him to date me a few times before moving things beyond some kisses and touches, and oddly enough, I'd been OK with that idea.

But oh, how wrong I had been. Once dinner was finished and we'd digested it over another glass of wine and some chat in the lounge, he'd slid closer on the sofa, taken my hands in his, and knocked the air from my lungs with a kiss so fucking fantastic that I'd been left breathless, wet, and desperate for him.

Marcus had turned to me with a decidedly promising expression gracing his face, and then he'd stood, held out a hand and, without saying a single word, led me from the room with the grace of a predator who had just secured his prey for the evening.

And here we were, standing in the middle of his large bedroom staring at each other as if we both wanted to pounce and devour the other like wild animals.

I was often an initiator in the bedroom, but even though Marcus had been initially hesitant about taking this path with me, now we were here he seemed to emit some silent dominance that made me hold back. This was his space, and from his confident body language and stare, Marcus was clearly the one in control. After giving me a long, hard look that set my knees quivering, he made the first move, closing the gap between us and gently brushing my long hair back over my shoulders.

He was so close now that I could see all the different tones in his green eyes; the edge of his irises was a darker forest green with flecks of navy, whereas the centre was several shades lighter and almost reminded me of moss. It was so striking that I wasn't sure how I'd never noticed it before.

It felt so natural being with him that it was just instinctive for me to reach out my hands and rest them on his hips, but the moment I made contact I felt Marcus's entire body tense and realised my mistake.

I'd touched him.

Broken his number one fucking rule within less than a goddamn minute of being in his bedroom. Leaning back so I could look at him, I saw that his jaw was clenched and his cheeks had paled, removing all traces of his earlier confidence and calm. There was even a visible sheen of sweat on his brow, and from his raised breathing I started to seriously worry that he might be about to have a panic attack.

'Marcus… I… I'm sorry …'

He didn't respond verbally, but he did shuffle backwards away from me as he took a few deep breaths to calm himself. He closed his eyes for a second, then opened them, blinked once, and walked to a dresser to our right where he began to rummage around in the top drawer.

I was trying to think what to say to make things right again when he pulled something from the drawer and returned to me. As I glanced down at his lowered hand I realised he'd selected a length of black silk and a flutter of nervous excitement ran through me.

Silently he moved behind me and looped the material around my wrists until they were fastened together at the base of my back. I'd never been restrained by a lover like this before and a tingle of fear-laced excitement ran up my spine.

I wriggled my wrists to see how tight they were, but it was immediately apparent that there was no room for escape. My heartbeat began a panicked drum, but then I glanced over my shoulder at him and relaxed. It was Marcus doing this, and for some unexplainable reason I trusted him completely.

The idea that I was his to use, his to do whatever he wanted with, was erotic, dark, and on the borders of perverse. It brought with it a searing-hot need in my core that was matched by a heating of my skin. I desperately wanted to rip my clothes off, but now my hands were tied that was obviously no longer an option for me.

He stayed behind me, and he was so close that I could feel the heat radiating from his body, and a gasp slipped from my lips as he ran his hands up my arms to my elbows and then back to my bound wrists, tickling the skin as he went.

Everything felt like it was magnified, every touch, every breath, and every movement. I wasn't sure if that was a reaction to the bondage, or just down to the intensity of the connection we shared.

Hot breath skimmed across my neck as he leaned even closer and spoke by my ear. 'Is that OK? Or is it too tight?' The feel of him so close behind me, gripping my wrists, holding me captive, sent a shiver of lust through me and dried my throat so much that I had to swallow twice before I was able to answer.

'It's fine… it feels good.' And it did. I might not have experimented with bondage very much, but I was really enjoying this. After our lovely evening spent talking and flirting I felt completely relaxed in his company, and the thought that I was now at Marcus's mercy was really turning me on.

Giving my wrists a brief tug and finding them well and truly trapped, Marcus hummed in apparent appreciation and placed a lingering kiss on the nape of my neck. 'That's better.'

He walked around in front of me again. I glanced at his face to check if he was still looking stressed, but his earlier panic had dissolved completely and been replaced with such blazing desire that a second shudder rippled through my body.

'Now, where were we?' he murmured as he stepped closer and lowered his mouth to mine again.

For a guy who freaked out at accidental contact he certainly was confident with his moves. His kiss alluded to years of experience, his tongue moving with sure, practised moves against mine until my legs weakened and he had to grip my hips to help keep me upright.

He held me so closely that having my arms tied behind my back didn't affect the moment as much as I'd thought it might. In fact, with his fingers running across my body as he rolled his hips against mine, I quickly forgot about my tethered wrists and just let myself sink into his attentions.

Now I couldn't touch him, Marcus's demeanour had completely changed. His body was noticeably more relaxed, and all the tension from his face had gone. Clearly his touching trigger was just to do with hands, because he didn't seem to mind when I rubbed my hips against his or arched my back and pressed my breasts into him.

Marcus dragged his lips from mine. He took a small step backwards and raised his hands over his shoulders to grab the neck of his T-shirt so he could pull it off. Pausing, he gave me an intent stare and then frowned.

'I… I have some scars,' he mumbled. 'I hope they don't put you off.' After his announcement, he dragged his shirt off and threw it to the side.

Standing still for a second, he just continued to stare at me, as if giving me time to look him over. I did, my eyes greedily dropping to his impressively muscled torso and taking in how amazing his body was. He was like a model from a magazine; buff and firm, but not overly bulky. I'd seen a weights bench in the room next door, and it was clear from his impressive physique that he worked out very regularly, but as my eyes continued their inspection I found them being drawn to the scars he'd mentioned.

I'm not sure what I'd expected when he'd said he was scarred, maybe birth marks, but the puckered, red marks on his skin looked vicious. The lighting was dim in here, but I could see multiple lines on the sides of his chest and across his stomach and I frowned as I wondered what had caused them.

They didn't put me off like he'd worried, but I immediately wanted to ask how he'd got them. Lifting my eyes to his, I found him staring at me with an intense expression and immediately knew that he wouldn't tell me if I asked, so I didn't. Instead, I voiced a different question that had sprung to my mind. 'Do they hurt? Is that why you don't like being touched?'

Marcus's eyebrows tweaked in surprise, as if he'd been sure I was going to question him on the cause of the scars, but then he shook his head. 'No. Some of them are a little sensitive, but that's all.' Licking his lips, he glanced down at his torso and then looked back at me. 'Do they disgust you?' He asked the question so quietly that I almost didn't hear it, but the hoarseness to his voice gave away just how much weight had gone into his few words.

He was worried, *really* worried, that the scars would put me off him.

He glanced down at his body and made a self-disgusted grunt as he grimaced. 'It's fine if they do. I can untie you and take you home…'

'No.' I shook my head, and he looked up at me, perhaps surprised by the vigour with which I had replied. 'They don't disgust me, Marcus. Not at all.' And it was true. I could see why he might think I'd be that shallow – after all, whenever I saw him at the club I was always dressed up to the nines and wearing a ton of makeup – but his scars didn't put me off. They were just part of him. Part of Marcus, the man I was starting to fall for more and more each time I met him.

'They're just part of you.' I vocalised my thoughts and his shoulders relaxed slightly but he still didn't look entirely convinced by my statement. With my hands tied behind my back I wasn't sure how I could reassure him. After looking at his flat stomach again, I decided to act on impulse and dropped to my knees, immediately placing my lips on the closest scar and kissing it gently.

I heard him suck in a surprised breath, but I repeated the move to several more of the marks and then glanced up at him. Marcus's eyes were screwed shut, but as I continued my kisses and began to run my tongue across the taut skin of his abdomen he let out a deep, desire-filled moan and slid his hands under my arms to drag me roughly to my feet.

'I want to tie you to the bed.' His gruff statement wasn't worded as a question, but I could sense from his tone that Marcus wanted my agreement before continuing, so I nodded and smiled shyly.

'OK.'

Once he had my consent he didn't waste any time. Marcus untied my hands, stripped me naked, briefly explored my body with a heated growl, and gently laid me back on his bed. The sheets felt shockingly cool against my heated skin and I sucked in a breath as I tried to get control over my ragged breathing.

Marcus collected something from a dresser at the far side of the room. As he approached me again I saw that he was holding some leather cuffs. This was my first real exploration into restraint, so a swirl of anxiousness curled in my belly at the sight but seeing the purposeful look on his handsome face somehow helped relax me. This was his "thing", and if I could just relax I was sure I would enjoy whatever he had planned for me.

Once again, I noticed that Marcus grew more alert and tense while my hands were free, but as soon as he had attached the cuffs to the headboard and had my hands stretched above my head and secured tightly, he grinned down at me, his earlier cool, controlled demeanour slipping back into place.

Gently lifting my head with one hand, he used the other to pull my long hair out from underneath me and then took his time spreading it across the pillow with a sweetly intent look. The level of concentration on his features as he arranged my hair would have been quite comical if the gentle tugs on my scalp hadn't been quite so erotic, but they were, and after just a few minutes I was squirming on the bed and pressing my thighs together to try to quell my rising arousal.

'Beautiful.' Marcus stood and gazed down at me, and I blushed under his scrutiny. What was it with me when this guy was around? I hardly ever blushed, but put me within sniffing distance of Marcus Price and my cheeks had a life of their own. Not to mention my libido… *That* went crazy whenever Marcus was around, too. It was like he released a pheromone that appealed directly to my sex drive and lit me up like a firework. Maybe he did, I didn't know enough about biology to say otherwise, but he certainly sent both my mind and body wild.

'You are so fucking gorgeous, Sasha.' Marcus bit down on his lower lip as his eyes strayed across my body again.

My eyes copied his gesture and roved over his body and I grinned. He wasn't half bad himself.

'Ditto,' I squeaked, my voice all high and lusty. I'm not sure I'd ever been naked with a guy who had such a great body, and that in itself was quite a compliment to him, seeing as I'd been with a lot of men in my time.

Marcus lowered his head and I thought that he was frowning at my compliment, maybe feeling self-conscious about his scars, but as a dimple appeared in his cheek I realised he was trying to hide a huge smile. Even with the scars, Marcus's physique was amazing, and he was so handsome it made something inside my chest hurt every time I looked at him.

Lifting his head again, he grinned at me and my lungs tightened as if a band was squeezing them. God, he was just stunning. Especially right at this moment as he stood there, topless and staring at me with his head slightly tilted and a chunk of his wild hair falling messily over his brow. He still had his jeans on, although the zipper was now noticeably straining, but then he broke my ogling by kicking off his shoes and socks and moving closer.

I held my breath as he lowered himself to sit beside me on the bed. 'Now, where I should start?'

He moved his hand to my shoulder, gently brushing some of my hair back and then trailing across the skin, down over my collarbone before tracing the curve of my breast with the lightest of touches.

'Here?' He didn't go anywhere near my nipples, which were hard and achy and desperate for his touch, but a shudder of lust still ran through my body.

Marcus noticed my reaction and chuckled, before removing his hand and lifting it to brush across my lips. 'Or here?' He lowered his head and placed a feather light kiss on my lips that had me straining upwards to try to deepen the contact, but once again, he pulled back before I could get any real satisfaction, causing me to groan in frustration.

'Or maybe here?' he asked softly, his hand dancing across my belly before trailing down towards the thin strip of hair at my groin. Oh God. He'd barely touched me and already I felt on the brink of an orgasm. My legs were still clenched together in an attempt at sating the throb between them, but Marcus tutted and brushed his knuckles over my thigh. 'Open your legs.'

His command was soft, but I still followed it immediately, parting my legs and praying that he would put me out of my misery and touch me where I needed it the most. When his hand moved between my legs I thought I'd got my wish, but then Marcus's finger made just the slightest touch, brushing over the sensitive skin on the inside of my thighs and almost, but not quite, stroking my clit before he ripped it away and pounced forwards to lie over me and crash his lips against mine.

This time there was no gentleness, no teasing touches, it was a full-on, hot, open-mouthed kiss that dared me to join in, and then dragged me in whole when I did. I'd kissed a lot of guys in my time, but I seriously don't think I'd ever been kissed quite like this. His kiss was amazing, more than just a meeting of lips and tongues. It felt like a meeting of souls, and as our mouths continued to move together I found myself getting light-headed. This was when I needed my hands, because I desperately wanted to grab onto him to help ground myself, but instead I wrapped my fingers around the bonds at my wrists and gripped so hard that I was surprised they didn't rip from the pressure.

I might not be able to grasp him with my arms, but as Marcus continued to kiss me and tease me with his hands I lifted one of my legs and wrapped it around his hips, dragging him down onto me so I could get some much-needed contact.

He lifted his head and grinned down at me, showing his appreciation of my move, and trailed a hand along my raised leg from the ankle all the way up the calf and onto my thigh. Digging his nails in, he dragged them across my skin and pressed my thigh down to widen my legs before bringing his denim-covered groin into closer contact with mine.

'Marcus…' The gasped name slipped out like a desperate plea for more, and in response Marcus nodded and placed another kiss on my parted lips.

'I know, I feel it, too. Let me take care of you.' His kiss trailed over my jaw, and then he began to slip lower on my body, his hands, lips, and tongue leaving a blazing trail of need on my skin as he kissed and licked across my collarbones and finally reached my breasts.

Both of my needy nipples were finally showered with

attention until I was writhing below him, desperate for his touch to move lower to where I needed it the most. Marcus seemed to sense my need, because after giving a harder nip to one of my breasts he continued lower on his exploration, his lips trailing across my stomach and making it quiver with anticipation before he finally reached the sliver of hair at my groin. My hips rose of their own accord, and Marcus chuckled, his warm breath feathering across my clit and making me let out a low, lusty groan as he teased me by blowing a cooling breath across my soaked flesh several times.

Finally, after what felt like hours of teasing, Marcus made his first proper contact with me and laved my clit with his tongue before sucking it into his mouth. The touch felt so good on the swollen bundle of nerves that I cried out in pleasure, my arms tugging at the restraints on my wrists and my legs bucking from the bed and looping around his shoulders.

Using a firmer grip on my waist, Marcus held me still and upped his movements by adding one hand to the mix. While his tongue continued to lick and suck on my clit he slid a finger down through my folds and then teased my entrance with it several times before slowly sinking it inside me. 'Jesus. Fuck, Sasha, you're so fucking wet.'

There was no point denying it, because I was. I was aroused to the point where I could feel my own moisture wetting my buttocks and thighs, and it was all because of the man who currently had his head buried between my legs.

Marcus upped the single finger to two, or possibly even three, I couldn't tell, but the stretch increased, and then, while sucking rhythmically on my clit, he started to thrust his fingers in and out. His hand moved quicker and quicker, rubbing against my G-spot on each hard, deep thrust, and then, before I could even begin to catalogue just how multi-talented he was, my stomach clenched and my groin tingled as an orgasm raced up on me.

I groaned, and my back arched as my core clenched around

Marcus's fingers over and over again until the spasms started to ebb and he slowed his movements to ease me down from the explosive peak.

Holy fuck. That had been some seriously good oral sex.

My head flopped back, my arms hanging limp from the leather that held them captive, but then a movement on the bed was followed by the sharp sound of a zipper lowering and I dragged my lust-dizzy head up just in time to watch Marcus peel off his jeans and boxers.

My dry throat got even drier as my eyes trailed down over his body and landed on his manhood. Nestled in a trimmed clutch of blond hair was a mighty fine cock. Thick at the base, and not relenting much as it stretched upwards to an equally impressive head that was already shiny with a bead of pre-come. I had only just climaxed, but the sight of his huge erection bobbing away as he moved to throw his trousers aside had me wide awake and ready for round two.

Marcus moved back beside the bed, pausing to grab a condom from the bedside drawer and roll it on. He stood there completely unashamed of his nakedness. Not that he had anything to be ashamed of – he was magnificent. Even the vicious scars didn't mar his beauty. My gaze drifted lower to where he was sheathing himself. His dick was so big that the rubber was stretching and straining as he rolled it down his length, and I had to swallow hard to try to contain my excitement.

He climbed back on the bed with me, one hand casually working up and down his sheathed length, as if making sure I'd got a good eyeful of what I was about to have inside me, and then he moved between my legs, spread them wide, and lowered himself over me again.

Our mouths met in a deep kiss, and the weight of his cock laid heavily on my stomach. As he continued to kiss me, Marcus shifted his position, allowing his erection to drop between my legs and rub against my opening. I was so wet the tip slipped through my folds with ease, and then with one more small adjustment he lifted his mouth from mine and stared down at me as he thrust forwards and began to bury his length in me.

A gasp rose in my throat as he stretched me, his cock sliding deeper and deeper until I could have sworn he was tapping at my cervix and stretching my opening wider than it had ever gone before. I'd been with well-endowed guys before, but Marcus might just be the biggest I'd ever had, and it took several almost-but-not-quite moments of stretching and pain until I was ready for him to begin moving properly.

'OK, babe?' he murmured, watching me so intently that I almost felt embarrassed by his scrutiny.

I nodded and managed a soft reply of, 'Yes,' before he shifted his hips back and began to move in and out of me with slow, deep movements that were so perfect they shook me to my core.

I swear to God that each thrust sent me to heaven and back. The stretch was exquisite, and he was managing to hit my clit and G-spot with every move. Add to that the sensation of his chest hair rubbing at my sensitive nipples and I was fast approaching the best sex of my life.

Neither of us lasted that long, but I was the first to go, my second climax rearing up on me with force and causing me to shout out and wrap my legs around him even tighter as he continued to jab his hips into me over and over again in pursuit of his own release.

Only after my orgasm had subsided did Marcus really increase his speed, thrusting into me a few more times and letting out a loud bellow as he jerked his cock deep into me and started to come. He pulsed inside me for several seconds, and then, with another low groan, he collapsed down on top of me, supporting most of his weight on his arms.

Holy crap. Not only had that been the best sex of my life, but I'd felt a deeper connection with Marcus than I ever had with any of my previous lovers.

Talk about a potentially life-changing encounter.

We lay entwined and panting for what felt like hours. Snuggling, cuddling, or long conversations after sex had never been my thing; I'd usually been more concerned about how to get the guy to leave as quickly as possible so I could sleep, but tonight with Marcus those thoughts didn't even cross my mind.

I felt content, happy and replete, and in no hurry to leave at all. We talked a little, mostly Marcus checking that I was OK, and us both expressing how much we had enjoyed what had just occurred, and then we lay there connected in some little bubble of our own. He might be on top of me, but with the way he had his arms wrapped around and under me, he was protecting me from the full weight of his body and I could have quite happily stayed there all night.

Finally, he peeled himself up. He gazed down at me for a second and placed a brief kiss on the tip of my nose that felt so intimate it made me blush, and then he slid from within me and rose from the bed to quickly dispose of the condom.

I wanted to wipe myself off and eyed the box of tissues on the nightstand but, seeing as I was still tied up, there was no way for me to reach them. Marcus saw my glance, and with a sweet smile he grabbed one and did the job for me as I settled back into the soft pillows.

Marcus disappeared into the en suite to chuck the tissue and condom and then retuned. He gave me a scrutinising glance and briefly chewed on his lower lip as if considering something long and hard.

My brain felt seriously mushy after the amazing sex we'd just had. I could barely process even the simplest of thoughts so what he could be thinking so hard about I had no idea.

'Would you… would you like to stay over?' Ah. *That* was what he'd been pondering. I distinctly remembered him saying that "no staying over and no romantic lie-ins" were some of his rules, but he'd obviously changed his mind now, and that thought thrilled me. If he was relenting on that, then maybe he'd soften on some of his other rules and let me touch him at some point soon, too. I was dying to run my hands though his wild hair and explore the firmness of his muscles with my fingertips.

Marcus's tone seemed to hint that he was unsure about whether I'd agree, but after the mind-blowing time we'd shared so far tonight, and the connection we'd had while talking earlier, I certainly wasn't in a hurry to leave.

Perhaps his hesitancy was because of my one-night history with men, because I'd never exactly been a staying over kind of girl, either. I'm fairly sure he was aware of this, but whatever the cause, I decided to put his mind at rest by smiling shyly and nodding. 'I'd really like that.'

Marcus grinned at me, and then his expression shifted to one of anxiousness. That's when things got even more bizarre.

He moved to the bedside table and opened all the drawers in turn as if checking for something. After shuffling through them all he let out a deep sigh. He shifted the entire piece of furniture away from the bed and put it against the far wall.

By this point, I was frowning in confusion and wondering what the hell he was doing, or looking for, but then he turned back to me with a contented and relaxed expression and came closer to remove the cuff on my left hand.

After chucking it onto the armchair in the corner, Marcus paused and looked at me intently. My right wrist was still snugly wrapped in the leather cuff and attached to the bedframe, so I gave a cheeky smile and wiggled it. 'You forgot this one.' I giggled, but Marcus simply stood by the foot of the bed and slowly shook his head.

'No, I didn't. If you want to spend the night, then the cuff needs to stay on.'

It took me several seconds to process his words, and when I did I found myself almost speechless. The cuff had to stay on?

Had he lost his mind? 'Excuse me?' I retorted sharply, my voice coming out all strangled and high pitched from shock.

'You heard me, Sasha. I warned you I had some extreme rules, and you said you didn't mind. This is one of those rules. If you stay over, then the cuff stays, too.'

My mouth hung open in shock. This was all so unexpected that, at first, I didn't even know how to respond. Marcus remained where he was, butt naked and hovering by the end of the bed as he tilted his head and gave me a level look as if trying to work out what was going through my mind. He wouldn't have to read my thoughts. Now that I'd processed his crazy request I was more than happy to enlighten him vocally.

'Are you fucking crazy?' I shrieked.

He swallowed and looked across at me sheepishly. 'Probably.'

'So, if I want to stay over I have to be shackled to your bed like… like some sex slave?'

He shook his head, sending messy chunks of his hair falling across his brow. Just minutes ago, I would have admired this and thought it looked sexy as fuck, but now all I could focus on was my shock and irritation.

'No. You wouldn't be a sex slave… but yes, you would be cuffed to the bed. Just one cuff… you'd have plenty of slack to sleep comfortably.'

'*Oh, just one cuff?*' I repeated, my voice slick with sarcasm. 'Like that makes it better somehow? Are you some kind of caveman? Is this supposed to turn me on? Am I supposed to swoon at this show of… of… of…' I was totally lost for words to describe the complete bizarreness of this situation, so I frantically waved my free hand in the air instead. 'Of… whatever the fuck this is?'

I ran my hand through my hair, leaped to my knees, lifted my cuffed wrist, and glared at him. 'Take this fucking thing off my wrist right fucking now!'

Marcus let out a heavy sigh and looked up at me, his

expression almost that of a small, hopeful boy. 'I want you to stay.' His tone completely threw me. He sounded so torn up that it made me pause for a second.

What the heck was behind all of this? 'Tell me what this is about, Marcus.' I deliberately softened my tone, hoping he might let me in on whatever was troubling him.

His eyes grew visibly duller and he shook his head. 'I can't. Not yet. But I still want you to stay.'

Swallowing hard, I shook my head. 'I wanted to stay, too, Marcus, but not like this.' I shook the cuff again to make my point.

He stared at me for several long moments and then sighed. 'I… I can't do it any other way.' He slumped his shoulders in apparent defeat, but his gaze stayed resolutely trained on the carpet as if he couldn't bring himself to meet my eyes any more.

'Fine. I can't do it like this, either!' I exploded, my earlier compassion vaporising and my voice sounding wavy as shock settled in and mixed with my anger.

Marcus lifted his head and stared at me for several long seconds before frowning. 'I tried to tell you earlier that I had more rules, but you said it wouldn't matter.' He paused and then added eight words which seemed almost wrapped in pain. 'You said you wanted to be with me.'

Something in my chest tightened at the achingly sad tone to his voice and I winced and had to drop my gaze away as guilt burned through me. I had no retort to his words, because they were true, I *had* said that, but I'd never in a million years thought that his rules would involve me being tied up all night long. It was a step too far. Scrap that, it was a fucking giant leap too far.

Our silent stalemate continued, the air filling with an uncomfortable tension until Marcus pulled in a long breath and then made his way around the bed towards the dresser where his phone was. 'I've drunk too much to drive you home, and I won't let you get public transport at this time. Let me call you a taxi,' he mumbled.

I watched him with my mouth hanging open again – it was becoming a familiar expression this evening – but he was tapping away on his phone at this very second ordering me a goddamn cab. Jesus, he was really serious about sending me home? It was three o'clock in the morning! I'd thought that if I made enough fuss he'd take the cuff off and relent, maybe tell me why he'd felt the need for it in the first place, but clearly, I had been wrong.

Chucking the phone aside, he risked a brief glance at me, his eyes still dark and troubled. 'It'll be here in five minutes,' he murmured, leaning down and undoing the final cuff. 'I'll let you get dressed and then I'll walk you downstairs.'

When the leather slid free I jumped to my feet so rapidly that my head spun for a second, but it didn't put me off dishing out some of my frustration. 'It's a little late for gentlemanly manners, isn't it?' I stared at his back with such intensity that it felt as if I was trying to throw angry sparks at him. 'You tell me you don't want me to go, and then you add the little delight that you want me to stay here chained up all night! I'll walk myself out, thank you very much.'

Marcus straightened his posture defensively, and he glanced over his shoulders at me and nodded tightly. 'As you wish.' There was a heavy silence as I dragged my clothes on, and then Marcus let out a long breath. 'Maybe we should go back to avoiding each other. If I see you at the club, I'll keep my distance.'

I shoved my arms into my bra but paused as his mention of the club made me wonder something. 'Do they know? Your friends at the club, do they know that you like to keep women tied to your bed like some abusive serial killer?'

Marcus's body tensed. When he turned to me next his eyes were dark with anger as if I'd touched on a sensitive subject. 'I'm not abusive, and I'm not a killer,' he grated, his face reddening with annoyance.

My outburst must have hit a button, because it suddenly seemed like a completely different man was standing before me. The problem was he wouldn't talk to me, so I had no idea what had triggered all this in the first place and therefore couldn't help him. It was so exasperating that my frustration was quickly morphing into irritation. I'd finally opened myself up to a man and this happened – it was just bloody typical.

'And in answer to your question. Some of them do, yes. It's a sex club, Sasha. My need to restrain women is hardly the most perverse of habits among the members.'

To be fair, he had a point there. I knew from my chats with Natalia that some really freaky shit went down behind the closed doors of the club's private rooms, so Marcus's penchant for a little bondage was mild in comparison.

Sighing again, he turned away. 'Take care of yourself, Sasha.'

'Go fuck yourself, freak,' I spat back, still feeling decidedly off-kilter from this whole exchange and deciding to resort to my good old defence of swearing.

As he glanced back at me over his shoulder, his expression darkened. 'I'll pass, thanks, seeing as I've just fucked you.' He stepped into a pair of boxer shorts and strode to the bedroom door, pausing on the threshold. 'Thanks for the fuck. You might have lied about being fine with my rules, but at least you lived up to your reputation of being great in the sack. Must be all the practice you get.'

His spiteful words were so unlike the man I'd come to know that they caused hurt to spread in my chest, and my mouth fell open in shock at his unexpected insult. He threw me another glance before leaving the room, but the look in his eyes didn't back up his nasty comment at all. Quite the opposite, in fact; from the pained expression on his face I could only guess that his words had been thrown out in upset and haste.

I'd obviously hit a nerve with my outburst, and he'd retaliated. His remark about me still hurt, though. I was well aware that I'd led a bit of a slutty lifestyle over the years, but I still didn't want it thrown back in my face like that. Mind you, I'd hardly been complimentary to him either, had I? I'd called him a freak, abuser, and serial killer, and on top of that, he had tried to warn me that he had some extreme rules, and I had told him I didn't care and then gone back on my word.

What a fucking mess.

A growl of frustration left my throat as I sought out the rest of my clothes. Rubbing my hands over my face, I cursed my stupidly short temper, which had no doubt been the spark that had fuelled the whole heated row in the first place. But even as I begrudgingly accepted that some of the blame for this debacle was on me I still couldn't rein in my stubborn side enough to seek him out to apologise.

When I let myself out of his apartment I found the cab already waiting at the kerbside and slid into the back seat with a heavy sigh as I replayed the last few hours in my mind again. The night had gone from amazing to amazingly confusing within a matter of seconds. And had he seriously thought I'd be fine with him cuffing me to the bed all night?

What the hell was that about?

CHAPTER FIFTEEN

Robyn

The chiming of the doorbell was almost instantly followed by someone hammering on the front door, and I frowned as I sped up my jog down the stairs to get to it. Oliver met me in the hall with a matching frown on his face and held out a hand to stop me.

'Let me get it.' He was obviously feeling protective, and to be honest, with the amount of noise our visitor was making, I was more than willing for him to open the door.

Oliver checked the spy hole. He turned his head over his shoulder and gave me a surprised look. 'It's Sasha.'

Sasha? We hadn't arranged to meet up tonight, and I couldn't for the life of me think why she'd be banging on the door like a lunatic attempting to knock it down.

I went to Oliver's side as he opened the door, and we were both almost bowled over as Sasha immediately barged her way into the hallway with a dramatic huff of breath. 'About bloody time! I hope you've got some wine, we're going to need it.'

Oliver and I exchanged a confused look as Sasha stormed off in the direction of the kitchen without waiting for an invite. 'Why, Sasha, how lovely to see you. Come on in, make yourself at home,' Oliver muttered to her retreating back with an amused look that made me giggle. 'Looks like girl talk to me. I think I'll leave you two to it.'

He dropped a kiss on my lips, then winked and disappeared into the lounge, leaving me to follow behind my dramatic bestie.

Entering the kitchen, I found Sasha already standing at the wine rack examining one of Oliver's most expensive bottles of red and looking like she was about to crack it open. I dashed towards her, pulled the bottle from her hand, and selected a more budget-appropriate drink before guiding her towards the table.

'Sit. Let me open this while you tell me what on earth is wrong.'

Sasha flopped into a chair at the kitchen table and then crossed her arms defensively. 'How do you know something's wrong? I might just be visiting.'

An ironic laugh caught in my throat as I turned to her with raised eyebrows. 'Just visiting, at nine p.m. on a Monday night? Firstly, we didn't have any plans to meet up, so that's unlikely. Secondly, you practically hammered a hole through the front door trying to get in, and lastly, you stated, and I quote, "I hope you have wine, we're going to need it."'

Sasha screwed up her face at my observations, but still stayed silent. I unscrewed the wine, poured a generous portion into both of our glasses, and gave her an intent look. 'So, did I jump to the wrong conclusion, or is something the matter?'

She huffed as if irritated by my speculation, but then pouted. 'You were right.' Sasha grabbed the glass of wine from my hand before I'd even had a chance to put it down and practically drank half of it in one go before nodding glumly. 'Something *is* the matter.'

I joined her at the table. I'd brought the rest of the bottle with me – it looked like we'd be needing it – and I rested my elbows on the wood and smiled at her reassuringly. 'Come on, then, spill the beans.'

After another heavy sigh, Sasha pushed her glass away and met my eyes. 'Marcus and me … we slept together.'

Woah, I had not expected that! After all the uneventful months that had passed between them I'd started to assume nothing would ever happen. Clearly, I'd been wrong. 'When?'

'Saturday night.'

Sitting up straighter, I put my hands on my hips indignantly. 'Saturday? Why am I only hearing about this now?'

She rolled her eyes and gave a thin smile. 'It's only two days later, Rob, and this wasn't exactly the type of thing I wanted to discuss over the phone!'

Humming my disapproval of her tardy gossip transferral, I sipped my wine and then tilted my head as I observed her. 'And this is a problem how, exactly? I thought you fancied the pants off him?'

'I did!' Sasha lowered her head and rested it on her forearms, still looking decidedly glum. '*I do*,' she added softly.

So, she still liked him, and they'd progressed their relationship to a physical level… I was really struggling to understand why she looked so down.

'Was he not up to your usual standards in the sack?' I speculated.

Sasha's head snapped up and she fired a hard glance at me that shocked me so much I shifted backwards on my seat. 'I was a slut, *I get it*.'

Where had that harsh reply come from? It seemed like I'd offended her, but that hadn't been my intention at all. Besides, Sasha was normally the first person to make a joke about the loose way she led her sex life. Her choice of the word "was" was an interesting one, too, as if she had now decided to put that part of her life into the past tense.

'Sasha, that's not what I meant, babe,' I murmured soothingly.

Letting out a long sigh, she plopped her head into her hands again and then shook it so loose waves of her long hair fell around her face. 'I know. Sorry. It reminded me of something Marcus said which upset me.'

My shock instantly turned to a frown. 'He called you a

slut?' I'd always thought of Marcus as a good guy, but if he'd said that to my friend I'd be rapidly reassessing my view of him, not to mention having a bloody big word with him next time I saw him.

'No. Not in so many words. It all got a bit heated and I think we both said things we regret.' Lifting her head again, Sasha met my gaze. 'I know *I* did,' she added softly.

I was stunned to see her expression was glassy with unshed tears. Sasha never cried. *Never.* In fact, the only time I had ever seen her close to tears had been because of Marcus Price, so he obviously registered as something pretty damn serious for her if he was triggering emotions like this.

Getting details from her had always been like drawing blood from a stone so, hoping I didn't upset her again, I decided to try to be more specific with my questions to get to the bottom of it all. 'So, you slept together, but now things are terrible. Were you just not compatible in bed?'

'No, it was incredible. We had amazing chemistry. God, Robyn, it was the best sex I've ever had.'

The best sex she'd ever had? Wow. Coming from Sasha, who has had a *lot* of sex in her life, that was quite a statement. Sitting back, I frowned again, completely lost. 'I'm so confused. You fancy him, you shared an amazing connection *and* the sex was great.' I lifted a hand and scratched at my head as I tried to work out what I was missing. 'What exactly is the problem, then?'

'We used handcuffs…' Sasha admitted, twisting the stem of her wine glass as a distraction. 'I enjoyed it, *a lot*... but afterwards… he…' She seemed to be struggling with how to explain it. 'Afterwards, he wanted me to stay over, and I wanted to as well, but… but then he said I had to stay cuffed to his bed all night.'

Sasha's peculiar confession occurred just as Oliver decided to walk into the kitchen with an empty mug in his hand.

Oliver winced and drew to a sharp stop, apparently having

overheard her last sentence. '*Dios*. Sorry, bad timing, I'll come back in a minute.'

'No! Oliver, wait, please, you might be able to help me make sense of all this mess with Marcus,' Sasha pleaded, causing Oliver's brows to pinch into a frown.

'You were talking about Marcus?' He seemed as astonished by her random confession as I was and flashed me a wary glance as if he weren't entirely comfortable with being involved in a gossip session about his close friend.

Sasha nodded, and Oliver relented, coming to join us at the table with an even deeper frown on his brow. She gulped her wine and stared at the table top as she spoke. 'To recap, we slept together, then I was going to stay the night, but he said I had to stay cuffed to the bedframe.'

'He wouldn't let you go?' Oliver asked, his tone low and disapproving.

'No, that makes it sound worse than it was,' Sasha sighed. 'Let me try and explain… things were great before and during, but afterwards… he asked me if I wanted to stay over, and I said yes, but then he got this really strange expression on his face and told me that if I slept over I had to keep one hand cuffed to his bed.'

I spluttered in shock, so surprised that Marcus – one of the friendliest, most laid-back guys I'd ever met – had acted in that way.

'Yeah,' Sasha agreed, flashing me an ironic smile. 'That was pretty much my reaction, too.'

Oliver leaned on the kitchen table, his expression intense. 'Did he give any reasons for his request? Was it part of a scene you two were playing out?'

'Nope. It wasn't like that. We had dinner and then things moved to the bedroom. There was no scene, no kink, really, we just had some fun with the cuffs.'

Oliver rubbed at his chin and shook his head, apparently at a loss. 'I have no idea why he would ask that of you. I know he used to like a bit of bondage, but as far as I'm aware he's never been into sex slave play.'

Sex slave play? My eyes widened at Oliver's casual use of the phrase, and once again I was reminded of just how starkly imbalanced my level of knowledge of BDSM was in comparison to Oliver's vast experience. It was never a thought that sat very comfortably with me, so I pushed it aside and concentrated on Sasha.

'Was that what it was? He wanted you to be his slave?' I asked in a whisper, slightly horrified by the possibility, and once again having difficulty in matching up these descriptions with the Marcus Price I thought I had come to know.

Sasha shook her head and helped herself to a top-up of wine. 'I don't think so. I asked him if it was something like that, and he said no. He just said, "If you want to stay over then this is how it has to be."' She shrugged. 'Oh yeah, and he moved the bedside table right across the room away from my side of the bed, too. It was weird. I have no idea why he'd do that.'

After several seconds of tense silence, Oliver stood up and folded his arms over his chest. 'I'm afraid I can't offer you any further insights into why he behaved that way, either, Sasha. I assume the evening didn't end well after that?'

Sasha's face scrunched up into a grimace. She shook her head and took another huge gulp of her wine. 'No. You both know that I have a bit of a temper and a deeply rooted stubborn streak…'

That was an understatement if ever I'd heard one. Sasha was the most single-minded and stubborn person I knew. She was even less flexible than Oliver, and that was saying something, because my man *really* liked to get his own way.

'Once he said I had to keep the cuff on I might have kinda freaked out a bit.' Which I took to mean she had definitely freaked out, big time. 'There was a lot of shouting, and we both said a few hurtful things.'

'But he did release you?' Oliver questioned again. 'He didn't keep you there against your consent?'

Sasha immediately shook her head. 'No. Once I said I wasn't willing to wear the cuff all night he took it off.' She smiled sadly and twirled her wine glass in her hands. 'Then he called me a cab because he didn't want me getting public transport and he'd drunk too much to drive me home.'

Chivalrous even during a time of stress – now *that* sounded more like the Marcus I knew. His behaviour really didn't seem to make any sense at all.

Pulling in a deep breath, Sasha rubbed her hands over her face, seemingly attempting to hold back tears. 'Things were pretty tense. It was horrible.'

I could see how much Sasha was hurting. Since this was my bestie who had never shown even the remotest emotion about any of the guys she'd been with before I felt I had to push her just a little. 'If you both like each other, isn't it worth sitting down and talking with him? Maybe there's a simple explanation, or some way you can work around this?' I asked, certain I'd seen some really potent chemistry between Sasha and Marcus and hating that it might all just fritter away.

Sasha flicked her hair off her shoulders. 'Nope. He's not willing to compromise, and neither am I. I'm not being chained to his bed like some animal; it's fucking ridiculous.'

Her tone held a note of such cold finality that I knew I wouldn't be able to persuade her to change her mind. I completely understood what she was saying. I loved the kinky things I did with Oliver, but if he'd told me early on in our relationship that he wanted me chained up all night every night I'd have walked away, too. There was no way I'd consider something so extreme.

'So how did you leave things?' I was fairly sure I knew the answer to my own question, but I figured it was worth asking anyway.

'We decided it would be best to just stay away from each

other from now on.' Sasha glanced at me and gave her first real smile of the night. 'Then he disappeared off somewhere, slamming doors as he went, and I stormed out. It was all very flouncy.'

Flouncy? Oliver and I winced as we looked at each other. Oh dear. It didn't sound like there was any hope of them working through their issues. All I could hope was that it wasn't going to make things at the wedding uncomfortable for them both… or us.

CHAPTER SIXTEEN

Marcus

I'd been in a full-on foul mood all week; swearing under my breath at the slightest thing, hitting out at the gym punch bag until my knuckles had bled, and being short and snappy with anyone brave enough to speak to me.

Saturday night with Sasha had been at once both the best and worst night of my life. I'd felt a connection with her unlike any other before, and the sex had been bloody incredible, but then I'd gone and fucked it up with my insecurities by chaining her to my bed like some animal.

I growled under my breath as I recalled her fierce reaction, and once again chastised myself for my fucking weaknesses. And God, did she have a mouth on her when she was pissed off. A small amused smirk briefly curled my lip as I recalled her outraged swearing, but then I frowned, still irritated with myself about the way I had treated her.

Regardless of how the night had ended, her fiery streak was such a turn-on for me that even now my groin gave a twitch of arousal.

I had been tempted to call her on several occasions and try to apologise, but I just hadn't been able to think what to say to her. If I'd called her I'd have had to tell her about my past and the reasons for my obsessions, and that seemed too monumental to tackle, especially over a phone call. Unsurprisingly I'd had no contact from her, either. After my behaviour I very much doubted that she would ever want to hear from me again. It was going to make going to the club a hell of a lot more awkward, too, seeing as we were both members and regular visitors, but I guess that was something we'd have to deal with when it happened.

At least now it was Thursday, so I could vent some of my frustrations in my squash game with Oliver. Hopefully smashing a ball around the court for an hour would help me clear my mind a little, even if my thoughts were being dragged back to Sasha every few minutes.

I was midway through unzipping my squash racket when Oliver spoke. 'So, I overheard Robyn and Sasha talking this week.'

Shit. Sighing, I nodded in resignation. I'd suspected that Sasha would have spoken to Robyn about what had happened between us, and I'd also prepared myself for the fact that Robyn might have then confided in Oliver. What I wasn't prepared for was having this conversation now, on a brightly lit squash court.

Trying to play it cool, I kept my eyes averted and shrugged. 'Oh yeah?'

'Yeah. So, you and Sasha finally got it on, huh?' I could hear the interest in his tone but decided that I would try to get the game started quickly to divert him from asking too many details. Clearing my throat, I pulled my racket out and rolled my shoulders to warm them up.

'Yeah.' Maybe Sasha hadn't mentioned what had happened at the end of our night, and Oliver was just interested in dishing the dirt about the fact that we'd finally had sex. 'You want to serve first?'

'No, I want to talk.'

Glancing over, I noticed that Oliver hadn't even got his racket out yet and stood with his arms folded, making no effort to warm up or prepare for the game.

'What was with your use of the cuffs?'

My shoulders slumped. Fuck. So, it would seem she *had*

mentioned my freak-out. 'You know I like bondage, Oliver, that's nothing new,' I replied, hoping that if I used a casual tone he might drop the subject and let us move away from it.

There was a long pause, and then Oliver shuffled uncomfortably on his feet. 'I know that, but she said you wouldn't let her go, Marcus.' Straight to the point; that was so Oliver. He'd never been one to beat around the bush.

Closing my eyes, I allowed myself a second of calm before turning to face my friend with a frown. 'I *did* let her go. I ordered her a taxi for fuck's sakes.'

Oliver was still standing completely still. He didn't look interested in playing squash in the slightest, and I started to realise that I might not get the workout I'd been hoping for.

'You know what I mean, Marcus. She said she was going to stay the night with you, but that you told her she had to be cuffed to the bedframe while she slept.' Tilting his head, he observed me with a frown. 'I know you used to enjoy bondage during sex, but cuffing her all night? That's pretty extreme, mate.'

It was, and even though I knew it was born from my deeply rooted insecurities, I still felt some sense of justification in what I'd done. I'd warned her I had rules, and she'd said she was fine with them. It wasn't my fault she'd changed her mind. Or perhaps it was. My brain was so screwed up over this that I didn't know what to think any more.

'Have you developed some new tastes recently? Slave play, that sort of thing?'

'No!' My reply was instant and forceful – I had no interest in that type of scene – but it was easy to see why he'd jump to that conclusion. I raised a hand and rubbed it over my face. 'It's not like that… but it's difficult to explain.'

Oliver must have seen the anguish on my face, because the next second, he was across the court and standing at my side. He placed a hand on my shoulder and gave it a supportive squeeze. 'You wanna talk about it?'

I did, and I didn't. Talking would mean confessing my biggest, darkest secret, and as much as I knew that I needed to get this out, I wasn't sure I could do it. I'd kept it hidden for so long that it felt like it was festering inside me. It was now starting to affect my life, and the people around me, and it had become clear to me after spending the night with Sasha that I couldn't live the rest of my life as a celibate man, so I needed to deal with my baggage somehow. Perhaps it was time to get it off my chest.

'You know that whatever you tell me stays between us, Marcus. I wouldn't even tell Robyn if you didn't want me to.'

I nodded and swallowed, but my throat was so tight with nerves that it felt as if it was full of glass shards. 'Can we skip squash and grab a beer somewhere? Not the club… somewhere quiet where we don't know anyone.'

Oliver dipped his head in agreement and gathered up his belongings before leading me from the court.

Twenty minutes later, we were changed back into our normal clothes and walking into a small backstreet bar just a short walk away from the gym. After buying two bottles of beer we found a quiet table at the back of the room and took our seats. I'd wondered if Oliver might prompt me again, perhaps give away more of what he'd overheard Sasha saying, but he didn't. He stayed silent, letting me reflect on where I should start.

I guessed the beginning was probably the most sensible place. I lowered one hand and rubbed briefly at my belly, easily able to feel the ridged skin of the scars beneath. 'You remember the scars on my side? You saw them once after squash, but I wouldn't tell you how I'd got them.'

Oliver's brow dipped into a frown, but he nodded in recognition.

'This is all linked to them. The reason I cuffed Sasha to the bed… I don't like to be touched during sex, nothing beyond holding hands. I can't cope with it.' Even saying the words brought a panicked sweat to my brow.

Oliver took a slow sip of his beer as he digested my words, but his confusion was written all over his face. 'Are they painful, or are you worried about people touching them?' he asked, misunderstanding me completely.

Running my fingers roughly through my hair, I shook my head. 'No, it's neither of those things. Sorry, this is really hard to explain.' I swigged down half the bottle in my hand and decided to just get it all out there. 'This goes back to when I was in the US with Celia. She liked a little kinky stuff in the bedroom, too. Sometimes she took charge and tied me up.' I saw the shocked look from Oliver and laughed dryly. 'Just because you like to be in charge in the bedroom doesn't mean we all do, Oliver. From time to time I like it when a woman takes control. Well, I did. I doubt I'll ever trust like that again now.'

Tapping my fingers on the table in agitation, I took another large gulp of my beer and placed the bottle down. My hand was shaking, and from the deepening of his frown, Oliver noticed it, too.

'So, this one night she had my hands tied to the bedframe and she was riding my dick. It was all incredible, and then suddenly she stopped, jumped off me, and started digging in the bedside drawers. I had no idea why, but I figured she was looking for a sex toy or something to spice things up a little more, so I waited. I couldn't really see what she was doing, but a few seconds later when she came back to the bed she had something behind her back.'

Pausing in my tale, I looked at my beer sitting on the table and wished I'd ordered something stronger to help me get through this. 'She'd always had quite an explorative side, and she'd been hinting about anal for a while, so I assumed maybe it was lube, or something she'd hidden in there earlier like chocolate sauce or whipped cream.'

I pulled in a shuddering breath as images of that night

flooded my mind again. 'She climbed back on and sat astride me again, but this time she gripped my hips with her thighs and trapped my cock below her arse, and then…' I drew in a shuddering breath and spat out my last words in a hurried rush. 'Then from behind her back she pulled out a knife and just started stabbing me.'

There was a heavy second of silence as Oliver tried to compute my words. He put his beer down so sharply that a spurt of bubbles shot from the top and the whole bottle toppled sideways.

'*Mierda!*' he cursed as he grabbed the bottle and steadied it, and then stared at me in utter horror. 'She stabbed you? What the fuck, Marcus?'

'She'd obviously taken one of my knives from the kitchen earlier in the evening and hidden it in the drawers. Even as she was stabbing me I recognised the handle as one of mine.' I roughly ran both my hands over my face in an attempt to steady my frayed nerves. 'I was stabbed with my own fucking chef's knife.'

The final quarter of my beer didn't last long, and as I downed it I made the decision to get something stronger from the bar. I could always leave my car and grab a cab home. 'We'd been having issues for a while. Her moods had been swinging dramatically, and I'd been working long hours and barely ever seeing her, but I'd never in a million years expected it to go that far.' I paused, my hand instinctively going to my stomach and tracing the largest of the silver scars.

'The first one was here. It went deep, but somehow managed to miss all my major organs and arteries.' A chill ran through my body as I recalled in precise detail the feeling of the sharp point piercing my skin and then the agonising dragging of my flesh as she twisted it and used the jagged edge to stab deeper. 'As soon as I realised what was happening I tried to buck her off, but she was like a fucking prime bronco rider and manged to get another three stabs here, and around here.' I traced the smaller, deep scars up closer to my ribs.

'My fucking hands were tied, but I managed to use my legs and almost knock her off me. That's when she hunkered down and gripped on and these injuries happened.' Pulling up my shirt, I exposed my abdomen and showed Oliver. 'See the lines here?' I traced the numerous silvery lines that traversed my stomach from one side to the other. There were almost too many to count. 'These are from the serrated blade as it dragged across me in the struggle. I think she was trying to gut me.'

Oliver's face had paled so much it was now chalky white. He shook his head in obvious astonishment and swore under his breath again.

'Ironically, if it hadn't been such a good quality knife those ones probably wouldn't have even broken the skin.'

A wheezed breath broke from Oliver's lungs, and I turned to look at him. He was sweating and holding the table edge with a white-knuckled grip. 'Jesus, Marcus.'

'Yeah,' I agreed quietly, before shrugging. 'To be fair, I got off lightly.'

Seeing his disbelieving expression, I clarified what I meant. 'We'd been in the middle of sex. Man, when she came back to the bed my dick was standing up like a fucking flagpole. If she'd been thinking clearer she could had chopped it off before I'd even realised she had the knife in her hand.'

Oliver's eyes widened as understanding dawned, and I tried to hide my amusement as he crossed his legs.

'Exactly. So, I have a few scars now, but I'm alive and at least I still have my tackle.'

We sat in muted silence for a second or so. Then, apparently reading my earlier thoughts, Oliver abruptly stood up and disappeared to the bar before returning with two large glasses of whisky and two more beers.

Lifting the whisky to his lips, he gave me a thin smile. 'I don't know if you need this, but I certainly do.' He slung back the amber liquid in one go, winced at the burn, and sat back with a deep breath. 'So, what happened? And what the hell caused her to do it?'

I rubbed my hands over my stomach and settled back in my seat, glad that the worst of my story was now out. 'I got lucky, really. I managed to use my legs to throw her off me, and by complete chance she banged her head on the bedside table as she fell and knocked herself unconscious. I was bleeding heavily, but I managed to snap one of the bars on the headboard to free my hand and reach my mobile.'

Following Oliver's lead, I downed my scotch and relished the burn as it hit the back of my throat. 'I called the cops, and then passed out from blood loss, but thankfully the police and ambulance arrived before Celia came round. I probably should have been embarrassed that they found me buck naked and tied to a bed, but I was so fucking glad to see them. I managed to tell them what happened, and Celia was arrested, and I was rushed to hospital and taken into surgery.'

Oliver placed a hand on my shoulder and squeezed. 'Fuck. This is horrific. I can't believe I didn't know this. I'd have flown over to be with you, Marcus.'

Nodding, I gave him a grateful smile. 'I know you would have, thank you, but I didn't want people to know or fuss.' Starting on my next beer, I shrugged. 'I was embarrassed that I hadn't seen through her. Once I had been stabilised in the hospital the police told me that they'd done a background search on Celia and found three reports of domestic abuse filed against her back in the UK.'

Oliver frowned, but nodded and leaned in closer as he listened.

'She hadn't gone as far as stabbing in her previous relationships, but she'd been physically violent. On each occasion the charges had been dropped due to lack of evidence, though.' As a distraction I began to pick at the label on my bottle. 'She'd moved to the US, met me, and, well, you know the rest of the story.'

Oliver had only met Celia a few times when he'd visited me, but he'd never taken to her. I should have trusted his gut and got away, but hindsight is a great thing once you know the outcome.

'She's in prison for attempted murder. I told you guys we'd broken up because I was too embarrassed to tell you all the truth.'

Oliver tried to speak so suddenly that he almost spat out his mouthful of beer. 'She tried to kill you! There's nothing to be embarrassed about, Marcus.'

'I guess not. I was basically a victim of domestic abuse, though. I'm a big, strong guy, and I let that happen… I couldn't… I couldn't imagine telling everyone. I felt like such a fool. Once I started to think back over it, it was obvious to me that she was abusive all along, but with my preference for a little kink she managed to disguise it as her being in a dominant role. I was working such long hours that we weren't together much, so it helped hide the issue for longer.'

We drank in companionable silence for a few minutes, both of us stewing in everything that had just been aired, but it was Oliver who finally broke the silence. 'So, the cuffs with Sasha – that was because you're worried it might happen again?'

I grimaced and nodded. 'Not just Sasha. I've only slept with two women since everything with Celia happened. Both one-night things, and both times I've had a panic attack and had to cuff their hands to the bed,' I admitted quietly.

I closed my eyes as I recalled the outraged look on Sasha's face again and sighed heavily.

'Logically, I know it won't happen again, but… but cuffing them makes me feel in control. It kinda fits with my sexual choices of kink, too, so it hasn't been a problem until Sasha.'

'What happened with Sasha that was different?'

I let out a long breath and met Oliver's eyes. 'I wanted more than just a few hours of fun. I wanted her to stay the night, and she wanted that, too… but I… I couldn't get past the idea of sleeping in a bed with her free to wander around the apartment.' I let out a dry laugh and shook my head, knowing that I probably sounded like a complete lunatic. 'Even though I knew Sasha wouldn't do that to me I couldn't relax. I moved the bedside drawers out of her reach and figured that if I could leave just one cuff on she wouldn't be able to get to the kitchen where my knives are kept. At the time, it seemed like a good solution. She could sleep over, and I'd feel safe.' I rolled my eyes. 'I know it sounds crazy now.'

'Actually, it doesn't, not now I know what you went through with Celia, but if you want something more with Sasha I think you're going to have to tell her all of this. She was really freaked out by it. You need to explain it to her.'

My refusal was on my lips even before he'd finished his sentence. 'I can't.'

'What are you going to do, then? Be single for the rest of your life?' he questioned, obviously trying to knock some much-needed sense into me.

I let out an aggravated grunt and ran my hands through my hair, pulling out several strands as I did so. The idea of telling all this to Sasha made me feel physically sick. 'She'll think I need a straitjacket and a long stay in an asylum.'

Oliver shook his head and nudged my arm. 'I don't think so, Marcus. I know she puts on that brash, ballsy front, but underneath all that she's really kind-hearted. I didn't like her at all when I first met her in Twist, but I've seen a totally different side to her since being with Robyn. Sasha's caring, compassionate, and loyal.'

He was right, Sasha was all those things, and the idea that I'd never get to truly experience them pained me greatly, but it didn't change matters.

'She likes you a lot, Marcus. Robyn told me that she's never seen Sasha get messed up about a guy, but you've well and truly gotten under her skin.'

My ears perked up at that little bit of information. I'd gotten under her skin? Well, that certainly made two of us, because I had to fight to stop my mind from wandering to thoughts of her twenty-four hours a day.

'If you like her just as much, then maybe you two could talk and work through things. Maybe she could help you get over your issues?'

It had been hard enough telling this to Oliver, my closest friend, so opening up such a vulnerable part of myself to Sasha seemed like a complete impossibility. I just couldn't see it happening. Downing most of my beer, I decided to keep my glum thoughts to myself. Instead, I said the words Oliver obviously wanted to hear. 'Yeah, maybe.'

And maybe one day pigs would fly.

CHAPTER SEVENTEEN

Oliver

The car containing Marcus and David pulled up to the kerb and I immediately clocked the frown on Marcus's face as he saw that I was standing on the pavement with Sasha and Robyn. Once David had parked up, the two of them got out, but I noticed that Marcus was far more reluctant to leave the relative safety of the vehicle and only did so when David rapped impatiently on the passenger side window.

I narrowed my eyes as Marcus finally joined us on the pavement, dragging his feet and flashing Sasha a glower in the process. For her part, Sasha seemed equally as uncomfortable with his arrival; crossing her arms defensively over her chest and straightening her spine like a spear.

Hmm. So, it would seem things between our nearest and dearest friends were still on the frosty to arctic scale, then. To be honest, I'd suspected as much, and had secretly arranged today's little meeting in the hopes of smoothing things out between them before the wedding next week. They might both be adamant that their stalemate wouldn't affect the service, but I knew deep down that it was worrying Robyn, and so in turn it was now an issue troubling me.

'Thanks for coming.' I exchanged a brief handshake with Marcus and gave David a pat on the back – he wasn't really a handshake kind of guy. Don't get me wrong, beneath his tattoos and biker appearance he was a lovely man, but if anything, he was more into greeting people with a hug, which I personally found a little over the top. 'We needed some muscle to help us get Sasha's things up to her new flat.'

Marcus blinked, and then, casting his gaze over the pile of things in the back of the van beside us, he gave a small sigh as understanding finally dawned.

'You said you needed help shifting some stuff,' he said to me, his tone accusatory as if he was aware what I was up to.

I crossed my arms and smiled. 'I do. It's just not my stuff that needs shifting.' I kept my reply light, finding a perverse pleasure in watching all this play out.

Marcus ran his eyes over the gathered group again before giving me a despairing look. 'Who packed the van in the first place? Why aren't they unpacking it, too?'

'Sasha's brother helped, but he's had to go off for a meeting.'

For a few seconds, I genuinely thought that Marcus was going to just turn and walk away, but then he turned his gaze on Sasha again, his frown still evident, and still just as deep. 'You're moving *here*?'

'I am,' Sasha spat, her eyes lighting with a spark of irritation. 'I know it's just around the corner from your place, but don't worry, Marcus, I'll make sure not to touch you if we bump into each other on the street. I vividly recall how much it freaks you out.'

Ouch. Now that I knew the backstory of Marcus's issues with contact I could imagine how much her words were hurting him, and as I shot him a glance I saw his shoulders sag and his eyes drop to the floor.

Mierda. I was really regretting my plan of getting them together today. Yesterday, when I'd concocted it, I'd thought it was such a good idea, and I'd had visions of them reconciling, or at least smoothing things over a little, but with all my careful plotting I'd overlooked one thing – Sasha's sass and her sharp tongue.

David flashed me a confused look, and in return I just

shook my head and then gave him a short nod to indicate that I'd fill him in on the drama later. I was considering telling Marcus to head off home – after all, David and I could manage the lifting between the two of us – but to my surprise, Marcus rolled up his sleeves and, after flashing me a disgruntled glance, grabbed a box.

'Let's get on with it, then. Where am I going with this?'

Sasha

Fuck, fuck, fuck. Why was I such a hurtful bitch? The agonised look on Marcus's face when I'd made my snarky comments about how touching freaked him out had been enough to cause a sharp stab of guilt in my chest that still hadn't relented.

My mouth had always worked faster than my brain, and my bluntness had got me into trouble more times than I could count. But the big difference here – the *massive* difference – was that I immediately regretted my words and the obvious pain they had inflicted upon Marcus.

Not to mention the fact that I was a complete cow for saying it in front of a gathered group of his friends like some sort of public shaming. Shit. I literally couldn't feel guiltier.

Things between us had ended badly, and yes, his request to tie me to the bed all night had freaked me out, but from the distressed looks he'd given me I felt sure there was more to his phobia of physical contact than it just being his preferred sexual kink. I was convinced there was a reason he feared touch, and a reason he had wanted me tied up, and the fact that I didn't know what it was drove me insane, but it still didn't justify me being so awful to him.

Marcus gave me another heavy-lidded look, and then, just when I thought he was either going to fire back a returning insult, or turn around and walk away, he surprised the hell out of me by picking up a box and glancing around the street.

'Let's get on with it, then. Where am I going with this?'

His words prompted me into action, and I scooped up another box and headed up the steps towards my new home. 'It's this way. Top floor, I'm afraid.' I made an effort to ensure my words were softer this time, and even though I didn't aim my comments at him directly, he gave me a look of surprise at my gentler tone.

Yeah, the bitch is reining in her sass, I thought with an eye roll as I pushed open the front door and began the lengthy climb up the stairs.

Marcus and I managed to avoid each other for most of the afternoon, but after several hours of work, Oliver and David were working their way across the lounge with a large set of drawers destined for my bedroom and I found myself trapped with Marcus in the lounge area with no way out.

We exchanged a brief glance and stood there in awkward silence like two complete strangers forced to share a very small lift.

David and Oliver were now jammed between a sideboard and an armchair and didn't seem about to move quickly, and I shuffled on my feet, hating the tension that I could feel wrapping around us both.

Finally, I heard Marcus sigh beside me. 'It's a nice apartment. Quirky,' he murmured as his eyes roamed the space, seeming desperate to look anywhere but at me.

I pulled my gaze from his and glanced around my new lounge. I'd already moved most of the furniture into this room with my brother a couple of days ago, so it looked quite together, and I was pleased with how cosy I'd made it. Fairy lights dangled across the patio windows, the sofa was covered in cushions and blankets, and the wooden coffee table and bookcase were a light honey colour and gave the room a lovely warmth.

'It's very you.' I wasn't sure what his comment meant, but it seemed to be a compliment, so I accepted it with a nod.

‘It’s pretty small, though. Nowhere near as big as your place,’ I said lamely, at a loss for any other small talk to fill the void between us. Marcus frowned, and I winced at my words. Bringing up any reference to the night we’d spent together at his apartment wasn’t exactly the best idea given our current stand-off.

As we both continued to stand there awkwardly, I tried to pluck up the courage to apologise for my snarky attitude downstairs. ‘Marcus, I…’ I turned towards him to try to get a little privacy and without even thinking properly, I placed a hand on his waist in an effort at shielding us from prying ears.

My contact must have lasted no more than three seconds before Marcus sucked in a harsh breath and knocked my hand away before literally vaulting over the armchair that was blocking our exit from the room. He clattered down the stairs so fast I was surprised I didn’t hear him tumble down them in a panicked pile.

Oliver and David paused with the set of drawers balanced between them, gawking at Marcus as he hightailed it out of the room. In sync, their heads swivelled towards me, but upon seeing my crestfallen expression they quickly dropped their eyes and continued their task while attempting to pretend that nothing unusual had just happened.

Well, shit, weren’t we just disastrous when we were in the same space for too long? How the fuck had I managed to forget about his dislike of contact?

Unsurprisingly, Marcus went out of his way to avoid me after that, and I actually found myself feeling relieved when all the heavy lifting was done and he and David left.

Clearly there was to be no resolving the differences between us then, so once we’d carried out our joint duties at Robyn and Oliver’s wedding it seemed highly likely that Marcus Price and I would go our separate ways and have nothing to do with each other ever again.

It was a particularly depressing thought.

CHAPTER EIGHTEEN

Oliver

Marcus had grand plans of dragging me halfway around the world for my stag do, but in the end my demand for a quiet night with the boys had won out, and I was now sitting around a table with Marcus, Nathan, David, Nicholas, and Matías, who had flown in especially to join us for the weekend.

We were in The Vaults, an exclusive members club underneath the streets of Central London, built within old arches and tunnels of the underground system, and had just experienced one of the best meals I'd ever eaten.

The club was lavishly decorated with silks, velvets, and fine pieces of wooden furniture, and lit with the flickering light from oil lamps and candles. All in all, it had quite a Victorian Gothic vibe going on. The Vaults specialised in high class dining and also boasted one of the best wine and Cognac cellars in the whole of London, so Marcus had chosen our venue well.

So far, we had experienced the quality of the food and wine, and now it was time to begin sampling the spirits they prided themselves on.

'That was delicious,' Nathan declared, pushing his dessert plate away and giving an appreciative pat to his stomach.

Marcus wiped at the corners of his mouth and threw his napkin down. 'It was good,' he conceded. 'I could have done better, though.' His boast didn't last long, because he burst out laughing almost immediately afterwards. No matter how skilled he was in the kitchen, my friend had never had a big head about his talents.

'I have no doubt you could have, but I wanted you here at the table with us, not sweating away in a kitchen all night,' I informed him with a grin.

A server gave a polite knock on the door to our room and entered while balancing a large silver tray loaded down with sampling glasses filled with a range of their finest Cognacs.

She placed them on a side unit and then set about making sure that we all had five different glasses in front of us. Once she had handed an information card out to us with details of the grape varieties used, she made to leave the room. Pausing by Matías's chair, she leaned down and murmured something, her cheeks heating so much as she did that it piqued my curiosity.

As soon as she had left the room, Matías looked across at me with a devilish grin and rubbed his hands together. 'My stag gift for you has arrived, my friend.'

Something about his expression and the wicked twinkle in his eye automatically made me suspect the worst and I was shaking my head even before he'd had a chance to explain what his "gift" was.

'I said no strippers, Matías,' I warned on a growl, but he held a hand up and shook his head with a look of mock offence.

'You always think the worst of me, old friend, no?' he answered with a frown. I was wondering if perhaps I had made a mistake with my assumption, but then he cracked another huge grin and stood up to pull the door open. 'These are not strippers, they are very high-class lap dancers.'

Lap dancers were just as bad as strippers in my opinion, and I wanted nothing to do with any of it on my stag night. I groaned in frustration and then seconds later we were joined in our little archway by three beautiful women who all strutted in wearing high heels and flirtatious smiles.

Matías really was the devil incarnate. With his dark good looks, goatee beard, and the gleeful smile on his face all he needed was a little set of horns poking out of his hair and he'd look the part, too.

'Matías….' My protest was halted as the women removed their long jackets to reveal slender bodies encased in practically no clothing at all. Every pair of eyes around the table widened, and I think it would be fair to say that all of us were rendered temporarily speechless.

One of the girls made her way towards me and attempted to massage my shoulders. There were only so many ways you could avoid someone's touch without being overly rude, so I shrugged off her hands before turning to Matías, who was encouraging one of the women to dance with him. I say dance; what I really mean is he was grinding against her and she was seeming to love every second of it.

Giving the girl behind me a tight smile, I pushed forwards in my chair to fully remove her grip. 'No, thank you.' I shot Matías a warning glare. 'Matías, please remove your "gifts."'

At my words he stopped his dance and looked across at me in surprise. 'Really? You would turn this down? Even on your stag do?'

Holding his stare, I gave one small, sure nod. 'I would.'

He assessed me for a moment or two and shrugged. 'I can't decide if I'm disgusted or impressed,' he mused, sliding a hand around another of the girls and tugging her closer. 'Your Robyn must be quite the girl to have you so ensnared.'

'She is,' I replied with no hesitation. Now that I'd found Robyn I wanted her and no one else.

Glancing around the table, I knew without having to ask that Nathan and Nicholas wouldn't be interested in a lap dance or any other form of attention from these women; they were both far too happy in their own relationships to ever consider it. David and Marcus were both single as far as I knew, but neither looked particularly comfortable with the current situation.

'Feel free to take your "friends" elsewhere if you wish to entertain them,' I offered, knowing that Matías would no doubt get his full money's worth.

Matías raised an eyebrow as he passed a greedy gaze around the women. 'Don't be offended, my dears; these are a stuck-up bunch anyway. Come, let us get out of here,' he crooned, gathering the girls up and helping them back into their coats. 'I'll join you all later,' he promised us, but as the third girl gripped his belt and dragged him towards the door he flashed me a grin. 'Well, maybe I will...'

'He is quite a character,' Nathan remarked dryly as the door shut firmly behind Matías and the dancers, cocooning us in our alcove. David reached over and took Matías's Cognac tasters and shared the glasses out around the rest of us before winking at me. 'Waste not, want not.'

I accepted my extra shot with a nod and David raised his glass in a toast. 'Cheers. To you and Robyn.'

We chinked our glasses together and as we took our first taste I savoured the flavour and jerked my head towards David. 'I thought you might have joined Matías and the girls for some fun.'

David swirled the amber liquid in his glass and flashed me a cocky smile. 'Nah. I might be getting on a bit, but I've never needed to pay for sex in my life. Besides, they were a bit skinny for my tastes.'

The Cognac lit a gentle burn in my throat and I hummed my approval. This really was the good stuff.

'And I'm guessing that Marcus didn't go with them because he's too preoccupied with a certain blonde bombshell who frequents my club, eh?' David teased, giving Marcus a dig in the ribs.

Marcus visibly stiffened. 'I have no idea what you're talking about,' he grumbled, taking a large swig of his Cognac and nearly choking on the fiery liquid.

'Really? It doesn't take a genius to see that you've got the hots for Sasha.' David looked at me and rolled his eyes as the alcohol freed up his tongue and made him state what every one of us around the table was fully aware of.

'Fuck off, David,' Marcus gritted, looking quite a lot like he was about to get up and walk out at any second.

I was usually up for a bit of banter like this but, having witnessed how upset Marcus had been when we'd helped Sasha move house last week, I decided not to join in and instead shifted the conversation towards our drinks.

Thankfully, the distraction worked, and the rest of the evening passed with pleasant conversation about the quality of the Cognac and the arrangements for the upcoming wedding.

As much as I was enjoying the company of my friends, I couldn't prevent my mind occasionally drifting to Robyn and wondering what she might be getting up to on her hen do.

I loved my friends dearly, but as the hours rolled on into the early morning I couldn't wait to get home to my girl.

CHAPTER NINETEEN

Robyn

As soon as I stepped inside the front door, Oliver slid an arm around my waist and pulled me into him with a soft growl. It was as if he'd been standing behind the door waiting for me. Looking up at him and finding a possessive smile spreading on his face, I decided he had quite possibly been doing exactly that.

He looked so handsome wrapped up in his suit, and I could smell the faint scent of some sort of expensive alcohol on his breath, but other than that he looked just as pristine as he had when he'd left hours earlier.

'I'm not a jealous man, as such. Possessive, yes, domineering perhaps…'

'Perhaps?' I blurted in amusement, interrupting him as a huge bubble of laughter rose in my throat at his words. That was the understatement of the century!

Oliver put on a mock scowl as he attempted – and failed – to suppress a grin. 'OK, I *am* domineering,' he admitted with a wink, 'but I'm not jealous because I know without doubt that you are mine, just as I am yours.'

Happiness filled me as a blush rose on his cheeks. It didn't matter that we'd been together a while now, I would never tire of seeing how affected this incredible man was by me, and my heart swelled with love as I gazed up at him.

I gave his hips a squeeze and raised my eyebrows. 'But…?'

'How did you know there was a "but" coming?' he asked in

amusement.

Shrugging, I pouted up at him, glad that I was sometimes able to read him just as well as he could me. 'I could hear it in your tone.'

Chuckling, Oliver nodded. 'And how right you are. I was merely going to say that while I may not be an intrinsically jealous man, I am rather happy to have you home and in my arms after your night out.'

I ran my fingers down the buttons of his silk waistcoat and let out a mumble of agreement. Tonight had been such fun, but I couldn't deny that I was happy to be home with him, too. Once my hand reached his belt buckle I tucked my fingers into the waistband of his trousers and gave a small tug. 'Same. I didn't like the thought of you out with the boys all night dressed up and looking as handsome as this.'

Oliver grinned down at me and then took my free hand and placed it over his heart. 'This part deep inside me belongs to you and you alone. Along with the rest of me.'

Smiling goofily, I leaned forwards and placed a kiss on his chest.

'I love that you can be just as possessive as I can,' he murmured, before tipping my head back to place a lingering kiss on my lips. 'I literally cannot wait to marry you at the weekend.'

It was so soon, but I felt exactly the same way. I was so excited to marry him that I was wishing the days away.

Oliver shifted me in his embrace so that he could press his hardening groin against my stomach with a sexy smile. 'Did you have a good time tonight?'

With him hot and horny and pressed against me it was quite hard to concentrate, but I smiled and nodded as I thought back over the evening.

'It was great. We had drinks in Carnaby Street and Sasha had booked a table at my favourite restaurant in Chinatown. Afterwards we went to a karaoke bar and sang and danced until our throats hurt.'

While karaoke would be Oliver's idea of hell, I had loved it. We'd had our own private room with a huge sofa, massive screen projecting the music videos, and waiter service at the tap of a button. We'd sung to Abba, danced like idiots to Wham!, and crooned out our best attempts at some of the new chart toppers like we were pros.

Oliver nodded and bit down on his lower-lip as he gave a small thrust of his hips against mine. 'I'm glad you had a good time, but it's late. Let's go to bed.'

As he took my hand and led me towards the stairs I could tell from the cheeky gleam in his eye that, even though it was almost three o'clock in the morning, we wouldn't be sleeping.

Not for a while, anyway.

As if reading my thoughts, he paused on the bottom step and turned back to me, his brow lowering.

'I hope your legs aren't sore from the dancing.'

My legs? Frowning in confusion at his statement, I flexed one leg and shook my head. 'No, why?'

Oliver's eyes glimmered with wickedness, and then his lips curled into a sexy smirk.

'Because when we get upstairs I want you presented on your knees for me.'

Just those few words and my body was wide awake and alight with arousal. I couldn't think of one thing to say in response to his statement, so I licked my lips and stared up at him with wide eyes.

Oliver let out a low laugh and raised a hand to gently cup my face. 'You're going to have to indulge me, Robyn, but I'm feeling territorial. You've been out all night with God knows how many men eyeing you up, and now I wish to re-establish my claim on you.'

He had no need to re-establish anything – I was well and truly his and we both knew it – but I wouldn't point it out, especially not when he was looking as devilishly sexy as he currently was.

'OK, Sir,' I whispered hoarsely, my throat parched from the adrenalin rushing through my bloodstream.

He gave a satisfied nod at my acceptance and, tightening his grip on my hand, led me up the stairs. Oliver flicked several glances back at me as he strode forwards, taking two steps at a time, and from the heated look on his face I had a feeling I was about to be in for quite a treat from my delicious Dom.

CHAPTER TWENTY

Robyn

As the plane lowered towards the shimmering strip of tarmac below us, I gazed out of the window with excitement growing in my stomach. A short moment later and the cabin jolted as the wheels made contact and then Sasha and I shared a grin.

Touchdown.

We'd arrived in Barcelona, and in just two days' time I would be marrying Oliver Wolfe. I never ever would have dreamed that this would be the outcome when I'd first spotted him inside the walls of Club Twist all those months ago. With his intense stare, and dark, dangerous vibe he'd scared the shit out of me – that first night when we'd met I'd barely been able to comprehend the idea of talking to him, let alone dating him, or marrying him!

A sudden moment of utter panic clenched in my chest, and I turned to Sasha and grabbed her forearm with a steely grip. 'Holy shit, Sash! I'm getting married! *Married!*' I repeated, my voice rising to a squeal and drawing the attention of several nearby passengers who gave me amused glances before starting to gather their belongings for disembarking.

Sasha let out a chuckle and smiled broadly as she patiently pried my fingers from her arm. 'Yes, you are my dear. You're marrying your very own big bad Wolfe.'

My teeth started to nervously chomp on my lower lip, but I couldn't help sharing her smile as she once again referred to Oliver as my "big bad Wolfe". Her description couldn't be further from the truth; yes, he had a certain penchant for a little kink and could make my knees quiver with just one dark, disapproving stare, but I'd quickly discovered that he was a very sweet romantic underneath it all.

'But unlike Red Riding Hood, I'd place money on the fact that you're going to get a happily ever after ending.'

I drew in a steadying breath and smiled. She was right. Oliver and I were a perfect match, and besides my brief moment of panic, I just knew that this was the right thing to do. I loved him, he loved me, and I couldn't wait to be his wife.

'You're right.' I nodded, my body relaxing, but then immediately tensed again as Sasha leaned in closer and gave me a wicked, conspiratorial look.

'And if you get eaten by your Mr Wolfe, I guarantee you'll enjoy it far more than Red Riding Hood did.' My eyes widened as her rude joke sunk in and Sasha cackled. 'Sorry, I couldn't resist. But I bet Oliver's great at it, right?'

Brushing my hair back from my blushing face, I peered out the window at the terminal building, determined not to continue a talk about Oliver's oral abilities while we were in a packed airplane. 'Check out the weather, it's perfect!' I blurted, hoping to distract Sasha from any further enquires.

Leaning around me to look out of the window, she nodded. 'Much better than the cloudy skies we left at home,' Sasha agreed, before prodding me to get my attention and passing down my hand luggage. Thank God for that, my distraction seemed to have worked. 'Now, I believe there is a swanky hotel and jug of Sangria awaiting us!'

Grinning, I nodded and stood up. We had two days to go until the wedding, but Oliver had insisted on being traditional and staying in separate locations until the ceremony, so Sasha and I were booked into a small boutique hotel halfway between Barcelona and his home village for the night. Then tomorrow we'd move into the guest rooms at his parents' house to spend the night before the ceremony.

Tonight, Sasha and I were going for drinks with Chloe once she arrived – she'd had to work today, so would be joining us later. Tomorrow, Oliver and I were having a quiet meal with just our parents and direct family, then on Saturday I'd be getting married.

Married.

To Oliver.

Once again, a tingle of excitement ran through my body, but with a chuckle I absorbed it and followed Sasha down the aisle to exit the plane.

'So, I suggest we grab our bags, check in to the hotel, and then do a little sightseeing, maybe even seek out a cheeky cocktail. What do you think?' Sasha suggested as we stood waiting for our suitcases to appear on the conveyer belt.

'I also need to pick up my dress, but apart from that small detour I think your plan sounds bloody perfect,' I agreed with a smile before I felt the sharp jab of an elbow in my side as someone pushed past me to retrieve their suitcase from the carousel.

Why were people always so rude? A simple "excuse me" would have done the job just fine. I turned to send a disapproving frown at the culprit and tensed when I recognised Alexandra, Oliver's colleague from Club Twist.

'Oh! Hello, bride-to-be!' she cooed when her gaze met mine.

'Hello, Alex. I didn't see you on the plane,' I mumbled, not sure what else to say to her. We didn't exactly have the easiest of relationships. I still didn't really like her – she was always lovely to me if anyone else was around, but snippy and catty when we were on our own, and I was convinced it was because she was irritated that I had snagged Oliver, and she hadn't.

'You're here very early,' Sasha commented with a scowl, and I had to suppress a grin at her blatant show of irritation.

She disliked Alex even more than I did and wasn't afraid to show it. Her comment was irrelevant, too, because she knew very well that most of the guests were coming tonight and making the most of the weekend.

Alex ignored Sasha's strop and put her case down before blowing some strands of hair back from her face. 'Yeah. We thought we'd make a mini-break out of it.' Alex linked her arm with the tall blond man beside her who I recognised as Joshua, her boyfriend, and apparently her submissive. To be fair, with his servile posture and downturned gaze he fitted the submissive bill far better than I ever would. 'The weather here is so much nicer than the UK, isn't it? We're hoping to pick up a tan.'

Sasha still looked like she was sucking on a lemon, but I managed to maintain my smile. Alex was being pleasant enough today, so I might as well be mature and do the same. 'Yeah, it's predicted to be high thirties all week.'

'Ooh, fabulous. Well, I won't hold you up. I'm sure you must have lots of last-minute wedding things to organise. See you on Saturday. Bye, Sasha.' Alex waved at us both and then disappeared into the crowd, dragging Joshua along with her.

'She's such a fake cow,' Sasha grumbled, hauling her case off the carousel and flashing another look towards Joshua and Alex's retreating backs.

'She is, but at least she seems to be making a bit more of an effort recently.' I might not like Alex a great deal, but I was still glad that in the end we'd invited her to the wedding. Oliver had been reluctant because of the bitchy way she had acted with me when I'd thought I was pregnant, but it would have made things even more uncomfortable between us all at Club Twist if we'd invited everyone else and not her.

'Right, enough talk about her, we've got cocktails to find.'

Chuckling, I rolled my eyes and looked at Sasha with a grin. 'I though you said we were sightseeing first?'

Sasha bit on her bottom lip, trying to look remorseful and

failing. 'Yeah, that, too, but you know, let's get our priorities in order. You're getting married in two days; we need celebratory cocktails pronto.'

And with her intentions stated, Sasha added my case to the trolley and set off towards the exit, grinning at me over her shoulder.

CHAPTER TWENTY-ONE

Robyn

Yesterday had been lovely. After picking my dress up from the courier's office where Oliver had had it shipped over by a special service and seeing the florist for some last-minute checks, I'd spent the day with Sasha, sightseeing and having a lazy lunch. Once Chloe had landed, the three of us had sought out the cocktails that Sasha had mentioned at the airport.

This morning, after recovering from a mild cocktail-induced hangover, we'd taken all our things across to Oliver's parents' house where Sasha and I would be staying before the wedding tomorrow.

Oliver, given his traditional outlook, was spending the night in a hotel, but we'd decided it would be nice to at least spend the afternoon and evening together with both of our families having a pre-wedding meal at his parents' house.

My mum, dad, and brother Tom had all arrived from the UK earlier today, but Oliver's huge family dwarfed mine. All five of his sisters had rolled in about three hours ago with their various partners and children and so now Sophia's dining table was full to bursting, but she was clearly in her element and loving every second of it.

Sasha had been invited, too, of course, but she'd chosen to leave us to it and head out with a few people from the wedding party to continue her cocktail weekend. She had promised to be back here tonight and in a fit enough state that she wouldn't be hungover for the wedding tomorrow.

There was something very satisfying about seeing the people you loved looking content and happy, and that was exactly what I saw every time I looked around the table. Everyone was smiling, laughing, and getting along really well, and as I snuggled into Oliver's side I can honestly say I'd never felt happier or more relaxed in my life.

Sophia hadn't let me do a thing during the meal preparation and serving, so after we'd all finished our coffee and drinks I insisted on starting the washing-up, something that Oliver decided to help me with.

But instead of helping me by drying the dishes I'd washed, he moved in close behind me and placed his hands on my shoulders to give me a gentle massage. He kneaded my muscles with just the right amount of pressure, and it felt so heavenly that my skin began heating with lusty enjoyment. The washing-up became temporarily forgotten and I stood there with soapy hands as I absorbed the sensation of having his hands on me.

'I've missed having you with me these last few days, *cariño*,' Oliver whispered, his breath warm across my ear as he leaned in close. 'And I missed you in my bed last night,' he added hotly as he slid his arms down and around me, one hand coming to rest on my hip and the other pressing flat across my belly and tugging me backwards into him so that I was nestled against his strong body.

'Me, too.' I was pressed top to toe with Oliver – my favourite place to be.

'I can't wait until tomorrow when you'll become my wife.' He placed a kiss on my temple and rubbed his hardening groin against my bum with a low growl. 'I'd love to take you to the guest room right now and bury myself between your legs…'

'And they say romance is dead.' I tried to giggle, but it came out as a husky moan, so I gave up my pretence and ground myself back against him until his erection dug in the cleft of my arse. If only we didn't have so many clothes on this would be a very promising position.

The noise of a door opening beside us made me jump almost a foot into the air, and as I looked across I saw my mum and Oliver's mother entering the kitchen and chatting away. 'And to end the tour, this is my kitchen... *oh*!' Both women came to an abrupt stop as they caught us in our intimate position by the sink.

'*Olive-ee-air!* Leave your girl alone!' Sophia clicked her tongue affectionately as she came to stand beside us, and I saw that my mum was struggling to hold back a chuckle. 'She will be your wife tomorrow; can you not wait?'

Oliver tightened his grip on me and made a show of burying his head into my neck and kissing me with several hot, wet kisses that had me giggling and squirming in his arms.

'No, *mamá*. Absolutely not.' He started to tickle me then, his fingers finding all my areas of weakness until I was laughing out loud and wriggling in his grip, which clearly did nothing to tamp down his erection that seemed to be growing harder and harder by the second.

'Oliver, stop!' I blurted between laughs. Finally, he relented and loosened his grip, but even though the tickling had stopped Oliver kept his hands firmly on my hips so I stayed in front of him and kept his hard-on hidden. Wiping a tear from my eye, I glanced up at him with a grin and then risked an embarrassed glance at our mothers who were both still in the kitchen and gazing at us with affectionate looks on their faces.

Sophia turned to my mum and gave her arm a squeeze. 'Young love, so sweet.'

I'm not sure they would think it was "so sweet" if they knew that Oliver was currently grinding his erection against my bottom, but we both smiled at them anyway and then collapsed into giggles as soon as they had turned and left the room.

He gathered me into his arms, this time with us facing each

other, and reached up to brush some stray hairs from my face. 'As much as I would like to ravish you tonight, perhaps my mother is right. One more night of waiting will make tomorrow even more special.' Leaning down, he placed a soft, reverent kiss on my lips, which immediately turned into something more heated and had us both clinging to each other and moaning.

Oliver dragged his lips from mine with a growl and stepped back. 'It may give me a serious case of blue balls in the meantime,' he added wryly, adjusting his trousers so I could clearly see the outline of his jutting erection, 'but it'll be worth it.'

CHAPTER TWENTY-TWO

Sasha

The music here was awesome. Admittedly, I couldn't speak Spanish, so the lyrics made no sense to me whatsoever, but the beat was fast, addictive, and perfect for dancing off some calories, which was exactly what I had spent the last twenty minutes doing.

We were in Fantasia, the club owned by one of Oliver's mates, and even though it was a sex club and none of us were planning on hooking up, we'd still taken him up on the invitation because it included free drinks at the bar all night long.

We'd started the night at a local nightclub with the rest of the younger crowd from the wedding party, but as the evening had drawn on and they'd headed off to their beds for the night, those of us who were members of Twist had headed here. The whole wedding was like a secret society – those in the know about Club Twist, and those not. The kinky ones and the vanilla. I personally loved the fact that a group of us had a common secret. It made it all feel quite taboo and exciting.

As the big day was tomorrow, Robyn was spending the evening with Oliver and their families having a quiet meal, so my dancing companion for the night was Natalia, Robyn's friend who worked in Club Twist. I hadn't spent much time with her before this trip, but I discovered she was really nice once you broke through her painfully shy exterior. She also seemed very intrigued by the men here, asking me on two occasions which ones I thought might be dominants, and I couldn't help but wonder if her shyness was just the expression of a hidden submissive side.

Looking around me, I grinned as I made a quick assessment: Natalia could do a lot worse than the men in here. The Spanish guys were as impressive as the music. Granted, there was a lot more slicked-back hair than you might see in an English nightclub, which wasn't really my taste, but when added to dark eyes, intense stares, and tanned skin, it combined to create some pretty spectacular handsomeness.

It might have looked like I was window-shopping the Spanish men, which I was slightly, under the guise of chatting with Natalia, but in reality, my gaze kept drifting towards the only blond men in here – Marcus and Nathan.

Marcus had been on my radar all night, as he usually was these days if I was in the same room as him, but so far, he hadn't glanced my way even once.

We clearly hadn't managed to sort out our differences the other day when he'd helped me move my stuff, but that didn't mean I'd managed to move on from the way I felt about him. I tried not to think about him or look at him, but it just didn't work; the back of my neck would tingle whenever he was close, and eventually my brain and eyes would overpower my rational thought and drag me back to him again and again and again.

It was irritating as fuck. I never let men get under my skin like this.

Marcus stood at the bar with Nathan and his brother, Nicholas. They might not have the sun-bronzed tans of the Spaniards who surrounded them, but as a trio they still made for a spectacular sight. Something about their confidence and intensity oozed attractiveness, and even though Marcus was my main focus, it was clear to see that all three were very gifted in the looks department.

They were sipping beers and talking, and as much as I kept

glancing his way and hoping to catch Marcus's eye, I noticed that his shoulder was slanted away from my direction and he seemed to be resolutely ignoring me. Maybe the cluster-fuck at my apartment had been the final straw for him, or perhaps he just wasn't aware that I was here tonight. The idea that he had managed to move on from our connection – something I hadn't been able to do in the slightest – caused a pain to constrict my chest for a few seconds and I had to lift a hand and rub at my sternum in an effort at easing it.

Bloody man. A touch on my arm broke my depressing thoughts and I reluctantly pulled my gaze away from Marcus's broad back to find Natalia speaking to me. It was too loud to hear her properly, so I leaned in closer, glad of the distraction.

'I'm going to get some water, you want some?'

I nodded with a smile and fanned my face to indicate how hot it was in here. 'Yes, please.' This place might be air-conditioned, but once you added two hundred dancing, sweaty bodies to the mix it didn't seem to be making much impact.

Natalia disappeared into the crowd, and I forced myself to remain turned away from Marcus so I could concentrate on enjoying myself. Over the next few minutes I let the beat wash over me, lifting my arms and closing my eyes as I swayed to the rhythm and thought of nothing but the music.

OK, so the occasional image of a certain tall blond chef with skilled fingers and a magical tongue might have entered my mind from time to time, but overall, I managed to forget about him.

The feel of warm hands settling on my waist startled me from my trance, and a thrilled shiver ran up my spine as I imagined tilting my head up and finding Marcus standing over me. When my eyes flew open however, I saw a tall, broad Spaniard invading my personal space and grinning down at me as he attempted to match my rhythm and dance with me.

That was most certainly not Marcus.

My lip curled in distaste and as I abruptly stopped moving.

There was an awkward moment where he continued to dance against me while I just stood there, leaning away from him with a perturbed expression on my face.

How bloody dare he interrupt my dancing?

'¡*Hola, señorita*! Let me dance with you.' His English might have been a little broken, but I still frowned at the way his words had veered towards a demand and not a polite request.

Shaking my head, I stepped back to dislodge his grip. 'No, thank you. I'm with a friend.'

He glanced around and smiled with teeth that had definitely been whitened – just a touch too much in my opinion – before once again moving forwards into my personal space. 'But they are not here now, no? So, we can dance?'

He moved his hands to my waist again, this time gripping harder and digging his fingers in so I couldn't step back. 'No. Thank you.' I reached down to prise his hands off, but his fingers were like a bloody vice.

'Let go of me,' I grated with as much volume as I could, given the background accompaniment of loud dance music. He didn't, though; he moved closer still until his hips were brushing against mine, and then began grinding himself against me.

'Get off me!' I spat, wincing from the biting pain in my skin from his grip, and banging uselessly at his arms with my hands to try and free myself.

'You very beautiful,' he almost crooned, and I gawked at him in utter astonishment. Was this guy for real? I was stunned that he was completely ignoring my request for him to leave me alone. Maybe it was a language barrier thing, but surely me smacking at him and frowning was enough of a clue that I wasn't encouraging his attention?

Tiring of him disregarding me, I decided to revert to the international language of violence and swearing; after all, it was one of my strong points.

Shoving his chest as hard as I could, I rolled onto my tiptoes and got right up in his tanned, sweaty face. 'I said *no,* arsehole! Just fuck off, would you?' I yelled it so loudly that my throat rasped painfully, but at least he'd definitely hear me over the music. My push hadn't dislodged his meaty paws, though, so I began forcibly struggling in his arms, wiggling and slapping at him in an attempt to get away.

It was hardly a skilled performance of self-defence, and with my slapping and flapping I certainly wouldn't be winning any awards for my fighting prowess, but with him wilfully ignoring me I didn't see what other choices I had left. At least this might attract some attention from the nearby dancers so someone would help me get rid of him.

Just when I was starting to tire of wrestling, his hands vanished in a flash of movement. As I stood there rubbing at my sore hip bones where he'd been grabbing me, I tried to work out how and why he'd finally let go of me. I turned and saw that the guy was now on the floor with a very angry Marcus straddling him and raising a clenched fist to deliver a punch.

Bloody hell! Realisation dawned, and my eyes widened. The flash of movement had been Marcus rugby tackling the guy off me.

'She said no, you fucker!' Marcus rained punches down on the guy at such a rate that I could barely keep up. It felt like hours passed as I stood there with a hand clamped over my mouth in shock, watching him smack my unwanted admirer, but in reality, it was probably just a second or two until Nathan intervened and split them up.

Marcus and Nathan disappeared towards the exit, dragging the guy out of the club – or perhaps taking him to the bouncers to continue with his battering, who knew? – leaving me standing there frozen in shock.

CHAPTER TWENTY-THREE

Marcus

This fucker was so big, he must have weighed a tonne, but I was so ramped up on my fury that his bulk barely registered as I dragged his protesting body from the club out into the reception area.

My fingers were biting into his upper arm so hard that he was whimpering now, pleading with me in Spanish and trying desperately to pry my hand off, but there was no fucking way I was letting go yet.

Sasha had asked him to let go of her and he'd outright ignored her. Let him have a taste of his own fucking medicine and see how he liked it.

'Marcus, calm down.'

The words were slightly breathless, Nathan was jogging along behind me trying to catch up, but I had no intention of heeding his advice, not when this guy had just been pawing Sasha like she was a piece of meat for his forced pleasure.

She'd said no, for fuck's sake.

I wasn't usually a violent man, quite the opposite in fact. Most of my close friends would probably describe me as chilled out and laid-back, but at this current moment I was anything but. I felt explosive. I'd calm down once this arsehole had his face painted all over the pavement for daring to touch Sasha when she'd said no.

I threw the guy onto the carpet in the reception area with a growl and pulled my leg back, ready to kick him, but was suddenly jerked back by a sharp tug on my shoulder. The contact was so hard I nearly tumbled over, and I let out a manic roar when I realised it was Nathan restraining me.

How fucking dare he? I knew for a fact he would rip the balls off any guy who touched his girl, Stella, inappropriately, so he was a fucking hypocrite to try to stop me.

Not that Sasha was my girl, I reminded myself sharply, but still.

'Enough,' Nathan stated in a low tone, flashing a warning glance to his right. Following his gaze, I realised that instead of being hypocritical he was most likely protecting me from getting into trouble, because there was a burly security guard eyeing me suspiciously and seemingly ready to take me down if I so much as sneezed too loudly.

'Marcus.' Nathan drew my gaze back to his and gave a sharp nod. 'Get a fucking grip.'

I was so wound up that I could easily have ignored him and thrown a punch his way – my fist had already balled and was partly raised of its own accord – but the quiet fury burning in his icy blue eyes brought me up short.

What the fuck was I doing? Was I seriously lining up to punch one of my oldest and closest mates? He hadn't even raised a hand to stop me, so I could have thrown a punch if I'd wanted, but something in his quiet strength made me stop and drop my hand to my side. I totally got why he was such a good dominant; he had the whole cool, calm, controlled thing down to a tee.

'Fuck. Sorry, Nathan. I lost my head for a minute there.' I kept my eyes averted in embarrassment. Shaking out my fist, I felt an ache in my knuckles and suspected I might have a few bruises there tomorrow.

'You think kicking the shit out of him will impress her?' he asked quietly, his tone ladled with scorn.

Running a hand through my hair, I glanced across at the guy who was still on the floor, but now being restrained by one of the bouncers.

'I didn't do it for Sasha,' I murmured, responding automatically.

'Of course you fucking did.' Nathan scoffed. 'I see the way you look at her.'

I frowned and shook my head. 'He was just a dickhead who needed a lesson in manners,' I mumbled, wondering if Nathan believed my bullshit any more than I did.

'Let me give you a tip, Marcus. Sure, girls love all the macho protection shit, but watching you gut some guy just because he dared touch her? That would not be a turn-on, *that* would be fucking frightening.' Nathan jabbed at my shoulder to make sure I was listening and then continued. 'And getting arrested for having a brawl isn't exactly going to impress Sasha, either.'

I didn't do it for Sasha. *I didn't.* We were incompatible, a complete no-go. I didn't do it for her. Although no matter how many times I repeated the phrase, I couldn't quite work out why I'd reacted so violently to the man if it weren't because of Sasha.

If he'd been pushing some other girl around would I have wanted to smash his face in?

No. Probably not.

Gritting my teeth, I lowered my gaze as the answer played uncomfortably in my mind. I felt antsy and fidgety, my body filled with adrenalin that had nowhere to go now that my human punch bag was no longer an option.

Nathan spoke with the bouncers and informed them that the guy had been putting pressure on one of the female club goers and I watched with some small level of satisfaction as they dragged the bastard off into a side room for a "talk". I hoped it included them getting up close and personal with their meaty fists, but who knew.

'You OK now?' Nathan asked, placing a hand on my shoulder and giving a supportive squeeze. As much as I knew he meant well, I wasn't in the mood for getting all flowery and discussing my feelings with him, so all he got in reply was a sharp nod.

Reluctantly I accepted that what I wanted to do most was get back inside and check that Sasha was OK. My brain might understand that we were completely unsuited together, but no matter what I did I couldn't seem to persuade my body of that fact and I still craved her with an intensity bordering on compulsion.

Looking back at Nathan, I shook off the hand he had placed on my shoulder before striding back towards the club in search of the girl who I wanted more than my common sense could understand.

CHAPTER TWENTY-FOUR

Sasha

It had been at least two minutes since Marcus had dragged the sleazy guy off me and disappeared from the club, and the hand covering my mouth was still firmly in place, although it was now trembling from shock sinking into my system.

Wow. That had been quite a display. I couldn't help but assume that Marcus *had* been watching me a little tonight, then. He might have been pretending to look the other way all evening, but how else would he have known I was in trouble? I didn't like the fact that he'd had to get in a fight for me, but I was pleased – and very relieved – that he'd decided to step in and protect me because that guy had been a complete dick with a total disregard for personal space.

Not only had he saved me from making an embarrassing scene fighting the guy off, the fact that Marcus had stepped in must show he felt something for me… mustn't it?

Natalia was still nowhere to be seen with our drinks, and I'd been well and truly put off dancing now, so I moved to the side of the dance floor where my jacket was hung over a stool and took a few deep breaths to try to recover my composure.

A few seconds later, Marcus strode back in, closely followed by Nathan. Marcus paused on the threshold, his shoulders hunched with tension and his eyes scanning the area like a predator on the lookout for its prey. I found my breath stalling in my lungs as his stare moved around the room, and then, as he zeroed in on me, his eyes locked with mine and I felt a jolt of connection.

He looked lethal somehow, far more wrung out than his usual calm demeanour, and was still panting slightly and frowning.

Dragging up my manners, I decided not to let his look deter me, and I nodded my thanks, hoping he would understand what I meant, and how much I had appreciated his intervention.

Nathan leaned in and said something to Marcus before moving to the bar. Marcus began to move my way, his eyes not leaving mine once, and the frown remaining well and truly in place as he stalked ever closer.

He was moving with such deadly intent that all the hairs on my body rose with awareness, and I found myself unable to do anything other than stand there and stare at him as he approached.

He stopped just a few feet in front of me and ran his gaze up and down my body as if checking that I was OK after my run-in with the sleaze. I couldn't find the right words to say, but the connection between us was laying heavily all around me and I found that all I wanted to do in this moment was show him how grateful I was.

One second, I was staring at his frowning handsomeness, and the next I had thrown myself at him. I'm not even sure it was a conscious decision, but suddenly I was all over him. I'd literally leaped up his body, and somehow, I was now attached; my hands were in his hair, one leg was wrapped around his waist, and my mouth collided with his with such force that our lips would probably bruise.

Marcus might have been shocked by my sudden attack, but it only took him a split-second to respond, and as his tongue forced its way inside my mouth he walked us backwards into a darker corner where we crashed against a wall as our kiss deepened.

The impact of hitting the wall took my breath away, but

there was no time to focus on my breathlessness because the next second Marcus had removed my hands from his body and pinned them above my head in one of his warm palms. His free hand skimmed across my body, touching and arousing me before coming to rest around my throat.

I'd never been held by the throat before, and although I felt vulnerable I also instinctively knew I was safe in his arms. His grip was firm, but not hard enough to affect my breathing, and I found it such a predatory position that my arousal shot through the roof and warmth pooled between my legs and wetted my underwear.

'I didn't do it for you,' he growled, his grip twitching on my neck and his face still contorted into a frown, and it seemed to me that he was desperately trying to persuade himself he didn't feel the thing that was so obviously growing between us.

I had no doubt that Marcus was a chivalrous guy, he would have stepped in to help any woman in distress, but it hadn't been any woman, it had been me, and the violence of his intervention had spoken volumes. He *had* done it for me.

He'd wanted to save *me*.

'No?' Raising an eyebrow, I gave a small smile to indicate that I'd seen through his lie and leaned in closer so I could whisper in his ear. 'I think you did. Thank you.'

His nostrils flared, as if he didn't like admitting that his strong reaction had been because of me, but his mouth found mine again anyway, and then his hand was on the move again, skimming across my body and landing on my breast where he gripped hard and began to fondle my nipple through my dress.

Both my nipples pebbled until they felt impossibly tight and ached for his touch, and I arched my back to force more of his delicious contact.

As he swapped to my other breast with his hand, our kiss continued; frantic and open-mouthed and breathless and incredible. I wanted to touch him so badly, but just as I went to tug on my trapped wrists he shocked me into stillness by dropping his free hand lower still and digging it up under my skirt. Wasting no time, he pressed inside my knickers and then slid his fingers across my damp skin before circling my moisture around my clit.

Holy fuck. Talk about getting straight down to it. It was as if the tension between us had suddenly caught up with him and he couldn't contain himself. I was instantly flooded with more moisture, which he obviously felt, because he smirked and then tugged at the zip of his jeans before leaning back to stare at me with intense eyes.

'Do you want this, Sasha?' he ground out, his smirk disappearing as he seemed to come to for a second and realise what he was doing. His darker expression was back as he waited for my reply, and even though I'd rarely ever seen him looking this dangerous I couldn't deny that his show of power was turning me on immensely.

'Yes. Oh God, Marcus, yes.'

After that it all happened so quickly. As soon as I had given my consent, he tore his cock from within his jeans, adjusted my position in his grip, and thrust his hips forwards, impaling me in one hard thrust that banged me back into the wall with its depth.

I was wet, but his first thrust still hurt a little as he rammed his sizeable length home and I shrieked his name, the sound only muffled when he clamped his lips over mine again and kissed me as his hips started to jerk back and forth.

The initial discomfort only lasted a second, and I was now wriggling against each of his thrusts and loving every second of it. Managing to free my mouth from his savage kiss, I gave a tug at my wrists. 'I want to touch you.'

The hand that held mine imprisoned flinched for a second as if he were about to give in to my request, but then his grip tightened and my hope faded. 'No.'

Leaning forwards, I kissed his jaw and trailed my tongue up towards his ear, hoping to persuade him. 'Please, Marcus…'

A sharp jab of his hips pinned me to the wall and stopped me from speaking again, and then he shook his head slowly. '*No.*'

I wanted to touch him so badly it burned in my system like an obsession, but the potency of the moment hit me and was so pure that I pushed my need away for now. What we were doing felt amazing, so really it didn't matter if I could touch him or not. I was with him, Marcus Price, the man who had featured in all my recent fantasies, he was fucking me like a man possessed, and it felt incredible.

I gave a small nod of agreement and we continued to move together, Marcus leading the pace and me attempting to keep up, but with the urgency and eroticism of the moment I knew I wouldn't last long.

Even suspecting this, the feeling building in my belly so quickly took me by surprise. As Marcus continued to move within me in deep, hard thrusts, I rolled over into a blissful climax, silencing my cries of pleasure by burying my face in his shoulder and drawing out my orgasm by tightening my leg around his waist and grinding my clit against him.

Marcus swore softly beside my head, and then I felt his cock expand and hips jerk as he began to come, too, the warmth of his release flooding my insides and bringing it home to me that yes, I really was with Marcus again, and yes, we really were having unprotected sex in the middle of a nightclub.

How had I not thought about condoms? I was usually so good at remembering, but the tension of the moment had somehow distracted me. Fuck. Thank God I was at least on the pill.

Forgetting that issue for a moment, I turned my attention back to Marcus who was still buried deeply within me and panting as if he'd just run a marathon. We remained joined like that for several seconds as we both came down from the furiously quick encounter, and then Marcus silently let go of my wrists and slid from within me. Digging in my handbag, I found a tissue. Averting my eyes in embarrassment, I tried to wipe between my legs. I'd had some dodgy encounters in my time, but a bareback quickie in a packed nightclub was certainly a first for me.

Finally lifting my gaze up to Marcus again, I found him watching me, still with a half frown creasing his brow. As I stared at him, something inside my chest tightened painfully. God. I was really falling for him.

Me, Sasha Mortimer, the girl who didn't do relationships, was falling head over heels for a man who wouldn't let me touch him. I'd never be able to stroke his body, never explore his face with my fingertips, never dig my hands through his hair… Was that the price I'd have to pay to be with him?

The longer I stared at him, the more panic swirled in my chest at both the mountain of feelings I was developing for this man, and the seemingly impossible situation that surrounded us.

How the hell could this thing between us ever work out? And how could I bring myself to walk away from him if it didn't?

'Jesus Christ, Sasha, you could at least attempt to look like you enjoyed it.'

I was so shocked by his tone that I frowned and looked up at him in surprise. 'What?' I had no idea what he was talking about, because aside from our lapse with the condom, that had been incredible.

'I guess it must be a let-down, breaking your famous "never have sex with the same guy twice" rule, huh?' His lip curled with distaste as he hurriedly pulled his zipper back up with a violent jerk of his hand.

Suddenly I started to piece together what his words might be referring to; presumably my expression must have looked panicked when I'd been thinking about how badly I was falling for him, and he'd mistaken my look for one of regret. Could that be what he meant? Because if it was, his guess couldn't be further from the truth. 'Marcus…'

But before I could properly explain he stepped back with a shake of his head and turned away, disappearing into the crowd before I could finish my sentence.

'Shit!' My clothes were scrunched and pulled aside, my thighs were still wet from our encounter, and my breathing was frantic.

In short, I felt like I'd just been well and truly fucked, and I no doubt looked like it, too. But still, I didn't exactly want to be running through the nightclub in this state.

I sorted out my clothes as best I could so I looked halfway decent, but by the time I dashed to find Marcus he was nowhere to be seen. I pushed through people and peered over dancers, but whichever way I turned there was no sign of him.

Marcus was gone.

CHAPTER TWENTY-FIVE

Marcus

I charged out into the balmy evening and let out a roar of frustration as soon as I was a safe distance away from the club. My rage drew the looks of several people around me, but I didn't give a shit. They could stare all they liked.

Dragging a hand through my hair, I realised I was trembling all over, and I stopped and tried to shake the adrenalin out of my body. It didn't help. My nerves felt jagged, and my whole body was jumping with the need to burn off some energy.

Fuck this shit. I was such an idiot for allowing my obsession with Sasha to draw me back to her time and time again. Even though I knew things between us would never work, I seemed to lose all my common sense when she was near.

Especially when she was leaping into my arms and grinding herself against me. My eyes fluttered shut as I recalled her heated reaction to me and lust burned in my system again. Christ, I'd have had to be a saintly monk not to have been affected by that little display.

A low burn of arousal hummed in my veins even now, joined by the heat of a mortified flush running up my neck as I was hit with the painful recollection of just how horrified she'd looked afterwards. It had been one of the best sexual experiences of my life, but clearly from her narrow-eyed grimace Sasha had not shared my enthusiasm.

Sasha Mortimer, the girl who never fucked the same guy twice, had just had round two with me, and she'd looked utterly dismayed at her slip. Quite apparently for Sasha that hadn't been the earth-moving experience I'd thought it had.

Just remembering how beautiful she'd looked afterwards with her flushed cheeks and swollen lips made my cock lurch to a half hard state, and I growled my irritation that my body wouldn't bow to my brain's orders to forget about her.

The look of revulsion in her eyes was one I would never forget, and I curled my hands into fists at my side as it played in my head over and over again.

I might have been feeling protective and predatory after her run-in with the Spanish sleazebag, but she had been the one to initiate things between us, I was almost certain of that, which was what made it all the more difficult for me to try to understand. Why jump up at me with such lusty moves only to regret it afterwards? Had my performance really been that bad?

Self-conscious worry mixed with my frustration and wriggled restlessly in my bloodstream until I could barely keep still. I needed to work off this restless energy before I did something I might regret later. In short, I needed to find my go-to relaxation method – a gym – and I needed to find it now.

CHAPTER TWENTY-SIX

Sasha

I glanced up at the hotel name again to check I had the correct place and then strode in, trying to look confident. I didn't feel confident, though. Not at all.

'Good morning, I was hoping you could tell me which room my friend is staying in? His name is Marcus Price.'

The receptionist glanced at the clock as if making a point of the early hour and gave me a scrutinising look before smiling politely. 'I can place a call to his room for you?'

I'd fully expected her to be cagey about giving out personal information, but as she lifted the phone from its cradle my reply almost squawked from my throat in my desperation to stop her. 'No!'

I didn't want her to call him just to have him hang up on me, which I was fairly certain was exactly what Marcus would do when he heard my voice down the line. I'd tried calling his mobile already, but he'd ignored all my calls, so I couldn't see how this would be any different.

I was desperate to speak to him to iron out the misunderstanding of last night, but as he wouldn't speak to me on the phone I'd decided I needed to pluck up the courage to do it in person.

Which is why I was currently standing in the lobby of this fancy hotel staring at a woman who didn't look like she was going to help me out at all.

Quickly formulating a plan in my mind, I held up the small

carrier bag I was holding and waggled it, hoping she couldn't see that all the bag contained was my discarded cardigan, a bottle of water, and my battered sunhat.

'I'm with the wedding party. Marcus is here with the groom, Oliver Wolfe? They've asked me to drop in a few last-minute essentials.' I knew Oliver was friends with the owner of this place, so I was hoping that dropping his name might get me the information I needed.

The receptionist's eyes widened slightly and then she chomped down on her lower lip. 'Ah, *Señor* Wolfe. *Sí*,' she nodded, her voice sounding slightly husky, and a blush heating her cheeks. Ah, it was like that, was it? I smirked at her reaction; it would seem Oliver had a fan – with his good looks she was no doubt one of many among the young female staff here – so I used this knowledge to my advantage. 'You know how Oliver can be. He was very insistent that I drop this off with Marcus… I'd really hate to disappoint him.'

'*Sí, sí*. Of course.' She nodded keenly, glanced down at a screen in front of her, and, after tapping a few buttons, looked up with a smile. 'Mr Price is in the City Suite, next to Mr Wolfe who is in the Presidential Suite. Both are on the top floor, level six. The lifts are just over here to the right.'

I gave her an appreciative nod, turned towards the lifts, and tried to suppress the nerves now tumbling around inside my stomach. I still couldn't believe Marcus had mistaken my panicked look for one of regret and stormed off, but now that I had come to terms with the fact I really liked him and wanted to try for more I had to at least attempt to talk to him. I needed to explain that my expression hadn't been regret, but panic because I'd realised I was falling for him.

Falling hard. In such a short space of time he'd become all I could think about.

I exited the lift and walked along the fancy corridor, checking the names on each room and not making a sound as my feet sunk into plush grey carpet. Glancing around at the silk wallpaper and oil paintings on the wall, I raised my eyebrows. This was a seriously fancy hotel.

Finally locating his suite, I stopped by the door and chewed on a fingernail as I tried to work out what the hell I was going to say.

In short, I had to face a man who no doubt thought I was a complete bitch who had only used him for sex, and tell him that not only did I like him a lot, but that my feelings for him were so strong they were terrifying to me. Terrifying, but also exciting. For the first time in my life, I actually wanted to move forward with a guy.

Shifting on the spot, I drew in a shaky breath. It certainly wasn't going to be an easy conversation to have, but I needed to dig up some confidence and get it done.

I very much doubted that he would be expecting me to turn up at his hotel like this, but now I'd managed to get past the security I had to at least knock on his door.

Whether or not he'd open it to me was another matter entirely.

CHAPTER TWENTY-SEVEN

Oliver

Breakfast had just been delivered to the room, and it smelt divine; cured ham and potato omelettes with a large pot of fresh coffee. The staff had also included a side plate of lightly sugared churros and two chilled glasses with a pitcher of Mimosas – neither of which I had ordered but were presumably an added extra because I was paying for not only one, but two suites in the hotel and it was costing me an arm and a leg for the privilege.

I carried the tray back out onto the balcony, glanced at the beautiful view, and placed the food down. I would have loved to be sharing the cityscape and breakfast with Robyn, but as I had insisted on separate hotels until our wedding night I was instead having breakfast with my best man, Marcus, in his room.

Just that brief thought of Robyn made me smile, and I felt the now familiar tug of love inside my chest as I allowed my thoughts to linger on her for a few moments.

Today she would become my wife, and I could barely stand the wait.

'It's only a few more hours, mate,' Marcus said with a chuckle, breaking me from my daydream and correctly interpreting my apparently lovestruck expression. Giving a wry smile, I nodded and poured the cool champagne cocktail before handing him a glass.

'I know. My apologies, I'm acting like a horny teenager.'

Holding my glass up, I grinned. 'Cheers.'

'Cheers.' Marcus laughed and clinked his glass against mine. 'I don't need to know the details of your horn, thanks, mate, but in all seriousness, I'm really pleased to see you so happy.' He knocked back a swig of his drink and gave me a long stare. 'You always seemed so set in your single ways I literally never thought I'd see the day.'

I could easily see why he'd think that; I had been happy as a bachelor, more than happy. I'd been untethered and free to share the bed of whoever I chose, and I had chosen many, *many* different beds over the years.

It was a lifestyle that had suited me perfectly until a certain wide-eyed brunette had stumbled into Club Twist and caught my attention. Never in a million years had I ever expected to fall in love, but fall in love I had. Hard and fast and so deeply that I couldn't ever imagine not having Robyn in my life now.

'She's incredible. She's so perfect for me,' was all I could manage as a response without getting overly sentimental.

He nodded, and even though I was now staring out across the city view I could feel that Marcus was still watching me intently. 'I can see that. I'm chuffed for you, both of you.'

Marcus and I were close – he was one of the best friends I had – but we were both proud men and I didn't want to show quite how much Robyn had softened me, so I decided to turn my attention to my breakfast as a way of ending the conversation.

He obviously sensed my diversionary tactic, because he smiled and joined me in eating. 'How was the family meal last night?'

'Good. I thought it might be a bit intense with everyone there, but actually, it was incredibly relaxed. What did you get up to?'

A peculiar expression crossed Marcus's face, one that I couldn't quite pinpoint but had momentarily looked like misery, and then he shrugged. 'Went out with a few of the wedding party for a bit and hit the gym later before bed.'

His earlier pained look had gone, and none of what he'd done seemed particularly out of the ordinary, so I decided I must have misread his expression.

It didn't surprise me that Marcus would use the gym at night. He wasn't addicted to exercise, but he certainly liked to hit the weights several times a week, regardless of the time of day.

I had just bitten into a mouthful of omelette when there was a knock at the door to the suite that caused Marcus and I to share a confused look. Swallowing my food, I frowned. 'You expecting someone?'

Marcus shook his head. 'No.'

'Maybe room service forgot something?' Although I couldn't imagine what; we already had enough food here for a small army.

'I'll see who it is.' Marcus stood up and chucked his napkin on the chair before heading towards the door.

I was just lifting another mouthful of food onto my fork when I heard Marcus give a loud curse from inside the suite. Frowning, I pushed my plate away and went to investigate. He stood beside the door with a scowl on his face and his hands clenched at his sides, but when he saw me approaching he hurriedly came towards me and steered me back out onto the balcony.

'Did you need Sasha for something?' he asked tersely, giving me a heavy stare. The strangely pained look from earlier was back again, but I still had no idea what it meant.

'What? No. Why?'

His scowl deepened, and he jerked a thumb over his shoulder. 'She's outside.'

Now I really was confused. Sasha was outside the door, but he wasn't letting her in? My mind immediately went to Robyn, and worry settled in my stomach. 'Maybe it's something to do with Robyn and the wedding?' As I ripped my phone from my pocket it vibrated in my hand, and my panic grew as I saw that it was a text arriving from her.

Good morning husband to be. I can't wait to marry you! See you soon xx

Her words instantly relaxed me, and after sending out a quick reply I glanced at the door again, wondering why he wasn't opening it. If Sasha wasn't here about Robyn, then why was she knocking on Marcus's door this early in the morning?

'Aren't you going to see what Sasha wants?' I asked in confusion.

Dropping back into his chair, Marcus downed the rest of his Mimosa and then refilled his glass. 'Nope.'

I paused briefly before asking the obvious question in my mind. 'Do you want *me* to let her in?'

'Nope.' His eyes remained averted and his newly poured Mimosa disappeared down his throat quicker than a flash. At this rate we were going to be needing another jug.

Clearly something was going on that I didn't know about, so I took my seat and sipped my drink in silence as I waited patiently for Marcus to open up. It didn't take too long. Barely ten seconds after I'd sat down, Marcus sighed and began to pick at some non-existent fluff on his trousers. 'We had sex. Last night. In the club.'

It was only three short sentences, but they almost made me choke on my drink.

'It was just a quick fuck. No big deal,' he added dismissively. Even though Marcus seemed to be aiming for a casual tone, his stiff posture and deep frown made it obvious that there was more to it than a simple "quick fuck". It also explained that weird expression I'd seen on his face earlier.

Recovering my composure, I put my glass down and cleared my throat. 'But now you're not speaking?'

'We had sex and afterwards she regretted it, so no, I'm not

speaking to her.'

She regretted it? Did that mean that he didn't? I could only assume that for Marcus this had started out as more than just casual sex. His bombshell made my eyebrows jump in my hairline but, trying not to look too shocked, I sat back and folded my arms. 'Want to talk about it?'

'No.' His answer was immediate, but so was his confused grimace. A second later, he banged his nearly empty glass down on the table. 'Yes.' Marcus rubbed his hand over his face and sat back, pushing his breakfast away. 'Fuck it, I don't bloody know! It's just screwed up, that's all, because I really like her, and the sex was incredible, but she clearly doesn't share the feelings I have.'

'She told you she regretted it?' Sasha might be brazen, and she was also one of the bluntest speakers I'd ever met, but even I was struggling to imagine her saying something so hurtful to Marcus. 'She actually said those words?'

Huffing out a breath, he raised his hands and ran them through his hair, leaving it sticking up like he'd been struck by lightning. 'She didn't need to, it was obvious in her expression. She looked horrified.'

And yet she had just been here knocking on his door… Surely, she couldn't have been that horrified?

I knew the history between Marcus and Sasha was messy and complicated, but I was a good enough reader of people to see that regardless of whatever differences they might have, they were undeniably attracted to each other. I couldn't help but wonder if perhaps Marcus had misread the situation somehow and jumped to the wrong conclusions.

'But it was consensual, yes?'

Marcus's eyes bulged as he leaped out of his seat and started pacing the balcony like a caged animal. 'Of course it was fucking consensual! Jesus, Oliver, I'm not a monster.'

Holding up my hands in a calming gesture, I shook my head. 'That came out wrong. What I meant was you said it happened in Fantasia, so I was wondering if you were using one of the private rooms and if perhaps things might have got a little out of hand? It's easily done. I know from personal experience.'

A brief memory of Robyn flitted to my mind, and the first time she'd agreed to let me show her some submissive positions. I'd promised her I would be on my best behaviour, but in the heat of the moment I'd gotten so carried away that I'd made her come in my arms. At that point in time we hadn't been at a place in our relationship where that was appropriate, and I'd overstepped my boundaries big time, causing her to run away from me looking horrified – just as Marcus was describing with Sasha.

'No, it was nothing like that. Some guy was hitting on her and she was telling him no, but he wouldn't get the hint so I dealt with him.'

Dealt with him? Glancing down at his clenched fists, I saw some blotchy bruising on his knuckles and raised an eyebrow but chose not to say anything.

'When I came back, Sasha and I shared some insanely intense eye contact and then the next second we were all over each other in a dark corner.' Marcus shook his head. 'I think she started it, but the more I think back to it I'm not even sure, to be honest.'

'And it was good?'

His eyes fluttered shut briefly, as if he were remembering every detail of their encounter, and then a telling flush filled his cheeks. 'Yeah, really good. The chemistry between us is so potent. It's like she makes me lose all control. I've never felt that with a woman before.'

I was well aware how that sensation felt. One sexy glance from Robyn could have me hard and throbbing within seconds.

'If she regretted it I don't see why she'd be here at your door now,' I murmured, stating the obvious. 'I can't help but think maybe you're missing something here, mate. I think you should talk to her.'

Marcus gave a defiant shake of his head and flopped back down in his seat, looking like a deflating balloon. 'Nope. I've made the same mistake twice, I won't be making it again. Anything that might have been between Sasha and me is finished.'

He topped up his glass yet again and sat back with a completely clear expression on his face as if he had wiped all memory of our conversation, and their sexual encounters, from his brain.

'So, it's your last morning as a free man. Anything you want to do before we start getting ready?'

It was quite clear from his expression that the topic of Sasha was closed. For now, anyway. Maybe once the dust had settled I could have a go at playing Cupid, because my thick-skinned best mate was clearly besotted, and from everything Robyn had said over the past few months it seemed to me that Sasha shared the sentiment.

They needed their heads banging together, and maybe I was the right guy for the job, but first I needed to get ready to marry my girl.

CHAPTER TWENTY-EIGHT

Robyn

I woke up with nervous excitement swirling in my belly, but when I went to find Sasha to share my exhilaration I got no answer from her bedroom door. Thinking she might be sleeping off a hangover, or had perhaps had such a good night at the club that she'd hooked up with someone and not come home, I quietly opened the door to check. When I ventured inside I found a messy and unmade bed indicating that while she wasn't here now, she *had* slept here.

It wasn't even eight in the morning yet, and Sasha usually loved her sleep, so even though she'd promised me she wouldn't be hungover for today, I was surprised that she was up at this early hour.

Assuming she was in the main house having breakfast, I got dressed and then composed a good morning text to Oliver.

Good morning husband to be. I can't wait to marry you! See you soon xx

I pressed "send" and stood there hugging myself in excitement. Husband! We'd be married today, and that thought had me grinning like a loon as I eventually got my feet moving and made my way across the pretty cobbled courtyard to the house.

Despite the early hour, there was a rush of activity going on; several people were carrying delicate white chairs across the yard towards the fruit grove where Oliver and I would marry later that day, and on the main lawn I saw the marquee being erected ready for the garden party that would follow the ceremony. It was just a canvas roof, really, and had no sides so any breeze would pass through. Its sole purpose was to provide people with some shade away from the blazing summer sun, because as lovely as this garden was, there wasn't enough shade for a hot group of wedding guests. From what I could see of it so far, it had been a good pick and looked perfect for the job.

Just as I arrived at the stable door to the kitchen a text pinged to my phone, and when I saw it was from Oliver my smile stretched my lips even further.

Good morning, cariño. I'm counting down the hours until you'll be my wife. I love you to the moon and back xx

Tucking the phone into my pocket with a buzz of happiness, I entered the kitchen and was immediately swallowed up in hugs from my mother and then Sophia. They were both filled with obvious excitement and faffed around as they settled me in a chair and began bringing a huge selection of breakfast items to the table.

'Good morning.' I eyed the mountain of food apprehensively. My tummy was so full of nervous butterflies that I didn't feel very hungry at all. 'This looks delicious, but I'm not sure I can eat anything.'

My mum clicked her tongue disapprovingly and dished me up a slice of granary toast and some scrambled eggs and placed it in front of me.

I glanced up at her and was met with a raised brow that I remembered well from my childhood – it was her "you will do what you're told" look, and so I dutifully scooped up a small forkful of egg and popped it in my mouth.

The taste of melted butter and perfectly cooked eggs hit my

tongue and my mouth instantly came alive with interest. 'Hmm, these are great.' I gave a moan of pleasure, and as my stomach caught up with the fact that I was ravenous, I tucked in with gusto, cutting a corner off the bread and loading it with eggs before bringing it to my lips.

'Have you guys seen Sasha this morning? She wasn't in her room,' I asked between mouthfuls.

Mum came to sit beside me with a fresh pot of coffee and poured us both a mug. 'Yes, she came across early, about six, I suppose. She had a bite to eat and then headed off in the hire car at just gone seven. Said she had something last minute to sort out.'

First of all, six a.m.? That was almost unheard of for Sasha, and secondly, what last-minute things were there to arrange? As far as I was concerned everything was done bar the setting up, and that was currently being performed by the lovely people outside who we'd hired.

Where the heck had my bridesmaid disappeared to?

CHAPTER TWENTY-NINE

Sasha

'So where did you go this morning? You never got around to telling me.'

I turned my back on Robyn and looked out of the window as a way of deflecting her question. She'd already asked me three times now, but I was deliberately avoiding having to explain the whole "sex in a public place with a guy I like but can't have" thing. There was no point telling her anyway, seeing as Marcus hadn't even opened his door to me so the whole drive had been a wasted trip.

He'd been in his suite, though, I was sure I'd heard movement behind the door after my knock. Presumably he'd checked the spy hole and decided he didn't want to speak to me. In usual circumstances I'd probably have been pursuing it a little harder, but today wasn't usual, it was Robyn's wedding day, and so I'd boxed up my problems and was now pointedly ignoring them.

'Well?'

God, she really wasn't going to let this drop, was she? I smiled and held up my hands as Robyn approached me. 'Nooo, don't come near the window! Oliver's out in the garden with the guys and it's bad luck to see the groom before the wedding.'

Robyn paused mid step and her cheeks flushed, so it looked like my attempt to distract her had worked this time. It was a shame Robyn couldn't see him yet. Her big bad Wolfe looked perfectly sleek, all suited and booted in his wedding gear and grinning at something that Nathan had said before the two of them threw their heads back in a laugh. I'm not sure I'd ever seen Nathan laugh before; he was always so serious. But with his arm slung around Stella and his posture relaxed they looked such a happy group that it made me smile, too.

Oliver appeared so excited about the prospect of marrying my bestie that a little lump of emotion formed in my throat and, seeing as I'd just finished doing my makeup, I had to forcibly push aside the tingling of tears that rose behind my eyes.

My gaze left him and scanned over the group he was standing with: Matías, Oliver's Spanish friend who I'd met briefly last night at the club, Nathan, Marcus, David, and a dark-haired guy who I'd never met personally, but knew to be Nathan's brother, Nicholas.

All of them were in similar smart suits, apart from David, who was wearing suit trousers, a white shirt, and a black waistcoat, but had skipped the jacket and tie and was currently in the process of rolling up his sleeves and exposing his tattooed forearms. I'd never seen him in anything other than jeans, casual shirts, and leather jackets, and it was clear to see that he was the most uncomfortable in the smart clothing. Funnily enough, he looked pretty good in a rough around the edges bad boy sort of way.

Finally, my traitorous eyes drifted across to Marcus and something inside my chest grew tight and uncomfortable as I recalled last night's events in my mind, and the horrific way it had ended between us. *Again.*

He looked stunning. Totally at ease and man, did he rock a three-piece suit – it fitted him to perfection. His hair almost looked bleached in the bright summer sunshine, and was just as wild as ever, reminding me of my constant urge to run my hands through it. Not that I'd ever get the chance, because for one thing, he hated being touched, and for another, he hated me.

'Does he look handsome?' Robyn asked.

'Mmmm. Yes. *Really* handsome,' I murmured.

A sharp nudge in my left arm had me turning away from the window in shock. 'Oi! That's my future husband you're lusting over!' she exclaimed with a giggle, but then, narrowing her eyes, Robyn gave me a knowing look. 'Ah, you weren't looking at Oliver, were you?' Her expression turned curious and she jerked her head towards the windows. 'Is Marcus out there, too, by any chance?'

Busted.

With a heavy sigh, I nodded.

'He likes you, Sasha,' Robyn stated with complete confidence.

After the fiasco in the club last night, I very much doubted that. He might fancy me, lust after me, even, but like me? No. The disgusted look on his face as he'd walked away flashed in my mind and I felt sick to my stomach. Seeing as Robyn didn't know about our quickie in the club, I tried to formulate a casual answer. 'Nah. He'll have moved on by now.'

'Nope. Oliver said he played squash with Marcus just last week and their conversation focused around you. *Again*. Apparently, he talks about you all the time. He's still punishing himself for the way things went down between the two of you that night when you slept together.'

Just like I was berating myself for the way things had gone last night. God, what a bloody mess.

Turning fully away from the window and the distracting sight of Marcus, I rolled my eyes at Robyn. 'Come on, Rob, this isn't what you want to be discussing, it's your wedding day. Forget about me and Marcus and focus on not sweating off your make-up in this Spanish heat.'

Robyn was looking in the mirror and fiddling with the clips in her hair, but she met my eyes in the reflection. 'Actually, this is exactly what I need to be talking about. I'm excited, but

I'm nervous, too. Gossiping about your love life is a great distraction.' Picking up another clip, she gave me an expectant glance. 'You still like him, don't you?'

Huffing out a breath, I scrunched up my face in frustration, but after an almost sleepless night thinking things through and coming to the conclusion that yes, I *did* like him, and yes, I *did* want more – even if that meant letting him cuff me to his bed all night – I could at least admit it now.

'Yeah.' Letting out a low exhale, I decided to confess my little secret. 'We… er… we had sex at the club last night.'

My words certainly grabbed Robyn's attention, because she dumped down the remaining hair clips so hard that they scattered on to the floor, and then she spun around to face me with wide eyes.

'*What*? How? Does this mean you're giving him a chance, then? What happened?' she squeaked, her hands flapping in excitement and the questions falling from her mouth in one big jumble.

I grinned at her reaction and the multitude of questions she was firing at me, until visions of what had occurred between Marcus and me sobered my mood. Flashes of our incredible connection flitted through my mind, followed by the tension between us afterwards and the way he'd stormed off.

'Some weird guy was all over me and wouldn't back off, and I started to yell at him. Marcus dragged him off me and threw him out, then he came back and… I found it pretty hot that he'd saved me… and we shared some big eye contact and then we were all over each other and then the next second we were having sex.'

'Just like that, huh?' Her eyes bulged as she nodded and came and sat next to me.

'Yup. Pretty much.' My shrug was meant to look casual but felt painfully forced.

'Are you OK? Did the first guy hurt you?'

Bless Robyn for always thinking of my safety first, even

when there was clearly some juicy gossip to be had. 'Nah. He was just being a dick. Marcus laid into him pretty badly, though. Punched him in the face and everything.'

Robyn let out a low whistle. 'Wow. He was protecting you. It's kinda romantic, really.'

It was, and it wasn't. The protecting me part was romantic, but the frantic public sex afterwards maybe not so much. I winced, desperately hoping we hadn't been caught on CCTV or, God forbid, recorded on someone's mobile phone to forever grace the airwaves of YouTube.

Robyn leaned closer, her eyebrows rising in curiosity. 'And you had sex in the club? In one of the private rooms, or right out in the public bit?'

Closing my eyes, I grimaced in embarrassment. Fantasia might be a sex club, but still, public sex was a bit brazen, even for me. 'Not quite, we were in a pretty dark corner.' I admitted quietly. God, I still couldn't believe we'd had sex in the club like that.

Robyn's eyes were the biggest I'd ever seen them. 'So who initiated it?'

'It was sort of mutual. It felt like the air around us was thick with sexual tension, and then the next second we were kissing like it was about to be the end of the world.'

'And was it just as good as the first time?'

I drew in a long breath, my cheeks heating as I recalled just how incredible it had been when he'd pressed me up against the wall, slid his hand around my throat, and pressed his body against mine. A little shudder of desire danced over my skin, and I glanced up at Robyn and saw her eyes latch on mine, watching all my reactions gleefully. 'Yeah. Just as good, if not better.'

'Wow.' Robyn breathed softly, obviously seeing just how much this was affecting me. I hated to admit it, but it really was. *He* really was. Marcus Price, the man I couldn't seem to move on from.

'Yeah. It was pretty hot.' I sounded sad, frustrated with the way it had ended.

'And the cuff issue obviously wasn't there if it was spontaneous and inside the club?'

'No cuffs, but I still couldn't touch him because he held my wrists above my head.'

Robyn started to thoughtfully chew on a fingernail, but I quickly reached across and slapped her hand away. 'Hey! We just painted your nails!'

She flushed and examined her nail for damage before smiling at me. 'Sorry. I was just thinking that there must be a reason he doesn't like contact. He seems fine with it around the guys. Do you think something happened in his past?'

'I was thinking along the same lines, but I don't know anything for sure. I guess now I'll never know.' I let out a breath as my face crumpled into a sad expression.

'Why? How did you leave things?'

I grimaced as the discomfort of guilt caused my stomach to cramp up into tight knots. 'It wasn't good… I was starting to realise just how much I liked him, and the panic must have shown on my face, I guess. I think he misread it as me regretting what happened between us, and then he walked away.'

Robyn's face creased into a wince of sympathy, which was probably directed at Marcus, and not me, because let's face it, whichever way I looked at it, the way things ended last night had been my fault. Instead of bottling it all up inside and panicking about my feelings I should have just opened up and told him like a normal person would.

Collapsing forwards, I buried my head into my hands. 'God, it was a train wreck, Robyn. It's *always* so fucked up between us.'

'Shit, Sasha. Why didn't you set him straight?'

I scrubbed my hands over my face to try to erase some of the guilt flooding my system. 'I panicked. I… I realised just how much I was falling for him, and it terrified me, and I totally freaked out Robyn!' I wrung my hands together and gave her an imploring look, desperate for her to understand. 'You know what I'm like, this is some seriously big shit for me. I tried to talk to him, but then my words got all jumbled and I just couldn't seem to explain it quick enough to stop him leaving.'

'Have you messaged or called him since?'

'I tried, but he didn't answer.'

'His phone might be out of battery, or switched to silent?' Robyn pondered.

'Yeah maybe, but that was also where I disappeared to so early this morning… I tried popping in at his hotel, but there was no answer. He was there, though. I could hear him moving around so I guess he's just avoiding me.'

'He could have been sightseeing?' Robyn suggested, doggedly sticking to her optimism.

'At seven o'clock in the morning on his best mate's wedding day? I don't think so,' I stated sadly.

Scrunching up her face in a grimace, she nodded with visible reluctance. 'OK… so maybe he was feeling messed up, too. He might have needed some time to work out what to say to you.' Robyn slid even closer and gave my arm a supportive rub. 'I know why you've always avoided relationships, and I get it… but surely you can see the positives to taking a risk with someone that you really like?' She bumped her shoulder with mine to force me to look at her and then raised her eyebrows hopefully. 'See how today plays out. It is going to be a boozy party, after all. Maybe once you're both feeling a bit more relaxed you can talk to him and apologise.'

Letting out a dry laugh, I smiled at her enthusiasm, but I didn't hold out much hope. I couldn't see Marcus coming within a hundred meters of me after the way things had ended. 'It's all been such a mess. It's like neither of us can make our mind up. It's either him keeping me at arm's length, or me freaking out. Now I've come around to the idea of maybe being with him and I still manage to screw it up. Talk about a complete fuck-up!'

Deciding that we'd had enough of this bloody frustrating subject, I checked the clock and grinned at Robyn. 'Enough of this depressing conversation. I think it might be time for me to lace you into that gorgeous dress.'

CHAPTER THIRTY

Robyn

The chatter of the crowd in the marquee ahead of me lulled. My stomach clenched with excitement as I leaned to the side, trying to get a clear line of sight down the aisle so I could get a look at Oliver, but I couldn't see past the gorgeous plumes of flowers that decorated the entrance. This was when the soft piano music was meant to start, but the space in front of me was totally silent. A room of bated breath.

Suddenly, through the sea of pink and white flowers I saw glimpses of a three-piece suit coming towards us, and grinned. I was so hyped up about the proceedings that it took me a second to register that it wasn't Oliver coming down the aisle as I'd excitedly assumed, but the blond head of Marcus.

Marcus, who was clutching something in his hand, and wearing a dark, troubled expression on his face.

My earlier excitement drained away and my stomach suddenly gripped with nerves, twisting so violently that I couldn't pull in a proper breath.

His expression… something was wrong. Very wrong. I didn't know what, but I'd never seen Marcus look so pale and anxious and it immediately made me feel like throwing up. Sasha must have picked up on the tension in him, too, because she took a step closer to me as if preparing to support me.

As soon as he reached my side, Marcus glanced between me and Sasha and chewed frantically on his lower lip.

'Marcus, what is it? What's wrong?'

He fidgeted on the spot for a second and swallowed loudly. 'It's Oliver, he's not coming.'

He's not coming?

Oliver isn't coming?

Those three simple words reverberated around inside my head and brought my entire world crashing down around me.

I don't recall leaving the garden, but I had obviously been guided out by Marcus and Sasha, because the next time I blinked and focused on my surroundings I realised I was sitting on the bed in the guest cottage.

What was I doing in here?

Sasha was hovering in front of me with a glass of water in her hand and that same anxious expression on her face, and Marcus stood behind her reading something on a crumpled piece of paper.

I couldn't think straight. My brain felt sluggish, as if I'd just woken up from some really deep sleep. I glanced down and saw that I was still decked out in my wedding dress, with my bouquet discarded at my side.

It was my wedding day? Why was I sitting here, then? Rubbing at my temples, I tried to get my brain to wake up, but I honestly couldn't remember anything of how I got here, or why I was in the guest cottage of Oliver's parents' house.

I racked my brain. What was the last thing I could remember? I'd woken up and looked out of the window and the weather had been perfect, then Sasha and I had got dressed together and shared some prosecco before heading down to the ceremony and then Marcus had come up to us with his message…

A rasping breath caught painfully in my throat as I suddenly remembered Marcus and his bombshell about Oliver.

It's Oliver. He's not coming.

Pain so excruciating that it almost blinded me erupted in my chest, scorching through my veins and making my head pound in agony. Every attempt at a breath felt like my lungs were trying to claw their way out of my chest, and my eyes started to burn as tears blurred my vision. My skin tingled with panic, sweat burst on my brow, and my chest still wouldn't relax.

I couldn't breathe.

Oh Jesus. I really couldn't breathe.

'Robyn? Fuck!' Hands gripped my shoulders and shook, and I just about managed to make out the image of Sasha as she stood before me looking pale and stressed. 'Breathe, Robyn. Take a fucking breath for fuck's sake.'

Oliver was gone. He didn't want me.

Another ripping, sawing half-breath dragged its way from my lungs and I folded forwards in agony as I desperately tried to get some oxygen into my system and calm the devastating panic that had me in its grasp.

Gradually I managed to relax my cramping lungs and pull in some cool, much-needed air.

'Here, drink this.'

I stared at the water glass in Sasha's hand for a few moments, focusing my foggy attention on watching a droplet work its way down the side of the glass and then drip from the bottom and plop onto the carpet.

It was our wedding day, but Oliver wasn't coming?

It made no sense to me at all, and my brain felt fuzzy from the stress of repeating it over and over again and still not managing to understand it. It was like some sick, surreal nightmare.

As my brain finally clicked back on and everything started to come into focus once more, I pushed away the aching pain of my devastation and leaped to my feet. Finally, I felt some composure returning.

Pushing the glass away, I shook my head. 'I don't need a drink.'

There was an insistent knocking at the door and Sasha

glanced at it before looking at me. 'That'll be your mum again. Shall I let her in?'

Seeing Mum when I was so heartbreakingly confused would no doubt make me cry, so I shook my head. 'No. I don't want to see anyone. Just tell me what the hell's going on.'

Sasha took a nervous step backwards and glanced at the paper in Marcus's hands before heading to the door to speak to my mum.

Marcus shifted on the spot looking anxious and then stepped forward to speak. 'I was waiting with Oliver for things to get going, but then he got an email through to his phone. He said he wondered if it was from you, so he checked it and then said he needed to make a call. He… er…' He paused as Sasha returned. His eyes wavered between her and me before he averted his gaze altogether. 'He never came back, but he sent me a text asking me to pick up a note from the kitchen and give it to you.' He fidgeted on the spot. 'I tried calling you, but your phone was off, and then I tried Sasha, but you weren't answering my calls, either.'

With that statement he flashed her a glare which could have melted plastic with its ferocity. The two of them shared a heated stare, but when Sasha's lips tightened as she prepared a comeback my eyes dropped to the paper.

They could argue about their stupid standoff for as long as they wanted; all I was concerned about was finding out what the hell was going on and what had spooked Oliver.

My stomach plummeted. What if something hadn't spooked him and he had genuinely changed his mind? Fear-laced pain stabbed at my chest and I sucked in a sharp breath at that idea before adamantly shaking my head.

No. I knew Oliver loved me, and I knew he wanted to marry me. I'd seen it in his eyes yesterday at the dinner with his parents. That kind of love couldn't be faked. Could it? I refused to entertain the idea that Oliver had changed his mind; something must have happened in that phone call he'd taken, that had to be it, but what could be bad enough to make him walk away from me?

Outside my confused bubble of thought the argument between Marcus and Sasha continued to rage. 'It's my best mate's wedding day. That's why I didn't answer your call! What's your excuse for not answering my calls yesterday? Or your door this morning!' Sasha spat, frustration obvious in her tone.

'I didn't answer my door because I'd hate for you to *regret* anything you said or did again!' Marcus replied in a near yell.

Looking up at them I could practically see the bristling tension arcing between them; both their backs had straightened, they were glaring at each other, and their mouths had popped open as if preparing to respond.

For fuck's sake. I needed to think this through in peace and quiet! I did not have time to deal with their shit right now, so I stepped between them and threw them both a savage glare.

'Jesus Christ! Shut up, both of you! You may not have noticed, but it's supposed to be my fucking wedding day and Oliver has disappeared! Sort your fucking sex life out later, not now!'

Marcus and Sasha both froze at my words. They looked suitably contrite as they flashed each other a wary glance and nodded rapidly.

'Sorry, Robyn. Here, you'll want to read this,' Marcus mumbled apologetically, before holding out the paper.

Looking again at the note in his hand, I tried to steady my composure, but I still felt a slight tremble in my fingers as I reached out and took it. It was slightly scrunched from where Marcus had been holding it, but other than that it was just a normal piece of printer paper. It was hard to believe that something so innocuous could hold my entire future.

I opened up the paper and my chest tightened as I saw Oliver's familiar slanted writing. Taking a deep breath, I began to read.

Robyn,

I apologise that this is last minute, but I just can't go through with it. I don't want to marry you. I've changed my mind. Don't look for me or contact me.

Oliver

The note didn't contain any of his customary kisses that he always used at the end of text messages or emails, and there was none of his teasing flirtatious humour showing through, either. It was just blunt, clear-cut, and straight to the point.

He couldn't go through with it.

He didn't want to marry me.

A scraping noise sounded through the room and as I bent forwards and clutched at my stomach I realised that it was a rasping breath trying to tear its way from my lungs. I felt like I'd been punched in the gut and winded, and my legs folded beneath me as I sank down onto the nearest armchair, still clutching the note in my hand.

After five minutes of sitting there rocking in shock while Sasha nervously hovered around me I stood up and drew in a long breath. None of it made sense – we'd been blissfully happy just yesterday – so instead of sitting here crying like an injured child I needed to think. It was time to get to the bottom of all this.

There was one clear option which would give me the best chance of finding out answers – the man himself – so I dragged my phone from the small clutch bag, pulled up Oliver's details, and pressed "dial".

The phone rang, and rang, and then went through to voicemail. So he wasn't even man enough to speak to me? Shaking my head in irritation, I redialled, only to have it ring out again.

God fucking damn it! I stabbed at the cancel button with my finger and immediately hit "redial" again. Fine. I'd just keep calling, then. I'd phone him until he picked up, or his bloody battery ran out.

Which is exactly what I did. Marcus left Sasha and me alone, no doubt keen to escape the tension hanging in the room, and even though I was getting no answer I kept routinely calling Oliver's number, cancelling it when it went to voicemail and then hitting redial.

It was a seemingly pointless task, but in all honesty, I didn't know what else to do. I was just thinking that perhaps I should give up, when suddenly, to my surprise, I heard the call connect and I pressed the phone to my ear, straining to hear something.

'Hello? Oliver?'

The pause that followed felt like it lasted an hour but was in reality probably no more than a few seconds.

'I told you not to call me.' The ice in Oliver's voice chilled me to my very core and sent a shudder of goose pimples across my skin. He hadn't even said hello. I'd literally never heard him sound so blank and emotionless, and it caused a crippling pain to erupt in my chest that almost prevented me from speaking.

'We need to talk,' I rasped, my strained voice barely even sounding like me.

'We have nothing to talk about, Robyn. Like I said in my note, it's over.' He sounded robotic. There was nothing in his voice that I recognised, not one part of it sounded like the passionate, intense man I knew and loved. It was like listening to a complete stranger, and as stupid as it was, I found myself numbly checking the phone screen to make sure I had dialled the right number.

Dragging up some grit, I took in a deep breath, stood taller, and shook my head as anger began to replace my fear. How bloody dare he do this to me?

'You don't get to just dump me at the altar on our fucking wedding day and then not explain yourself!'

There was a moment of silence as if my outburst had shocked him, but then his strangely mechanical voice sounded down the line again. 'It's over. I had a long think about things and we won't work in the long run.'

The harshness to his words made me dizzy, but I just about managed to stumble out a reply. 'Why not? Things… things have been going so well.' I knew I was starting to sound desperate, but what else could I do? We'd been blissfully happy until about four hours ago. Or at least I'd thought we had.

'There are things I need, Robyn. Sexually. Things you would hate. I thought I'd suppressed my desires.' He paused, his words hanging in the air incomplete, and my stomach knotted as I waited for whatever he was going to say next. 'But it turns out I want them more than I want you.'

I choked on my breath as his wounding words sunk in. *Them?* He wanted *them* more than he wanted me? Was he talking about sexual acts, or other women? My brain spun as I tried to comprehend what the hell he could be talking about. 'What type of things? You know I'm open to exploring new stuff… we could talk about it…'

'No.' His retort was immediate and cripplingly final.

'Is it another woman… or women?' I croaked, feeling precariously close to throwing up.

As if he wanted to really make me suffer, Oliver let out a short, humourless laugh before adding his final nail in the coffin of our broken relationship.

'I miss the mindless sex I indulged in before I met you. I fucked hundreds of women, did you know that? Hundreds. You could never satisfy a man like me.'

A pained cry left my lips at the hurtful finality in his statement. When I realised that the line was now dead because he'd hung up on me, I allowed my grief to overwhelm me as I sunk to the floor sobbing and clutching at my tear-soaked face.

'That motherfucker!' Sasha spat, coming straight to my

side. The call hadn't been on speaker, but the room was quiet enough that she must have heard most of it, and she bundled my numb body up into her comforting arms and rocked me.

But nothing could comfort me. Not now that my heart had been ripped out from my chest and my life left in tatters.

I felt like my entire world had just come to a sickening halt. I'd had everything planned out in my mind, every forwards step – marriage, new house, a dog, and perhaps even kids – and they all included Oliver.

Now there was nothing.

No Oliver, no wedding, no future.

He'd become everything to me so quickly, and I'd thought that I was his everything, too. It might sound dramatic, but at this moment in time I literally couldn't see how I'd ever manage to pull myself together and carry on.

So I didn't.

I sat surrounded by the deflated meringue of my wedding dress and cried on Sasha's chest. I cried until I could feel her dress was soaked with my grief, and my body was so exhausted that it fell into a disturbed sleep right there in the middle of the floor.

CHAPTER THIRTY-ONE

Oliver

I pressed the "end call" button to hang up the phone and took a deep, unsteady breath. The utter craziness of all this was dizzying, and my stomach reeled with sickness at the horrific words I'd just uttered to the woman I loved more than life itself.

I stared across at Alexandra where she was reclining on the bed grinning like a Cheshire cat. She pouted at me, and then casually began undoing another button on her shirt to reveal more of her pale white cleavage.

The sight revolted me to my core, and I turned away, scowling and looking down at the piece of paper in my hand. It was the script of what I'd just said to Robyn, the hideous, hurtful words written by Alex and handed to me so I could say them when Robyn called back.

Frustration made me clench my jaw until it squeaked. Why had Robyn been so insistent and kept calling me? If I could have had just a few more hours I might have managed to sort out this fucking nightmare without having to say those unbelievably hurtful words to her.

Fuck me, I'd be lucky if she'd ever speak to me again after the things I'd said to her.

Mind you, if the tables had been turned and she had walked away from me, I would have been just as persistent with my phone calls. I'd have turned heaven and earth upside down to find her, so I couldn't really blame Robyn for her actions.

My stomach was churning violently, and I wanted to throw up, but I swallowed down the sickly bile that kept rising in my throat and stood tall. I had to stay strong; I couldn't let Alex see me so weak.

Don't believe those words, cariño, trust in me. I'll sort this out, I thought over and over, but the agonising cry of pain I'd heard Robyn give out over the phone would haunt me forever. She had believed every word.

She'd had to, though. With Alex here threatening me I'd had to make Robyn believe me; it was the only way I could progress and try to sort this mess out.

I also wanted to try to keep hold of this phone. It felt like a lifeline to me. Perhaps if Alex was distracted enough I could slip it into my pocket and manage to send a text to Robyn later.

Cupping my hand around the mobile, I lowered my arm, trying to keep my movements casual and sending up prayers to whichever god might be listening. When I reached my trouser pocket, I loosened off my fingers and felt a swell of hope erupt in my chest as the phone slid into my pocket unnoticed by Alex.

As I looked back at her, every muscle in my body tensed and I only just held myself back from leaping across the room and strangling her. As much as I wanted to, I couldn't, because not only did she have her sick threat hanging over me, she also had a gun in her hand.

She'd pulled the weapon out shortly after I'd met up with her, and although I didn't know much about guns, I was informed enough to know that she had definitely loaded it and cocked it with apparent proficiency, making it seem real, and not a fake as I had first hoped.

I needed to distract her from thinking about the phone, so I decided to try to strike up a conversation.

'Happy now?' I murmured, only just managing to keep the hatred from my voice.

'Hmm. Yes, that speech was very good. You're quite the

actor, Oliver.' Alex uncurled herself from the bed and strutted towards me, a smile of pure wickedness spreading on her face and the gun glinting in the sunlight.

She walked with a swagger, her shirt almost completely unbuttoned now, so I suspected she was trying to be seductive, but all I could see was the evil bitch who had arrived five hours ago and blackmailed me into cancelling my wedding.

Alex reached my side, ran her knuckles down the buttons of my shirt, and then hooked one finger into the buckle of my belt and tugged gently.

She was almost acting flirtatiously, and I was momentarily convinced that my trick with the phone had worked, but my heart sunk as she traced the belt around to my pocket and dipped her hand inside.

For a second, she deliberately avoided the phone and tried to tease my cock with her fingertips, but when I made no outward response to her move she retrieved the mobile. 'I think I'll keep hold of this for the time being,' she whispered, giving an over the top flutter of her eyelashes. She slid the phone inside her bra cup before lowering her hand again and cupping my groin.

My teeth clenched at her gesture, but my cock stayed as limp as a lettuce leaf – not that Alex seemed to care. I stood as still as a marble statue as she gave me a squeeze and fondled my balls.

'I'm sure I can change this with a few of my tricks,' Alex purred. She gripped me harder and I winced, glad that her continued caressing wasn't having any effect on my soft dick.

She lifted her gun-wielding hand, the cool metal of the barrel chilling along my neck before she rested it on my shoulder and rolled onto her tiptoes so her mouth was beside my ear. 'I'll get you harder than you've ever been,' she promised thickly. 'I still remember all the kink you liked in my bed, Oliver.'

I'm not sure what she thought she was remembering,

because we'd only shared one night together, and while we might both have gotten off in the end, it had been blatantly obvious throughout that we were incompatible. We were both too dominant and unwilling to compromise; it could never have worked between us.

'The only thing I like in my bed these days is Robyn,' I stated blandly, not caring if it pissed her off. Thank fuck it worked – for now, anyway – and Alex dropped her hand away as she made a noise of disgust.

I felt a cool touch to my neck as Alex ran the nub of the gun around my skin and then down my chest and over the buttons on my shirt. 'Careful, Oliver, it's not too late for me to carry out my threat, you know.'

Gritting my teeth, I let out a sigh of exasperation. 'What exactly do you hope to gain from this?'

Alex smiled and threw her head back to let out a single bark of laughter.

'You, Oliver, that's what. It's simple, I want you.' Poking me in the chest with the gun, she giggled, but to me it just looked like the actions of a madwoman. 'You might think you love that naïve little bitch, but she could never satisfy you the way I can.'

This time it was my turn to make a sound of disgust, but Alex didn't seem to care that I was dismissing her idea and merely smiled up at me. 'And if you can't find it in yourself to be with me, then I'll simply find your silly little fiancée and kill her.'

Ice slid through my veins at her threat, and I swallowed down any caustic reply that I had been about to throw at her.

'If she's dead you won't need to be distracted by thoughts of her ever again and you can concentrate on being where you're supposed to be – with me.'

I immediately realised that I was going to have to reel in my anger if I wanted to keep Robyn safe. I couldn't risk talking back to Alex and her reacting and going after my *cariño.*

'So, what's it to be, lover boy? Me or her?'

I racked my brain for a solution to this seemingly impossible mess, but with a sickening feeling rising in my chest I knew that no matter how I approached it, there was only one thing that would appease Alex and distract her from Robyn.

Me. She wanted me.

Numbing my mind, I did the only thing I could think of. I stepped forwards, pulled her into my arms, and shoved my hand down her skirt as if my life depended upon it.

In reality, of course, it was Robyn's life hanging in the balance, and as much as it sickened me to do so, when Alex's hand moved to my groin this time I didn't push it away.

CHAPTER THIRTY-TWO

Robyn

It was now a day and a half since *he* had disappeared and left me standing in my wedding dress behind a marquee full of shocked guests. A day and a half from the wedding that never happened, and I hadn't seen or heard anything else from him.

We were stuck in Spain because of a lack of available flights out, and I literally couldn't take it any more. Everyone around me was being so overly nice it was painful, but the thing was, it wasn't real niceness; it was pity, mixed with a fair dose of worry and concern, and it was driving me insane. I wanted to scream at them to bugger off, shout, and have a flailing tantrum on the floor like a kid.

The worst was the shock on people's faces when I walked in a room and caught them in mid-conversation. They'd go silent and start fidgeting and it was screamingly obvious that they were talking about me and my absent groom. No doubt speculating about why he'd left me, or what I'd done wrong to prompt his disappearance.

The exact same questions that were spinning repeatedly round and around in my head.

Nobody knew what to say or do around me. I was the girl whose husband-to-be had dumped her seconds before the wedding; the reject, the failure, the one left behind to pick up the pieces.

Sasha was pushing me to the point where I wanted to kill her because she was hovering so close to me all the time, talking incessantly about nothing in particular. And his family didn't seem to know where to look whenever I came near them. I think they felt guilty, unable to believe that their gorgeous little boy had done this.

But he had. I was alone, hurt beyond repair, and confused, and it was all because of *him*.

I'd started to move forwards in tiny steps, the first of which was to avoid using his name, so he was now "him" or "he" in all my thoughts. After the painfully harsh phone call with *him,* I hadn't attempted to make contact again, either. Even my mum was at a loss for what to do. She was so stressed that all she did was faff around me, bless her, and even though I knew they all meant well, all I wanted was some peace and quiet to try to absorb everything that had occurred.

Sophia had insisted that we stay at the house, saying she knew her boy and he'd return with a plausible explanation that we would all laugh about in years to come, but I'd heard how cold he sounded on the phone and I wasn't fooled.

It was over, he was gone, and now it just felt alien being here with all his family and not having *him* at my side.

It was awkward beyond belief, smothering and so oppressive that I desperately needed to get away before I had a major meltdown.

I had to bide my time, though, because I knew they wouldn't just let me leave so I had to wait for moments where Sasha was out of the room to plan my escape. When she took her morning trip to the toilet, I shoved a random selection of clothes into a small bag, then later, when she went to make us a cup of tea, I located my passport, wallet, and phone and popped them in the front pocket. Finally, later in the afternoon when she popped to the toilet again, I made my escape.

As soon as I heard the bathroom lock click shut I grabbed the bag from under my bed and, without looking back, I snuck down the stairs, out of the side door, and jumped in the hire car to set off.

I drove without knowing where I was going to go, but preferably I would end up somewhere nobody knew me. Right now, it felt like anywhere would be better than that pretty house on the hill and the painful memories it held.

CHAPTER THIRTY-THREE

Oliver

I'd never experienced frustration like this. It was now day two with Alex, and I felt like a fly stuck in a web. With her threat on Robyn's life still prominent in my mind, I'd decided yesterday that my best bet was to give up on my arguments and anger and just play her game. It was agony, and went against every fibre of my character, but I'd started acting like an obedient puppy.

I glanced across at Alex from the corner of my eye and gritted my teeth in an attempt at holding in all the furious words I wanted to yell at her. Currently, she sat at the table in our room doing God knows what on her laptop, but no matter how much the screen demanded her attention, her right hand never left the gun which lay on the table beside her.

The frustration of knowing that if the gun wasn't part of the equation I could physically overpower her with ease was driving me insane, but the bloody thing never left her side, and so there seemed to be very little I could do. I wanted to attack, but the action would be almost pointless if I got shot and wasn't around to share my life with Robyn afterwards. So, as much as it was killing me, I needed to bide my time.

Alex stood and, after sending me a sultry glance which I did my best to return, walked into the bathroom and shut the door.

I stared at the closed door and my mouth dropped open in shock. She had finally made a mistake – she hadn't tied me up – and my heart began pounding in my chest as I immediately stood up and wondered what to do.

Every single time she left the room she had handcuffed me to a solid metal pipe on the wall and gagged me, but not this time. Perhaps she had fallen for my show of obedience, or maybe she'd just forgotten, but whatever the reason I suddenly had a glimmer of hope at an escape.

I took a step towards the exit door, but then stopped. If I ran then Alex's threat over Robyn might never go away, and I couldn't live knowing that Robyn might never feel safe.

Grimacing, I grabbed the handcuffs that Alex had used on me so many times and turned back towards the bathroom door, knowing that I had to act now if I stood any chance of capturing her while her guard was down.

Placing a hand on the door knob, I took a second to swallow down a ball of nerves in my throat and prepare myself. I knew the layout of the small bathroom, but I had no idea where the gun would be, and that thought was terrifying enough to seriously make me question my sanity. Would she still be holding it? Or would it be on the unit with the sink? Perhaps it might be on the side of the bath?

It was a question I couldn't answer from out here, so, pulling in a deep breath, I tried to steady myself for entry, but it was impossible because I'd never felt so anxious in my life.

Shaking myself into action, I placed my shoulder on the door and barged my way into the room with a roar that would hopefully shock Alex enough that she wouldn't immediately fire at me.

Luck was on my side, and as I stumbled into the room I saw that Alex was at the sink washing her hands and the gun was on the counter beside her. Both of our gazes dropped to the weapon. A second later, we did a synchronised dive for the gun. Alex was closer, so her wet hands grabbed it first, but as she went to raise it towards me I swung out with the back of my hand and managed to knock it from her soapy grip.

The gun clattered to the tiled floor and I dived at Alex. I grabbed her and forced her backwards until we both tumbled over the toilet and staggered around the room in a whirlwind of clutching hands and fiercely spat words.

Alex dropped to her knees and my position behind her meant I could easily grab her in a choke hold, which I did, my arm like a steel band around her slender neck. Even though one of her hands managed to grab the gun I tightened my grip, confident that I now had the upper hand.

I was wrong, very wrong. Barely a moment after I'd grabbed her I heard the muffled crack of the gun going off and something ripped through my shoulder with such heat and intense agony that I roared out with pain.

We continued to struggle, but I could see the red patch of blood on my shirt growing larger and larger by the second. My body started to feel weaker from the blood loss until black spots of unconsciousness rose before my eyes and swamped me.

My last thought as I slumped to the ground was of Robyn, and how much she must hate me.

CHAPTER THIRTY-FOUR

Oliver

'*Señor*? Sir?'

The voice sounded distant and muffled, and as hard as I tried to focus on it, I couldn't quite seem to manage to bring it properly into my foggy mind.

'*Sir*?' The voice grew more insistent and was accompanied by the feel of someone taking hold of one of my arms and giving several hard jerks. The movement caused a sharp pain to tear through my shoulder and brought me slightly out of my stupor, and I forced my eyes to open to find out who the hell was shaking me like a tambourine.

A man dressed as a paramedic was hovering over me. As he went to shake me again I hissed in warning and glared at him. I didn't care if he was wearing a uniform; if he tried to touch me when I was in this much pain he would be getting a punch in the face.

Thinking about it, why was I in so much pain, and why the hell was a paramedic leaning over me?

My mind was blank, and everything still felt blurry around the edges.

I lifted a hand to the agony in my shoulder and my fingers immediately slid through wetness before rubbing at a rough, torn area of skin that hurt so much when I touched it I thought I was going to throw up.

When I pulled my hand away I saw it was slicked with crimson, and it was this sickening sight of my own blood that started to bring some of my sense back.

The fight with Alex.

The tussle.

The gun going off…

That was why I was in so much pain and currently lying on the bathroom floor.

The man had sensibly backed away from me a little but was holding a large medical backpack as if intent on doing some tests on me. 'Were you attacked? Can you describe who did this?'

Who did it? I could do far more than just describe Alex; I could give him her full fucking name, address, and date of birth. My eyes frantically moved around the room, and then I almost deflated with relief when I saw she was lying beside me, also being tended to by paramedics. From the look of it she was out cold and bleeding from a head wound.

'Her,' I croaked. Clearing my throat, I gave the man a desperate look. '*Policía*… we need police… she needs arresting.'

After giving me a shocked look, he turned to one of his colleagues and in rapid Spanish told her to go and put another call in to the police to hurry them along.

Looking at Alex's pale face, I could only assume that luck had been on my side during that fight, and when I'd passed out from the pain of the gunshot I had knocked Alex over and she'd banged her head. Or perhaps she'd slipped in my blood, because the tiled floor was slick with crimson.

Thank fuck. Whatever had happened didn't matter. I was just glad she was still here because if she had escaped and acted out her threat to kill Robyn I would never have been able to carry on.

The police arrived barely a minute later, and once I had given a statement and was happy that Alex was secured, I lay back with a sigh and nodded at the paramedic who still hovered over me with a wad of bandage in his hand.

CHAPTER THIRTY-FIVE

Oliver

Alexandra was safely locked away in police custody, and I was patched up and desperately searching for Robyn.

As soon as I'd been allowed to get my phone in hospital I'd called her over and over again, but her mobile was turned off. So, with difficulty – and much to the disapproval of my doctor – I'd dragged my clothes on and promptly checked myself out of the clinic.

There was no way I could lie in a hospital bed while Robyn was still under the impression that I had left her. Besides, my wound was stitched up and I'd had fluids pumped into me for the last two hours, so I felt much better than I had.

Unfortunately for me, there was no trace of her. My feisty little fiancée had seemingly disappeared into thin air. I'd hoped that she would still be at my parents' house, but a quick phone call with Marcus had dashed my hopes. He said that she had been staying with my family for the days following the failed wedding, but she'd disappeared this afternoon after lunch.

This afternoon, while I was busy getting shot.

Thank goodness I hadn't dared go to my parents' house in person to look for her, because there would have been too many questions thrown at me that I simply didn't have time to answer, not while Robyn was still AWOL.

Marcus had been understandably curious as to where I'd been but, being one of my closest friends, he'd accepted my promise that I would fill him in later and not pushed for further details.

I'd now been to practically every hotel in town to see if a young Englishwoman had checked in within the last few hours, but with no luck. Apparently, there was a music festival starting on Monday which meant that all the hotels were fully booked. I'd been convinced that I'd find Robyn back at the hotel we'd stayed in on our first visit here, but it too was full, and the receptionist couldn't remember having seen Robyn in there enquiring after a room.

Following the failed hotel search, I'd contacted Marcus again to get his help searching and had sent him to the airport with a wad of cash to bribe someone into checking today's flight records, but that too had drawn a blank. Robyn hadn't flown out, her rental car hadn't been returned, and she wasn't in any of the city's hotels.

While I was relieved that she hadn't left and was presumably still somewhere in the region, I was now worried sick, because she didn't know the city like I did and if all the hotels were full she'd soon be finding herself in unfamiliar streets at night with nowhere to stay.

'Fuck!' I threw my hands up and ran them through my hair in agitation. Spinning on the spot, I stared around the pretty square. Attempting to search the countryside outside Barcelona had seemed too daunting a challenge, so I was laying my hopes on her being in Barcelona itself. It felt like searching for a needle in a haystack, but I wouldn't give up, and had spent the last few hours walking the streets checking any bar, hotel, or restaurant that I could find.

The lights were starting to come on for the evening, but I had absolutely no idea where to look next, or what to do. I felt utterly helpless, which was not a feeling that sat easily with me.

Just then I caught a glimpse of familiar bright blonde hair through the throngs of people in the square and found myself pushing through the crowds as I made a beeline for Sasha.

Sasha and Robyn were best mates. Where one was, the other was often close by. Could my girl be here somewhere? My heart accelerated as I fought through the crowd, trying to simultaneously reach Sasha and scan the surrounding people for a glimpse of Robyn.

After my multiple unanswered calls to Robyn earlier, I'd tried Sasha, but also had no luck. She no doubt hated my guts as much as Robyn did, but if there was even a vague chance that she might know where Robyn was, then I was willing to risk the foul-mouthed outburst she would no doubt send my way.

When I caught up with her, I stepped around her tall frame and caused her to come to a skidding halt. Her eyes widened for a fraction of a second and then immediately lit with anger and her spine straightened out a few inches to make her seem impossibly tall and bristling with murderous rage.

'Sasha, don't hit me.' I held my hands up in a gesture of surrender and tried to give her an appeasing look. From the murderous sparks still flying at me, it had failed completely. 'I can explain everything, but right now I really need to know where Robyn is.'

'I'm not telling you where she is, you utter piece of shit.' Sasha looked lethal. Eyes bulging, fists clenched at her sides, her entire frame tense as if she were struggling to hold back from pounding me into a pile of hamburger meat. She probably was. 'How the fuck could you hurt her like this?'

'I didn't mean to… there's been a whole pile of fucked-up-ness going on that will take too long to explain here, but I swear to God, Robyn means the world to me and I'm going to make this right.'

'The only reason I'm not punching your fucking lights out is because there are police standing just over there and I can't afford to spend the night in jail because Robyn's going to call soon, and when she does I need to *not* be incarcerated.'

A stabbing pain shot through my heart at her reminder that

my girl was out there somewhere alone, and I shifted on the spot, wondering how the hell I could pacify Robyn's loyal best friend. I needed to know where she was. I needed to be the one to find her and fix everything.

'Where is she, Sasha? Please, I need to see her,' I stated bluntly, keeping it short and sweet but throwing a plea into the mix in the hope that it might help my case.

'Why? So you can rip her fucking heart out all over again just to watch her break in person? I don't fucking think so.'

My hands shot to my hair in frustration and tugged, the sharp movement causing a jab of pain in my bullet wound. 'Is she OK? At least tell me that much,' I said hesitantly, desperate for something to appease some of the guilt I was carrying.

'OK? *Is she OK?*' Sasha repeated, her volume rising with each word, her eyes piercing into mine with such ferocity that I had to look away. 'Do you even have any idea the pain you've caused her? She fucking adored you, you son of a bitch! You were her entire world and you finish things with her on her wedding day in a letter! *A fucking letter!* You absolute coward.' Sasha jabbed out a hand and poked me in the chest hard enough to make me wince and take a step back. 'Think about it carefully, Oliver, how the fuck do you think she's feeling?'

To be frank, I couldn't even begin to imagine. Broken, hurt and confused, I supposed. This was all my fault. She was broken hearted, and it was all because of me. The slow ache of this realisation came in cold, relentless waves sickening me to the core. Pulling in a breath, I lifted a hand to my hair and scrubbed at my scalp until it hurt.

'Do you know Alexandra from the club?' I asked, making my statement brief in the hopes that I could make a quick explanation to Sasha and get her to tell me where Robyn was.

Sasha frowned at my question, but she nodded slowly. 'Yeah. The blonde ice queen you fucked once upon a time.

What about her? If you left Robyn for that fucking bitch I really will kill you, Oliver, police or no police.'

I winced at her description. Clearly Robyn had shared my history with Sasha. And "ice queen"? It was quite apt, really, because the entire time I'd been stuck with Alex in that hotel room I hadn't seen one shred of real emotion cross her face.

'On the day of the wedding she contacted me and told me to call it all off.' Sasha's eyes lit with anger and immediately I realised that she might be imagining all sorts of incorrect things about me and Alex reigniting our romance. 'She blackmailed me, Sasha. She had a video of… well, it was basically a sex tape containing footage of me and Robyn and other images of someone that looked like me doing all sorts of unspeakably violent things to some woman.'

Sasha's mouth dropped open in shock, her ballsy demeanour briefly calming down. 'What the fuck?'

I nodded grimly and went on. 'She had a full list of contact details for Robyn's family, and she was planning on sending the tape out to them all if I didn't call off the wedding.'

'Why?'

'Because she wanted me,' I stated simply. There was no other way of sugar-coating it.

'Jesus Christ, Oliver. You should have just told her to fuck off.'

Exhausted, I shook my head. 'No, I couldn't, believe me.' My teeth gritted together from tension, making it difficult to continue speaking. 'I couldn't risk her parents seeing that tape.'

Frowning, Sasha tilted her head, no doubt trying to work out if I was bullshitting her. 'Was it really bad enough for you to worry about? What exactly did it show?'

I nodded, grimacing as I recalled the explicit images. 'It was horrific. She was planning on passing off the man in the tape as me and telling Robyn's family that I liked to beat her till she bled. You know her father had that heart attack last year; I couldn't risk the tape being sent to him… the idea that someone would hurt his little girl like the man in that tape?' I shook my head. 'I couldn't imagine how it would make him feel.'

Sasha let out a whooshed breath, and her posture grew marginally less defensive as if she had finally decided to believe me. 'Fucking hell. You're right, he's always been massively protective of her. It could have given him another attack.' She nodded thoughtfully and then frowned. 'But why the awful note and the hurtful phone call? It was torture to see Robyn as she read that letter, Oliver. And the conversation? I swear it nearly killed her when you said you didn't want her.'

Pain and guilt stabbed at me with such force that I felt momentarily winded and had to recover my composure again before speaking. 'I wanted to tell Robyn what was going on so badly, but Alex was very prepared. She had a gun aimed on me the whole time.'

'Holy shit!' Sasha exclaimed, her anger seeming to soften further as she leaned in closer to hear the rest of my tale.

'So, basically, she was very set on winning me and she wanted to cause Robyn as much pain as possible in the process. She scripted that phone call. They were not my words.'

Sasha spun around on the spot and ran her hands roughly through her hair. 'Jesus, this is screwed up. Where's Alex now?'

I drew in a breath and tried to resist the urge to rub at the wound on my shoulder. 'In jail on charges of attempted murder.'

Sasha's eyes widened, but for once Robyn's mouthy best mate seemed lost for words, so, with a heavy sigh, I elaborated.

'She decided if she couldn't have me she'd rather no one did,' I informed her quietly. 'She took a shot at me, but luckily it only scraped my shoulder and in the chaos that followed she got knocked unconscious.' Pausing, I ran a shaky hand gently over the bandage under my shirt, a small dot of rust-coloured blood already seeping through. Scraped was a slight understatement, but it seemed easier than going into too many details.

Tiring of recounting my ordeal, I was now desperate to find Robyn. 'I can explain it all in detail later, but right now I really want to find Robyn, Sasha. Please, where is she?'

Sasha folded her arms and blew out a breath. 'Look, I don't know where she is either, OK? She's been with me for the last two days, but then this afternoon at lunch she was talking about needing some time alone. I nipped out to go to the toilet and when I came back she'd taken the rental car and gone.' She chewed on her lower lip and fidgeted on the spot. 'I'm really fucking worried that she'd going to do something stupid, Oliver. I've never seen her this upset.'

My blood ran cold at her words and I stiffened. Robyn wouldn't do anything to harm herself. Would she? The Robyn I knew wouldn't, she was independent and feisty. Together we were unstoppable, but what about apart? I'd never thought I would be so reliant on another human being, I'd always been arrogant and sure of myself, but the thought of being without Robyn made me feel like the weakest man on the planet.

Shit. I needed to find my girl, and I needed to find her fast.

'I've checked all the hotels in the city, but maybe she's gone back to the place you stayed on your first night here?'

Sasha nodded. 'Maybe. I've just been scouring the city on foot, but I'm headed back to the hotel to check.'

'Keep in touch, OK?' I urged her, backing up my request with a firm stare.

'Yeah, will do. You, too. Let me know if you find her.'

I agreed with a nod, and then we went our separate ways, but I still had no clue where to begin looking. As I stood in the evening sun, feeling totally lost and helpless, my phone began to ring in my pocket and I practically ripped the lining out of my suit in my haste to retrieve it.

Disappointment seared through me when it wasn't Robyn's number that greeted me, and I let out a sigh as I read "Matías Mobile" instead. I wasn't really in the mood to speak to my old school friend but, seeing as he knew about my cluster-fuck of a week, I accepted the call and lifted it to my ear just in case he somehow had some news for me.

'Matías,' I greeted him bluntly, knowing that if he made one attempt at a joke about how I'd come to my bachelor senses and left Robyn at the altar I might well have to go over there and kill him.

'Evening, Oliver. Hell of a few days, hmm?'

So far, all Matías knew was the same as the other wedding guests – that I'd snubbed my bride-to-be ten minutes before our wedding ceremony. He didn't know about the shit with Alexandra, but he did know that I'd spent this afternoon phoning every goddamn person I knew in Barcelona – him included – asking them to keep their eyes open for my girl.

'You could say that.' I closed my eyes and tipped my head back, still unable to fully grasp all that had occurred. 'It's a long fucking story, but I'll have to fill you in later, Matías.'

'I have something here at the club which may cheer you up.' There was nothing at Fantasia apart from people in search of sex and alcohol, and neither of those would cheer me up. Nothing could lighten my spirits except for finding Robyn, and even then I'd no doubt have a massive battle on my hands trying to get her to talk to me after the way I'd treated her.

My jaw tense, I let out a harsh irritated breath. It was just like Matías to think that sex could solve my problems, but a conversation like this was just a waste of my time. I needed to be looking for Robyn.

'*Mierda*, Matías. I know you've never been in love, but seriously? This is going to take more than sex to fix.' I heard a snort of laughter at the other end of the line.

'I realise that, Oliver, I'm not a complete nympho.' I rolled my eyes. Matías might be one of my longest standing friends, but he was also the closest thing to a sex addict that I'd ever encountered. He would fuck anything as long as it had a pulse.

'Chill out, Oliver. I have her here.'

He what?

'E-e-excuse me?' I stuttered.

'Your Robyn, she is with me at Fantasia,' he repeated calmly, as if he hadn't just said the very thing I'd been desperate to hear someone say all afternoon.

My feet were already moving before I'd fully digested his news. 'What? Why the fuck is she with you?' I was monumentally relieved to have located her, but to find out that she was with Matías – the biggest rogue I knew – in his sex club wasn't exactly reassuring. 'If you've laid one finger on her, Matías, I swear to God…'

'*Olive-ee-air*, breathe, my man.' His Spanish pronunciation of my name purred from his tongue in an attempt at soothing me, but it didn't work. Nothing could soothe me in my current mood.

'Of course, I haven't touched her. I may not understand why you left her at the altar, but I know she is yours and yours alone. Believe it or not, she sought me out.'

Why the hell would Robyn go to Fantasia on her own? None of this made any sense to me, but I was nearly at the square where the club was located, so I hurried my pace, determined to find out for myself.

'I'll explain it all when you arrive.'

'You're damn right you will.'

Hanging up the phone, I broke into a run for the final leg of the journey, ignoring the pain in my shoulder as I sprinted over the cobbles.

CHAPTER THIRTY-SIX

Oliver

I slammed a hand onto the huge front doors of Fantasia so hard that they swung open and crashed into the walls behind them with a resounding boom. My entry announced itself, and seconds later I was surrounded by two burly security guards who obviously took offence to my violent entry and were fast attempting to drag me back out the way I had just come.

'¡*Deténgase*! Stop! He is my guest.' Matías's steely voice broke through the chaos surrounding us, and as soon as the bouncers let go of me I stood tall and straightened out my clothes before sending a narrow-eyed stare towards them.

Matías didn't get a much friendlier glance. He was looking decidedly smug as he waited for me, casually leaning on the reception desk of the club with his usual air of arrogance seeping from every pore.

He was in his favoured dark attire; wearing black leather trousers, a black shirt, and a navy-blue velvet jacket. I approached him, feeling unusually wary. Had he pursued Robyn after I'd left her at the wedding ceremony, perhaps? I knew he had always looked at her with interest on our visits here. He did have charm and looks by the bucket load, and Robyn must have been really upset, but even I was struggling to see her turning to a player like him for support or affection in her time of need.

Waving an arm toward the stairs, he nodded once. 'Come, let us talk in private.'

I wanted to demand to see Robyn right this second, but this was his territory and making demands had never worked on my stubborn friend in the past so was unlikely to work now. Drawing in a calming breath, I gave a tight nod and followed him towards the offices.

Once we were away from the curious ears of the reception staff, Matías stopped in the corridor and turned to me. 'I have broken the confidence of your pretty little lady by calling you, Oliver, but you and I have been friends for a long time now, no?'

I nodded my agreement, but the frown still stayed embedded on my brow. 'We have indeed. What do you mean you're breaking her confidence? What's going on Matías, why is Robyn here?'

Matías folded his arms across his chest and gave a shrug. 'I was as surprised as you when I found her on my doorstep this afternoon, but you must believe me, she came here of her own free will.' He raised a hand and rubbed at his perfectly trimmed goatee beard, his shrewd eyes watching me carefully the entire time. 'About three hours ago I was here in my office when the staff told me a girl was downstairs asking for me. I went down, and to my surprise I see your Robyn there. She was very upset, but she said she needed a place to stay where she could have some alone time. She made me promise that if anyone came looking for her I wouldn't tell them she was here.'

I nodded but was still clueless as to why Robyn had come here.

As if reading my mind, Matías went on. 'She said her best friend was very well meaning but a little over the top in her concern and that she needed some space. Robyn said she had attempted to leave the country, but all flights were full, as were the hotels she tried. In a panic, she ended up on my doorstep asking if I could provide her with a secure place to sleep.'

Matías turned away from me and quietly opened the door to

his office. He swung it back to reveal Robyn, curled up in a ball and asleep on the sofa.

The relief of seeing her well and unharmed was so overwhelming that I felt dizzy, it was as though I could finally feel my heart beating again, and for several seconds I had to steady myself on the doorframe so I didn't collapse into an exhausted slump. I couldn't stop myself from greedily taking in every detail of her; she was facing towards us, but even with some hair falling over her face I could see that her cheeks looked deathly pale and she was frowning in her sleep.

'I offered her a proper bed in one of the private rooms, but she looked horrified at the idea and asked for the couch instead.'

A small, fond smile quirked my lips as I remembered how squeamish Robyn still was when it came to the rentable rooms in Club Twist. I sensed Matías turn his gaze onto me and then he gave a full-on smirk.

'She's quite a sweet innocent, isn't she? Was she a virgin when you met her?' Looking across at him, I bristled with irritation at the filthy grin on his face. She hadn't been a virgin, but it still pissed me off that he was even asking such a personal question.

'None of your fucking business, Matías.'

He pursed his lips as he tried to hold in a grin at my heated response. 'Quite. My apologies.' He cast his gaze to Robyn again and back to me. 'Although I'd place money on the fact that she's not quite so innocent now she's with you, my friend? Hmm?'

My nostrils flared as I drew in a breath and tried not to lose my temper with him, but in response Matías merely chuckled and held his hands up in defence. 'I am merely guessing. I know your experimental appetite in the bedroom, Oliver, and young Robyn here clearly has you entranced. I was just curious as to what it was she did to steal your heart.'

My gaze turned back to Robyn and my irritation melted

away as I stared at her. My entire body felt like it was coming alive again, just because I was near her. 'She did nothing other than be herself,' I murmured. 'She's incredible.'

There was a quiet moment between us and then Matías caught me in his interested gaze again. 'If she is so incredible why did you leave her on your wedding day?'

Once again, the mention of my actions made me feel like I'd been punched in the gut and my eyes flickered shut. 'Long fucking story, but let's just say it wasn't by choice, and that I plan to make everything right again now.'

I knew he was staring at me, no doubt in open curiosity about the events of the past few days, but I didn't have time to enlighten him now. I loved Robyn with all my heart, and I didn't want to waste another second in making sure she knew it.

'I'll explain it all to you later over a nice glass of Spanish red from your expansive cellar,' I suggested, but my eyes remained fixed on Robyn as she slept on the sofa. 'She looks upset even in her sleep,' I added, still focusing on how deathly pale she looked.

'I swear to you that I have not placed a finger on her, Oliver. My only role in this was to give her somewhere safe to stay.'

Dragging my gaze to his, I held out a hand toward him. 'I see that now. Thank you, Matías, I owe you.' Shaking his hand, I held on to the grip and gave him a grateful look. 'And thank you for calling me. I know she asked you not to tell anyone, but I really appreciate it. I desperately need to make her understand what happened.'

'You owe me nothing. It is no problem. But once you two are sorted I shall take you up on that offer of the story. I am most intrigued. Perhaps we could even crack open one of my special bottles of Cognac.'

Giving a heavy sigh, I nodded. 'Yeah. It's a pretty stressful story, so we might need the strong stuff.'

'I hope you sort things out; you two are clearly a perfect match.' Pausing, he sighed and then turned to leave me in the room alone. 'You may need to grovel your arse off, my friend. I'm fairly sure she cried herself to sleep,' he informed me grimly, and my chest tightened uncomfortably.

I hated that I'd done this to her. Caused her so much distress that she had cried herself to sleep not just tonight, but probably the past night as well. Fuck. It was killing me inside.

Once I was alone with her, I closed the door and then moved closer and watched her as she continued to sleep. Now I was just a few feet away I could see that Matías was right: Robyn had tear tracks across her pale cheeks, and that sight alone caused me to let out a pained wheeze. This week was supposed to have been the happiest of our lives, and yet one unwelcome intervention from Alex had turned it into the stuff of horror films.

I wanted to touch her so badly, wake her immediately, and set her straight about it all. But I didn't want to startle her, and I knew that after my behaviour this week she might not want me to touch her anyway. So instead of leaning in and scooping her into my arms as I yearned to, I softly cleared my throat instead.

Her eyelids fluttered, but then she seemed to drift back towards sleep again, so I repeated the action, coughing a little louder and watching as her muscles tensed and she blinked as she woke up.

As she focused on me there was a second or two where Robyn was obviously still sleepy enough that she didn't remember the events of the week, because her face filled with a smile and her eyes shone with happiness and love like they always did when we were together. Then a cloud of shock and anger swept her features, and as her expression turned to panic, she abruptly sat upright and shoved herself backwards on the sofa away from me.

'Robyn, *cariño*, it's OK, it's me, we need to talk.'

Her eyes were glassy as tears instantly built, and she shook her head rapidly. 'You said plenty on the phone, Oliver, just leave.'

'Fuck! I'm not going anywhere. The things I said on the phone were bullshit, they weren't real. Let me explain.' I tried to reach for her, but she let out a horrified squeak, scrabbled even further along the couch, and pulled her knees up to her chest in an attempt at making herself small and unreachable.

'Don't touch me!'

A disgusted grunt left my lips as she tried to avoid my contact. She was mine, and I needed to feel her just as much as she did me. I shuffled closer until she had no further wiggle room and then clasped both of her hands in mine, letting out a small satisfied sigh as our connection sparked and fizzed between us like normal.

Normal. Dios, I couldn't wait until things between us were back to boring ol' normal.

I could see in her eyes that she felt the spark fire up between us, she always did, so it would be no different now just because she was angry with me. In fact, anger was no doubt intensifying her feelings. We didn't argue as such, but *dios*, on the occasions that we'd had a disagreement the makeup sex was always incredibly potent and explosive.

She tried to pull her hands from my grasp with impressive strength, but she could never out-tug me, and I held on tight and gave a firm shake of my head. 'We're meant to be together, Robyn. Nothing can stop me touching you.'

Her face screwed up into a frown, and I could clearly see confusion as it began mixing with her anger. I understood perfectly well why – just a few days ago I had told her I no longer wanted her in my life, and now here I was declaring that we were meant to be together and grabbing hold of her hands. It must be quite a mind-fuck for her.

'Robyn, I need to… *oooff…*' My explanation was halted as the air was forced from my lungs on a sharp inhale. Robyn had thrust a leg forwards and kicked me in the chest. I was so shocked that my grip fell away from her hands as I clutched at my solar plexus, gasping for breath and completely winded. I watched in astounded pride as my feisty girl jumped up from the couch and stood in the furthest corner of the room, glaring at me.

'I said, don't fucking touch me. Don't make me repeat myself again, Oliver,' she spat, her entire frame bristling with determination.

A choked bark of laughter left my crippled chest at her words – words that I had often said to her at the start of our relationship when I'd told her how much I hated repeating myself. But Robyn wasn't laughing today so I sobered my expression and nodded once to signal my compliance.

I stood with difficulty. My shoulder was now burning with pain, and my chest was still cramped and winded. One hand rubbed at my sternum in an attempt at helping my poor lungs get some breath back in them, but it was no good, I was still gasping and wheezing.

Glancing at Robyn, I saw her wincing with guilt and hope flared in my chest. If she felt guilty about hurting me then that meant through all her anger and pain she still cared about me.

In my mind everything was fixable as long as she still wanted me.

I held out my arms to my sides and offered her a free shot. 'Hit me again. I fucking deserve it for what I've put you through.'

She frowned, her eyes briefly dropping to my torso and then slowly dragging up my body until she found my face. Normally it thrilled me when I caught her doing a slow perusal of my body – it was a nice little affirmation that she still found me just as attractive – but today I couldn't for the life of me decide if she were thinking about ripping me to pieces or ripping my suit from my body.

'No.'

My heart cramped at the realisation that she didn't want to hurt me, not even after all the shit I'd put her through. The kick had been a knee-jerk reaction brought about by her panic to break our touch, nothing more.

'You can leave, or you can talk. Just don't touch me,' she whispered, before swallowing loudly. Her eyes clouded over, and she wrapped her arms tightly around her middle as if trying to shield herself from me and the pain I had inflicted. 'I can't cope with that.'

Her words were far more agonising than any punch or kick could have been, and I accepted her demand with a sad nod of my head and moved across the room. I stopped dead when I was about three paces from her and she held up a hand to tell me that I was close enough.

We stared at each other in silence for at least a minute until she raised a hand and gave a tired rub at her temple. 'Oliver, I'm so confused…' Her voice was pleading now, the anger in her tone had evaporated and her eyes were latched on mine as if she were totally adrift and had no idea what to do. It seemed she was looking at me to lead the way, which was just fine by me, because I certainly had some explaining to do, and the quicker I did it, the quicker I could have her in my arms again.

'This is going to sound like utter bullshit, but you have to trust me, Robyn. Every word I am about to say is God's honest truth.'

She stayed silent, but I saw a minute nod of her head to indicate that I should start. With a grimace, I cast my mind back to Saturday morning and began.

'Saturday morning, while I was waiting for you before the start of the wedding, I got an email. It was from an unknown sender, which I would usually ignore, but the subject of the email was your name…' I paused and ran a hand through my hair. 'I was curious, so I opened it. It contained a video, a phone number, a list of email addresses, and a simple message: "*watch this and then call me. If you don't call me I will send this video to every email address listed.*'"

So far so good. Robyn was still listening to me, but her eyes reflected the confusion I had felt when I'd first pressed "play" on that despicable video.

'It was a video of you and me having sex,' I stated bluntly, watching as her eyes widened in surprise. I still had no idea how Alex had got that footage, but it appeared to be from one of the rare occasions that we'd had sex at Club Twist. I'd be checking all the private rooms for hidden cameras as soon as we got home, that was for sure.

'Both of our faces were clear, and at the start of the film a caption came across the screen that said…' I drew in a breath, knowing that Robyn wasn't going to like the next part. 'It said, "*See what Oliver does to Robyn when he fucks her.*"'

Her frown deepened, and she tightened her arms around her chest. 'What?'

I saw her bite her bottom lip and had to fight every urge in my body not to reach out to her. 'After showing a brief video of us, the clip changed to a man beating the shit out of a woman. Obviously, it wasn't us, but the camera angle made it look so much like us…' I shook my head, the violent visions still engrained in my memory. 'They were in the same room, and both were naked. She was tied to a bed, and he was…' *Dios*, it repelled me so much I could barely even say it. 'He was using whips and floggers on her body until she was crying and bleeding and then…' I swallowed, and tasted bile in my mouth. 'Let's just say that as things progressed it didn't seem consensual.'

Robyn's eyes were bulging with horror, but I needed to make it very clear for her, so she understood why I'd taken the actions I had on Saturday. 'He raped her, Robyn. Brutally and repeatedly, and the whole thing looked like it was me doing that to you.'

After her loud gasp, shocked silence hung heavily between us, then she shook her head. 'That's… that's awful. But why did it make you call off the wedding? I don't understand.'

My eyes held Robyn's the entire time I spoke, desperately hoping that she could see I was telling the truth. 'The author of the email told me to call off the wedding and go to her, or else she would send the video out to a whole load of people.'

'She? Who was it?'

'Alexandra.' Lowering my head, I let out a long sigh and then joined my gaze with Robyn's again. 'Seems you were right when you said she still wanted me. Once I had watched the video, I called the number in the email and she answered. I couldn't believe it at first, but she got straight to the point, saying that she wanted me for herself.'

It was clear from the clouded expression on Robyn's face that she still didn't quite grasp the whole story.

'If I didn't call off the wedding she was going to send the video out to all the email addresses on her list, and at the top were your parents.' Robyn gasped at my words and I softened my tone as I continued. 'Alex was also kind enough to remind me about your father's weakened state of health since his heart attack.'

Robyn was finding it difficult to breathe now, and all I wanted to do was hold her and comfort her, but I refrained, knowing that she must be struggling to straighten this mess out in her head.

'You thought it might give him another attack...' she guessed quietly.

I nodded slowly, glad that she was latching on to the important details. 'I did. Honestly Robyn, when I first saw the video, even *I* thought that both the clips showed you and me... Except obviously we never do anything violent and non-consensual like that. If I could confuse the two of us with the people on the tape, then the chance that your parents might was too great to risk. If your father had suffered a heart attack because of the shock of that tape I would never have been able to forgive myself.'

'It was really that bad?' she asked softly.

My face contorted to a grimace. 'It was. Honestly, it was so brutal that it's actually in a police evidence locker right now.' Robyn seemed to be accepting what I was saying, and I felt the days of tension starting to slowly release from my shoulders. 'I decided to go and meet Alex as she had demanded, and I was planning on overpowering her, deleting the video, and then returning to the wedding. Unfortunately, she had considered that I might do something like that and when I arrived she turned a gun on me.'

Robyn sucked in a breath so rapidly that it hissed through her teeth, and in response I felt my gunshot wound give a pulse of pain as if reminding me of how bloody lucky I had been. 'I'd never in a million years expected her to have a weapon, so I ended up trapped there.'

'What was she expecting? That you would just give up on your life – on me – and settle down with her?'

I ran my hand along my jaw, still unable to get my head around what exactly Alex had been thinking. 'I think that's exactly what she hoped for. She told me we would be happy together, and that if I didn't put in the effort the video would be sent out to not only your family, but my parents and my colleagues in the accountancy world. In short, she was willing to risk your father's health, my family's opinion of me, and my career to get what she wanted.'

I could see shock in her face, but confusion, too, and I realised that she hadn't fully grasped what I was getting at. 'If I couldn't prove it wasn't me in that tape I would have gone to prison for violent assault and rape, Robyn.'

Robyn shivered as my words sunk in.

'With the gun in her hand and her threats on the table I had no choice but to comply with her demands until I got the opportunity to overpower her.'

'So, she was with you when I phoned?' Pain flashed in her eyes as she mentioned my hurtful phone call on the day of our wedding and I immediately wanted to set her straight.

'Yes. I couldn't try to pass any message to you, or tell you it was all a lie, because she would have sent the video out. I'm so sorry for what I said. For the record, they were her words, not mine. She wrote down exactly what I had to say to you.'

'She wrote it down?'

'Yes,' I replied grimly. 'After your first few calls Alex realised that you weren't going to stop phoning until you spoke to me, so she wrote down what she wanted me to say. Told me if I deviated from it at all she would press "send" on the emails.'

Robyn nodded slowly and puffed out a sigh. 'I can't deny that I'm relieved to hear that... I... I can't stand the thought of you with other women.' Her eyes dropped away from mine. '*Hundreds* of other women,' she added in a pained whisper. It was immediately obvious that Robyn had been dwelling on what had been said between us, and even though I'd told her they weren't my words she was still bloody well lingering on it now.

'Hey. Enough. I haven't been with hundreds of women, *cariño*. Like I said, that was just spiteful talk Alex made up. She knew it would hurt you to think that, so she made me say it.' In truth, that total probably wasn't far from the mark. I'd certainly led a far from salubrious life before I'd met Robyn, fucking anything that had taken my interest, but that was all in the past now, and dredging it up wasn't going to help put the sparkle back in my girl's eyes.

Robyn silently absorbed everything I'd said so far and then a deep frown creased her brow.

'So you were with Alex for two days, and she wanted you for herself... Does that mean you and she...?'

My heart sunk as I realised I was going to have to confess what had happened between Alex and me.

As much as I wanted to lie to reassure Robyn and help me feel like less of a shit, I knew I couldn't keep it from her. Our married life would not start on a bed of secrets and lies; no good would ever come of that.

Keeping my voice level, I stared at her and prayed that she would hear the truth in my words without pushing me to actually say it. 'I did what I had to do to keep you safe.'

Robyn sucked in a small breath and stared up at me. 'You fucked her,' she stated softly, her eyes widening with obvious pain.

'No…' It was technically the truth, but I still felt the weight of this explanation weighing heavily on me.

'Oliver, just tell me,' Robyn demanded. 'It's OK if you did. She had a gun and she was threatening both you and me… I might not like it, but… but I get it.'

'She tried repeatedly to initiate it, but I swear I didn't have sex with her, Robyn. Eventually she started to threaten your life and that was when I realised I couldn't avoid it any longer so… so I… I used my hand to get her off. Tried to fool her into thinking that I was coming around to the idea of being with her. It seemed to keep her satisfied and bought me a little more time.'

Robyn's jaw had tensed so much that I could see a muscle jumping along it, but I persevered with my confession, determined not to keep anything from her. 'I'm so sorry. I hated doing it because I knew it would hurt you, but at the time I couldn't see any other option.'

Robyn stayed silent, but eventually I saw her give a small nod of acceptance. She'd thought I'd had full sex with Alex, so perhaps the reality was a bit of a relief. 'I stayed fully dressed, and if it makes you feel better my dick was as soft as a marshmallow the entire time.'

She gave a small, dry laugh, but kept her eyes lowered away from mine as if she were struggling to take it all in and I started to panic that I was going to lose her all over again. 'You're the only one I want, Robyn. I had to do it to keep you safe.'

Pulling in a wheezy breath, Robyn nodded. 'I understand. It's OK.' Her words sounded sincere, but her gaze was still lowered, and a little crinkle between her eyebrows indicated her continued uncertainty.

'Look at me, *cariño*.' My voice was firm, and her head immediately popped up as if she were unable not to follow my command, a reaction which I fucking loved and instantly aroused me. '*You* are the only woman I want. You are the only women I will *ever* want. Understand?'

Deciding that I'd had enough of her no touching rule, I took her by surprise and pulled her towards me. I tucked her into my chest and wrapped my arms around her tense frame until I finally felt her relax against me.

Thank God she was accepting my touch. I'm not sure what I would have done if she'd tried to fight me and push me away again.

We stood like that for several silent seconds, and then, without saying a word, Robyn took hold of my wrist and pulled me towards the small en suite bathroom attached to the office. I wasn't entirely sure what she was doing, but from the intent look on her face she had something in mind, so I kept quiet and watched with curiosity as she unbuttoned my right shirt cuff and began rolling it up.

Once my sleeve was neatly tucked up by my elbow she tugged me towards the sink and silently began soaping up my hand. She washed each finger with care until my entire hand was surely the cleanest it had ever been, but I was still in the dark about what she was doing.

'Was it just that hand?' she asked quietly, staring down at my fingers and chewing on her lower lip.

'I'm not sure what you mean. Was what just that hand?'

Robyn raised her head and looked at me with a determined gleam in her eyes. 'That you touched her with. Was it just that hand?'

Ohhh. Now it all made sense. Robyn was cleaning me up,

removing the traces of Alex and claiming me back as hers. Was it wrong that her little show of possessiveness really turned me on? Probably, so I tried to hide my growing arousal by turning my body, and then nodded. 'Yes, just that hand.'

Her eyes drifted from my gaze and settled upon my mouth. She frowned and lifted a thumb up to graze across my lips. 'Did… did you kiss her?' she asked, her voice coming out in a dry croak.

'No. I swear to God.' And it was the complete truth. We had not kissed, not even once. I wouldn't tell Robyn that Alex had tried to kiss me, though, and the only way I'd avoided it was by upping the moves with my hand until she'd had her eyes rolling back in her head and was boneless in my arms from the strength of her orgasm.

'Good,' she mumbled. Giving a swift nod, she picked up the nail brush and gave my hand another going over until the skin was actually starting to sting a little. I didn't complain – if it appeased my fiery little Robyn then I would take the slight discomfort.

While she was washing me, I decided to make sure she knew that I hadn't wanted any of this. 'I never wanted to leave you at the wedding, Robyn, you have to understand that. I was forced by her sick video, and the threats to show it to your family. I really had no choice.'

Robyn continued to scrub at my nails, but she glanced up at me and nodded. 'I get it. I understand.' She drew in a breath and nibbled on her lower lip, her scrubbing faltering slightly until she was just holding my hand in the sink. 'And… and I satisfy you? I… I'm enough?'

My eyes flickered closed at her question. Fucking Alex. I hated that she'd put these doubts in Robyn's mind. 'Fuck, yes. I don't want or need anyone else, OK?'

My words seemed to start to sink in because she dried my hand off and pulled us out of the bathroom before snuggling herself into my chest with a soft sigh. I matched her contented sound with one of my own and leaned down to place a gentle kiss on the top of her head.

'You are everything I've ever dreamed of and more.' Robyn looked up at me from where she was snuggled against my chest and blinked, as if she were struggling with my compliment. She blushed the most gorgeous shade of red as she seemed to pick up on the depth of sincerity in my gaze. 'You and me. We're meant to be together. Don't question it, and don't ever doubt it. OK?'

I felt her body completely relax against mine and she nodded with a soft smile. 'OK.'

Stroking a hand over her hair, I thanked my lucky stars that she was accepting me again after all this bullshit. After my awful confession that I'd had to get Alex off in order to buy myself some time, I'd started to doubt if she would ever forgive me, but Robyn seemed to be taking it all rather well. If she'd told me that she'd pleasured another man I think I would have killed someone. Not to mention my story of blackmail, sex tapes, and guns… It did sound completely made up.

'If you need proof of any of this I have the email, and I could get one of the detectives to speak to you. Alex is being detained here while they question her.'

'She's in jail? For what, blackmail?'

'That… and attempted murder,' I added with reluctance. I'd been hoping to hide that from Robyn to save her worrying but, seeing as I had a bandage covering my wound, I supposed it would have come out pretty soon anyway. 'They also want to know who the people in the tape are, so they can find the woman and see if she's OK.'

Robyn heard my words, but only focused on two of them. 'Attempted murder…?' she whispered, her voice high and thin.

Swallowing hard, I nodded slowly and then pulled the neck of my shirt to the side to reveal the bandage there.

'She… she hurt you?'

'She shot me,' I clarified.

Robyn sucked in a horrified breath and her face paled as she scrabbled onto her tiptoes and gently ran a finger around the edge of the dressing.

I let her fuss over me, enjoying the feeling of having her touch me again, even if it was to ease her worry. 'Yes. When I realised that she really was crazy enough to try and follow through on her plan I knew I had to do something, so I waited for her to be distracted and then I tackled her. Unfortunately, she wasn't quite as distracted as I had thought.'

'Oh my God… Oliver…' Robyn now sounded as winded as I had felt when she'd kicked me earlier, and tears brimmed in her eyes.

'Hey, it's OK, it only skimmed the surface of my skin. It's barely even a graze.' Her eyes darted to my neck and then back to the bandage. She was obviously thinking that if it had "grazed" me a few inches to the left it would quite possibly have hit my main artery and things could have been a whole lot worse, which was exactly what the paramedic had said.

From the trembling in her lip and shaking in her hands I realised that all the stress was becoming too much for Robyn. I dragged her back into my arms and gently rocked her until I finally felt her calm and settle against me.

Time passed slowly by as we stood like that, both of us silent and absorbing everything that had gone on, but finally Robyn pulled in a long breath and leaned back. 'I want to see it.'

For a second, I thought she was talking about my wound, but then she frowned and looked me straight in the eye. 'You said you have the email. I want to see the video.'

I shook my head. 'You really don't, it's not pleasant watching.'

'I do. I want to see how far she'd go to take you from me.'

I could see from her eyes that Robyn wasn't going to be deterred, so with a reluctant sigh I pulled out my phone. I'd let her watch a little, just enough to satisfy her obvious curiosity, and then stop before it got to the really abhorrent parts. Drawing in a deep breath, I nodded. I unlocked the phone and scrolled through my emails before bracing myself as I pressed "play".

The first shot started, and I knew Robyn would recognise the setting as one of the tamer rooms at Club Twist. She had never been a huge fan of using the private rooms at the club, she didn't like the idea of how many people had used them before us, so we tended to do our sessions at home, but on the occasions where we did do a scene at the club this room was her choice.

Robyn and I were naked and caught in a passionate embrace. Our hands were moving everywhere, lips devouring each other, and eyes burning with love whenever we broke for air and shared an intense glance.

It was sexual, and erotic, but not perverted, and certainly not violent. To me, the love we felt for each other seemed obvious in every reverent touch and shared stare. We were making love, pure and simple, and if it wasn't for the fact that our nakedness would no doubt embarrass them, I really wouldn't have cared if my family and Robyn's had seen this part of the video.

Unfortunately, that section only lasted a few seconds, and after a moment of dimmer lighting the view cleared and the horror show began. The room was the same one, but the girl in this film was no longer Robyn. Unfortunately, with her face averted, her slim body and similar hair made it hard to see the difference. She was kneeling on all fours with her head hanging down, and the man, who looked a hell of a lot like me in his build, was standing with his back to the camera, naked and holding a whip in his left hand.

Alex must have gone to some fairly arduous lengths to find footage of people with such similarities to Robyn and me. The editing was so smooth that it honestly just looked like a later snippet of the first film.

On screen the man began hitting the woman over and over, throwing in hard slaps with his hand and pelts with his whip until her shoulders were shaking with her sobs and her back was reddened and bleeding in several places.

This continued for several minutes until the woman was visibly distressed and struggling to get away from him, only to be held back by the restraints on her hands and ankles. Finally, the man dropped the whip and took hold of her hips. He dragged her thrashing body backwards and subdued her with his strength.

Grimacing, I moved my thumb across the screen and stopped the video. 'You've seen enough,' I whispered. Robyn didn't need to see the viciousness with which he took her, forcing his cock into both of her openings and throwing his head back in triumph when she finally gave up fighting and collapsed below him in a limp, sobbing heap as he continued to have his way with her for a further fifteen minutes.

'Jesus…' Robyn wheezed, fisting my shirt with trembling fingers and looking up at me with wide, horrified eyes. 'You're right… They look so much like us. Fuck, Oliver…'

'I know. You see now why I couldn't let your parents see that film, yes?'

She nodded, rendered mute from shock for a second or two. 'My dad would have freaked if he'd seen that. We could have proved it wasn't us eventually, but the damage could already have been done.' She stared at me, pale and obviously thinking back over what she had seen. 'We both know that you're not left handed, and he had tattoos on the insides of his wrists, which you don't, but Dad wouldn't have realised that. He would just have seen you doing all those terrible things to me.'

I hummed my agreement and nodded, relief pouring into my expression when it became clear that Robyn completely and utterly believed me and fully grasped how seriously I'd had to take the video when it had first arrived on Saturday.

'She's a lunatic.' Robyn absently fiddled with the buttons on my shirt.

'She is, but after the hell of the last few days I want to forget about her now and reconnect with you, OK?'

Robyn gave a small smile and nodded her agreement. 'OK.'

I stooped down, took hold of her arse cheeks, and lifted her up my front until our eyes were level. She wrapped her legs around my waist to keep herself steady.

'Oliver! Your wound, be careful!' she yelped, trying to free herself from my grasp.

'It's fine, Robyn.' In truth there was a slight sting, but nothing I couldn't cope with. 'Hold me, please?'

At my request she gave a small nod and then looped her arms carefully around my shoulders before she buried her face in my neck on a long, contented sigh.

'Now I feel like I'm home,' she mumbled against my skin, and those few words were filled with such emotion that I felt like my heart was going to burst.

Totally overwhelmed by everything that had happened, I cuddled her to me even tighter, ignoring the burn in my shoulder and not wanting to ever let her go. I would *never* let her go, not again. I'd literally do anything to keep this woman with me until the day I died.

'Fucking hell, Robyn, this week has been hideous.'

'You swear in English a lot more than you used to,' she observed mildly, pointedly ignoring my comment about the past week as if she couldn't bear to think about it anymore. She was right in her observation, too. I'd never sworn in English until I met Robyn, but God, did she drive me wild enough to swear in every language known to man.

'I'm so sorry for everything I put you through.' Whatever hell I had been going through while I dealt with Alex, I knew it must have been ten times worse for Robyn because she'd been totally in the dark about it all. She had thought that I'd left her. For three whole days, this girl who I treasured more than my own life had thought that I had turned my back on her and gone.

I could barely begin to imagine how that must have felt, but I tried to consider it… How would I have coped if things had been reversed and Robyn had told me that I could never satisfy her, and she was leaving me? Just thinking it made me feel sick to my stomach and so fucking vulnerable that I shuddered.

Swallowing down a lump in my throat, I tried to settle my anxiety by losing myself in the one thing that kept me sane – Robyn – so I indulged in a deep inhale of her hair. I had no clue if it was the scent of her shampoo that I so adored, or her natural smell, but whatever it was, I bloody loved it.

Robyn lifted her head and met my gaze with an understanding stare. It was tinged with tiredness, and I could still see the evidence of her recent stress in the blue smudges under both of her eyes and the paleness of her complexion. I'd put my girl through hell and back, and I hated myself for it almost more than I could bear.

'I feel like I've aged ten years in the last three days,' I murmured, adjusting my grip on her so I could rub up and down her back with one hand.

Robyn leaned back slightly to create some space between our bodies and then, to my surprise, she dragged my shirt from within my waistband and dipped her hands under the hem. Her fingers began a slow inspection of my belly, and then moved upwards over the bumps of my abs until they were resting on my pecs. Fluttering her eyelashes at me, she nibbled on her lower lip and smiled.

'You don't feel like you've aged to me,' she whispered huskily. Her gaze didn't leave mine as her hands continued to tease me, and as I stared into her beautiful bluey-grey eyes I saw a distinctly lusty twinkle settle in them. 'In fact, from where I'm sitting you feel mighty fine.' She squeezed her thighs around my waist and then scraped her nails gently across my pecs before digging them in just enough to make me suck in a breath and send a bolt of blood to my cock.

Feeling playful, was she? After the stress of my recent confessions I had not expected this at all, but Christ, I couldn't say it was unwelcome.

Ever since I'd laid eyes on her again I'd desperately wanted to bury myself inside her to claim her back. She was mine, and after all the rejection she must have been feeling these past few days, I wanted to make things right between us again. *Needed* to. As I stared at her it suddenly became of utmost importance to show her how much she meant to me, how important she was to me, and how much I craved her more than my next breath.

Gripping her tighter so she wouldn't fall, I spun us around and backed Robyn into the wall. In a much-practised move, I cupped the back of her head to make sure she didn't hurt herself if my move was too hard. Which it usually was, because whenever I was pressing Robyn to a wall like this I was usually hot, hard, and desperate for her, and not in full control of my strength.

Who was I kidding? I might play it cool and composed, but I was always desperate for this woman, had been since day one.

Breath gushed from her lungs as she hit the wall and I was glad I'd taken the time to at least protect her head. Her eyes opened wide in surprise at our new position, but then, to my delight, she took the lead and fisted my shirt before dragging my mouth down to meet hers.

Dios. Her taste. It was incredible, and I simply couldn't get enough. These last few days had felt like forever. It was the longest I'd gone without touching her or tasting her for months, and I never wanted to go that long again in my lifetime. It was the most explosive of reunions, teeth clashing as our lips melded together and breaths mixed in a desperate haze of desire. It was hurried and lusty and untidy, but utterly perfect. Utterly us.

Robyn clearly wasn't content to leave our reunion at just a kiss, because after several minutes of our mouths melding passionately she began fidgeting against me, the heat of her core rubbing against my trousers right over my solid cock until I growled and thrust it against her.

I wasn't convinced that sex was an entirely sensible idea with the images of that awful video fresh in both of our minds, but like always, Robyn seemed to read my thoughts perfectly. 'Distract us, Oliver. Good memories to wash away the bad… please? I need you back. I need you inside me.'

Needed me inside her? Well, when she put it like that I was hardly going to turn her down, was I?

There was barely a second to gasp a breath, because the next moment her mouth had found mine in a kiss so desperate and hungry that it was all I could do to keep up with her.

I knew exactly what Robyn was doing; she was trying to claim me back after I'd been with Alex, reassure herself that I was hers and only hers, but what she wasn't considering was that I wanted to do exactly the same. I felt dirty and disgusted with myself every time I remembered how I'd made Alex come, and all I wanted to do was erase that memory and claim Robyn back, too.

Besides, she seemed to be trying to take the lead, and there was only one dominant persona in this room, so I pressed her into the wall to support her weight and then captured her hands. I pinned them above her head and attacked her mouth with a new hunger that seemed to surprise both of us.

A low, lusty moan left her mouth at my raised tempo, but after kissing me back for a few minutes she twisted away from my kisses and made eye contact with me, her gaze filled with desire and love so obvious that it made my dick swell even harder than before.

'I want to touch you, Oliver.' She briefly dropped her eyes to my shoulder where the bandage was once again hidden by my shirt. 'I need to feel you below my fingertips.' It seemed fairly obvious that my girl was still dwelling on my gunshot and the fact that I could have been injured far more seriously. After staring at her for a few more seconds, I nodded and released her hands so that we could unite in our desperation to reconnect.

I would never admit it to Robyn vocally, but it had felt like my life had flashed before my eyes when I'd heard that gun go off, so I needed her touch to reassure me just as much as she needed to give it.

Robyn ran her fingers across my body, touching and rubbing gently for a few seconds before her desperation won out and she began scrabbling at my clothing. I was craving the feel of her skin on mine, and I didn't have to wait long, because she gripped the hem of my shirt and peeled it up until it was looped under my arms.

'Off…' she begged, tugging at the material, and as I leaned away I saw her face was flushed and her gorgeous lips were slightly swollen and moist from our desperate kisses. Possessiveness rose inside me and I nodded, shifting my stance to support her weight and raise my arms above my head.

As soon as she could, she peeled the shirt from my body and threw it to the side. Her fingers scratched across my arms, my back, and dug through my hair, but things abruptly slowed down as Robyn's eyes settled on my bandage again. She made a small, mumbled noise of concern as her fingertips rose and flitted across the area, and so I instantly set about easing her concerns by kissing her again and gripping her hips so I could thrust my groin against her stomach.

'It's fine, don't worry.' I'd had enough of being soft and reassuring. I needed her, and I needed her now. 'I'm yours, Robyn. You are the one I want to spend my life with, the only one I want to touch, the only one I want to fuck until you scream so hard you can't speak. Understand?' My tone was low and urgent, and I knew she needed to hear the reassurance just as much as I needed to give it.

She bit down on her lower lip as my blunt words sunk in, and my cock lurched even further as an embarrassed blush coloured her cheeks at my deliberately blatant word choices. Then she nodded. 'Yes. I know. I love you, Oliver.'

'I fucking adore you.' I crashed my lips down onto hers and kissed her until she moaned into my mouth and went limp against me.

CHAPTER THIRTY-SEVEN

Robyn

'I fucking adore you.' His words made my heart swell, and I repeated them over and over in my mind until I was almost frantic with the need to have him inside me. It had been way too long, and now I was over the shock of finding out everything that had occurred between him and Alex in the past three days – well, almost over the shock of it – I desperately wanted to reconnect with him.

Our relationship wasn't just about sex. It might have started that way, I suppose, with my research mission at Club Twist, but that definitely wasn't how it was now. However, the physical side of things would always be a big part of who we were as a couple – we just clicked when we were together, and that connection was even more potent during sex.

'Let me put you down while we undress,' he muttered, sounding irritated that he had to separate us, even if it was only for a few moments. Oliver lowered me to the floor, and as soon as my feet touched the carpet I ripped off my clothing in record speed. I sunk to my knees and pushed his hands aside as I began tearing at the fly of his suit trousers.

My fingers were shaking from the mixture of lust and adrenalin in my system, but finally I succeeded in ripping the fabric apart and dragging his trousers and boxers down his legs in one go.

Oliver kicked them aside, and as his cock sprung free I froze in my kneeling position and just stared up at him. What a sight. From down here he towered over me, looking even taller and more muscular because of the angle. His thighs were right in front of my face and so gorgeous, all muscled and broad, and then there was his cock… It was already fully erect and bobbing around as if daring me to touch it.

The sight of him, so hard and excited because of me, did nothing to cool my lust, and as a bead of pre-come escaped from the slit I couldn't help but descend upon his shaft, taking as much of him into my mouth as I could until he bumped against the back of my throat.

'*Dios*, Robyn!' His breath escaped him in a hissed curse as I set about sucking on him as if my life depended upon it. He was solid but got even harder when one of his hands slid into my hair and grasped at the long strands before guiding my head back and forth along his shaft. I smiled around him, finding it amusing that regardless of the situation he always felt the urge to be in control, and that I always wanted it that way, too.

'So deep… Fuck…' he groaned, and I smiled around my mouthful of him, pleased to be having such an effect. My tongue teased the thick veins on the underside and swirled around the broad top until he gripped my head and attempted to pull me away.

'I need to be inside you.' His commanding tone always sent desire and lust shooting through me and I instantly stopped my movements and looked up at him, wondering if he planned on taking me against the wall – it was one of his favourite positions.

Oliver smiled down at me, but behind his expression I could see tension in his jaw and shoulders showing just how much he was currently struggling to hold himself in check. He wanted me – badly – and that realisation thrilled me to the core.

I placed my hands on his thighs and slowly slid them up his body as I stood, making sure to tease him plenty along the way and trail my fingers over all the spots that I knew drove him wild. Once I was standing, I found Oliver watching me in delighted fascination, as if seeing me so affected by him was reassuring to him somehow. Perhaps it was; he might have been worried that I would be angry with him for what happened with Alex, but that couldn't be further from the truth. The stuff with Alex was done now, and I was just so bloody relieved to have him back in one piece.

He took my hand, dragged me towards the sofa, and then laid himself down on the leather before patting his lap. Grinning, I practically leaped onto him, straddling his body and immediately moving myself into position.

I lifted my body, lined up the tip of his shaft with my opening, and prepared myself for something seriously special. I could feel it in the charged air around us, but even if I hadn't been able to, I just knew this was going to be good because we never went this long without something physical occurring between us.

The thick head of his erection began to enter me, pushing apart my sensitive flesh until I had to pause, my leg muscles quivering with the attempt at holding myself up. As much as I was tempted to drop down onto him, I knew from experience that he was always a tight fit, and with nearly a week since he'd last been inside me I was going to need some stretching. I edged him into me a little at a time, absorbing the delicious stretch with a low, drawn-out groan.

'Fuck, Robyn. Yes. Take me. I'm all yours, baby.' As I neared the end of him the fullness became almost too much. There was a hint of pain, but it was mixed with exquisite pleasure. Pleasure and pain, but it was the exact perfect balance for me.

Our eyes were joined in a burning stare that seemed like it would last for eternity, and as I sunk down onto the final inch of him I felt so connected to him that my emotions nearly overwhelmed me.

Oliver's hands were flexing repeatedly on my hips, which I knew was his way of holding himself back from taking over the control, so I began to move to give us both the friction we were craving. I circled my hips over and over again, feeling his length inside me hitting against all the right places and quickly driving me towards an orgasm.

This was incredible, but my slow movements obviously weren't enough for Oliver because he gripped my hips and I found myself turning and being flipped onto my back. In a mere millisecond, I was caged below Oliver as he let out a lusty growl and plunged back inside me again.

'Mine,' he stated, his expression filled with possessive desire as he reared back. From the dark look on his face I knew this was about to be some of his rougher, harder sex, and oh God, was I right. His entire body jacked forward on a plunge that was so hard and so deep I could barely deal with the intensity of it. He'd managed to rub my G-spot and slam against my clit with such perfection that my vision blurred for a second and a yelp flew from my mouth as pleasure sliced through my body.

I clung to him as he continued to relentlessly slam in and out of me, and the feel of us reconnected in such a base way suddenly triggered me to climax, the pleasure rushing at me so intensely that my whole body tensed for several pulsing moments as I came and then went limp below him.

His hips slowed, but the depth of each of his thrusts continued to send aftershocks of my climax rushing through me, making my internal muscles clench around him on each one. A growl escaped Oliver's throat as my body clutched at him like a fist and triggered his own release, his cock throbbing within me, jerking and filling me, until his head fell forwards and rested on mine.

He continued to roll his hips lazily against mine, his cock still buried deep within me and seeming to want to stay there for the foreseeable future. This was just fine by me – I was pinned below the weight of the man I loved more than anything in the world, surrounded by the smell of his clean sweat and the feel of his reassuring closeness, and there wasn't a single place in the world that I'd rather be.

Finally, he stilled his hips and rolled us over so I was collapsed and panting on top of his body. He snuggled me to his chest and I felt his hot breath whisper across my temple as he placed a kiss on the top of my head. 'You're fucking perfect, Robyn. I love you so much.'

Grinning, I leaned up so I could look into his eyes. 'I love you, too, Oliver.'

He was gazing at me as if I was the only woman on earth, and I soaked up his attention like a sponge, allowing it to calm all the anxiety and worry that I'd gone through over the last few days.

We'd always had such a strong connection; right from the first day we'd met it had been electric between us, and that bond hadn't dimmed in the slightest during our time together. I suspected it would always be like this between us, even ten years down the line. No matter if we had children running around our feet and pets getting in the way, there would always be Oliver and I and our unbreakable chemistry. When our eyes met I felt complete, and it would seem from the glow in his gaze that Oliver felt exactly the same.

'So, now we've sorted out all the crap of the last few days, how do you feel about marrying me tomorrow?' he asked with a playful smile tweaking at the corners of his lips.

'I'd love to,' I said, my words becoming lost as he pulled me into him for another deep kiss.

CHAPTER THIRTY-EIGHT

Oliver

Today was the day, albeit our second attempt. After sorting out all the shit from last week I was finally marrying Robyn, and I'd barely been able to keep a smile off my face since I had woken up a few hours ago. It was so bad that my cheeks were aching, but in less than an hour I wouldn't care about that because my sweet girl would be standing before me and we'd be exchanging our vows.

I'd finally get to make her mine, once and for all.

Glancing across at Marcus, I smiled to myself and shook my head in amusement. I was fairly sure that Robyn had bribed, ordered, or paid Marcus to keep an extra close eye on me today, because he'd arrived at my room two hours earlier than we'd planned and hadn't left my side since. Literally. He hadn't let me go to the restaurant for breakfast – food had been ordered on room service – and the two times he'd needed the toilet he'd gone with the bathroom door open so that I was never out of his sight.

It was now my turn to use the bathroom and Marcus was propped in the doorway watching me like a hawk, presumably in case I tried to leg it and escape out of the window. I had no intention of running again, but even if I had, the window was about the size of a postage stamp, so the chance would be a fine thing.

'Are you sizing up my cock and wondering who has the biggest?' I asked him with a smirk.

Marcus flushed, his eyes jerking to my dick and then back up again as he laughed. 'No.' He pushed off from the doorframe, crossed his arms with a grin, and wiggled his eyebrows. 'I already know mine's the biggest.'

I tipped my head back and laughed before finishing off and zipping my trousers back up. It wasn't like we'd ever laid our junk on a table and measured them but, seeing as we were both members of Club Twist and had, in the past, indulged in the many pleasures to be found there – a shared woman here, an orgy there – we'd seen each other's tackle on numerous occasions. I was fairly confident that mine was bigger, but neither of us were exactly small, so I'd let his boast go.

'So, if you're not eyeing my impressive dick with jealousy, then I'll have to assume Robyn is to blame for me having you stuck to my side like a shadow today, then?' I asked with a chuckle as I moved to the sink to wash my hands.

Marcus eyed me in the reflection of the mirror and nodded sheepishly. 'Yeah, there's no point denying it. Your bride-to-be has the jitters. She's worried you're going to leg it again.'

My teeth clenched at the idea that Robyn might be waking up on her wedding day with feelings of dread instead of joy, and I turned to face Marcus with a grim expression. 'I didn't leg it,' I ground out, my mood plunging to some seriously dark depths as memories of Alex's blackmail sprung unbidden to my mind.

'I know, don't look like that, Oliver. Robyn was just joking.' He shrugged and grinned sheepishly, obviously trying to raise my spirits. 'Well, mostly joking. She called me last night and demanded that I didn't leave your side until you were at the altar.' He moved closer and gave me an affectionate punch on the shoulder in an attempt at lightening the mood. 'Considering you're supposed to be the control freak dominant in the relationship, your girl certainly has a possessive side where you're concerned.'

My cheeks flushed with pride as I thought about Robyn

getting possessive over me, and then I nodded in agreement. My little Robyn might be the sweetest, most loving woman I'd ever met, but boy, did she have a fiery side too.

'I'll call her, set her mind at ease.'

Robyn

Here we were again. My wedding day, take two.

Pulling open the curtains, I grinned at the bright sun blazing outside. Perfect. It was a beautiful day, again, and another cloudless blue sky. Today I would *definitely* be becoming Mrs Robyn Wolfe… Now that Alex had been dealt with nothing could stop me walking down that aisle to Oliver.

Sasha was busy applying her makeup in the bathroom, and I was picking at my breakfast of smoked salmon and scrambled eggs when my phone started to ring beside me. Seeing Oliver's number flash up, I immediately felt my heart accelerate. It wasn't the excited speeding up that I usually got whenever he called me, though; it was a sudden pang of nerves clutching at my heart and making my pulse race. Glancing at Sasha, I bit down on my lower lip and frowned.

'It's Oliver. Do you think something's gone wrong again?' I rasped, my voice seeming to have deserted me.

I heard the noise of Sasha swearing and dropping something in the sink, and then she appeared in the doorway with a frown that matched my own. 'No. Absolutely not. Oliver wouldn't do that to you.' She didn't look entirely convinced by her words, but she came and sat at my side, and when I continued to stare at my phone as it vibrated about on the table she picked it up and placed it into my hand.

'Answer it, Robyn.'

Taking a deep breath, I connected the call. My pulse was

thumping so loudly in my ears that I was worried I wouldn't be able to hear Oliver over the sound of it. 'Oliver? Is everything OK?'

'Good morning, *cariño*.' The rich warmth of his voice poured down the line, and even from those three simple words I could hear that he was smiling. Instantly, my shoulders relaxed. 'Today I get to marry you, so everything is wonderful.'

At his words my smile turned to a full-blown grin and beside me I saw Sasha flash me a wink and stand up. My expression obviously put her at ease because she headed back to the bathroom to continue with her makeup, leaving me to my call with Oliver.

'I was worried when I saw you calling. I thought maybe something had gone wrong.' I refrained from adding "again" onto the end of my sentence, but we both knew it was hanging there in the air.

'I just wanted to hear your voice. Nothing is wrong at all.' Oliver chuckled down the line and I relaxed back into the sofa while cradling the phone against my shoulder. 'Well, apart from the fact that Marcus is stuck to my side like a shadow and has just watched me take a leak for the second time this morning.'

I laughed, and my cheeks heated guiltily. 'Really?'

'Hmm, yes. I believe that may be your doing, my love?'

Oliver had never called me "my love" before, and I had to say I rather liked how it sounded rolling from his tongue with his slight Spanish accent. The endearment didn't stop me giggling, though, as I realised that Marcus must have grassed me up in the little reconnaissance mission I had tasked him with. 'Sorry. I was just nervous.'

'It's OK, *cariño*. I find it incredibly hot when you get all possessive over me.' Oliver almost purred his words down the line this time, and I grew warmer and had to squirm on my seat to try to settle the sudden arousal bubbling in my system.

'And just so you know, I'm not going anywhere. In fact, if it were possible to bring the wedding forwards to right this second, I would. I can hardly wait to have you as my wife.'

I took a moment to let his affectionate words sink in and grinned, wishing that he were here with me instead of being down the other end of the phone line. 'Me, too, Oliver. I can't wait.'

'So, is that all settled, or do I need to come over there and put you across my knee to remind you who you belong with?'

His low, teasing words took me completely by surprise and I sucked in a shocked breath as arousal ignited in my system and licked through my veins.

Erotic images of his hand reddening my backside and warming my skin filled my mind. As my fingers started to tremble, I found myself completely incapable of replying.

Down the line, Oliver let out a deep laugh. 'As tempting as that idea is, I was just joking, Robyn. So, are you at my parents' house yet?'

I was so turned on now that his abrupt return to normal conversation took me a second to adjust to.

Oliver's parents had invited me to stay with them last night, but in the end Sasha and I had opted to stay in a hotel so we could relax with a spa and some champagne. It had worked a treat, because I felt well and truly rested today.

Shaking off the remnants of my arousal, I nodded. 'Yup. Me and Sasha got here early so we could take our time getting ready. Your mum has been amazing, and my parents should be arriving soon.' I wandered over to the window as I spoke and looked out at the orchards and the valley beyond. The setting here really was stunning. It was still relatively early, so the gardens behind Oliver's parents' house were empty except for a few people tweaking the flowers for the day and primping the dinner tables inside the marquee, but I still got an excited tumble in my belly as I looked down upon the wedding preparations taking place below.

My wedding preparations. *Our* wedding. Me and Oliver. An excited giggle burst up my throat and I turned away from the window with a happy sigh.

'Hmm. I love it when you make that noise, *cariño*. I love it even more when I make you make that noise… like I will tonight… over and over again…' His tone had dropped lower and was now just a rough, seductive rumble down the line, promising all sorts of delicious wickedness to come later.

I fanned my face and bit down on my lower lip as I grinned. 'Stop it, Oliver! You'll get me overheated if you carry on like this.'

'I'd like nothing more, but if I got you overexcited and wet for me then you might need to change out of those gorgeous lace knickers I know you're wearing right now. You are wearing them, aren't you?'

Swallowing hard, I nodded, and then belatedly realised that he couldn't see me down the phone. 'I am. And the suspenders…' Oliver let out a growl so lusty and rough that I'd place money on the fact he was now sporting a raging hard-on.

The underwear set was a wedding gift from Oliver that had been delivered to my suite first thing this morning. Beautiful lingerie to wear under my wedding dress that included white lace panties, a matching strapless bra and, of course, a set of stockings and suspenders that would sate his obsession with peeling them from me with his teeth.

My skin heated further as I imagined him doing that exact thing to me tonight, and I had to really focus on not letting myself get carried away. 'They're stunning, Oliver. Thank you.'

'You are more than welcome. But seeing as I wish to be the one removing them, I think perhaps I should behave myself and leave you in peace now to finish getting ready.'

I would be seeing him in less than two hours at the wedding, so the pang of disappointment that I felt at our imminent goodbye seemed a little silly.

'OK,' I murmured reluctantly, and as I did I had a feeling that this might be one of those moments where neither of us wanted to hang up.

Oliver chuckled down the line as if thinking the exact same thing, and then he clarified that yes, he had indeed accurately read my mind. 'I don't want to hang up either, Robyn, but I will, because the sooner I do, the sooner I can be on my way up to the house to marry you.'

Hmm. When he put it like that maybe I could bring myself to hang up. 'OK, that sounds good. Really good.'

'Really good. Yes, it does. Now, you have two hours left as a free woman and then you'll be mine, Robyn, and there will be no escape.' His words were teasing, but knowing Oliver's possessive tendencies as well as I did, I suspected there was also an undercurrent of need in them as well.

'I don't want to escape,' I replied huskily, knowing it would soothe him. 'I'll happily accept an entrapment in your lair, Mr Wolfe.'

'My lair?' Oliver sounded amused, but confused, and I giggled as I heard Sasha bark out a loud snort of laughter in the bathroom.

'It's nothing, it's just a joke Sasha has. I'll see you really soon.'

'Hmm.' He made a contented humming noise that vibrated right to my core. 'You will indeed.'

'I love you.' I'm not sure why I felt the need to splurge the words out, but I did, and in response I heard Oliver give another hum.

'I love you, too, Robyn.' The call was still connected, and I sat there listening to his breathing, amazed at just how attached I could feel to another individual. It was as if we were two halves of the same whole. 'And now, because I know you won't hang up, I will,' he murmured, a smile evident in his tone. 'See you very, very soon, *cariño*.'

And just like that the line went dead and I was left with the biggest, soppiest smile on my face.

CHAPTER THIRTY-NINE

Robyn

I'd planned on being fairly casual in my preparations for the wedding. I mean, I wanted to look nice for Oliver, obviously, but I never wore that much makeup, and the most lavish treatment my hair usually got was an extra shot of conditioner when I visited a salon for a cut and blow dry.

Sasha, Sophia, and my mum had other ideas, though, and over the last hour I'd found myself being primped to within an inch of my life; my hair had been washed, dried, and styled thanks to a friend of Sophia's, Sasha had lovingly done my makeup, and my mum had given my nails a slick of pale pink polish.

I felt like a princess with this much care being showered upon me. Being the centre of attention like this wasn't something I'd usually enjoy, but as I slipped on my wedding dress and let Sasha secure the back I had to admit that it had all made the day feel even more special.

'Wow. You look fucking gorgeous!' Sasha blurted, before blushing and holding a hand over her mouth. She flashed an apologetic glance at my mum and Sophia, who were both suppressing smiles at her foul mouth. 'Sorry, but you do. Even more than last time.'

Last time. Sasha's gaze widened as she realised what she'd said, but I just rolled my eyes. Her words could have upset me, but I was so excited about the day that I let them wash over me.

‘Let me see a mirror, then.’ I hadn’t been allowed to look in a mirror since their fussing had started so I had no idea what to expect. Sasha had spent ages on my face, and I was slightly worried I might look like a hooker dolled up and ready for her first client of the night. If that did turn out to be the case, then I’d be grabbing some makeup removal wipes and cleaning it all off regardless of how much Sasha might complain.

‘I’m a bit worried the makeup might be a bit much… *oh…*’ Reaching the full-length mirror in the bathroom, I caught a glimpse of my reflection and my breath caught in my throat.

Wow. I looked… well, I didn’t have a big ego, but even I could admit that I looked beautiful. My hair was styled in a messy up-do, elegant, yet totally me, and the makeup Sasha had done was incredible. It was there, but not obvious; my skin looked flawless and natural, my lips plumper somehow and with just a hint of coloured gloss on them, and the light eyeshadow and mascara she’d used made my eyes look wide and clear.

I loved it, and I was pretty sure Oliver would love it, too.

The dress was the cherry on the cake: strapless, simple, and falling to the floor so that it managed to flatter my waistline at the same time as giving me a great cleavage.

It was official – I was ready for my wedding.

Just ten minutes now separated me from becoming Mrs Oliver Wolfe, and a ball of emotion built in my throat as I watched my eyes become bright with unshed tears.

‘Don’t you bloody dare cry, you’ll set me off,’ my mother chided, and the sound of her swearing was so rare and so comical that instead of crying I found myself turning to the gathered women and laughing instead. Sasha’s love of bad language was clearly rubbing off on us all.

‘Shall I open some more fizz?’ Sophia asked, holding a bottle up expectantly. ‘The bride is allowed to be traditionally late, after all.’

As much as some Dutch courage did hold a certain appeal,

I shook my head almost before she'd finished her sentence. 'No. I don't want to be late. I don't want to wait another second.' After everything that had happened, all the ups and downs we'd faced this past week, I wanted to be at Oliver's side as soon as was physically possible.

Passing my gaze around them all, I saw nods and looks of understanding. Both my mum and Sophia pulled me in for delicate, non-creasing, non-makeup-smearing hugs before disappearing off to join the wedding guests below.

Sasha sucked in a deep breath and joined my side in front of the mirror. She gave me a gentle bump with her shoulder. 'So, let's go get you married, eh?'

With a nod and a nervous giggle, I picked up my bouquet and followed her from the room to find my husband-to-be.

The ceremony was beautiful; we exchanged vows while nestled under the citrus trees on Oliver's parents' estate – it was exactly as I'd dreamed – and now that it was over I almost felt guilty that I hadn't absorbed as much of it as I should have. Once I'd joined Oliver at the altar I'd found myself too captivated by him to listen to much of what the priest had said. Oliver had looked beyond stunning in his sleek tuxedo and navy-blue tie. I was so distracted by him that I'd spent the best part of the ceremony ogling him greedily instead of paying attention.

He really was mine. The gorgeous, powerful man by my side was about to become my husband. It had almost seemed hard to digest.

His eyes had gleamed with amusement when he'd caught me staring, and from the way his blue gaze had heated, I knew that he was just as affected by all of this as I was.

Luckily, through my haze of lusty love I had managed to hear the prompt for my reply of "I do", and instead of ogling him I'd become ensnared in Oliver's captivating eyes as he'd repeated the promise and then leaned down and captured my lips in a kiss to seal the deal.

As always, his kiss was so much more than just a simple meeting of lips. When his tongue had demanded entry to my mouth it had been more like a meeting of souls. Our hands had clutched, and mouths melded as we became one in both name and body, and we'd both become so carried away with it that we'd only stopped when the crowd had woken us from the trance by whooping and hollering about our erotic public display.

As embarrassing as that had been, no one had looked particularly put out by our passionate embrace, and even my mum had been grinning goofily at us as we'd made our way down the aisle towards the rest of our lives.

The food afterwards had been delicious – a spread of Spanish delights that had been rich and tasty but not too filling – and now we were in mid-flow enjoying the after party.

So far, I'd danced with my dad, Oliver's father, Richard, David from Club Twist, and now I was working my way through the official wedding party, starting with Nathan. Bless him, he was trying his best, but his body was so tense that it was like dancing with a well rooted tree. From what I'd witnessed since knowing him, this man only ever relaxed fully when he was with his partner, Stella, and from the way his eyes kept darting across the room towards her I could only assume that he was desperate to get back to her right this second.

We made it about halfway through a song before Nathan cleared his throat and stepped back from me. 'I think it's time for you to dance with the best man. Marcus, you're up.' Nathan held my hand out towards a startled looking Marcus who had been lounging in a quieter corner of the marquee.

'Oh, I don't really dance…' Marcus protested, but Nathan was already dragging him onto the dance floor and shoving him towards me.

'The bride needs to dance with the best man; it's tradition.'

Marcus's usual easy demeanour seemed to be missing as he stepped in front of me and placed a hand on my hip. As I copied the action and laid my palm on his waist, Marcus stiffened up.

'Um… do you mind just putting your hand on my arm instead?' he asked tightly, and, with a small frown, I did. Weird. So, the no touching thing that Sasha had mentioned wasn't just confined to her, or the bedroom.

Marcus took a deep breath as if struggling with this level of intimacy, and then took my other hand so we could start dancing.

'Sorry. I'm not very good at this,' he mumbled.

'You're doing great,' I reassured him, thinking it was funny how all of Oliver's closest friends were similar in their stiff, uncomfortable dancing styles.

'You look beautiful, Robyn. Today has been amazing, and I'm so pleased to see you and Oliver so happy.'

It had been a day filled with happiness and grins, and my cheeks ached as I smiled broadly yet again. 'Thanks, Marcus, it's been such a special day.'

As we swayed to the music a more comfortable silence fell between us. It wasn't often that I got Marcus all to myself like this so, after a few moments, I decided to use this opportunity to take a risk and play Cupid. 'You know Sasha feels terrible?'

Marcus's frame visibly tensed, and his eyes shot to mine. 'Oh, yeah? Hungover?'

'Hmm, no.' Licking my lips, I decided to just say what I knew my best friend hadn't been able to. 'She told me what happened at the club, Marcus, and she hates the way it ended. She feels terrible.'

His cheeks flushed as I mentioned their tryst, but his eyes darkened as he seemed to close himself off from me. 'Well, she doesn't need to worry, I've got the hint. She doesn't do guys twice, apart from me, and that was a mistake. I'll be staying away from now on.'

'No! That's not what she meant at all! Think about it, Marcus, she didn't actually say those words, did she? That's just what you assumed.'

Marcus stilled as he thought back, but the deep frown was engrained on his forehead.

'Sasha was panicking afterwards, but not because you were a mistake.'

He listened to my words but then shook his head. 'She certainly looked like it was a mistake to her.' His eyes flashed briefly with hope and then dropped away from mine self-consciously. 'If it wasn't regret, then what was she panicking about?'

'She said that she finally understood just how much she likes you and she started to freak out a bit. I suspect what you thought was regret on her face was actually shock.'

'But…'

Squeezing his hand, I interrupted him and then gave him a look which encouraged him to let me finish.

'She's not good at opening up with guys, Marcus. She has her reasons, but basically, she doesn't do relationships with feelings and when she realised how much she liked you it scared her to death. She told me herself that she's falling for you.'

Marcus completely stopped any pretence of dancing and raised his eyes to mine. 'Really?'

'Yep.' I let go of his hand and stepped back to give him his personal space again. 'I wouldn't tell you this otherwise, but honestly I've never seen her like this about a guy before. She's absolutely gutted about the way things ended between you two.'

Marcus nodded slowly and shoved one hand into his trouser pocket. 'Thanks, Robyn.' Leading me with his other hand, he took me towards our other groomsman, Matías, who welcomed me with open arms and a wide, wicked grin.

As Matías took my hand I watched Marcus move away to

the side of the garden. If my chats with both him and Sasha didn't prompt them into doing something about the connection they shared, then perhaps they just weren't meant to be together.

From the twinkle in his eye as he'd given me over to Matías, though, I would place money on the fact that Marcus was on his way to track Sasha down right this very second.

Matías brought my attention back to him by squeezing my hand and offering me a small tilt of his head in greeting 'Ah! It is finally my turn with the beautiful bride!' He wrapped me in his arms and literally spun me onto the dance floor with such gusto that I let out a yelp of shock and had to cling on to him as I giggled and tried to keep up with his skilled moves.

OK, so David, Marcus, and Nathan might have been stiff and uncomfortable in their moves, but boy, could this man dance! Matías had the skill of a professional, and after just a minute or so of twirling and dipping we had drawn a crowd and were being cheered and clapped from all around.

Strong hands landed on my waist from behind and halted my movements, and I watched as Matías grinned over my shoulder at whoever had interrupted our dance.

'I think that's quite enough of that.'

The sound of Oliver's deep tone just beside my ear sent shivers through my body, and I glanced over my shoulder to see him giving Matías an amused but disapproving stare.

Matías threw his head back and laughed before winking at me. 'I think I have upset your very protective husband.'

Oliver's hands tightened on my hips as if he very much liked to be called my husband, and I couldn't help but wiggle backwards into his touch.

'You spoil our fun, old friend,' Matías said. 'Just one more dance, no?'

With a growl, Oliver swept me into his embrace and twirled me so that his strong body now separated me from Matías. 'No. The next dance is mine.'

Matías held up his hands in defeat but was grinning from ear to ear. 'Fair enough. I must say it is good to see you so ensnared by this beautiful woman. It gives me hope that maybe one day I, too, will be able to find such fierce love.'

From the slightly sad tinge to his eyes as he spoke, I could only assume that all Matías's playfulness and flirting was actually hiding a deeper loneliness. He bowed at me as he stepped backwards, then grabbed Chloe and, with a howl of laughter, began to spin her around the dance floor with relish. Rolling my eyes, I rewound my earlier thought. Perhaps he wasn't lonely; maybe he was just a playboy through and through.

'Wife.' Oliver's growled statement brought my eyes back to his and I grinned up at him with a small nod before slipping my arms around his neck and stepping into a slow dance with him.

'Husband.' I tried out the title for him, instantly loving the way it sounded.

Oliver hummed his appreciation and tucked me closer into his embrace as we continued to sway to the music. 'Now and forever, baby. Now and forever.'

CHAPTER FORTY

Sasha

As expected, the wedding had been amazing. After all the craziness of the last few days I had finally got to watch as Robyn walked down a tree-lined aisle towards Oliver. I'm not sure I'd ever known a couple who were so well suited for each other. They were like two halves that completed each other. It was clear he was besotted with her, and I'd never seen Robyn so head over heels – Oliver was undoubtedly the absolute love of her life.

They had picked possibly the most beautiful setting I could ever have imagined; flowers had been scattered amongst the fruit trees, the summer air had been heavy with the scent of orange blossoms, and the valley view behind them as they exchanged their vows was utterly breath-taking.

Every single person gathered to celebrate their union had been grinning from ear to ear. It had been so fucking perfect that it was like something out of a movie.

Sniffing, I swiped at a stray tear on my cheek and rolled my eyes. What the hell was wrong with me? I never cried, but spending the whole day surrounded by all this bloody romance was ruining me.

The ceremony was done, meal eaten, and the first dance had been danced, but it was still warm as the evening drew near and the wedding party lazed around the beautifully decorated gardens of Oliver's parents' house.

I'd moved away a little to have five minutes in the sun, and

I closed my eyes, letting the warmth relax me. All I could hear was the quiet lull of voices in the distance, crickets in the tall grass behind me, and the gentle rustle of the breeze in the trees. It was utterly tranquil.

But my moment of peace was suddenly broken by the sound of approaching footsteps and then Marcus's tentative voice. 'Sasha? Can I have a word with you, please?'

Everything that had occurred between us last week was still so raw that my initial reaction was to throw out a sarcastic reply and try to protect myself by pushing him away again but, using an incredible amount of self-restraint, I managed to follow Robyn's advice and control myself.

Apparently, miracles do occur.

Sarcasm might be my defence mechanism, but I really needed to work on tamping it down, because this was a guy I was seriously attracted to, and yet I'd been on the verge of snapping at him before I even knew what he wanted to talk about.

Swallowing my nerves, I looked up and met his gaze. Pain, stress, and tension were swirling across his features, and those emotions resonated with the feelings currently stuck within my own body.

This thing between us really was messed up. It was either me being a bitch to him, or him cuffing me to a flipping bed and not explaining his reasons. His behaviour that night might have made me uneasy, but he hadn't hurt me in any way, and when I'd asked him to release me, he had immediately done so. And there was also no escaping the fact that the sex both then and the other night had been incredible.

We'd fucked frantically, and it had been hot and hard, but his behaviour hadn't been that of a sadistic weirdo.

It seemed clear to me that the no touching thing was because he was struggling with some inner turmoil, but what could cause a man to need to cuff a woman to his bed all night? I guess there was only one way I'd ever find out, and it was standing before me right now.

Marcus must have taken my silence as a rejection, because he sighed and went to turn away.

Panicking that he was going to leave, I quickly found my voice. 'Wait! Marcus.' My words had the desired effect, and Marcus paused and glanced back at me over his shoulder.

Knowing that I needed to apologise for the way I'd reacted last week, I decided to get it out of the way right from the start. 'I can be a real bitch sometimes. I'm… I'm so sorry that you misunderstood my expression. It… it wasn't true what you thought. You thought I regretted what happened in Fantasia, didn't you? I didn't, not at all. Please… come and sit?'

Marcus's gaze intensified at my confession, and then he gave a small, hesitant smile as he swivelled back around and took the sun chair beside me.

'So, was last week a mistake, or not? Because you certainly looked like it was,' he asked quietly.

I had no idea how I could have looked so horrified the other night but, judging from the wary expression on his face, it had obviously made him feel like a complete shit. Lowering my mortified cheeks, I shook my head.

'No. Being with you again… It wasn't a mistake, it… it was incredible.'

Marcus's breath seemed to stutter at my whispered words, and even I was struggling with the fact that I was finally saying them out loud. Confessing emotional feelings to a man was certainly a first for me, and it was just as difficult as I had always imagined it might be.

After staring at my twining hands for a minute or so, I finally plucked up the courage to raise my head and look at him. 'I have no idea why you're interested in me. I'm such a bitch.'

Marcus frowned and shook his head. 'You're beautiful, determined, funny as fuck, and caring. You might want people to think you're a bitch, Sasha, but I know you're not.'

'Yeah, I can be.' I gave a dry laugh and tried to shrug off his compliments, even if his words had made something inside me feel warm and gooey.

'Not deep down. I've seen your softer side, remember?' Instantly I was taken back to the night we'd spent together at his place. He was right, he had seen my softer side then, because for whatever reason, this man made me open up like no one had managed before. I could feel the connection again now, and for once in my life I felt like letting my guard down. I *wanted* to. The idea of letting him in scared me, but Robyn was right; if I didn't take a chance with someone like Marcus, who I felt a genuine bond with, then I'd probably be alone for the rest of my life.

'Look, I... I like you a lot, Sasha, but I need to know one way or the other how you feel. I can't keep going round and round in circles like this; it's driving me insane. I know I screwed things up that night at my house, but...'

'I like you, too,' I blurted, interrupting him halfway through his sentence. My words caused hope to flare in his eyes, and then I made the move to shift my chair closer. 'I feel so dreadful about what happened last week, Marcus, but I was panicking. I didn't know how to deal with everything I was feeling, and you obviously saw that reflected in my features.'

I desperately wanted to reinforce my words with contact, but I knew he had issues with touching. Remembering how he'd told me that holding hands was OK, I tentatively reached across and laid my palm across his.

The brushing of our skin caused goose pimples to fly up my arm. Marcus gave a low chuckle and squeezed my hand. 'It's still just as potent,' he murmured, and I let out a relieved breath that he hadn't rejected me or pushed me away.

'It is,' I agreed, my entire body singing with happiness at our proximity. The heat between us intensified until I felt like it was swirling in the air around us. No matter what issues we'd had in the past, or how insurmountable our differences had seemed at times, we'd always had this explosive chemistry and obsession that seemed to be stronger than any I'd experienced before. It was more than lust, more than desire… So much more that I couldn't even think of a word that was adequate to describe the enormity of it.

One certain emotive word beginning with L did keep springing to my mind, but I wasn't quite ready to contemplate it just yet, even though I strongly suspected it was what I was starting to feel for Marcus.

We shared a silent gaze for a moment or two, as if he was thinking the exact same thing, and then his brow lowered into a frown.

'I figured you probably hated me after what happened at my place with the cuffs. And then the other night happened so suddenly, I wondered if maybe you had just got caught up in the moment and afterwards regretted it.'

'The only thing I regret was not stopping you to clarify what I was feeling. I'm so sorry. And for the record, it had nothing to do with that night with the cuffs, and I definitely don't hate you.' Giving his hand a squeeze, I softened my tone. 'It was obvious something was troubling you that night,' I ventured, wondering if he might trust me enough now to explain his need for the restraints.

'Yeah,' was the only reply he gave, but I could see in his eyes that he wanted to confess more. I ran my thumb gently across the back of his hand, and in response I heard Marcus give a soft, approving hum.

Perhaps if I opened up a little he might reciprocate? Gently massaging his hand with mine, I dropped my gaze away as I made my first confession.

'I… I don't let people close. I mean I haven't, not for a long time. It started when my parents died… It hurt so much losing them… I didn't know how to cope with all the emotions, so I started to avoid relationships. Quick flings were easier, no heartache involved.'

Marcus's eyebrows rose at my blurted admission, and then he nodded in understanding.

It wasn't easy talking about this side of me. In fact, it was painful as fuck. For years I'd turned myself into a slut to avoid getting hurt. It wasn't something I was particularly proud of, but it was me, and he needed to know.

'But then I met you.' My voice softened to a whisper. 'And as well as feeling an attraction to you, I felt a genuine connection. It fucking terrified me,' I confessed with a dry chuckle. 'That's why I freaked out so badly after that first night. I'd opened myself up to you and agreed to spend the night – something I never do – and then you react by wanting to tie me up all night. It… it hurt me, Marcus.'

'Fuck.' Marcus cursed under his breath and slapped a hand down on his thigh before gripping so tightly that his knuckles turned white. 'I'm so fucking sorry, Sasha.'

Nodding, I gave him a reassuring smile. 'And so yeah, the cuff thing was weird as fuck, but I should have talked to you about it all, not freaked out and yelled abuse at you.' Tilting my head, I reconnected our gaze and found his eyes burning with hope which somehow gave me the courage to continue. 'I'd known then that I liked you more than I had other guys, and the connection between us had been incredible, but I didn't know how to deal with it, and that terrified me, too.'

'So, when things get too emotional you resort to being sarcastic?' he speculated with a smile, and I nodded.

'And bitchy. Over time I guess I just built a wall around myself. Deflecting things with a snarky comment seems easier than dealing with what's really going on.'

'I can understand that.' He paused, running a hand through his thick mop of blond hair and giving me a long look that seemed to say so much more than words could about how he felt about me.

'I don't know how things between us are going to pan out, Sasha, but I can tell you now that I feel more for you than I have for anyone in a long time, and I would never intentionally hurt you.'

My pulse jumped with both excitement and nerves at his words, but to steady myself I drew in a breath so deep that my nostrils flared, and then I nodded.

'I never wanted to fall for someone… I never wanted to care… After losing my parents, I… I can't imagine going through the pain of losing someone again…' I murmured. My eyes fluttered shut at how vulnerable I sounded. I hated exposing my weaknesses like this, but he needed to see this side of me. I wrapped one arm tightly around my chest as if holding myself together. This was the most open I'd been with anyone for… well, forever.

He gave my hand a gentle, reassuring squeeze. 'You *do* let people in, though. Robyn is your best friend, isn't she? That involves feelings, albeit slightly different ones.'

He had a point there. I'd never considered it that way. I loved Robyn fiercely, just like a sister, so what he was saying logically made sense – I *could* let people in. My fear had just created a distance between me and whoever I let in my bed – as though sexual intimacy was more intense than any other closeness.

'That's true,' I admitted quietly, before starting to gently rub my thumb back and forth across his hand. It felt so lovely that we both sat there in contented silence for a few moments, staring at our joined fingers.

After a while, Marcus started to move around restlessly as if there was something he wanted to say. 'Your use of sarcasm to deflect what's really going on is probably quite similar to what I've been doing for the past two years.' Sitting up straighter, he turned in his seat to face me, seeming to be about to open up, just as I'd hoped he might. 'Not with sarcasm, but I've been deflecting, too. Avoiding facing up to my fears, I guess. It's… it's not an easy subject for me to talk about, but I'd like to try and explain…'

Nodding keenly, I gave him a supportive smile. 'I'd like that, but only if you want to tell me.'

Marcus took a moment to adjust our hands so that our fingers were intertwined. He dipped his head in a nod. 'I would. I want you to know.' Clearing his throat, he smiled. 'We're actually remarkably similar in some ways.'

We both had our demons, that much was already clear, and so I joined him in his smile and waited quietly for him to continue.

'You said just now that for a long time you have avoided relationships so you wouldn't get hurt. Well, in a way so have I.' He paused, shifting uncomfortably in his seat and then looking up at me ruefully. 'My need to secure you to the bedframe or stop you touching me… That's not an entirely new thing for me, but I haven't always had that compulsion. I used to enjoy being touched, sometimes I even liked it when a woman took the lead in the bedroom… but… but not any more.'

I pushed away the stab of jealousy that hit as I imagined him with another woman, and then remembered my suspicions that maybe he'd been hurt physically at some point. I frowned and leaned in closer to him, curious, but not wanting to overly force his confession.

'What happened?' I asked softly, making sure that I was close enough to give support, but not so close that I was intruding on his personal space.

'When I was in America I was seeing a girl. Celia, I think I mentioned her to you once before.' I stayed silent, but nodded, remembering the way he'd slipped up and mentioned her name and then quickly changed the subject. 'We'd been together a while, but it was a kind of on-off-thing because she was busy, and I was working crazy shifts at my restaurants trying to make a name for myself.'

The idea of him being in any type of relationship with someone else still made my stomach knot uncomfortably with jealousy, and I had to work really hard to hide the emotions from my face.

'One night we were in bed together. She was leading things. I was tied to the bedframe and halfway through having sex she jumped off the bed and started rummaging through the bedside drawers. I figured she was getting something to spice up the evening, but when she climbed back on the bed she …' Marcus's eyelids fluttered shut for a second, and when he opened them again his blue eyes looked stormy and troubled. 'Well, she… she tried to kill me.'

A rasping gasp of shock tore from my throat and my fingers tightened around his until I had to force my grip to relax so I didn't break any bones in his hand. She'd tried to kill him? What the fuck?

'She stabbed me, over and over again with my own fucking chef's knife.'

'Holy fuck, Marcus!' I shrieked, not able to control my bad language, or the volume of my voice, given the severity of what he had just confessed to me.

He gave an ironic smile and shrugged. 'Yeah, it was pretty fucked up. So obviously that's where my scars come from.' Locking his eyes with mine, he licked his lips. 'And my insecurities. I always lock my knives up now, both at home and at work, and that night with you… I started to panic, so I moved the bedside table away. You probably thought I was a complete weirdo doing that halfway through the night.'

I gave a small smile as I remembered him rearranging the furniture. 'It was a little strange,' I agreed, giving his hand a squeeze. 'But completely understandable now I know why.'

Pausing, I tried to imagine what he must have gone through. 'Why would she do that?' I asked, unable to imagine anyone wanting to hurt Marcus. He was so charming, so lovely. Apart from when I hurt him, I reminded myself, feeling guilty that the only occasions where I'd seen him bitter and reactive were when I had lashed out with my spiteful words.

He distracted me from the uncomfortable memories by giving a self-conscious shrug. 'I wondered that, too, at first.' He ran a hand through his hair and dropped his gaze. 'I blamed myself for a while. It made me question things, I thought maybe I was the cause… Maybe I wasn't a nice person and I'd done something to push her to it.'

'No!' My grip on his hand intensified and I shook my head firmly. 'You're one of the most genuine, laid-back, lovely people I've ever met,' I stated with certainty. My defence of him was so rapid and so fervent that Marcus looked almost as shocked as I felt. But it was true. We might not know each other that deeply, and yet somehow, I still knew my words to be true.

Marcus's face softened as he gave a shy smile in response to my statement and nodded sadly.

'I'd never realised it while we were together, but she's ill. The doctors treating her now think it's some sort of psychopathic issue.'

My eyes widened in shock. Jesus. I'd read enough thrillers to know if that really was the case then Marcus was probably quite lucky to be alive.

'I haven't been able to be with a woman since without tying her up.'

'It's not exactly surprising,' I mumbled, almost unable to think of one helpful or supportive thing to say. His psychopathic ex-girlfriend had tied him up and tried to kill him! That was surely as dramatic as it got.

'I've only slept with two women since it happened.' His face flushed, and he gave me an embarrassed smile. 'Well, three including you.' Swallowing hard, he sighed. 'Each time I've had panic attacks of varying degrees. I didn't really care with the other two, because it was just sex, there were no overnight stays involved so I could get away with tying them up. I just said it was part of the scene… But with you… I knew as soon as I met you that things between us would be different if we went down that path.'

Squeezing my hand, he smiled at me, and it was so sweet and affectionate that I wanted to crawl right into his lap and snuggle him until the fear in his eyes went away. But seeing as he'd just admitted to having issues with contact and touching, I refrained.

'That's why I tried to keep you away when you first came on to me. I didn't want it to be just sex with you, and I was worried that my need to tie you up might freak you out.' Throwing his head back, he let out a lovely deep laugh. He looked at me with twinkling eyes. 'Which it did. I know you would never do what Celia did… But I can't seem to move on from it… Keeping one cuff on you all night seemed the only solution I could think of to help me stay calm, but obviously it completely backfired.'

'It kinda did, yeah, but it makes sense now. Thank you for telling me.' I gave his hand another supportive squeeze, desperately wishing I could wrap him in my arms and soothe him. 'So, the no touching thing, that's all linked to it as well?'

Marcus blinked and then stared down at our linked hands. 'I never had issues with intimacy before the stabbing, so I guess so. I think in my mind I sort of convinced myself that I was safer if I could keep a distance between me and the girl. Holding hands was OK, because they couldn't reach for a weapon if I had a grip on them.' Pausing, he shook his head. 'Fuck, I sound like a complete lunatic.'

He lifted his free hand, rubbed it over his face, and then stared at me intently. 'I trust you, Sasha, and I don't want it to be like that between us, but you might need to be patient with me at first. It's been a while since I've let my guard down. I'm kinda fucked up,' he stated as a closing summary, his lips twisting with apparent self-irritation.

'I think we're both a little fucked up, Marcus. I've been emotionally shuttered for so long I don't know how to handle all these feelings I'm experiencing. That won't exactly make me the easiest person to be with, either.'

'Maybe that makes us a perfect match?' he speculated hopefully.

'A perfectly imperfect pair?' I joked.

'Yeah.' His eyes were glowing now, and he moved just a fraction closer. 'I really like you, Sasha. I know it won't be easy, but I'd really like us to try again.'

Me in a relationship. It seemed such a bizarre concept. It had been so long since I'd contemplated something like it that I had to take a moment to think it through. Marcus was the first in… well, forever, to make me want to share my life with a man and not just my bed. I chewed on my lower lip for several moments and finally nodded. 'I'd really like that, too, Marcus.'

Clearing his throat, Marcus stood up and held his hand out to me again. Jerking a head towards the dance floor up on the lawn, he gave a shy smile. 'Would you, uh… would you like to dance?'

My eyebrows rose with pleasant surprise, but I took his hand and let him help me to my feet. 'You know that dancing involves touching, right?' I asked cautiously as we made our way back towards the wedding marquee and the soft strains of music that were floating out into the afternoon air.

'Yup, but if I want to make this work with you, which I do, then we've gotta start somewhere, right?'

My chest clenched at his declaration, and I nodded, giving his hand a squeeze.

By the time we got back to the tent, my heart was pounding with excited nerves and even though I caught both Robyn and Chloe giving us curious glances I kept my attention solely focused on the gorgeous, sweet, damaged man who was walking beside me.

We found a spot on the side of the dance floor and then I turned to him expectantly. I knew how I usually danced with a man – closely entwined and touching pretty much everywhere – but with his contact issues I didn't want to push

Marcus too fast, so I simply waited for him to take the lead.

At first, it seemed like he didn't know what to do, but finally, after fidgeting on the spot for a few seconds, he stepped closer and tentatively placed his hands on my hips.

Smiling at how intensely focused his gaze was, I decided that touching his waist might trigger him as it was so close to his scars, so I raised my hands and laid them on his shoulders. As soon as I made contact with him, Marcus tensed and stopped swaying to the music. Leaning back to see if he was OK, I noticed a sheen of anxious sweat on his brow and immediately began pulling my hands away.

Marcus caught me by the wrists and shook his head. 'No.' Keeping his grip gentle, he guided my hands back to his shoulders again, then resumed his hold of my hips, drawing me in closer so he could rest the side of his face against mine as we slowly moved to the music.

My wrist was against the side of his neck, and I could feel his pulse racing under the skin as if his heart were trying to break free of his chest.

The thing that struck me the most about this situation was that I knew from first-hand experience just how skilled this man was in bed. He was right up there with the best lovers I'd ever been with, and yet right now he was attempting a simple cuddle and shaking like an inexperienced kid who'd never even touched a woman before. It made my heart clench for him, and I felt myself falling for him even more.

'You don't have to force this, Marcus, we can take it slower. I don't even like dancing that much.' I tried to push back from him again, but he tightened his grip with a little growl, pulling me flush against him and not letting me go.

'Liar. I know you love dancing, I've seen you at the club.'

My cheeks flushed with embarrassment about how many guys he must have seen me dancing with, rubbing against and kissing, but I pushed it away. That was the past. This man here in my arms was my future. 'OK, I do enjoy dancing, but it doesn't mean you have to put yourself through this.'

His grip still didn't relent, and so, after a second or so, I began to relax into our dance. Now he was so much closer it was a little awkward to have my hands around his neck because he was taller than me, so I slowly lowered them and wrapped them around his waist instead. I placed them more across his back so that they were away from his scars and made my movements as slow and as gentle as I could.

He didn't seem to mind the change of position, so I leaned my head onto his shoulder with a contented sigh. He smelt incredible; I didn't know if it was aftershave or just his natural scent, but I wanted to nuzzle into his skin to get more of it. I didn't, though. I reminded myself that we needed to take small steps, and so held myself back.

His heart was still pounding in his chest like a speeding freight train so, after a few minutes, I raised my head again and met his gaze. 'Is this OK?'

The sheen of sweat had gone now, and Marcus's eyes were dilated and heavy-lidded with lust and not the trace of fear I had seen earlier, which were certainly all good signs.

'Yes. God, it feels so good. *You* feel so good.'

I grinned at his words and allowed him to pull me back against him. He trailed a hand down my back and then sighed happily.

His grip intensified, and he drew his head back to stare deeply into my eyes. I could tell from his expression that his next words were going to be important in some way.

'No one knows what the future holds, Sasha, so I can't promise you'll always want me around, but I can promise that I will never hurt you. If you can trust me with your heart, I will cherish it, and treat you like a fucking queen.'

A warm feeling spread through my body at the protective determination in his tone. I reached down and took one of his hands and lifted it up to lay it flat on my chest, right over my heart. 'It's yours,' I murmured softly. 'And I'm not walking away, either. Now we're doing this thing you'd need to pry me out of your life with a crowbar.'

My words clearly pleased him, and then, to my surprise, he copied my action, taking one of my hands and laying it over his heart.

'Ditto. It might be trying to break its way out of my ribs right now, but this is all yours, too, baby.'

It was a big step forwards in the contact between us and his chest tensed below my touch. He was obviously anxious, his heart was rapidly hammering under my palm as evidence, but as I glanced up, his smile was contented and as we swayed together I felt his body begin to relax.

The song playing was quite an upbeat number, but Marcus and I continued to dance to our own private rhythm as we both absorbed all that we had confessed to each other, moving slowly together and ignoring the excited jumping and dance moves of the people who shared the space with us.

I felt utterly content and happy, but the entire time we danced I was hugely aware of the zinging chemistry passing between us. It was like this whenever we were near, but now we were taking our first tentative steps towards togetherness it seemed even more potent. It was like magnets pulling us together, an addictive feeling, and one that I no longer had to try to fight against.

I wanted to kiss him, touch him, explore his body, and then fall into bed with him in a bundle of sweaty limbs, but I knew all of that would probably have to wait, or at least be done in careful, small steps.

Tipping my head back, I gazed up at him with a grin and my heart exploded with excitement when Marcus returned the expression with just as much gusto. He looked relaxed now, and so handsome that it made my stomach flip.

'I really want to kiss you,' he murmured, his eyes dropping to my lips.

'Why don't you, then?' I offered coyly, wanting him to

make the first move.

'With our rather explosive history I'm a little worried that it might get a bit explicit for the middle of a wedding.'

A giggle erupted in my throat and I buried my head into his shoulder to try to quieten it. Explosive history? I suppose that was one way of putting it.

'I can't seem to control myself when I'm with you,' he continued. Gripping my waist tighter, he ground his hips forwards and the hard length of his erection, trapped between us, throbbed against my belly.

Oh… I hadn't noticed *that* earlier. Must be because it was confined in the tight suit trousers he wore.

'Yes, it's all getting a bit uncomfortable down there,' he commented with an amused quirk of his lips that had me breaking into another loud laugh. I couldn't remember the last time I'd felt this relaxed and carefree with a man, and it was quite a refreshing feeling. 'Seeing as my poor balls are already in near agony I might as well kiss you. Just stop me if I try and drag you down to the floor and strip you naked, though, will you? I'm not sure Oliver's ninety-six-year-old grandma could cope with the sight of my arse bouncing in the air.' Both of us laughed, but then our eyes seemed to lock and as we shared a heavy gaze our smiles gave way to the heat simmering below them.

Marcus lowered his head. His lips brushed over mine and I can honestly say it was such a special moment that it felt like the first time we'd ever kissed.

Our lips met. At some point, he gathered both of my arms and held them gently at the base of my spine. I was so lost in the kiss that I barely noticed the move, and to be honest I'm not sure Marcus was aware that he'd done it, either.

With a groan, he finally dragged himself back from the kiss, parting our mouths but keeping me firmly ensconced in the circle of his arms. 'God Sasha, I…' Marcus seemed to bring himself up short with whatever declaration he'd been about to say. With a shy smile he lowered his face and placed a chaste kiss on the corner of my mouth. 'You're incredible.'

I let out a contented breath. Over his shoulder, I saw Robyn giving me a double thumbs up. I grinned at her and then snuggled into Marcus as I absorbed the way he was gazing down at me with such affection.

He was giving me that deep look again, the one that made it seem like I meant everything to him. It had terrified me when he'd first looked at me like that in Club Twist, but rather than scare me this time, it made something inside me vibrate with warmth. I could now accept it without panic, because as much as I'd never thought I'd say it, he was starting to mean everything to me, too.

CHAPTER FORTY-ONE

Robyn

As the wedding party started to thin out and our guests began leaving in the shuttle of taxis towards the glittering city skyline, Oliver and I took a little time to speak to some of our closer friends. Stella and Nathan had grabbed us to offer further congratulations and we had shared a glass of wine with them on the terrace.

We'd been friends for a few months now, but the very first night I'd met Stella both of us had spotted the collar the other was wearing; a possessive claim from our respective men, and one only those in the know would understand. It had led to us bonding almost immediately. It helped that she was laid-back, down to earth, and lovely, too, but the fact I could ask her any questions I had about the Dom/sub lifestyle had been brilliant.

From the snippets she'd told me, she and Nathan were a little more immersed in the lifestyle than Oliver and me, but seeing her again today – with her collar firmly secured at her neck – had given me an idea for this evening.

Oliver and I were now heading back to the guest cottage at his parents' house, and I was working out when I could prepare my surprise. We'd chosen to spend the night here because it was well separated from the main house to give us privacy and had the added bonus that we wouldn't have to get a cab or drive back to the city.

As he opened the door we were met by a glorious display of lights and the scent of vanilla filling the air.

'Wow!' Looking up at Oliver, I grinned.

Someone – presumably my mum, Sophia, and Sasha – had filled the cottage with fairy lights and there were jars of scented candles littering the table tops and fireplace. I looked up and was surprised to see an expectant expression on Oliver's face that made me start to suspect perhaps my original guess had been wrong.

'Did you do this?'

My new husband smiled down at me and slid his arm around my waist. 'That depends, do you like it?'

'I love it!' Stepping inside, I took in all the details of his hard work; as well as the candles and twinkling lights, the bed was topped with a gorgeous bouquet of red and white roses, and there was a chiller beside the bed with a bottle of champagne in it. As I turned to him something else caught my eye that had me sucking in a breath and moving to the wall beside the window.

'Oh my God, Oliver…' On the wall was a frame containing a collage of photographs that all had one thing in common – us. Pictures of us from our last trip in Barcelona, one of us from outside a café in London, and several inside Club Twist which I immediately recognised as the night that Oliver had proposed. I didn't even remember those ones being taken.

'Sasha gave those ones to me. Caught on her camera phone.'

Oliver was proving to be even more romantic than me, and my eyes misted up as I gazed over the pictures again. 'Wow. I love it, Oliver.'

Oliver stepped up behind me and slid his arms around my waist from behind so I was tucked in with my back against his chest. 'I'm glad.' Reaching an arm over, he pointed to one photograph. 'This is my favourite.' The picture was from the night we'd got engaged and mostly contained me, grinning from ear to ear and looking so happy I was almost bursting. In the background, behind me but connected to me with a firm handhold was Oliver, looking equally as happy and proud as punch. I could see why he liked it so much; it had perfectly captured our special moment.

'Now, as much as I want to throw you on that bed and ravish you, I've drunk too much champagne and I need to use the bathroom.'

As soon as he disappeared I quickly set about getting my own surprise ready. I stripped down until all I was wearing were the stockings and suspenders and then ran to my suitcase to retrieve my jewellery bag. I removed the single pearl necklace that my mother had lent me as my "something borrowed" and replaced it with my collar. Then, wearing just the suspenders, my collar, and my wedding ring I knelt in the centre of the floor and presented myself in the submissive position that Oliver loved the best.

The bathroom door opened a few seconds later and I immediately heard Oliver draw in a shocked breath and then hum appreciatively.

'Utterly breath-taking,' he murmured. His praise made my cheeks heat, but I kept my gaze averted like any good submissive would.

Oliver placed a hand on the top of my head and slid it down to the nape of my neck before trailing through my hair until he found the strip of my collar. His fingers traced the collar until he touched the small disk at the front that held his initials and my nickname – *cariño.*

'I see you came prepared.' He slipped his hand through my hair again and tilted my head back so I was gazing up at him. I wore the collar most of the time back home, but as soon as my mother had offered me the pearl necklace for the wedding day – she had also worn it on the day she married Dad – Oliver and I had immediately agreed that it was a lovely gesture, and I'd removed the collar before flying out.

What he hadn't known was that I'd packed the collar, too, just in case the opportunity arose.

'As gorgeous as you look, can we save that for our honeymoon tomorrow?'

I frowned, wondering if that meant he didn't want any sex at all tonight. It had been a long day, not to mention a stressful couple of days beforehand.

I couldn't deny that I was a little disappointed. I'd been hoping to consummate our marriage in this beautifully decorated room, but I'd be happy as long as Oliver held me in his arms as we fell asleep.

'Of course.' He helped me to stand and I reached for my silk nightgown before lifting it to pull it on but was stopped as Oliver gripped my waist and shook his head. 'Uh, uh, you won't need to be dressed,' he murmured, a sexy grin spreading on his face.

'But I thought you just said to leave it until tomorrow?'

He chuckled, and as he took a step towards me I noticed a large bulge in the front of his trousers which looked decidedly promising. 'I asked if we could leave the submission until tomorrow, not anything else.'

Suddenly it dawned on me that perhaps he was feeling romantic. It was our wedding night, after all, and even though he always took care of me during our scenes, his dominant persona wasn't perhaps his most romantic side.

'Tonight, I just want this to be about us, together, no leading or commands.' He was gazing down at me now with such heat that I felt completely and utterly frozen to the spot by the intensity in his eyes.

Oliver might not be intending on dominating me tonight, but he certainly had plans for something hot in his mind, that much was very clear, and a shiver of lust shook my entire body.

He saw my shudder and let out a low, sexy chuckle as he reached my side and slid a possessive hand around my waist.

'Come here, Mrs Wolfe, we have a marriage to consummate.'

CHAPTER FORTY-TWO

Oliver

As I gazed down at Robyn I could hardly deal with the intensity of the emotions I felt for her. I wanted to worship this woman for the rest of my life. Love her, protect her, make her laugh, make her come apart in my arms, and make all her dreams come true.

I'd never in a million years thought that I would meet someone who would make me want to settle down, but now the idea of being with anyone else sickened me. No other woman would do. I wanted Robyn, and Robyn alone, to the point where I literally couldn't imagine a life without her by my side.

She had looked so gorgeous today at the ceremony that I'd been hard for most of the afternoon, but she was even more stunning now. My eyes skimmed down her body again. She was naked except for the suspenders, her collar, and her wedding ring.

Dios, I was a lucky man.

She was perfection in human form: silky smooth skin, slender waist, long legs that I loved to feel wrapped around my waist, breasts so perfect they made me want to fall to my knees and worship them, and those were just her physical qualities. She was also the sweetest, most loyal and loving girl I'd ever encountered. Quite simply, she was the ideal counterbalance for me. Together we were whole.

I had no idea what I'd done to deserve her, especially given the less than salubrious life I had lived up until meeting her, but I would grab hold of the gift I'd been given and treasure her with everything I had in me.

'You said we had a marriage to consummate,' she murmured, 'but you seem intent on just gazing at me.' She was teasing me, picking up on my moment of silent contemplation, and I grinned at her.

Nodding, I leaned down and nibbled at her neck, running my teeth over her collar and giving a gentle tug. 'Hmm, yes, you are quite correct.' She shivered under my touch and I grinned against her heated skin. 'Let's rectify that, shall we?' Instead of continuing to kiss her neck, I nipped the tender skin below her ear and laughed as Robyn let out a lusty moan.

I stepped back and walked a circle around her, wondering just where I should begin. I wanted to throw her on the bed and plunge inside her, but this was our wedding night, and my need to fuck and claim like an animal needed to be replaced with romance and love – I wanted to make sure that tonight would be a perfect and unforgettable experience for her.

The glint of her wedding ring caught my eye, and so I took hold of her wrist, pulled her hand to my mouth, and placed a lingering kiss on the band of platinum.

Mine. She was mine now and forever.

Placing a hand on her hip, I savoured the feel of her soft skin below my touch and then completed my circle of her, dragging my hand around until we stood face to face again. Her skin was flushed now, eyes wide and lips parted, and it was an invitation that I just couldn't resist.

Lowering my head, I caught her mouth in a kiss that Robyn immediately returned. She rolled onto her tiptoes and slid her arms around my neck, licking at the seam of my lips and giving a soft mewl of happiness when I parted them and let her have her way with me.

The feel of her warm breasts pressing against my chest reminded me just how unbalanced our state of dress was and I lifted my hands and began to shrug out of my waistcoat.

'Need to be naked…' I mumbled against her lips, and with a soft giggle Robyn joined in, ripping at the buttons on my shirt and tugging it free from my trousers.

'I should have stripped first. Would have made my romancing a lot smoother,' I murmured with an amused smile as I peeled my trousers and boxers down and kicked them aside.

Once I was naked I glanced down and had to try to supress a grin at the sight of my cock lurching around as if reaching out for Robyn.

She noticed it, too, and as I raised my head I saw her watching my desperate display with a heavy-lidded expression. Biting down on her lip, she loosely gripped the base of my cock, sending shock waves shooting through my system like little daggers of pleasure.

'Someone looks keen,' she whispered, her cheeks heating with desire as she ran several gentle pulls up my shaft and back down again.

I was more than keen, I was near desperate to be inside her. But, still intent on romancing my new wife, I lowered my hand and gently removed her grip from my throbbing dick and then led her towards the bed.

I crouched down, scooped her into my arms and crawled onto the bed. I was nowhere near as graceful as I'd have liked, because my legs were trembling from her recent teasing, but once we were in the centre of the bed I placed Robyn down and kissed her again until my rocketing heartbeat had slowed a little.

Once I was confident that I had control over myself again I knelt up and gazed down at Robyn as she lay sprawled below me like the ultimate temptation.

The beautiful lace stockings I had bought her for the wedding had not been a waste of money. They looked stunning, especially now they were the only clothing she wore.

They sheathed her lower legs and ran to mid-thigh and then clipped to the delicate belt at her waist, drawing my eyes to her bare pussy.

Mierda. She was so wet her juices shone on her upper thighs and I placed a hand on the suspender belt and gripped as I massaged over the lace before beginning to trail my fingers higher.

Bending down, I placed a kiss on her belly before dragging my mouth over her hot skin and down to the top of the suspenders. I rested my lips on the lace and gave it a tug with my teeth to free the clips before deciding that, actually, the stocking could stay on.

'You look sexy as hell in these. I think we'll leave them on.'

Robyn parted her lips as if about to say something, but whatever words were on her tongue melted away as I moved my lips from the top of the stocking and began working higher until they found the moisture at the tops of her thighs. I lapped at it, growling at the taste of my girl, and running a swipe of my tongue from her soaking entrance up through her delicate folds. *Dios*, she tasted so good.

'Oh God… Oliver…' Her encouraging moan was all I needed to hear to know that she was loving this, and as she dug her hand into my hair and gripped, I flattened my tongue against her clitoris and circled it before sucking the bundle of nerves into my mouth and giving several rhythmical pulls.

Suddenly it wasn't enough. I needed to be closer, deeper, so I slid both my palms up her thighs and pressed her legs open wider until she was splayed and displayed for my eyes only.

Shifting my weight onto my elbow, I continued to suck at her and then introduced a finger, circling it around her sensitive flesh until Robyn was writhing below my touch and mumbling incoherently as her nails bit into my scalp.

'Oliver… please!'

I loved how wild she got when we were in bed together,

and I also loved how I could make her beg.

She was loud tonight, my new wife, and, smirking in satisfaction, I grinned up at her. 'Patience, Mrs Wolfe, let me take care of you,' I murmured. I lowered my mouth again, loving how I could feel her flesh quivering against my lips.

I was nearing the limits of my own self-control but decided to push her limits just a little more before I finally allowed myself the prize of driving my cock into her.

First, I upped the finger inside her to two, crooking them so I could locate her G-spot and then massaging it as I gave several deep, slow thrusts of my hand. Once she was mewling and writhing against my hand, I eased a third finger to join the first two, loving the feel of her body stretching and allowing me in.

Now for the test. My fingers were by no means small, and I knew that adding any more would be pushing it for her, but I just couldn't resist. Pressing her legs as wide as I could get them, I began adding another finger, having to work it in with small pushes and twists of my wrist. Watching the way her entrance stretched for me was fascinating, and the feel of her channel rippling around my fingers was so extraordinary that my cock gave a desperate lurch.

I lowered my mouth and licked at her clit as I started to move my hand back and forth with more vigour. The little bundle of nerves was swollen with need and slick with her juices and I couldn't resist sucking it hard.

My actions were causing gurgled moans to slip from her mouth, but when I swapped my lips for my thumb and circled it on the slick nub Robyn let out a shout. Her hands left my head and started to clutch and grab at the bedsheets beside her. She was wild below me, and the sight was the most beautiful I had ever witnessed.

'I'm close, Oliver… Jesus… I want you inside me…'

Her body arched into my touch, and even though I'd been intent on making her come before taking her I would never turn her down if she asked for me to be inside her. With a twist of my wrist that made her eyes bulge with pleasure, I carefully removed my hand from her and shifted my body over hers. Like a homing missile my cock found its way to the cleft between her legs and nestled there, ready for action.

'I love you so much, Robyn.' I murmured. Gazing down into her eyes, I pressed my hips forwards and sunk into her, causing her to let out a wheezed yell of pleasure.

Robyn looked lost in the moment, but her eyes met mine and held. 'I love you, too, Oliver. You're my entire world.'

I circled my hips, losing myself in the warmth of her body and the dizzying sensations it was causing in my head. I could feel her heating below me, her skin flushing and her channel tightening. As I plunged in deep again, the contact of my body grinding against her clit caused Robyn to stiffen below me and start to come in huge pulsing waves of pleasure. Her channel gripped me like a fist, her hands sliding to the back of my neck and dragging me down for a desperate kiss.

Her body convulsed below mine for what seemed like an eternity, her climax going on and on until, finally, she let out a long, shaky breath and blinked up at me, looking totally overwhelmed by the power of her release.

'Was that good, *cariño*?' I remained deeply planted inside her, just giving the smallest circles of my groin to help her ride out her orgasm, and once she started to come to from her high she grinned and nodded at me.

'That was bloody brilliant, Mr Wolfe.'

I couldn't help but laugh at her description, but then my cock jerked inside her as if urging me to move, so I sunk my hips down again and let out a moan as my belly flattened on hers and I was buried to the root.

Robyn began moving below me, undulating her gorgeous hips so I was buried gloriously deep and felt like I was about to explode from the pleasure building in my balls.

I had wanted to draw this out – it was our wedding night,

after all – but I was so close now, my body desperately urging me to chase my climax. Besides, we could always continue things later.

I began to move my hips again, dragging my length slowly out before pressing back in with a low groan. She felt so good I could happily stay buried within her body for the rest of my life.

My control was fading now, the need to fuck hard and fast starting to build in my system like a potent drug, and eventually, with the encouragement of Robyn's grinding hips below me, I started to thrust faster and harder.

Even though she'd only just climaxed, Robyn's body tightened around my cock again as my deeper thrusts rubbed repeatedly over her G-spot. If I were lucky, I might be able to take her over the edge with me when I came.

So much for my idea of romancing my new wife. I was now fucking her madly, my hips like a piston and our desperation obvious in the harsh breathing and the way our hands were clawing at each other's skin and leaving marks.

My balls had risen, and the searing feel of my climax rose uncontrollably in my belly. Robyn was just as frantic, but no matter how hard I had tried to hold back, suddenly my body gave in and it rushed at me in a wave of pleasure. I jerked my hips deep and, with a low moan, I came in huge great pulses that soaked her insides and coated my cock until I felt like I would never stop coming.

The jarring of my body against her over-sensitised flesh triggered Robyn's second release and below me she gasped, her head rolling back in pleasure as her overheated channel clamped around me and drained the last of my climax from my body.

Dios. Talk about a successfully consummated marriage. As I gazed down at her, I almost felt overwhelmed from the intensity of it.

She was incredible.

My wife. My lover. My best friend. My submissive.
My everything.

ACKNOWLEDGEMENTS

As always I want to start my acknowledgements by extending a massive thank you to all of you lovely readers – without you I would have no reason to write, so thank you! Your support and encouragement really does mean the world to me.

A huge thanks must go to my fabulous editor, Liz for the time and dedication spent on finding all the typos that I love to splatter about liberally within my manuscripts. You must have the patience of a saint!

I must also extend massive thanks to my publisher, Accent Press, for their continued support of my writing. In particular, Hazel and Katrin for the time and effort you put into working with me.

Next to my beta readers on this project - I love you all for the constructive feedback and encouragement: Leah Weatherall, Grace Lowrie and Katie Newman, thank you!

I mustn't miss out the never-ending support of my husband, family and besties Helen Lowrie and Karen Wilmot – I love you all and am so lucky to have you in my life.

I think that's everyone, but huge apologies if I have missed anyone out …

Thanks again for reading,
Alice xx

THE *UNTWISTED* SERIES

When schoolteacher Allie Shaw took an impromptu cleaning job to cover for a friend, she never expected to wind up snowed in with a devilishly handsome sex God.

THE *REVEALED* SERIES

An all-consuming affair with famous pianist Nicholas Jackson engulfs Rebecca in a whirlwind of passion and dominance. But is she ultimately destined for heartbreak?

Proudly published by Accent Press

www.accentpress.co.uk